THE NUCLEAR CATASTROPHE
a Fiction Novel of Survival

by:
Barbara C. Griffin Billig

Dedicated to:
Edward Billig, for all his love and support

In Memoriam: Bett Pohnka
(1935-1991)

4th Edition

Copyright: 2011 by Barbara C. Griffin Billig

4th Edition

Also published in paperback as:

"The Disquiet Survivors of The Nuclear Catastrophe"

ISBN: 9780615479828

INTRODUCTION

Set in Southern California, this is the story about the people living and working near a nuclear power plant that experiences a large earthquake. The book follows the paths of Ben Harrington, head of the nuclear power plant and Sara, his pregnant wife. Frank and Paula Waring with two children live in San Mirado, an adjacent town. Althea Carr is their school teacher, and Cecil Yeager is employed as an accountant at a nearby chemical plant. Each chooses different solutions to deal with the problems that arise after the catastrophe. This book brings home the reality of what would or could happen. No one can be so arrogant as to believe it will NEVER happen, especially after the events of March 11, 2011, in Fukushima, Japan. History has shown us time after time that...what can go wrong...will go wrong.

This is the 4th edition of the original published hardcover novel. Technology has moved with lightning speed since the story was written many years ago predicting this type accident would occur. Now we actually know for sure what was denied for thirty years - that this accident can happen. Sadly Fukushima, Japan, was a replica of this novel's story line. And since years have passed since the Fukushima disaster, we now know much more realistically what the aftermath is like.

Unfortunately, the United States and many other countries also have nuclear reactors that are over forty years old that are the same design as those that experienced meltdowns in Fukushima. It is a foregone conclusion that as these reactors age, or new ones are operated by incompetent third world countries, or attacked by terrorists, more nuclear catastrophes are in the future.

Radiation is a boring subject – you can't see it, you can't hear it, you can't feel it – until it's too late. But what if you were warned that more than the normal amount was released into your area? What would you do? Where would you go? This fiction novel is about what should NEVER happen. But what if it did...near where you live...or work?

An example of radiation we all recognize is the rays of the sun. Staying out unprotected in the sun too long produces a painful sunburn. Sun rays can only penetrate and irritate the outer layers of skin. Nuclear radiation byproducts can travel through thick layers of concrete. When they pass through the body, each particle acts like a bullet as it penetrates the body cells, damaging and killing those cells.

The building blocks of our world are atoms. Some atoms such as Uranium or Plutonium are constantly breaking down, releasing particles and rays. Put those radioactive atomic substances together in the right configuration and they create such heat and energy as they decay that an ATOMIC BOMB is generated. A nuclear power plant is built to control the speed of the decay processes and the heat generated from the processes – until something goes wrong.

Read what these fictional characters experienced and the choices that they made – and be better prepared to make your own choices.

As of January, 2015, there are 439 nuclear power plants that are operational in the world with another 69 under construction. The United States has 104 of these plants, France has 59, and Japan has 50. (1)

(1) European Nuclear Society web site home page.
www.euronuclear.org

4

Chapter One

The crisp sheet of parchment fell from his fingers to the top of the polished desk, the letterhead standing out like a flag against the white background. Ben Harrington knotted his fist and slowly, rhythmically, brought it down on the letter. The Southern California Society of Environmentalists was a loud, outspoken body of malcontents. It was more and more vocal on any issue that even remotely pertained to the environment, and its protests were being heard. Now he was beginning to worry. The unanswered question in his mind was whether the Society's protests had set something else off - like causing the confab with the politicians this afternoon. If so, he wanted to make sure of what he could do about it.

Ben reached across to the intercom and punched a button.

Without waiting to hear who would answer, he ordered, "Mike, get in here!"

In agitation he shoved his chair back, rose to his feet and paced back and forth behind the desk while he waited for Mike Percy. This kind of thing spoiled his day. In his precise, meticulous manner, he had maintained White Water as a smoothly functioning electric utility plant. He kept himself on his toes, and he expected nothing less from his subordinates. When there was a goof it was because someone was careless, and carelessness couldn't be tolerated.

The knock at the door was immediately followed by the entrance of the big, affable assistant supervisor. Mike wore his usual wide grin, the disarming smile that stretched completely across his face and was illuminated by large innocent eyes. His features belied his actual age. "Hello, Ben. What's up?"

Ben's private thoughts were momentarily checked by the appearance of this mild, good-natured man. He hadn't wanted Mike for the position of second-in-command, but his choice had been by-passed—over-ruled in fact—out of deference to the wishes of someone on the company's board. Indeed, Ben had always considered Mike the least competent of the two men who worked the control room with him, a point that had been clearly made on the last personnel evaluation form submitted on the employees. He shoved the letter over to Mike. "Read it."

After a moment, Mike looked up, his expression now one of concern. "I don't get it, Ben. They wouldn't do anything like that, would they?"

A conscious snort of air escaped Ben's nostrils, a sign of his annoyance. "Of course they would! They've just been waiting to catch us on something, and now, thanks to you, it looks like they've got what they want."

Mike glanced down at the sheet once more. "This is ridiculous—it's pure harassment to start an action like this."

Ben clenched his fist, getting satisfaction from the feel of the muscles tightening into a ball of bone and gristle. He was going to get Mike straightened out once and for all, he decided. If the letter had come a day later he wouldn't have been alerted to prepare for this afternoon. One screw-up leads to another.

"They've been aching for this," he said angrily to Mike. "All this time those busy-bodies have had their noses stuck into this facility out here. Well, now they've got an excuse to sound off!" He stared hostilely at Mike.

Aware of his boss's wrath, Mike dropped the letter on the desk and shrank back. "Ben, I know what you're thinking, but I swear to God, it slipped my mind. It just slipped my mind."

"That's no damn excuse, Mike! You've got a responsible position. You can't let matters slide just because you've got other things to think about. I told you over six weeks ago to get that report filed!"

The reprimand was sobering to Mike. He replied humbly, "It didn't seem very important at the time. I kept putting it off until I completely forgot about it." Shrugging, he continued, "A report to be filed at the county library—good grief, what's so important about that?"

"The Southern California Society of Environmentalists thinks it is and that's sufficient. They probably had someone especially assigned to read that report," he said, eyes still flashing anger.

"There couldn't be a thing in it that would interest them, Ben. A propeller blade broke on one of the turbines and we had to shut down for a couple weeks. So what?"

Ben leaned toward Mike and snapped, "So we are obligated to file a report in a public office on every single incident out here that results in the reactor in this plant being out of operation. That is a safety report that must be presented under state law, Mike! It's not for us to decide whether we'll do it or not." Ben softened his tone. "Look, Mike, I'm trying to be fair about this. It's not something I'd be any less rough on myself for. You think it's not important, but we're in a business where there's no room for error."

"It was such a minor problem, Ben," objected Mike. "The...."

"We were out of action for sixteen days!" Ben interrupted, exasperated. "Sure, you and I know it was minor, but the public has to be informed. That's why S.C.S.E. is sniffing around. They want to catch us doing something wrong!"

Mike shook his head worriedly. "But we didn't file a report when our stack emissions exceeded the maximum level."

"Hell no," snapped Ben. "We simply cut back production until we got the emissions under control, which we did within a day or so, if you remember. Nobody knew we were running a little high except for you, me, and Des Anderson. But when the operation comes to a halt, everyone knows about it, and I can promise you that when we don't tell them why, we're going to be getting this kind of flak," he retorted, and thumped his fingers on the letter.

Mike frowned, "They won't sue, will they!"

"Sure they will," Ben answered heatedly. "There's nothing for them to lose by stirring up a legal mess with the company. This group has been itching to get us into court for a long time. It'll get them a lot of publicity—which is exactly what they want."

"But a law suit?. That's going pretty far," Mike protested. "Look, Ben, I don't think they're serious about a lawsuit, but since they seem intent on making trouble, I'll get that report ready this morning and send it right out."

Ben waved the suggestion aside. "No! They sent a copy of this letter to the president of the board and it's my guess that they're already working on legal action. Do the report, but you email a copy to everyone and take the original to the library yourself, Mike. I want to be certain it gets there." As an afterthought he added, "Make a copy and send one by messenger to the S.C.S.E. headquarters."

Mike grumbled to himself, then spoke outright. "I don't think they ought to get away with these high-pressure tactics they're using, Ben. Giving them their own personal copy of the report sets a bad precedent."

"Listen," said Ben, "it's not your butt that's going to be in hot water with the board. It's mine! Since you screwed it up, you can get it straightened out! But I want it done today! I've got a group of company executives coming here with two big-wig politicians after lunch. You make sure that report is on my desk before they arrive, Mike!"

Mike stepped back at the onslaught of words. "All right, Ben. All right. I just didn't think that filing that document would be so important. I....well, paper work isn't...."

Ben interrupted, "I don't like the desk job, either," then hesitated over that comment which was absolutely untrue. He did enjoy the administrative end of the power facility. "But these things have to be done." What had seemed an almost insignificantly simple task for Mike had become a blunder that could set reverberations sounding all along the company's chain of command.

Humbled, Mike said, "Maybe they'll ease off when they get the report."

"Yes, if we're lucky. Meanwhile, I'm left to face this myself when the board reads that letter. And on top of that, there's that bunch coming in today—the last thing I need is a couple of senators snooping around the plant," said Ben wearily.

With a feeble attempt at reassurance, Mike replied, "At least the subject of this report won't be brought up by anyone from the company. And I don't see how the senators could know anything about this complaint of S.C.S.E."

The muscle at the angle of Ben's jaw popped out as he stared at his colleague. Most of the statements he wanted to make to Mike were left unsaid as he listened to the other's appraisal of the situation. Unable to do more, he nodded and said, "Just do the report, Mike. I'll handle whatever develops here this afternoon."

Mike knew he was being dismissed and turned toward the door.

"By noon," Ben reminded him as he stepped outside.

Up the walk they came. Seven men, dressed in conservative business suits, and led by J. Rufus Pettengill, vice-president.

Ben watched them as they reached the bottom steps. Then he checked his tie once more, nudging it securely under his collar, straightened the lapels on his fresh white lab coat, and marched through the door to greet them.

His superior of West State Utility Company, Mr. Pettengill, made the introductions with a flourish of complimentary remarks which he grandly bestowed on his plant supervisor's head.

8

When at last it was Ben's turn to talk, he spoke distinctly and with clarity, with not a hint of nervousness that had plagued him during his long wait for their arrival.

"Gentlemen, welcome to White Water Nuclear Power Facility. We are honored to have you here. It is a rare day when we have the opportunity to welcome two distinguished United States Senators." He nodded in the direction of two of the men. "Senator McCauley. Senator Jackson. And we are always pleased to have officers from our plant on the grounds." Pausing, he nervously touched his tie.

He looked over the faces before him, then continued with his speech. "White Water is recognized as a model facility for the generation of electric power from nuclear fissioning processes. We are most anxious to grant your request of a tour through our plant; thus within the next few hours you will have a first-hand observation of the most technologically perfect system to replace the antiquated fossil fuel electric generators. As we guide you through these buildings, we hope to answer any and all questions you may have regarding not only this facility but nuclear installations in general."

He paused to catch his breath, then noticed that the short, lively Senator McCauley had begun to gaze about, as though he had lost interest in Ben's comments. Suddenly, the realization hit him that in being overly zealous, he had kept everyone standing on the steps.

"Since we are outside, perhaps we should begin with a walk around the external plant," Ben said quickly. "From the freeway, the most noticeable structure is the huge dome-shaped building behind us."

"Is that where the reactor is?" asked the junior senator, Jackson in a slightly high-pitched voice.

"Yes, it is, sir, along with a variety of coolant pumps, a steam-electric generator, and a few other things."

Although Benjamin Harrington, Ph.D., took great pride in being well versed in the subject of nuclear energy, he hoped the questions would not be too inane, or too disruptive to his discourse. While it was nice to invite their questions, ill-timed ones became a nuisance, often causing him to break his chain of thought.

"That pipe going up the side of the dome, the one that looks like a smoke stack, what's it used for?" asked McCauley.

"We call that a primary vent stack," answered Ben.

"Yes. And what comes out of it, Dr. Harrington?"

Ben cleared his throat, hoping to avoid a lengthy explanation. "When the reactor is in operation, there are radioactive wastes that form as by-products. Many of those wastes are in the gaseous state, and as such, are eliminated through the vent stack." There, he thought, that should be clear, senator.

"Radiation goes out that stack into the atmosphere?" asked the senator.

To Ben, the man's question, although innocuous, seemed to somehow convey a hidden implication. "Well yes, Senator. You surely are aware that this is a standard practice throughout all such plants. Of course," he hastened to add, "we keep our emission levels within the guidelines established by the Radiation Emission Council."

The senator looked at Ben carefully. "Have you ever exceeded the maximum level for emission?"

"Never, sir," snapped Ben. "When emissions come close to the maximum level, we reduce capacity—reduce our productivity, so to speak." At this moment he wished he could talk privately with Mr. Pettengill. These questions seemed unusually probing, and Ben began to wonder if the senators' motive for coming was indeed in response to the Southern California Society of Environmentalists. Perhaps that group had already reached an attentive ear. No matter, he decided. Nuclear power was here to stay.

Continuing the tour, Ben led the group from the Visitor Information Center, where they had met, around the turbine building, service building, past the effluent-control room, to the waste holding tanks, all the while elaborating on the complexity of the plant and its size. To camouflage his nervousness, he kept his left hand slipped into the pocket of his lab coat. His demeanor seemed one of self-assurance, as he strolled confidently around, expounding on the various aspects of the facility. "And this area, gentlemen, is where a large percentage of the radioactive wastes are removed prior to shipment of the spent fuel rods. Fuel rods, you see, are enriched uranium-235. Uranium atoms are the ones that are split by neutrons to release tremendous heat energy.

"During reactions, radioactive wastes accumulate on those rods, choking out, or smothering the reaction, eventually, unless the rods are replaced. Approximately every twenty-four months the old fuel is replaced with new, and much of the wastes are

10

collected right here."

"These wastes are dangerous, I presume?" asked Senator McCauley blandly.

"Oh, yes indeed, unless handled very carefully," said Ben.

"Exactly what is done with them, afterwards?"

"They're kept in these tanks until they decay."

"They are? I didn't realize that they could all decay right in those vats," said the senator with a note of doubt in his voice as he appraised the huge holding tanks.

Ben was hesitant to amend the statement. Then finally, "Actually, a small part of the wastes are passed out through effluent tubes."

"Into the ocean?" asked the senator as he stared at the vats.

"Into the ocean. However, they cause absolutely no detriment to marine life in the vicinity," said Ben reassuringly.

"Interesting," the senator said under his breath.

Being appointed one of the youngest chief supervisors to ever command a nuclear facility had certainly not happened because of Ben's disdain for dealing with the public. It had been due, in part, to his total enthusiasm for this particular form of energy and its potential, but it was mainly due to his brilliance in the field of nuclear physics. Having to deal with skeptical politicians and critical environmentalists taxed his patience. Always eager to display the ingenuity of modern science, his spirits were always quickly dampened by comments that verged on impertinency, especially those which cast doubts on the effectiveness and safety of the nuclear plants.

To his way of thinking, it would be far better if lay persons, who lacked knowledge of such installations, simply left well enough alone and let the aim of science run its course. Fortunately, the comments thus far were not the impertinent variety. Perhaps he had been mistaken to expect such from the senators. Maybe they were here simply to view the plant and nothing more.

The executive officers of West State followed quietly in the entourage, making occasional light remarks that neither added to, nor detracted from, Ben's elaboration. The supervisor suspected that their contributions were so meager because they, themselves, had no thorough understanding of what was before them.

"Shall we enter for an inspection of the interior?" he invited, training his eyes directly on Senator McCauley.

Sensing that the most concern was with the reactor, Ben led the way into the huge, ball-shaped building that housed the core of the reactor. The area was a maze of catwalks, cranes, generating units, and the tall, cylindrical steel vessel containing the core.

"This gentlemen, is the container that surrounds the reactor core. The core is, of course, the center region with its thousands of fuel rods, and fortunately," Ben smiled benignly at them, "the control rods."

"Ah yes," said Senator Jackson, "the control rods govern the speed of the reaction. Right, Dr. Harrington?"

"Yes. That's correct. They are the means by which the reaction is controlled. It can be slowed down, by inserting additional rods, or speeded up, by withdrawing rods. You might say that the rods are the insurance that a nuclear reaction never proceeds uncontrolled." He smiled easily as he finished.

"Dr. Harrington," said Senator McCauley, "I was under the impression that an uncontrolled reaction would cause an enormous explosion—not with the ferocity of an atomic bomb, but an explosion, nonetheless. Could that happen in one of these things?"

"Absolutely not, sir! That bit about an explosion is a myth perpetuated by....our opponents. Oh, theoretically, whenever the proper amount of fissionable material comes together in the right place, a critical mass could form and an explosion could ensue. But there is positively no means by which this could occur in a nuclear power plant. None, sir!" Ben was smug with the certainty that what he said was true. "In fact, the very beauty of this system is that it's not only a clean and efficient method of producing electrical energy, but it is also fool-proof."

The men paused beside the reactor vessel. Aware that the fissionable fuel was deep within the steel container and hidden from view, they were comforted by the knowledge that as they stood there, near enough to reach out and touch the container, they were well protected and shielded from its inner core. A certain degree of awe and reverence is reserved in every man for those forces too great for his comprehension, and Ben never failed to recognize this on the faces of those few important persons who were treated to the grand tour of White Water.

"Without belaboring the virtues of our establishment, gentlemen," Ben continued, "I should mention that while initial loading of the fuel assembly tends to be very expensive, the

12

overall cost is minute when compared with the vast amounts of fossil fuel used in conventional processes. The estimate is made that one pound, a mere sixteen ounces, of uranium fuel, yields the equivalent of several million pounds of coal. That in itself is the crux of this new industry."

Senator McCauley had drifted away, and was now climbing a metal staircase, leading to a catwalk overhead.

By the time Ben noticed him, he was carefully examining a fuel chute. Although wanting to yell out to the inquisitive little politician, and tell him to stay with the group, Ben instead collected the remaining people and hastily ascended the steps behind the senator.

Bringing up the last of the column, Ben found himself shoulder to shoulder with the vice-president of the utility company. "Mr. Pettengill," he said in a low, worried voice, "the senator...."

He wasn't given the chance to finish his statement before Pettengill clapped him on the arm and replied in an equally whispered tone, "You're doing fine, my boy. Fine. Just keep it up." An expression of pride was registered on his plump face.

Hurriedly Ben pushed up to the front of the group and again started to explain, only to have the senior senator interrupt him and move away. Suddenly the inspection was assuming an awkward trend. As they toured the remainder of the plant the jaunty, inquisitive Senator McCauley was charting the course the group followed. Pausing at points of interest, he asked for explanations from the supervisor, then, often as not, began to stroll off before Ben had completed the more lengthy responses —a habit that the nuclear physicist found particularly annoying.

When at last every nook and cranny had been presented to the visitors, Ben gladly returned them to the small conference room off the main office. A bright, cheery young lady served the men beverages, then subtly withdrew.

Leaning forward over the long table, Ben endeavored to firmly resume his leadership role. "You no doubt know that West State has requested authorization from the A.E.C. for an expansion of these facilities. Our intent is to develop—over the next few years—three more nuclear units at this site. The need for the extra reactors is obvious. It lies just beyond us— metropolitan Los Angeles."

"Dr. Harrington, White Water is a fairly recent addition to southern California. How large is it?" asked the senior senator.

13

"This plant has an eight-hundred megawatt capacity, Senator McCauley."

"And those that are on the drawing boards for future development?" asked the senator.

"The same size. Eight hundred megawatts," Ben said flatly.

"Would those four, the combined total, be sufficient to supply a substantial amount of the electricity required by L.A.?"

"Substantial, yes sir, but not all of the power needed. There are plans, being developed at this moment, which will involve the construction of a fourteen billion dollar nuclear power complex to the north of Los Angeles—for the exclusive provision of power to that city."

Senator McCauley seemed surprised by this. "Is that right? Well, before too many more years have passed your fair city will be the center of a huge circle of nuclear power plants."

Ben shoved his black horn rims a little farther back on the bridge of his nose, then smiled at his guest. "That's right, sir, all to meet the demands of one of the world's most rapidly expanding cities. And, of course, in a broader spectrum of terms, it is nuclear energy which will allow the industrial nations of the world to avert a major energy crisis."

The younger senator, who had been largely silent through these last hours, spoke up, "You aren't giving much credit to the potential in solar, or geothermal methods of capturing energy, Doctor."

"No, I'm not, am I?" asked Ben. "It is my feeling that those forms you have mentioned are nothing more than remote possibilities for yielding the tremendous quantities of energy required by this country. In my opinion, research need look no further for the solution to the increasing problem of energy shortages. We have it," he said adamantly.

Without warning Senator McCauley began getting to his feet. "Dr. Harrington, we appreciate your kindness and your patience. We know we must have torn you away from very serious duties to guide us through this facility. We thank you."

Ben breathed a quick sigh of relief and protested weakly at terminating the session. "Oh, we have a film which traces the history of White Water from its inception to present day, Senators. Wouldn't you like to view it before departing?"

"No, no. Time doesn't permit our presence here any longer, Doctor. Besides, with the exemplary facility you have, and the dedication of its personnel, we feel sure that we will be hearing

14

of White Water again," said the senior senator.

Chapter Two
Tuesday

The day began like any of a thousand others, with Sara's voice summoning him from bed, while she went about the preparation of breakfast.

Slowly, Ben slung his feet onto the floor, and walked across to the bathroom. His movements were sluggish, for the events at the plant on the previous day had drained his stamina. Bloodshot eyes stared back at him as he leaned toward the mirror and began the daily routine of shaving off the dark, thick bristles.

A mourning dove cooed to its mate in the canyon below the house. It was a soft, pleasing sound, one that was rapidly becoming an oddity in the heavily congested stretch of land that bordered on the Pacific, extending southward from Los Angeles. The gentle, sweet cooing had become such an integral part of the beginning of each morning that Ben had wondered about the eventual time when houses would be thrown up on the sides of the canyon, driving the birds away. When they moved, he and Sara would search for another quiet spot still near a natural habitat, unspoiled by giant earth-moving machines and the strange glass and wood affairs that were designed by eager, far-seeing architects.

A strong aroma of coffee drifted into his nostrils, luring him into the kitchen. "Ah, good morning, sweetheart." He placed a kiss on his wife's neck, lifting her long blond hair away.

The tall, lovely woman returned his show of affection by brushing his chin with her lips, while never taking her eyes off the omelet. She flashed him a tender look of concern. "You're tired, dear. But, then, you didn't rest well."

"No. I had trouble unwinding after the staff meeting last night," he said as he ambled toward the table.

"I'd wanted to wait up for you, but as it got closer to midnight, I finally had to go to bed. Suddenly I need so much sleep."

"You shouldn't have waited at all. I told you I'd be late." He picked up his glass of juice and quickly drained it. Then he noticed the glass by her plate, and its burgundy colored liquid. With his back to her, and wondering about the unusual breakfast drink, he asked, "Did you go in for your examination yesterday?"

"Yes. I had a one o'clock appointment, remember?"

He vaguely recalled she had told him that, but the previous day was such a jumble of events that his wife's visit to the physician had been pushed far aside in his mind. "Well?" he asked, as he turned to her. "What did he say?"

She lifted the omelet onto a dish and moved toward the table. "He said I shouldn't have any trouble carrying this one if I'm careful."

"Careful?" he asked quizzically. "What does that mean?"

"Follow his advice, I think," she answered as she took a seat. He was still standing, absorbed in what she would say. "Did he have any advice about why you had the miscarriage?"

She shrugged, "He couldn't know, Ben. He wasn't the attending physician. Besides, he says there are dozens of reasons why pregnancies are naturally aborted."

Ben lifted the glass of deep red fluid to his nostrils. The scent of wine wafted through the air. Puzzled, he asked, "Is this what you're drinking for breakfast?"

She looked at him out of huge brown eyes, and smiled warmly, "Is there something wrong with it?"

Ben scrutinized the high cheek bones and the rich full lips of his wife. Her head was regally tilted to the side, letting the shining blond hair fall like a curtain behind her as she awaited his answer. "It doesn't seem to me that drinking this stuff in the morning is going to help you with the baby one bit, Sara."

That she had poured it at all was a shock to him. Sara was familiar with the best wines, the gourmet drinks, but she had never cultivated a taste for them. Ben recalled his first visit to the home of her parents. Her father possessed a lavishly-equipped wine cellar, the pride of the older man. Yet, Sara was totally unconcerned with its stock. "Is this a fetish or something —a craving that you suddenly have?" he asked as he set the glass down.

She took the glass and lifted it toward her mouth, paused, then returned it to the table. "It's a foul-smelling substance," she said. "No, Ben, as strange as it may sound, the doctor prescribed an alcoholic drink three times a day, so I thought wine would be the easiest to take this early in the morning."

"He prescribed it for a woman during pregnancy? He must be insane, Sara. You'll have to find another obstetrician," Ben said.

"You'll never have a child if you listen to some nut like that."

Sara reached out for his arm and pulled him toward his chair. "But you don't understand, Ben. The doctor says that small amounts of alcohol will slow contractions of the uterus. He thinks premature contractions could be the reason why I lost the first one."

"You're only three months along—that seems pretty early to worry about contractions," he said as he watched her pour the coffee. She did it gracefully, as she did everything.

Smiling, she pushed the toast toward him. "You wouldn't allow the doctor to tell you how to run White Water, dear. I would imagine that your qualifications in medicine are as limited as his in nuclear energy. So perhaps it would be best if we did this his way." Shifting the conversation, she asked, "What were your visitors like yesterday?"

"Who? The senators? They were all right, I suppose. One, the older fellow, a short, snoopy little guy, was kind of irritating. He came on fast—interrupting to ask something, then switching off to another interest of his—without waiting for the rest of the group. For a while I thought that he was being too curious, like he had some ulterior purpose for being there. But then I decided it was my imagination. The other one was a nice guy."

"Did you find out why they were there?" she asked.

"Visiting—or at least that's what I was told. You know how politicians are, always trying to get a finger in the pot." He was reluctant to tell her about the flare up over the shutdown report, and about his earlier suspicion that the senators were inspecting the facility as a result of a request from the Southern California Society of Environmentalists.

"They must have been there quite a long while," she said.

Ben knew that she had obliquely referred to his arriving home at a very late hour. "Actually, they weren't. I had anticipated them spending much longer in the plant, but Senator McCauley seemed anxious to be on the way."

She was silent, apparently waiting for him to explain his delay more fully.

"After the politicians left, Pettengill decided we should have one of his infamous meet and confer sessions. On the spur of the moment he decided on it. When I phoned you I had no idea of being as late as I was."

Raising her eyes to his, she replied, "It must have been a very important meeting."

He had no wish to assuage her curiosity by explaining that the S.C.S.E. letter had filtered down to Pettengill, and the long hours spent in conference were in regard to that. "Routine business, just routine," he said off-handedly. "What are your plans for the day?" he asked. "A meeting of your sorority alumni club, isn't it?"

"No, I'm not going to those gatherings anymore. Didn't I tell you about the last one I attended?" she asked.

He shook his head, "I don't recall. But you didn't say you weren't going back."

"Well, no matter. I'm not. It's the same thing all the time. Vacationing."

"Videos?"

"Yes, camcorder home made videos. Sue Anna's vacation to Hawaii, and Joan's last trip to Europe, and Debbie's three children in their pool—and those because they haven't been able to afford to go anywhere since they built it. It's just all so inane."

"You're bored with them."

"Yes, I suppose. But what I really would like is to find them on some subjects that are meaningful, instead of discussing the color of tea napkins. Just once."

"Whatever you think, Hon. I'm sure you have every right to be bored with that group." Having other things on his mind, he glanced at the clock above the sink. "I've got to go. Must get a backlog of paperwork done before this day ends."

"So soon?" she asked wistfully.

"Maybe I'll manage to be home early this evening. How about it?"

"I'd like that," she answered softly.

For the briefest second they stood close with their arms around each other. His very tall, lank frame dwarfed her as he held her to him. Her wan, porcelain skin was in marked contrast to his dark complexion. Releasing her, he turned and walked out the door.

It was a beautiful morning. Later, there would be smog creeping in to blanket the sky; but as yet, it was a day free of the troublesome, tainted air. Out to the right the ocean was clearly visible, a sailboat bobbed gently up and down on the calm blue water.

Edging the German-made sports car deftly into the parking slot, Ben grabbed his briefcase, and with a dozen long strides, stepped into his office in the front of the control room.

At 8:28 a.m. the huge reactor was already underway, splitting the U235 atoms and producing tremendous amounts of heat. Ben smiled to himself, the self-satisfied smile of a man who had complete understanding of the complex working of this monstrous unit. It gave him a comfortable feeling to be in this dust-free room, with computerized control boards and buttons, and with the ocean less than six hundred feet away.

Donning his lab coat, he picked up a clipboard and began making his rounds as he routinely did each working day. This would be the last round he'd make for a month. His vacation began at the end of the day. He casually nodded to his colleagues as he checked his readings against previous records and dutifully noted them in the proper spaces. The main control center was a sterile, ultra-modern room, its control consoles in white and the men in white lab uniforms. All screens, indicators, buttons, and levers for the normal and emergency operations of both the reactor and the generating plants were contained within these four, heavily-insulated walls. The plant represented the finest in engineering design, the ultimate in construction. The facility was built on the beach because of the need for vast amounts of cooling water for the reactor. No other spot had been feasible in arid southern California. The area was laced with old fault zones, the San Andreas fault itself being nearby, but the structures were created to withstand the most violent earthquake.

The reactor was housed apart from the control center. Dome covered, the reactor building was equally well constructed to take the shakings from the earth without being split or damaged. Inside, the reactor core and its thousands of fuel rods were protected from the incoming coolant by metal jackets within their steel reactor vessel, which was completely encased by a thick, steel drywell.

It was an extremely efficient operation and Ben appreciated that efficiency as much as any physicist. He wasn't blind to the potential dangers of nuclear energy, but he knew that so long as the machinery functioned properly, and there was no human error, and no accidents, then there was no way that the enormous quantities of radioactive poisons could escape into the environment. True, every two years the fuel rods would have to be removed and transported to a reprocessing plant for cleaning, removal of plutonium and burial of the remaining radioactive wastes; but again, it was simply a matter of everyone doing his job properly. It was over a year ago that White Water had been refueled last. Ben remembered getting a queasy sensation in his stomach as the diesel truck, groaning, had pulled onto the freeway with its heavy load of radioactive fuel rods en route to the reservation. But the two year accumulation of radiation was well contained. Nothing short of sabotage could release its deadliness to the air.

Glancing at the clock Ben noticed that the time was 8:42 a.m. Precisely at that moment, the cement floor began to slide under his feet. His head snapped around in surprise as he instinctively reached out to steady himself, grasping onto the edge of a console. His feet were firmly planted on the floor, perhaps twenty-four inches apart, yet he felt like he was on a large skate board as his body was thrown first forward, then backward. Attempting to regain his balance, Ben dropped his papers and held firmly to the console with both hands.

Across the room, Michael Percy had been cast broadside into the front of the master control board. Scrambling to latch onto something stable, Mike's hands frantically waved over the instrument panel. "Jesus Christ!" he yelled, "what's happening?"

"Mike," Ben shouted, "it's an earthquake! But watch it! Get your hands away from that panel!"

He didn't think Mike heard him. The man seemed to be yelling, his mouth wide open and his face contorted in shock.

Desmond Anderson, the third member of the crew was lying partially under a desk, his back and feet exposed, but his head securely protected.

In what seemed like minutes but was actually less than sixty seconds, the shaking ended. California experienced numerous earthquakes each year and, as would be later determined, this one was not particularly forceful. To the three men frozen in the control room, however, the trembling seemed quite intense. After all, this building had been especially constructed to withstand the most violent rigors, and yet their bodies had been flung about with the swaying motion like tiny rag dolls.

Finally tearing his hands loose, the knuckles as pale as the console to which they had been firmly attached, Ben switched on the scanning screen to the reactor building. No one was in sight. Strange, he thought, there should be someone down there. Snatching up the intercom speaker, he began calling, expecting

21

any minute to see white coated figures moving about. Ben's absorption in the eerily empty picture before him was interrupted by a shout from Mike.

"Ben! There's something wrong! The reactor temperature's rising!"

"Shut it off! Drop all the control rods." Ben's command was instinctive as he wheeled away from the screen and strode over to the master control board. He quickly checked the instruments for the cause of the problem, eyeing the temperature-gauge needle. Mike was seated at the other end of the board intent on the switches in front of him. About to speak to him, Ben was distracted by the crackling sound of static from the intercom switching on. Then a voice came through the speaker, a voice filled with fear.

"A coolant pipe has cracked! We're getting flooded with water over here!"

Ben spun toward the screen in time to see the floor of the reactor building take on a shiny, liquid glaze.

"That may be hot!" he bellowed, grabbing the microphone. "Get out of there!"

Turning aside, he roared, "Des, make sure the emergency coolant switch has activated! Fast, man!"

Without coolant, the interior of the reactor core would quickly become overheated. As the intense heat built up to a sufficient level, fuel rods would melt and the fission process would cease, with tremendous damage to the reactor. Theoretically.

Two orders had been issued by the supervisor, both of which should bring the problem under control.

"Done!" Des answered as he checked the computer screen that showed the switch was activated that shot the stand-by coolant into the superheated core.

"Ben, there's something wrong! The control rods won't go down!" cried Mike as he worked the program controlling the release buttons. In response to Ben's first command, he had quickly located the buttons that, when remotely pressed, would lower all of the cadmium control rods into the reactor core. Those rods absorbed the excess neutrons and were the brakes for the fission process. Without them, the reaction within the core would continue unchecked, and an unchecked nuclear reaction would result in a great explosive force building up until it was released in a violent discharge.

"I don't understand it! The red lights are on!" bellowed Mike.

"And I can't get these damned rods to drop," he said as he feverishly alternated the buttons.

"What do you mean, they won't go down? Why not? They've never failed to before!" Ben shouted.

"They won't! They won't. I think I may have accidentally entered something during the quake that raised the ones that had been down."

"Do you mean there aren't any controls in there? Jesus Christ! If we don't get those rods to drop we're going to have a blowout." Red lights flashed all across the panel of computer screens as Ben stood there frantically mashing buttons.

"Ben, the temperature is still rising in the core," said Mike excitedly.

"What? Still rising? Isn't the coolant...?"

"The emergency coolant must be evaporating," Des yelled out. "The fuel rods can't take too much more before they start melting, Ben!"

"At least the goddamned reaction will stop once the fuel rods melt!" said Ben, reassuringly.

But the situation was becoming critical to the reactor. The men, relying on what they knew to be the best opinions of certain scientists, were convinced that a burn-out would destroy the reactor but would prevent a nuclear explosion. There was no reason not to believe this since a burn-out was commonly touted as a built-in safety factor with the reactor core. Still, a burn-out would be an extremely costly occurrence for the company.

"Des, keep an eye on the temperature gauges! Mike, come with me," snapped Ben.

Taking his assistant, Ben left the consoles and passed into a smaller, circular cubicle. "There's one other chance for dropping those control rods." By now they were in front of a gray metal console with the face closed off. "There's an emergency lever that can be used as a last resort....maybe it'll jar them loose."

Instructing Mike to hold the door back, Ben reached inside, grasped the metal lever, and yanked. Nothing happened. The lever hadn't budged. In surprise Ben hurriedly searched for the cause. To his dismay, the cabinet had become warped and its metal surface had squeezed the lever into an immobile position. The earthquake had done some damage.

More damage was done than was obvious to Ben, in fact. The sudden shifting of the earth beneath the plant had caused a hairline fracture to traverse the top of the reactor dome. This

23

meant damage to the pressure suppression system.

"It's no use," Ben said dejectedly. "The damned thing is jammed."

"Ben, what are we going to do? Without those rods...?"

Ben ignored the question and ran back into the master control room. Des looked up as

he entered.

"It's still going up, Ben! That core is an inferno!" said Des.

The scanning screen showed the reactor building to be empty of people. The crew working around the reactor had exited at Ben's order. Now the scene was a flooded, innocent-appearing chamber with its gigantic steel reactor vessel and metal catwalks overhead. In the center of the vessel was the multi-ton core of radioactive fuel, and it was quickly, with deadly accuracy, speeding toward a monumental release of its immense powers.

Realizing that the members of the crew had escaped from the reactor area, Ben turned his attention to the board again. In the absence of liquid coolant, internal temperatures within the reactor continued to rise. Although the theory had never been tested, Ben just assumed that the very worst that could happen, if the emergency coolant failed to reach the interior of the core, would be the melt-down of the overheated radioactive fuel rods, which would in turn shut down the chain reaction of splitting atoms.

Although some skeptical scientists had warned of the possibility of the melt-down actually resulting in a pooling of molten radioactive substances in the bottom of the reactor, the consensus from most nuclear physicists was that even with such a pooling, there would be insufficient fissionable matter present for the formation of a critical mass. Relying on these conclusions, Ben considered the danger of an explosion from the nuclear source to be almost non-existent.

Having exhausted his efforts at forcing the control rods to drop down inside the over-heating core, Ben returned to the temperature gauges. The needles were rapidly climbing t their limits on the dials, A melt-down would completely destroy the reactor, but at least the damage would be confined to that area, and the remainder of the plant would be spared.

Ben stood, watching the needles as he ground one fist against his other palm. Mike stood behind him, and together they heard Des say the program was initiating to throw the switch that would release the second stand-by emergency coolant. This was their last resort to forestall the meltdown.

"Is anything happening?" yelled Des from his console, hoping Ben would announce a temperature reduction, showing that coolant had entered the core.

"No!" shouted Ben as the needles continued their upward swing. It was apparent that the water which should cool the reactor was not getting to it.

Mike grabbed Ben's arm. "Why hasn't it burned out?" he asked as his fingers clamped into flesh. "That's what it was supposed to do, wasn't it, Ben? Melt, then die out?"

Ben nodded dumbly. "Yeah. But I don't think it's going to do that. Look at the gauge!" The needles had reached their limits. They could go no higher.

Des was suddenly behind them. "It's not burning out!" he shouted. "The reaction isn't stopping, Ben."

Mike wheeled away from them and broke into a run toward the door yelling, "I'm getting out of here. This thing is going to blow!"

For a split second Ben took his eye off the dial to glance at the clock overhead. It was 8:46 a.m. In the next instant an unearthly hell exploded over White Water.

Ben thought he had been dreaming of the pain, but when he opened his eyes it became a reality. It seared his body, seeming to touch each nerve as it sliced through the tissues. And it worsened with each inhalation that was more than the briefest gasp, tearing at his lungs with every effort of breath. Slowly, carefully, he blinked, the dryness of his eyeballs causing a raspy sound that carried to his brain. It was funny that he should hear that when all else was quiet.

The sun neared its zenith—it was nearly noon. Ben tried moving his body but the slightest motion made the pain more acute. He lay back under the rubble, waiting. Surely a rescue squad would be here soon.

The next time he lifted his lids the sun had gone far past its zenith and was beginning its descent. Was this possible, that no one had attempted a rescue mission? Aware that the reactor had exploded sometime before nine o'clock and he had lain there for hours without anyone making an attempt to help, Ben was convinced that aid would never come.

Gazing overhead, he saw that the day had become smoggy. It was the kind of gray foggy haze that always accompanied a temperature inversion. A high pressure system had trapped the heat near the earth's surface, forcing the industrial and auto wastes of smog to blend with whatever other particles might be present in the lower atmosphere. The pollutants, including the radioactive fallout, would hang suspended low over the area until winds blew them away, or rains carried them to the ground. An inversion was most deadly when confined by a natural basin, as in Los Angeles. Open to the sea on one side and closed off by mountains on the other, the Los Angeles basin was sure to lock in the poisoned clouds.

Tugging painfully, Ben began working his body from under the chunks of rubble. Discovering that his left arm was tightly wedged beneath a slab of building material, he concentrated on getting the limb free. At last it was exposed, and to his dismay he found that about midway between the elbow and wrist, the forearm had been turned around. The palm faced out instead of in. Grimacing, feeling jagged ends of bones scraping flesh, he gingerly lifted the wretched hand up and folded it into his shirt, close to his chest. Clearing the last of the rubble away from his legs, he cautiously tested each one and learned that they were capable of motion.

The stillness was a foreboding of things to come. Not even the slapping of ocean waves could be heard. The plant had been destroyed. Piles of metal and concrete littered the grounds. Warped, twisted bodies of automobiles were scattered over the land. The nine o'clock crew had been arriving at the moment of the explosion. Normally there would have been thirty-two people within the plant; now, Ben saw no one.

The stupendous release of energy had virtually flattened White Water Nuclear Power Plant. Its personnel were as ragged and ripped as its reactor. None escaped who were in their cars or defenselessly walking across the parking lot or on the grounds.

Disoriented, Ben pulled his painful body to its feet. It had become obvious that having alone miraculously survived the blast, he would have to try to help himself. He reached inside his jacket pocket for his smart phone. The screen was black. He punched the power button. It lit up. He dialed 911. Nothing. Nothing happened. He brought up the district office number. Nothing. There was no signal - not for sending or receiving.

Home. Home was his goal, but the direction to take was the problem. Spying the chain link fence in the distance, he started toward it in hopes that upon reaching it, he could continue eastward until reaching the freeway. Then, with luck, he would be picked up and carried home.

Once he was moving, the pain became less noticeable; not less intense, but less noticeable. Complete concentration was required to avoid the hunks of wreckage that lay in his path. Only strong- willed determination to live forced him to place one sluggish, bone-weary foot after the other.

The fence, the dully metallic, heavy wire wall that enclosed the White Water facility was still standing. He could see it more clearly as he lifted his glance. A huge dark blob seemed trapped in the mesh of wire a short distance above the ground. The blob became no more distinct, however, as he laboriously closed the distance between himself and the fence. Then finally he was there, directly abreast of the elongated mass. By now it assumed human characteristics. Two arms thrown back in surrender. It was Mike Percy.

Mike had evidently been running across the parking lot after dashing out of the control room. His body was horizontal to the ground and about two feet above it. He had been blown into the chain link fence with such force that the metal links had sunk deeply into his back, firmly attaching him by the meaty shoulders, buttocks, and thighs. The charred features were barely recognizable.

Ben stared in horror. Unwilling to leave the corpse grotesquely snagged by the fence, he determined to pull it loose until it could fall to the ground. Suppuration and body fluids had plastered the clothing to the body. Selecting a hem of the dead man's shirt, Ben closed his fingers weakly around it. The fabric crumbled into ash. Steeling himself, he placed his hand behind the nape of the neck and gave a short tug. The skin slipped. Indeed, the skin and the prickly hairs at the base of the skull slipped off into his hand, adhering its wet, yellowish pink tissue to his own flesh. With revulsion, he disgustedly slung his hand, throwing the sticky mass aside. It was no use. He simply didn't have the stomach to pull Mike free. The heat had literally cooked the body to the point where flesh was beginning to fall from the bone.

Ben wanted to be sick. He felt his intestines churning and a hot bile-tasting odor rose into his mouth, but for some reason nothing came up. His parched lips and throat desperately needed water—but vomiting would only dehydrate him that much more. It was just as well if the regurgitate would stay down.

27

Stumbling along the length of fence, nearly blind with pain and fatigue, he finally found the opening. The journey to the freeway, less than two hundred yards, seemed interminable. Yet somehow he made it. His reasoning faculty had not been functioning well, for he'd thought that once he made it out to the highway, he'd be picked up and carried to safety. Now the six lanes were before him, stretching endlessly in opposite directions. But there was not a single vehicle, not a single evidence of people, in sight. Nothing moved. There were no birds in the sky and no glittering reflections from airplanes up in the gray overhead. It was almost as if he were the last man on earth.

Chapter Three

The Calmar Chemical Company was the nearest industrial operation to the White Water Plant. Situated thirteen miles directly south, it, too, was within a stone's throw of the Pacific. At eighteen minutes until nine o'clock that morning the day shift had already been there nearly an hour.

Up front, in the administration section of the plant, sat Cecil Yeager, assistant director of marketing, in his tiny, glassed-in office. Cecil brushed his coarse hair back and pulled himself in closer to his desk piled with paperwork and glanced at his computer screen. It was at that moment, as he glanced outward, that he noticed Mr. Hargrove standing on the other side of the glass. Hargrove seemed intent on the young man before him. Cecil could see his boss's lips move and imagined that he could hear the words. He continued to watch as the younger man broke into a broad smile and pushed his hand into an eager grasp with the boss. A knot twisted in Cecil's gut. This was it. He watched as Hargrove clasped the other around the shoulder and turned to walk off. The bastard, Cecil murmured under his breath.

Instead of returning to his office, Hargrove, his face tinged with the redness from too many years of boozing and from the morning's pleasantries with his young employee, pushed the door in and stepped into Cecil's office. Calmly he withdrew a thin, dark cigar, held a flame to the end until he was puffing smoke, then looked Cecil squarely in the eye as he spoke. "Guess you saw that out there."

Cecil lowered his glance, without nodding.

"Yeager, I'll get right to the point. I've just had a talk with McCormick."

Cecil looked up, his eyes cool. Here it comes, he thought, that old fart is going to hand me a line of bull next....a lot of 'you're a fine man, Yeager.'

Hargrove puffed deeply, then continued, "You've been with us a lot of years....a fine, a really fine addition to our staff." Hargrove paused, inspected the tip of the cigar. "I know you were next in line for promotion, Yeager, but the job went to McCormick.

A hot spasm of anger passed through Cecil's body, but he sat unmoving.

Hargrove opened his mouth to continue when the shaking began. It was not a violent quake, hardly more than a tremor to Californians who had experienced many such rumblings over the years. But the man registered a trace of surprise and waited for the movement to cease. Within a fraction of a minute the quake was over.

Papers on the desk had shifted and Cecil scooped them back into a pile. As yet he had had nothing to say to his superior.

Hargrove cleared his throat. "Calmar, you see, is taking a new course in the advancement of its employees. We're going toward younger men....men who have a lot of years to give us....men with new ideas, fresher drives."

Cecil lifted himself from his chair and went over to gaze out through the glass wall.

"You're an excellent chemist, Yeager, and you've done all right in marketing, but," Hargrove flicked the ash from his cigar, "we need someone who is, well....more personable for public relations."

With his back to Hargrove, Cecil replied, "McCormick is an ambitious young man. He won't disappoint you." And he's a butt licker to make it after less than two years, he didn't add.

"Yes....well, I'm glad you understand." Hargrove drew a short puff on his cigar. "What's best for Calmar, eh, Yeager?"

Cecil saw Hargrove's reflection in the glass as the man reached for the doorknob. "Yes sir. Calmar," he said to the departing form.

Returning to his chair, Cecil sank down into it. His palms were wet and he dried them on his trousers before starting up the marketing program and beginning his work. He hadn't time to get to the second tab on the screen when suddenly a terrific boom sounded.

It was much, much stronger than the occasional sonic booms that people had grown used to. In the older wing, in the packing department behind the administrative offices, the windows high on the stucco wall shattered, sending splinters of glass raining down on the workers feeding the assembly line. At the same instant the south wall of the thirty-year-old building began to buckle and chunks of mortar cascaded through the haze of mortar dust to the floor.

Immediately conveyor belts ground to a halt, lights went out, and the ventilation system shut off. Within seconds the entire operation at Calmar had ceased.

For the space of two or three good breaths the only sound was falling mortar and workers scrambling to take cover.

Clerical workers and officials of Calmar drew themselves into a tight group on the main floor of the newer part of the building. Cecil, feeling the shock to the structure, rushed from his office into the large central room. In the dimness of the interior, it was apparent that many of the staff were frightened. This was no ordinary sound reverberation, and following so quickly on the heels of the quake, it seemed ominous.

Hargrove pushed his way through the group until he reached Cecil's side. "Here, Yeager," he said, shoving a small bullhorn into Cecil's hand, "find out what's happening in the packing department!"

Holding the bullhorn, Cecil watched Hargrove rush across to a telephone with intercom and start yelling into the speakerphone. It was dead. The phones were down. A dark thought passed through his brain as he saw the older man's concern. So where's your fair-haired McCormick, Cecil wondered, as he started down the corridor to the back of the plant.

At first the darkness of the older wing and the accompanying quietness sent a wave of fear through Cecil. Had they all fled— or was it worse? "Now hear me," he yelled. "Are you there? Is everyone all right?"

His voice, strangely hoarse in the bullhorn, loosened the tongues of the workers. Questions were hurled out amidst isolated moans and more than a few, near hysterical screams. By this time everyone who could was frantically talking at once. It took several minutes for the din to die out so that Cecil's voice could be heard again.

"Folks, try to stay calm! We've got to stay calm!" he commanded.

"What the hell has happened?" yelled someone from the darkness.

"Is it the Russians?" shouted someone else.

"Or the Red Chinese?" bellowed another.

Calmar employees had been shuffled about some by the shaking four minutes earlier, but recognized the source of the movement. Once they had regained their equilibrium, they had calmly gone on with their chores. This new jolt though—this was something entirely different.

"It's the Japs again! I knew this would happen," came from one of the older men.

"Naw. Not them. They own half of California by now," someone snorted.

"Listen! People! Take it easy! This is Cecil Yeager speaking. As soon as we know, we'll tell you, but right at this moment, we don't know what has happened. Please vacate this department and meet out on the parking lot." He stared at the south wall which seemed likely to collapse at any second. "Just gather in the parking area until I get back to you."

"Well, that's that," someone remarked as the workers quickly moved outside. "They may as well let us go home because there won't be any work done in that wing for a while."

Assured that everyone was out of the damaged wing, Cecil hurriedly returned to the office area. The workers there still milled around the center of the floor, speculating on where the explosion had occurred. Having no knowledge of the collapsing wall in the rear area, they were loudly expressing their views but otherwise showed less concern than the packagers.

It was Hargrove dashing wildly into their midst, yelling and flailing his arms, which brought the group to quietness. "Listen! Listen! It was at White Water....there's been an accident at White Water! A car just stopped out front for a moment, then drove off."

"The explosion?" Cecil asked.

"Yes, yes! White Water has been leveled! There's radiation everywhere! " Hargrove started off again, then hesitated momentarily as he passed Cecil. "Yeager," he ordered, "tell the people in the packing department that we've got to get out of here...''He moved off before the words were finished.

Cecil watched him scurrying off, a lemming now. Then grimly thinking of the workers outside on the parking lot he grasped the bullhorn more firmly and headed for the door.

Outside the employees had convened on the asphalt lot and were showing signs of recovery from their earlier shock. Most had their phones out and were trying to get on the internet or call or text someone. Relief that they had escaped without injury was evident in their hushed conversations. Occasionally laughter would break through from someone who felt very lucky to be standing there at all. As far as they were concerned, though, the danger was over. But there was muttering that they had no cell phone reception.

Cecil appeared on the steps with his bullhorn and began shouting. "Everyone back inside!! Get inside now! Come in through here!" He motioned frantically, beckoning to them.

The group exchanged glances of bewilderment but began to move in the direction of the building. When Cecil repeated his message and then darted inside himself, the stragglers sensed the urgency in the man and speedily closed the distance to the building.

When they were assembled, crowded inside a small meeting room, Cecil climbed on a chair in front of them. Trying to keep his voice from shaking, he made the announcement. "The White Water power plant has just had an explosion!" He waited for the reaction of panic from the people. Instead there was a moment of silence.

"Is that why we don't have any cell phone service?" someone called out and others assented.

"Then can we go home?" a voice asked finally.

"When will we be called back to work?" someone else queried.

"Wait. Wait! You don't...." Everyone was talking suddenly; he couldn't make himself heard above the noise.

"Yeah. How long will it take them to get this wall repaired so we can work?"

"Didn't you hear what I said?" Cecil shouted. "White Water has had a major explosion!" His emphasis was lost on the people.

"So we're without electricity. Big deal," came the retort.

"Yeah. They'll fix it. We'll have power soon."

Could this be? Cecil wondered. Could these human beings, crowded here in this room, possibly be ignorant of the catastrophe that had just befallen them? His background as a chemist made the significance of the accident deadly clear to him, but surely other people....

"Look, folks! White Water was a nuclear power plant. It has exploded! Don't you know what that means?" Cecil asked.

"Sure. We're going to be out of electricity until they get it repaired."

"They? Who are you talking about?" he questioned, appalled by their incomprehension. Here stood the backbone of the country—and they hadn't the vaguest idea of the horrifying meaning of this accident. "There is no 'They' who will go out

33

and repair White Water. It has been destroyed, people!"

Their faces reflected the lack of understanding, the incomprehension of lay persons who had never heard of beta or gamma rays, radioactive wastes, or fission reactions. The word reaction, itself, had no more meaning to them than the collection of angular buildings that sat on the horizon thirteen miles southward.

They were a younger generation for the most part. Atmospheric testing of nuclear bombs was internationally banned at the time they were listening to the latest music on their ipods, surfing the web, and getting their first automobiles.

As adults, they'd periodically notice an article in a local newspaper dealing with the installation of a nuclear plant or some group that was against the installation. Occasionally a blurb would appear about a leak of radioactive wastes and comments by a scientist as to its dangers. But that would be followed by officials denying that danger existed and stating that the public was ignorant for being spooked. These articles, though, had little bearing on the average man and woman as they thumbed cursorily through the news on the way to sports, the comics, and the food section.

The day of the fallout shelters was gone. The shelters had only served as havens for down-and-out winos. Since the threat of the cold war had ended and atmospheric testing had ceased, the shelters had been eliminated.

Perspiration rolled down from his armpits as Cecil tried to communicate the full scope of this disaster. "Don't you see," he pleaded. "It's not a simple matter of the lights being out, for God's sake. It's an atomic explosion that we've had!"

There were some murmurings at this. An older man spoke up. "Like an atomic bomb? Is that it?"

"I'm afraid it is something like an atomic bomb. Do you remember what the radiation did to the Japanese when we dropped our A-bombs?" How could people who had been babies in 1945 or not even born yet grasp this? Unless they'd been educated with the facts, they couldn't understand. He absently wiped sweat from his forehead. "Well, we've got that same kind of radiation in the air right now....right overhead."

"Lordy, I remember reading about where those Japanese got burned to death. And others got real sick from something in the air and died." Someone had begun to catch on.

"What are we going to do?" begged a voice from the crowd.

"I don't know....I just don't know," said Cecil, relieved that he had at last aroused some concern. "But there's no reason for you to stay here. Maybe try to get your families together, because there'll certainly be an evacuation."

"Leave our homes?" asked a chorus of voices.

"I guess so. With the radiation in the air the longer we're around here the more of it we're going to absorb," he said.

A female voice, near hysteria, shrieked, "But where do we go? Which way?"

"Away from here—from the White Water site—I don't know. Someone will have to direct us. Turn on whatever you can get to work when you get home. Hopefully you or someone in your neighborhood will have an emergency generator. Somebody is going to have to tell us the safe routes....but stay away from White Water!" Cecil cautioned from the darkness.

A few people began to panic at this. They turned and ran to their automobiles. Outside, one lady dashed across the lot, her head covered with a packing box as though to protect herself from the penetrating rays. The disbelievers in the strange danger of the airborne particles strolled, their lack of haste indicating their disdain for the fright that had begun to flow.

"Hell, I don't feel anything in the air. I'll bet you that guy Yeager is a crock," said a young man.

"Yeah," agreed his friend. "He don't know what he's talking about. There's nothing burning me."

"Naw. Me neither," agreed the other as they walked slowly toward their automobiles.

Screeching tires and the mad rushing of employees quickly became contagious to many of the skeptics—and there were many. Seeing their fellow workers dashing away set them to thinking, and before many more steps, they, too, began breaking into a run. Their private thoughts failed to assure them that this was some sort of monstrous lie, that nobody would have let anything that dangerous be put up on the edge of a megalopolis that contained nearly eleven million people.

Because metropolitan Los Angeles and its neighboring Orange County were crisscrossed with a massive, arterial system of freeways, a public transportation system of buses or trains was virtually nonexistent. So, as the Calmar workers piled into their automobiles, they wheeled either north or south to get to minor routes near their homes. All southbound traffic passed within a few hundred yards of the White Water site. With car

35

windows securely rolled up, most felt that even if those strange foreign things were really in the air, then they certainly wouldn't get inside a car with its windows closed.

While others, in the offices, frantically snatched their belongings from desk drawers and files and exited in a headlong rush, Cecil Yeager methodically pondered on those few articles which he thought might be useful in the days to come. Company records that he had been personally responsible for were not among his list of considerations. The computers had automatic back up systems. Anything that wasn't backed up now, it was too late. His employer had been too cheap to put in emergency power generators. But no one was going to stick around to do any work, anyway.

He leaned against the edge of his desk, his head lowered in concentration, when the last employee raced through the clutter, en route to the parking lot.

Frank Waring, a junior accountant at Calmar, paused only long enough to ask, "Hey, Yeager! What are you doing standing there? I had you figured to be the first one out!"

"I....I'm just trying to decide on what to take," Cecil explained. "I expected you to be long gone," the man said, dashing out. This comment from his fellow worker was the kind of stinging, acid barb that people often threw at him. For some reason, unexplained to him, others seemed to picture him as the first one out, the one least likely to cope, the one who was always intimidated and easily frightened. That image was inconsistent with his picture of himself. He knew he was probably one of the best-read and most knowledgeable men in the chemical company. His lack of aggressive behavior was simply due to a deeply ingrained timidness in his relations with other people.

An unmarried, lonely man, and without kin, Cecil sought refuge from his loneliness by embedding himself in piles of books, journals, and papers. Naturally scholarly in his early life, he had read to learn, but as the years began quickly ebbing away, he continued to read, not only to learn, but also to fill the vacuum that was the solitude of his evenings, his weekends, even his vacations. A promotion to public relations would have plugged the hole in his life, would have made him become more outgoing. But it wasn't to be, now.

In his assessment of the situation, he concluded that the dangers of the radiation hung like a giant lethal cloud above his head—nothing short of a rapid evacuation from the region could save him from its horrors. In the brief span of a few moments, he could not determine the course to follow, the direction to take. Whatever seemed the easiest, and the most expedient, that's what he'd do. Meanwhile, he must prepare for the eventuality that he may never see Calmar Chemical again, nor perhaps, even this once beautiful countryside.

From the corners of his memory came the knowledge that metals absorb large amounts or radiation, and if worn close to the body, served as pools for the deadly rays that would steadily and continually irradiate his tissues....ultimately destroying cells of his body.

Carefully he removed his watch and laid it on the desk. Next, the class ring was tugged off his finger and placed beside the watch. Metal coins were removed from his pocket and dropped into the collection.

With these things done, Cecil went into the small room used by the night security guard. Swiftly he pried the lock off the guard's locker. Inside he found the oily thirty-eight caliber pistol that was carried on night rounds, which he slipped into the outer pocket of his jacket. It was metal but he would stow it away from his body once he got outside.

A last glance around, and he moved past the conference room into the business office. Hesitating for a mere second to scan the office, he stooped to the huge gray safe. It was a new security device, recently installed, and with a flick of the lever the safe was open. Brushing aside the coins, he removed the bills and stuffed them into a money bag. Dropping the bag into his pocket, he turned and walked out the door.

In the rear-view mirror of his car, the squat, sprawling plant seemed a deserted, forsaken structure. He wondered when people would again darken its portals

Sixteen years Cecil had given to Calmar Chemical and in those years he'd worked himself from a laboratory chemist doing dilutions to a minor executive position. And today it was over. His decision had been hastily formed but Cecil knew that once his mind was made up he wouldn't change it. On some future day this plant would be operating again, but it wouldn't be for quite some time, and it would never include Cecil Yeager's services. He wasn't unhappy to be leaving Calmar, wishing only that it had been for a different reason. With his course of action now firmly fixed in his mind, Cecil made the journey from Calmar to his townhouse. Traffic was a nightmare. Everyone seemed to be in their cars.

Damn, he wished he hadn't bought the place. As soon as he quit making payments it would be repossessed. He cast the thought aside as he rushed into the bedroom. There was only one thing he'd take, but the reflection in the mirror stopped him in his tracks. He'd never been a man to smile easily and catching a view of himself, the heavy, bushy eyebrows knitted in concentration, the thin lips a gash in his lower face, he halted momentarily. He stared at the somber, serious reflection of himself. For an instant he tried relaxing the muscles that had pulled the crows feet into deep trenches. But it didn't work. They had been there forever, the lines. They were permanent fixtures to the side of each of his eyes, firmly ingrained in the flesh of his face. He grabbed some clothes and his cash that he had stashed and rushed out the door, back to his car.

An hour and twenty minutes had elapsed since the explosion at White Water. How quickly had the news spread? As he accelerated onto the freeway ramp traffic was congested moving south away from Whitewater and only dribbles of northbound vehicles were on the freeway. The morning had turned hot and stuffy and it was uncomfortably warm in the car but Cecil elected the heat in favor of drawing in more air from the outside.

Nature was inflicting a cruel joke on Californians this morning. The temperature inversion was becoming a crucial barrier to dispersion of the fallout. Under ordinary weather conditions, offshore winds would be whipping the heavily-laden air higher in the sky and carrying it eastward, over the less populated desert regions. Or, under more unusual conditions, a good strong Santa Ana wind coming in from the deserts would blow the foul air over the Pacific. But neither of these wind systems was present this morning. There were only the meager puffs that occasionally circulated under the heavier layer of air. If this inversion persisted for more than a day or so, Cecil knew, there could be thousands of casualties from radiation exposure.

Cecil had always had a fear of flying. Even during the war he'd had to steel himself against this unreasonable fear and literally force himself onto the planes. And Dramamine and mild sedatives did nothing to quell the churning in his stomach and the tightness in his chest. Still, this was the moment to throw caution to the wind....wind? He grimaced at having formed the word in his mind. He needed to get away from here—out of the radiation—as soon as possible. Ahead lay the landing strip, looking dull in the gray haze.

The money sack formed a bulge in his jacket pocket and he reached down and patted it, secure with the thought that for enough money one could buy anything. He drove up to the one person in sight.

"Yes sir?" the man in dirty coveralls asked. "What can I do for you?"

"A plane," Cecil replied. "I want to charter a plane."

"When do you...?" began the attendant.

"Right now. I want one right now," said Cecil in a rush of words as he alighted from the car.

"Well, now, I don't know. My other pilot is out and I can't leave the place," answered the man. "There's no way...."

Cecil snorted testily, "You run a charter service, don't you? Can you fly?"

"Well sure, but mister, we're a shoestring outfit."

"I'll pay you—pay you well. All I want is to get away from here." In his eagerness Cecil was pressing the man. He wondered if his approach was becoming suspicious to the other.

The appearance of another man interrupted the conversation. He gestured to the pilot to come over. It was minutes before the pilot returned to Cecil. Wiping his hands on a greasy cloth, he seemed to appraise the chemist closely.

In his anxiety to be gone, Cecil exhibited a nervous fidget as he shifted from one foot to the other and glanced, once, back over his shoulder. Physically, he was not unprepossessing with his coarse brown hair and stocky build. An intense man, Cecil's alert dark eyes stared at the pilot as he awaited the man's decision.

"Sorry, I can't do anything for you," said the pilot.

"Wait," protested Cecil. "I said I'd pay you—more money than you'd earn in a dozen flights." He glanced out toward the runway at the shiny small plane.

"You from near Los Angeles?" asked the man suspiciously. "I just got told about what happened." He looked up at the sky as though expecting visible evidences of the disaster.

Reluctant to admit to his reason for haste, but knowing that the pilot now understood, Cecil admitted, "Yes. I was pretty near when White Water had the explosion. The freeways are going to be jammed soon with people trying to escape. I want to

39

beat the rush."

The pilot nodded and switched his gaze to the horizon. "It's going to be bad, they say." Returning to Cecil, he remarked, "Look bud, out there is a twin engine Comanche, fueled up and ready to go. But when it leaves this strip it's going to have me and my family aboard."

"You'll have room for an extra passenger?" asked Cecil hopefully.

Shaking his head, the pilot began moving away. "Man, I won't even be able to get all my family in that cabin. You're out of luck."

Cecil stepped in closer and grabbed the pilot's shoulder. "Listen, you won't make this much money again on a single flight. I'll triple what you think a trip to Mexico is worth."

Without looking at him, the man answered, "Sorry....you don't have that much money." Noticing the chemist's car, he said, "Drive out. That's what everybody else will have to do."

It became apparent, as the man started rapidly walking away, that his answer was final. As he got into the car, Cecil thought of the gun that he had. He could force the man to fly him out. With the muzzle of that pistol in his ribs, the pilot would have to do it. But what if the guy got obstinate? There's no telling what he'd do at five thousand feet. "Hey!"

The pilot hesitated and turned back. "Yeah?"

Cecil had his arm through the window of the car, his fingers gripped around the handle of the gun as it rested on the seat.

The pilot was waiting, but Cecil couldn't bring himself to raise the weapon into sight. Realizing the uselessness of further arguing, he let the gun drop and the pilot continued on to his truck. In a few seconds the vehicle was kicking gravel against the bed as it raced past Cecil and out toward the highway.

Sitting dejectedly in the car, Cecil began mentally, researching other avenues of escape open to him. Every additional minute of exposure to the radiation would do excessive damage to his tissues, and yet, the quickest escape route was now obviously closed to him, he knew. By-passing the freeway and driving the county roads would take him forever to get away from the area, and deciding that he knew what to expect by going due east, he elected to go in another direction. The trip was approximately a hundred and forty miles by freeway, but that route was out. The freeway would be packed. He'd have to travel backroads even if it would probably double the distance. With decisiveness, he headed the car south.

Chapter Four

San Mirado's main street was coming to life. Local coffee shops had unlatched their doors for the early morning trade. The post office and department of motor vehicles had opened at eight, but excluding these and several service stations, no other shops were prepared for daily business as yet; a typical pace of the downtown of a suburban, bedroom community.

Downtown was no more active than the surrounding subdivision. However, there suburban housewives had seen their husbands off to work and their children on their way to school. With the day stretching before her, Paula Waring had called across the fence and invited Flo Winton over for coffee. It was a not unusual practice that the two shared—spending some time in the morning over a breakfast roll while they traded gossip. For Paula the kaffeklatsch frequently was the highlight of her day.

They were sitting across the dinette table sipping the hot brew when the quaking began. Coffee sloshed out of the cups as the two women stared at each other, both firmly gripping the edge of the table top. The shaking movements ended within seconds. In San Mirado it had been felt as a relatively mild tremor.

"Whew," Flo laughed nervously. "For a moment there I thought this was going to be the big one."

Paula was more annoyed than concerned over the tremor. Getting to her feet she straightened a picture that had been knocked askew and then tore off paper towels to swab up the spilled coffee.

"Damn. Wouldn't you know it." Paula stopped her mopping motions and pointed. "Look at the end of the coffee-cake." There was a large soggy spot in the pastry. Coffee had spilled onto the plate and soaked in. "And I just bought that yesterday! Frank thinks I made it," she added as an afterthought.

Flo nodded knowingly as she cut off the wet end and found a clean plate for the rest of the pastry. Once everything seemed in place again Paula poured them a fresh batch of coffee and they took their seats. Except for a tinge of nerves, nothing had altered the outlook for the morning. Paula sliced the crusty pastry and was shoving it toward Flo as the second vibration hit the house, cracking a large window in the dinette.

"Now what the heck was that?" snapped Paula. It was not that either woman was frightened by this most recent event. Rather, Paula was irritated that damage was done. She jumped from her chair and went to inspect the shattered window behind her.

"Those fighter jets from the air station, I'll bet," Flo replied. "I knew that one of these times those booms would break some windows. Mine always rattle and shake when those things are up there on training flights." Flo sounded confident of the cause of the breakage.

Paula was inclined to agree, but the cost of replacing the windows was foremost in her mind. "I think the military ought to have to pay for this."

"Well, I don't know..." replied her bosom friend.

"Oh, come on, Flo! If their planes cause a sonic boom that breaks my windows, it's their fault. And they should have to replace what is damaged!"

"You've got insurance, haven't you? Just collect on that."

Paula considered the suggestion briefly. "I'm not sure something like this is covered. Frankly, I don't think it is, Flo. But even if it were, my rates would go sky-high if I tried collecting on every little thing that happens."

Paula stood, pondering the cracked glass as Flo got up and moved to her side. Reaching down, Paula removed a sliver of the broken window from the sill, just as a loud, extremely piercing siren began somewhere in the small town.

"What in the world?" she demanded, dropping the fragment and clasping both hands over her ears. She looked at Flo in bewilderment. In her four years in San Mirado she'd never heard anything like it. The shrill noises continued without let-up.

Flo finally grabbed up the telephone. "I'm calling the police to see what's going on."

"Maybe it's some kind of a drill," ventured Paula.

"For what? We've never had drills for anything before." She dialed several times before giving up. "Damnit, it's dead. Where's my cell phone?"

Both moved rapidly to the front of the house. The street running past the house now had a handful of neighbors standing in it, confusion on their faces as they attempted to talk above the piercing sound. At last the noise ended and Paula and Flo stepped outside to join them.

"Does anyone know what's going on around here?" asked

43

Flo. She had gotten no signal on her cell phone. The internet connection seemed to be down, too.

The best information seemed to have something to do with a dusty looking cloud that had speedily formed in the northwest.

Someone suggested, "There's not much up that way—that electric power plant, maybe."

Speculations on the cause of the strange, glass-shattering noise and the dirty cloud passed freely among the women. Receiving no answers to their question, they finally began to disband and drift back indoors.

Paula and Flo, however, were still leaning against a parked car, engaged in talking, when a van turned onto their street.

The vehicle, equipped with a mobile communication system, was issuing instructions as to evacuation procedure. The message was more puzzling then informative; but then, the vehicle and its hastily delivered bulletin had been the small city's initial effort at warning its citizens. The driver had been pushed into the cab with orders to drive up and down the streets of San Mirado while the public official at his side shouted out the news.

"What's he saying?" asked Paula.

They strained their ears to understand before the unit had driven out of hearing range.

"Something about evacuate southward on the freeway."

"Why? Why?" Paula asked as she stepped into the street to view the unit.

"Shush—I'm trying to hear," said Flo.

Watching the rear end of the truck turning the corner, she remarked, "Something about White Water exploding."

"White Water? What's that?" asked Paula.

"The power plant up the coast."

"Oh. Oh well, then the current's just going to be off," said Paula with a note of relief in her voice.

"I guess so," Flo said, frowning.

"Why evacuate, though? That doesn't make any sense to me," Paula remarked. "Do you suppose it's a prank—you know, kids are always doing dumb things. Maybe it's just someone trying to scare us."

"But the sirens, Paula—why were they being sounded?"

Paula shrugged her shoulders. "I have no idea. I've never heard anything except the periodic test sirens before. Do you think it's a test? But I can tell you one thing—I'm sure not going to leave my belongings here and take off down the road. Frank would be mad as hell when he gets home tonight if he finds me and the kids gone."

"Aren't you going to go get them at school? I mean, just in case there's something to this?"

"No, I don't think so. Not until I know more about this, anyway."

"Well, I am," Flo said. "It may be a hoax, but if it's not, I want to have my boy with me."

San Mirado public schools consisted of kindergarten through twelfth grades. The students attended campuses at three different locations within the community. High school classes began a little earlier in the day than the intermediate grades. Kindergarten began on the latest hour—at nine o'clock, to allow ample time for mothers to drop their tykes off after husband and older children had gone their way.

At Intermediate School the doors had been shut against the outside. Virtually every modern school plant built within the recent past had been structured for maximum utilization of the mild southern California weather. No long dark corridors extended the lengths of two-story brick prisons. Instead, the individual classrooms, identified by their varying colors of red, blue, green, or yellow doors opened directly onto the compound, and into open air.

Miss Althea Carr's seventh grade class students were in their seats. The tardy bell had rung promptly at 8:30 a.m. Like obedient children, they had saluted the flag in a sing-song voice, then politely waited for Miss Carr to call the roll. Attendance was very good. But then it was still early in the semester.

Being a stern disciplinarian made the teacher one of the less popular ones on the campus. The children respected Miss Carr, and slightly feared her. Some openly admired her, but she definitely was not the campus favorite. She never dilly-dallied, but got right into the lessons and stayed with them until her daily objectives were reached. She was impossible to be led astray from the subject under discussion by slyly contrived questions or flattering remarks. For all her lack of popularity among her young charges, she nonetheless managed to propel most of her pupils far beyond their usual levels of achievement.

Her concern at this particular moment was with a young man in the last seat in the back. He seemed to spend more energy kicking the chair of the girl in front than he did saying the pledge. Her continuing dread was this rebellious child who refused to say the pledge. He'd put his hand over his heart but wouldn't make any sign of mouthing the words. His was a bad example for the others to see and she knew she'd have to handle this subtly, lest others get the same idea.

The tremor rocked the room with a brief spasmodic quiver. San Mirado sat a respectable distance from the maze of fault zones, and the quake hardly moved the sandstone on which Intermediate rested. Actually the trembling had ceased before the principal had had the chance to ring the bell that signaled an earthquake.

"Well, class, it seems that we won't be having to duck and cover just now." Miss Carr smiled pleasantly to the children as they sat down. "Kim, would you mind collecting the homework papers, please?"

Moans and groans greeted this announcement. Althea smiled to herself while maintaining an outwardly stern expression. Other teachers sometimes forgot to gather the assignments, but not she. The ones who'd chosen to watch television the previous night instead of doing their work would be caught again.

Just as Kim handed the papers to her and she was glancing through them, a booming noise resounded through the acoustical tile. There were no windows in the classroom, the theory being that four solid walls cut down on the distractions to the pupils, and she chose to ignore the sound. "I can see by these papers that some of you have decided there are things more important than an education." She was going to make it a bad scene. Each failure to perform was a personal affront to her as a teacher.

She had just begun to warm to the subject with, "Perhaps you need an extra half hour after school to finish your assignment," when distant sirens started blaring. Shortly the buzzing of the school's own bell was added to the racket.

Althea quickly sorted the sounds out in her mind. The classes were required by the state education code to undergo one full-scale fire drill each month, and one duck-and-cover drill each semester. This was the signal for the latter. But they had had their practice for the semester only last week.

"All right, children! Quickly! Under the desks!"

She knew that in the event of an extreme emergency, such as an earthquake, the students were to drop to the floor and crawl under their desks upon hearing the special bell. Instructions required that the same procedure be followed for other

46

emergencies—duck down and get under the desks and stay under them until the clear bell was sounded. But this obviously was not because of the earthquake. That shaking had lasted briefly and ended several minutes ago.

The buzzing of the school bell continued after the sirens stopped. Her knees were beginning to ache and she wondered if the young students' legs fell asleep, too. In another room this might have been fun for them, but not here. She refused to allow any breach of regulations.

Eventually the buzzer also quit. There was silence in the room.

The whole episode was disconcerting to the teacher. A clear bell hadn't been sounded yet. Someone up there in that office hadn't learned to do his job properly. The clear bell always had to ring otherwise they'd be expected to remain here under the desks. Not knowing exactly what to do, Althea crawled to the intercom phone hanging beside her desk and dialed the office. No answer.

But as the school's back up emergency power generation system kicked in the intercom came to life with words broadcasting that had a coldly sobering effect. She had not even been born in 1945, but she vividly recalled the documentaries on TV, and pictures she had seen in a college classroom.

Coughing away the choking feeling, she finally got to her feet and faced the class. For a moment she didn't know what to say to them, how to explain. Finally, "Children, there is a deadly poison in the air. The White Water Nuclear Power Plant....has exploded. All its terrible invisible wastes are up in the air we breathe." Slowly she sank into her chair. "We will never forget this day." Althea sat there, immobile, with a vacant expression, as if her mind were elsewhere.

Young faces peered at each other from under the desks, perplexed by Althea. Then realizing that she had forgotten them, they slowly climbed into their seats and sat quietly before her—motionless—their young faces pale. Failing to understand the incident, but aware of its uniqueness, and sensing the graveness of the occasion, they waited patiently until their teacher returned the day to normal. But she couldn't, and she wouldn't, for as far as she was concerned, the children had ceased to exist.

Thirty minutes after the cloud of dust was spotted in the northwest, the citizens of San Mirado continued to discuss its cause and consequences. The public announcement issued from

47

the van cruising the neighborhood was indistinctly heard by most of the listeners, and those who received the message clearly were confused as to precisely what action, if any, they should be taking.

At first the message was believed by many to be a terrible hoax. Others, who were willing to accept the report verbatim, were disinclined to follow the advice to vacate their homes and businesses in a headlong rush to safety. After all, how would they ever become re-united with spouses, who were away on their jobs, or with other relatives? And what would happen to a house or business that had been left by the owners? Past experience had proven that a weekend was sufficient opportunity for burglars to denude a place of its contents. No, the people of this town weren't about to forsake their worldly possessions in a mad flight toward some obscure safety. In the average mind, if this emergency wasn't war then there couldn't be very much danger. Certainly nothing to get too upset about this early in the morning.

Safety at this point meant different things to different people, but very few believed it meant driving as far south as you could go with no destination.

Ever since Flo walked off mumbling about getting her boy Rickey from school, Paula had been considering the same idea. She was lifting the garage door by hand, in preparation for driving to the school when she saw her daughter running down the sidewalk.

"Mother! Mother!" screamed the child.

Paula waited until the child drew near. "Kim, what are you doing here? Have they let you out of school?"

The child's blond hair was a mess of tangles, an observation which momentarily irritated the mother. "What's happened to you? You look like you didn't even comb that mop this morning," admonished Paula, her own hair neatly coiffed.

"There was a duck-and-cover drill at school and we had to crawl under our desks," answered the girl in short gasps. "Mother, did you hear about it? The poison? Miss Carr was acting so funny in class, Mother."

"Slow down, Kimberly!"

"But Miss Carr was really weird! After the sirens stopped she told us that some terrible thing had let a lot of poison into the air and we're breathing it now." Her lips started quivering as she spoke. "Mother, is it true?"

48

"Kim, have you seen your brother? Do you know if he was let out?" asked Paula worriedly.

"Is it, Mother? Is it true?" The girl was starting to cry with big, colorless tears rolling down her cheeks.

Paula grabbed the child by her thin shoulders and roughly shook her. "I don't know what's going on! As soon as Jerry gets home we're all going to sit right in that house until your daddy comes in. He'll know what's happening. Now, did you see Jerry anywhere around the grounds?"

Paula heard her son yelling as he came bounding across the street. A sophisticated ninth grader, he was enthusiastic over the unexpected freedom.

"Hey, Ma, our teacher said he didn't know when we'd be having school again. Great, huh, Kim?" Seeing his sister's red eyes and hearing her sniffles suddenly sapped some of the boy's fervor.

"Hush, Jerry. I don't want to hear another word from you until Frank gets home from work," Paula commanded.

Now that her brood was together, she herded them inside the house. Pushing the two children toward a sofa she ordered them down as she sat across from them. The mother rarely lost patience with her children. In fact she usually took great delight in hearing her handsome, young son sound off. But not today. It was one of those days when everything seemed to be going wrong. Paula let her thoughts wander—maybe she should have stayed in bed that morning. Nothing had gone right, not since she had scorched Frank's shirt collar ironing it before breakfast and he had been late leaving for work. Sighing, she looked over at the shattered window, and tried to think where they'd get the money to replace it. Slumped down, she brooded that the day had overtaken her.

Within the quarter hour the door burst open with a giant heave and Frank Waring stood in the middle of the room. His sudden appearance was a shock to the wife and children.

"Frank! Did you hear anything about...?"

"Paula, we've got to get away from here!" He was agitated and in great haste. "Come on!"

"Wait....Frank. What in the world is going on, anyway? Did they let you off from work or...?"

"Calmar has shut down, Paula. According to one of the execs we're free to leave the plant. Right now we've got to worry about saving our hides and getting the hell out of here!"

49

Frank Waring had known Cecil Yeager only remotely since the first day of his employment at the chemical plant, but since Yeager had said this was dangerous business, then it was. No matter how others might spurn the chemist's admonitions, Frank respected his intelligence.

He was about to speak again when Flo burst in the door behind him. She was obviously upset and her husband Harry was trailing concernedly behind. Immediately she started to speak. "Oh, Paula, Frank....we can't find Rickey!"

Harry tried putting his arm around his wife but she brushed him off. He frowned, his brow wrinkling as she turned to the Warings.

"I knew it was a mistake to have given Rickey the motorbike. I argued and argued with Harry. He's too young to handle a machine at his age, and now he hasn't come home from school!"

Harry stepped up softly behind her. "I tell you, Sugar, there's nothing to worry about. He'll be home soon."

Flo shrugged helplessly, looking at Paula. "Your children were home long ago. Weren't they all let out together? The school couldn't tell me anything."

Jerry pulled himself up from the sofa where he was sitting with his sister. "I saw Rickey and Lesley White on his bike, Mrs. Winton."

Flo turned to the boy. "Do you know where they were going, Jerry?"

"Yes ma'am. Rickey said they were going all the way up to White Water to see what had happened."

Frank gasped. "White Water. Jerry, why didn't you say something about this sooner?"

"Well, gee...I don't know."

"Oh Jesus," moaned Flo. "Harry, we've got to go up there and get him."

Frank reached out toward his friends. "Now wait....you can't go up there! That whole area is hot with radiation!"

Harry peered around Flo to speak to Frank. "I don't think it's that bad. Sure, maybe there's some radiation but not all that much."

Frank stepped up closer to Harry and spoke softly. "Listen. It's suicide for you to go north. Hell, man, it's suicide for us to be right here."

Harry shook his head. "Aw now, Frank, it could be worse."

Grabbing Flo and shoving her toward the door, he said over his shoulder, "Don't worry so much about all this bullshit. We'll get in the car and go find Rickey. Everybody's in an uproar over this thing but I tell you it's just not that serious."

Paula watched her neighbors leave and then turned, confused, to Frank.

"Get some stuff together and let's go!" he said to his wife.

"Where, Frank? We can't just get in the car and start driving. Where are we going?" asked Paula.

"East—to Arizona," he answered.

Paula didn't oppose Frank's decisions, at least not often. But this seemed senseless to her. "What about the house? It'll be stripped of every solitary thing we own," she protested.

"Look, woman, we may not ever come back to this house. We may never see it again. And if we don't, it won't make a damned bit of difference to us if everything is stolen."

"Frank, we've spent years making just the home we always wanted. Now you're ready to throw it all aside and run screaming because of some rumor."

"It's not a rumor, Paula! Less than one hour ago a nuclear reactor went up in dust—and it's not but a few miles from us. If we hang around here, we're going to be dead ducks!"

Paula hesitated over the statement then looked at the children who had become alarmed at their father's words. Kim's face was stained with a fresh onslaught of tears. She moved over to comfort the girl.

"Frank, are you sure it's dangerous? I don't see how this could happen. Harry doesn't think it's serious."

"So what! I'm not going to stand here arguing with you any longer, Paula. I'm leaving and the kids are going with me. If you want to stay to protect your possessions, then that's your choice. But it's a damned foolish one, I'll tell you that!"

"We don't even have any cash in the house," she replied sullenly. "How far do you think we'll go without money?"

That was a fact Frank had not considered and it stopped him momentarily. "All right," he answered shortly, "we'll go by the bank and draw out what we've got in there. But get in gear, for Christ's sake, Paula. We're wasting precious time!"

"What'll we take?" his wife asked.

"I don't know, for crying out loud. Just grab some stuff. Some clothes. But hurry!"

Frank left them to their own as he rapidly selected a couple items he wished to take along. The M-1 carbine was illegal to have, but law or not, the wartime souvenir was picked up. Filling his pockets with the long, pointed bullets he re-entered the kitchen to help his wife.

And there she was. The ancient tea set that her grandmother had given her was sitting beside the door. A black Persian Paw stole, in its bug-proofed bag, was parked next to the silver pieces.

"Frank, I need you to carry this to the car," Paula said. "Be careful and don't drop it, it's an antique." With that she extended the old, hand-carved clock that had sat in the center of the mantle.

Frank glared at her. "You're unreal, Paula. I'm worried about saving our lives and you're dragging out every broken down piece of junk in this house. We're not taking any of it!"

She scowled at him and clutched the clock close to her.

Snatching up the tea service in exasperation he stalked outside and threw it into the trunk. "Let's go!" he shouted.

They tumbled into the car, Paula delaying until she was positive the door was securely locked.

Frank was a masterful driver. He whipped the vehicle into the street and had crossed the two blocks to stop in front of the bank before his family had settled down and fastened their seat belts.

He dashed from the car to the yellow stucco building of the only local bank in San Mirado, a small business with no branches. Because it was local it was popular. But in a flash he was back. "God! Wouldn't you know it! They've closed up the damned place! There's no people there and no electricity so the ATM doesn't work." He threw his body into the seat.

"Daddy, can't you write checks in Arizona?" Kim asked.

He threw a disgusted look at Paula. "And who would be in this bank to honor the checks, huh?

Chapter Five

After the students had been dismissed, Althea Carr began her own preparations to leave. The school administration had released the students prematurely—she thought in fact the manner in which the school day abruptly ended had reflected disorganization on the part of the staff. The children should have been kept in the classrooms until it was deemed safe to let them go, or until their parents were notified to pick them up. But then, she was simply a teacher, not an administrator, nor a maker of decisions regarding emergency policy. She was frankly amazed at the lack of established procedure. The school had numerous instructions on what to do in case of fire or earthquake—just as there were instructions regarding a high ozone count in the smog—but nothing existed within the school which outlined the procedure for this sort of crisis.

Although she had cautioned her pupils to run straight home and not tarry along the way, she wondered how many of them got the message and did her bidding, or were even so instructed by other teachers. At this moment the children could be loafing in the open air, observing the huge, dusky cloud which was still forming overhead.

Althea Carr was in her thirty-fifth year and had already learned a lot about life; enough at least to put priorities in proper perspective. She was one of a minority, in her native California, and had been born and raised in Los Angeles. Her parents lived there still, and that was her destination—big, sprawling L.A.

A meticulous woman, Althea smoothed her hair back, fastening a loose strand in her chignon. Her brows were plucked in arches, and the pale lipstick—her only make-up—blended with the tailored dress to define an image of a serious woman. Without looking she knew she was in order....now. After that first message of the disaster, she'd almost lost control, momentarily at least, but now she had her nerves calmed and her emotions restrained.

With a last glance around the room, she picked up the batch of homework papers and placed them neatly in a manila folder. She had them tucked securely in the crook of her arm and was reaching for her handbag when she realized what she'd done.

She dropped the folder on her desk. There was no need to grade those papers.

There were two cars left on the lot as she hastened to her coupe. Fastening the doors tightly and locking them, a habit she'd developed years ago because of driving alone, she guided the vehicle under the freeway and then onto it, traveling north.

Under optimum conditions the trip from San Mirado to her parents' home 70 miles away in Los Angeles was a good hour's drive. But these weren't optimum conditions today. The near absence of traffic coming from the Whitewater direction told her that the horrors of the disaster lay visible on the route and all traffic was detouring that area. A few cars still cruised northward in the direction of White Water and Los Angeles. Was it possible that these people had not yet heard the word? A shudder raced down her body at the thought of what would be found should she travel past the site. Should she do that....go by to see what had happened? But the impulse to satisfy a morbid curiosity was extremely weak, and she turned the car onto an off-ramp and headed due east for several miles, leaving the coast behind.

When next Althea entered the freeway system, her lanes of the freeway were empty. The lanes with traffic moving in the opposite direction were packed. People were pouring out of Los Angeles panicked, unaware they were also headed toward White Water. She mashed the gas pedal to the floor and grasped the steering wheel tightly, as if to steel herself to enter the city that everyone else was deserting.

In the lanes approaching Althea, cars were moving at a slow creep, almost pushing each other. The heat from the blacktop, the honking of the horns, was unnerving to these other drivers. All it would take would be one irrational person to convert a traffic jam into a free-for-all.

Like a mad bull one man began ramming his truck into the center divider, finally smashing a gap in it. Then he raced his truck through. There was a virtually empty stretch of freeway before him and he quickly accelerated. Other cars streamed in behind him. Instead of three lanes for traffic exiting Los Angeles there were now six....and Althea faced them.

Turning her attention to the highway in front of her, Althea gasped. What she saw was madness! Had she driven onto the wrong side of the highway? She slowed and looked wildly around. Approaching vehicles had at first appeared to be on the opposite side of the divider—now suddenly her lane was blocked by on-coming cars....cars speeding directly toward her!

Althea felt a weakness in her knees and wondered if she'd be able to use her legs. Every nerve was jumping as she braked with her left foot and began pulling as near to the edge of the road as she could get. The cars bore down on her, horns blaring.

They flew past her and cut in behind her, the nearest driver shaking his fist as he careened past. The embankment on her right was steep—a slope that dropped some twenty-five feet to a residential street below. Althea peered out at the edge. The right wheels of her coupe were barely hanging onto the brittle shoulder.

A jar brought her attention away from the shoulder. In front, a young man and his family were stacked in a land rover that was nose to nose with her coupe. She saw his motioning arm and heard his curses to move, but there was nowhere for her to go.

In his anger, the driver cut his rover sharply and pushed into her left fender. She heard the crunching of metal but its significance was lost on her as she felt herself begin to slide. The car teetered for a moment on the edge, than as the right wheels slid off, the machine began to roll. Over once, over twice, tumbling its contents around, it reached the street below in a battered state. Rocking back and forth on its wheels, it came to rest. Miraculously it had ended in an upright position in the flat dirt area below the freeway.

Althea was dazed. The flips had jostled her equilibrium. She loosened the restraining seat belts and laid her head back for a moment, breathing deeply several times. Her limbs trembled spastically, and a powerful urge to urinate came over her. With sheer will, she forced the sphincter valve in her bladder to close, and she continued with the deep breaths until most of the twitching had left her muscles. Finally she was sufficiently calm to pull herself upright.

There were numerous people rushing by but none had the slightest interest in her or her predicament. Then she almost laughed as she realized the motor of the little coupe was still purring despite its tumble down the embankment. Althea felt an almost human relationship with the car at that moment. At least it hadn't disappointed her.

The car went into gear with a strange crunching sound but moved forward regardless. Althea peered out of the cracked windshield at the neighborhood around her. This small satellite city of Los Angeles, with its poorer older houses, was familiar territory. By winding through its residential streets she would be able to get home.

Before long Althea drew to a halt before the aging frame house of her parents. The trip had taken over three tense hours. She exhaled loudly as she let herself relax for a moment. She'd made it....at last. But it wasn't over yet. She knew that.

Her mother was waiting on the porch. Tiny, steel-gray ringlets formed a halo around the ebony face of the older woman. She broke into a worried frown as Althea climbed out of the car and started toward her. "Did you come by that place?" she asked.

"No, Mama, I took the long way around," replied Althea as she walked into the house.

"Your car, Thea....what happened to it?" asked the mother as she noticed the collapsed top and battered sides of the vehicle.

Althea, inside, sank into the sofa. "Some white bastard shoved me off the road."

"Althea! Are you all right?"

"Yes, Mama. I'm okay." Once this morning, for a split second, she'd thought she wouldn't make it. She'd been afraid that she'd never see either parent again. Her father interrupted her thoughts. Coming up behind her he laid his hand on her shoulder.

"Your mama and I decided we'd better stay put until you got here, Thea. We figured you'd know what to do."

She reached up and patted his gnarled fingers.

Jess Carr walked around to sit on the stool at his daughter's feet. He was proud of his daughter—his only child. He'd worked extra night shifts to see that his girl got an education so she could lift herself above the level of other black people. He'd wanted a better station for Althea than he and Lou Ella had, and he'd helped her get it. She, in turn, had never given them reason to be unhappy with her.

"When we heard about it we couldn't believe it for awhile.....It seems like we're an awful long way away from that thing, Althea. Look, our lights are still on and everything. But that man on the radio just kept going over it and over it. If he's telling the truth, it's pretty scary." The old man blinked his eyes slowly.

"I know, Dad. Sometimes I wonder if any of us know enough about this accident to be properly frightened," replied Althea. "I wish I could believe we were safe up here." Then peering at her father closely, she asked, "Are you feeling all right, Papa?"

"Me? Oh, I'm doing good, Thea."

Three years it had been since the heart attack. Three years since he'd been forced to quit work and take life easy. Being without an income and with only the meager pension had hit him hard. He hadn't wanted to be dependent on anyone, not even his child. But he'd had no choice in the matter. "Do you reckon it's as bad as they say on TV?"

Althea rubbed her forehead trying to ease the pain of a headache that was just beginning. "I don't know....I suppose we must believe that it's that bad. What else can we think, anyway? At least you have power up here."

Jess watched as her slender dark fingers massaged her temples. His heart ached with pride every time he looked at the thin face, the aquiline nose, and the large black eyes. He was continually amazed that he and Lou Ella had been able to produce such a beautiful child. No coarse features or thick lips on his girl, but very definitely his child, nevertheless.

Althea got up to go into the kitchen for a glass of water. She moved with the grace of a lovely black swan. "What are we going to do," asked her father.

She returned with the glass. Without replying, Althea picked up the telephone and dialed. There was much static and interference on the line but she finally got through to her number. "Aunt Bertha? This is Althea... .yes, in L.A.....No, we're all right, all of us. Aunt Bertha, we're going to have to get out of here....yes, soon." Althea paused to listen. "Well, naturally St. Louis is a long way off but when we leave here we need to have some destination in mind." Again she listened. "Driving in the car will be our best chance....What?" For what stretched into a minute Althea listened. Then slowly she hung up the phone.

Her mother stood at her elbow, a small portable radio in her hand. Lou Ella was an inveterate listener of the box. Television was interesting but that was for evening. A radio was kept tuned in during the whole of each day. When her chores carried her away from the console in the living room or away from the kitchen and the pink Emerson that sat above the refrigerator, then Lou Ella pocketed the little transistor and carried the news

57

and music with her. Standing beside her daughter she asked, "What happened, Althea?"

Althea let her gaze wander around the room before she finally returned to her mother. Exasperation and anger filled her voice when she answered. "Aunt said we should not come to St. Louis, Mama. They've been told that anyone from this area will be contaminated with radiation and would pollute everyone we come in contact with. Pollute, can you beat that! It make us sound like some kind of garbage."

Lou Ella, surprised, threw her hand over her mouth. "My very own sister....Bertha said that?"

Jess caught his wife and laced his arm around her.

"Ohhhh," moaned Althea, "of all things.....Well, we've got to get out of here anyway." Grasping the phone determinedly, she said, "I'm going to make one more call. Maybe the airport...."

Los Angeles International Airport had had a typical, weekday early morning at the busy terminals. Passengers hastened to flights, to luggage centers and to ticket booths in preparation for arrival and departure.

George Kingsley, making the best use for the hour lay-over between Dallas and Tokyo, had walked down the concourse to the souvenir stand in the front of the terminal. He paid his dime and folded the copy of the Los Angeles Times under his arm. He had just turned and was about to thread his way to the coffee shop upstairs when a shrill sound from the public address system screeched through the air, immediately followed by the announcement .

"Attention all passengers! Attention all passengers! All flights are canceled. Repeat. All flights are canceled until further notice!"

Travelers stopped and listened intently, shocked looks on their faces. The announcement continued. "Due to an accident at White Water Nuclear Power Plant radiation has been released into this area. All air traffic in and out of Los Angeles is discontinued until further notice! All passengers and air personnel are advised to seek shelter for the duration of the emergency!"

The people were clearly stunned by this news—though not so much by the announcement concerning radiation as by cancellation of the flights. For many, and especially for those stranded between flights, this was more than simply inopportune. Where could they take shelter? Some could quickly return to their homes, but what about those caught between destinations?

The people stood fixed for a long moment, exchanging glances of bewilderment at this sudden development. Then a man broke ranks and began walking rapidly, breaking shortly into a run. That one person was the catalyst for the rest. Nearly everyone began hurriedly moving, then running, shoving and pushing those still immobile out of the way.

It was readily apparent to George that the sudden rush of people breaking toward the street indicated they had absorbed the impact of the news and were abandoning the airport. In an instant there was a mob around him, a bulging tide of bodies headed toward the exterior. He felt himself being pushed backward and reached out for leverage. Failing to grasp firm footing, the mass of moving people lifted him off his feet and hurled him into the concession stand and across its counter. Suspended over the counter, he saw the mob grow in the rush to the outside. In their frantic haste, the crush of people swelled at the double exit doors until it became a huge knot of squirming flesh. Only a few broke through and raced into the street, others piled into the congestion, making exit to the outside nearly impossible. Then stamping like stampeding cattle they pushed and kicked at each other until screams began to fill the morning air.

George heard the cracking of the thick floor-to-ceiling windows in tandem with agonizing screams. The forefront of the mob had been shoved through the wide windows and beyond the jagged glass. The wounded staggered about on the sidewalk, their cuts bleeding profusely, as more and more were swept through the gaping hole, pushed from behind.

It was a scene of madness.

Althea faced her parents. Their looks of expectation were plainly written on their faces. They were waiting for her to set some order to this....to their lives. She was the educated one, she was one who'd know how to cope with such as this. Even as a little girl Althea had shown her difference from other girls in the neighborhood. She'd absolutely refused to have her hair put in corn braids and she was only six at the time. Before she was ten she already knew that she wouldn't be scrubbing some white woman's floors as Lou Ella had done. No ma'am, not Althea. Althea was going to be a school teacher.

She heaved a short sigh. "Mama...let's get a few things together. Here, I'll help you," and she started off toward the bedroom.

Jess called out, "But what are we going to do, Thea?"

Althea hesitated before she answered him. She didn't have to worry about whether the airlines would take her credit card—or whether or not she and her parents could even get on a flight. A recording had answered her call to the airport. It had repeated the word 'closed' over and over again. She turned to reply. "We're leaving the area. To where I'm not sure, yet...but we're getting away from here." She walked out of sight.

The older couple followed her into the bedroom. "What can we do?" asked Jess.

Thea glanced at her father with concern. Would his heart stand up to this? "Papa, do you feel like loading the car?"

"Sure. What goes first?"

"Anything we have that's of value....anything that's small enough to be carried along."

She watched as he started away. "Papa! Do you have a good supply of digitalis?"

His tired face formed a soft fleeting smile as he nodded. "I got plenty."

Lou Ella caught her breath. "Thea," she whispered, "I'm nearly out of insulin."

"Oh, Mama, no!"

The older woman's dark skin suddenly turned an ashy gray. "I didn't know this was going to happen. I'd planned to buy it when I did shopping in the morning."

This recent crisis loomed before Althea with fierce intensity. She closed her fist and pounded it once against her forehead. To her mother, who was severely diabetic, the insulin was as essential to her life as food. But would there be a pharmacy open to dispense the precious hormone?

Jess returned to where the two women stood. He'd overheard the conversation. "I'll go down to Cole's."

"But what if they're closed, Jess?"

"Then, Lou, I'll just go upstairs to where Mr. Cole lives and get him to open up for me." The pharmacy was four blocks away and since the Carrs had traded there for years, there was no doubt in anyone's mind that Mr. Cole would provide the needed insulin....if he were around.

"No, I'll go," said Althea. "You two stay here and get things ready to throw into the car when I get back."

"I can drive down for you," offered the father.

Thea shook her head. "Uh uh. I'll do it." She didn't want either parent exposed to the air any more than necessary.

In the order of importance, Althea knew her mother's insulin ranked first as she headed the car toward the neighborhood pharmacy. There was no way of knowing how long this relative calmness would remain before all hell tore loose—which was sure to happen soon. Once everybody was convinced that this was genuine, panic and havoc would take over. And she wanted to be well removed from here when that happened; but they had to have the insulin.

Turning left toward the store, Althea looked at the changes that had occurred in the neighborhood, in this once strictly-white area. As it had aged, many of the old homes were claimed by businesses; now residences sat next to commercial structures. And with the aging process had come the lowering of values that allowed her people to move in.

Allowed....she grimaced at the thought. They hadn't been permitted to live here when it was new. Althea knew all the reasons why. Her education had made her acutely aware of the total black problem, not just what was going on in her community. But her friends had accused her of trying to forget their cause, of trying to forget she was black, when she had moved to San Mirado to teach. San Mirado was almost totally white. But her friends didn't understand her motivations. They didn't understand her at all.

Her old Uncle Linc, God rest his soul, had kept a protective mantle around his niece as she grew up. His advice to her was always stern and unending—and always the same. "Thea, never trust a honkey, girl, never trust a honkey." And he'd been right she'd learned over the years, partially right, anyway. She'd learned her lesson so well, in fact, that she didn't trust any man — black or white. No, it was men who went to war, men who raped and plundered. In a confrontation, it would never be a case of a woman matching her wits against a man. No, it had to be physical; and for the woman, attractive or not, she'd be the one to lose. Linc was right—there was no man to be trusted....except for Edward.

Edward? She set the thought of him aside. This was no time to entertain daydreams. Before this was over, before she got her parents and herself to safety, she was going to need her mind well in order. She had no one to rely on but herself, she knew; help would come from no quarter but her own.

Braking the car, she pulled it over to the curb and peered through the side window. Cole's Drugs still had a light on inside. How long, she wondered, before the older generators gave out and the city would be without electricity? In the darkness of night there'd be hell to pay in this neighborhood.

The store seemed deserted to her. Nobody was visible from where she sat in the car, but the front door of the pharmacy was open, hanging strangely askew on only one hinge. As she looked at it closer she saw the glass had been knocked from the door's window and lay in small fragments scattered over the sidewalk. Mr. Cole must be there, then, she thought.

Althea grasped her purse firmly and slid out of the seat. Always a creature of habit, the events of the day had shaken her normal routine. As she walked across the short distance to the store's entrance, the proof of this was left behind—the car keys were dangling from the ignition.

She had only taken one step inside the pharmacy before she stopped. Instinctively she knew that something was terribly awry. The shelves were stripped, their bottles and boxes lay piled in the aisles. Noises behind the high counter were proof that someone was here—but who?

She called out timidly, "Mr. Cole? Are you here?" Then louder, "Mr. Cole....where are you?"

A cold metal tube was suddenly pressed into her neck. A crazy laugh rang out. "Hey man, look what I got here!"

Althea froze with fear. Her intuition and the cold metal told her that this was a gun. She held her breath, afraid that the slightest movement might jar the gun into action. The man's laugh changed into a giggle as he stepped into sight. He was, she discovered, a youth in his early twenties. He grinned sardonically, his eyes feverish from what could have been illness—but she guessed it to be drugs.

A second youth stepped from among the prescription shelves. He, like his partner, carried a sawed-off-shotgun, and like his partner, he too was ablaze from the pharmacist's stock.

"Howie, what a chick!"

Howie forced the gun deeper into her neck, inching Althea forward.

"Yeah, man!" The second youth's eyes rapidly jumped around as they flitted from Althea, to Howie, and back to the spoils in front of him. He wasn't interested in Althea for long and he rapidly began filling his pockets with capsules as Howie backed Althea against a wall.

Althea kept her attention on Howie while he drew closer and closer to her. She glanced over at his dirty finger wrapped around the trigger of the gun, as Howie extended his free hand to Althea's hip and fondled the soft curve. She kept her face expressionless. Better not to show fear to the little creep. But, then, neither could she take much more of him. Every muscle in her body was taut with revulsion. Pounding through her brain was the single thought of what she could do to get the muzzle of that gun off her neck.

His hand started up her back, pulling her nearer to him. Turning her head away, she caught a glimpse of the other youth stealing toward the door. His action was furtive as he cast a look back over his shoulder in Howie's direction, then darted for the doorway. If she was going to take a chance it was now or never!

"Look!" she shouted. "He's leaving!"

Howie whirled Althea around. "Jimbo! Stop, you son-of-a-bitch!"

Jimbo whipped his shotgun in Howie's direction.

It was obvious he was going to fire. Summoning a surge of energy, Althea sprang out of Howie's grasp and lunged behind a shelf.

The first charge was released from Howie's gun and the front of Jimbo's face disintegrated into a thousand miniscule pieces of flesh.

Althea screamed, holding her hands over her ears.

The second explosion from Jimbo's gun followed before the first died, almost as an after-shock. The pellets peppered Howie but failed to catch him in the full of its blast.

By now Althea's screams had stretched into one long continuous wail. As Howie stumbled toward her, she jumped to her feet and fled around the end of the shelves. There, crumpled on the floor, was the pharmacist, his chest a mass of drying blood. She knew from the glaze of his eyes that he was dead. Leaping his form she swept over him and toward the dying

Jimbo. There was no time to question Howie's intention should he catch her, so Althea charged around Jimbo, leaving him twitching from what must certainly be the throes of death, and sped out the door.

Running to the curb, she expected to be in her car and driving off before Howie could reach the sidewalk. But the car was gone! In disbelief she hastily scanned the street. She'd parked it there....right in front of the store. She distinctly remembered stopping right in that spot. Then where...?

She saw the tail of the coupe as it turned a corner at the end of the block. Oh God, now she recalled. She must have left the keys in it.

Howie was somewhere near. She could hear him lumbering, his yells getting louder as he approached the front of the store. Throwing her head up, Althea began running, knowing her life depended on it. She ran until it hurt to inhale, then blocks later, gasping for air, she slowed to a stumbling walk. Looking back over her shoulder, she realized that not only was Howie nowhere to be seen but she had actually been running in the opposite direction from home. Grimly she altered her course.

What could be done now, without her car? They were stranded as surely as if they were on an island, she and her aged parents. "Damn!" she exclaimed. "Damn this stinking city...damn this whole mess where a car is the difference between....oh, damn!" She lowered her head and increased her pace.

Chapter Six

Ben stood, squinting into the sunlight, as he tried to orient his thoughts. The light lacked intensity as it filtered through the haze, and he decided it must be early afternoon.

His mind was a jumble. He had struggled to the freeway expecting to be immediately loaded into an automobile and driven to safety. Instead, he had found the major artery completely devoid of vehicles. Evidence of the morning traffic lay in twisted clusters. Although the vehicles had obviously contained people at the moment the tremendous force had hit the machines, there were no signs of life now. Bodies, yes, but no living persons were in the vicinity of the gnarled wrecks. It was evident to him that the traffic had been blown off the highway at the moment of impact. Survivors must have somehow straggled from the region—provided there were survivors.

Painfully, doggedly, he once again started the long trek toward home. It seemed hours that he'd been pushing his aching body forward. There had been periods when his mind had momentarily blacked out, shutting out his anguish; then he'd emerge from the mental darkness, feeling his strength somewhat renewed. Gathering himself, he continued to push forward, slowly, and each moment the searing pain renewed itself.

He tried mentally blocking out the agony, but that didn't work. With each step a sharp jolt of pain would shoot through his chest, setting off another tiny explosion of misery. Each swing of the leg was becoming more and more difficult until finally he stopped. Maybe it would be easier to simply lie down and wait. For what, though? To die? Thoughts like this only deteriorated what little will he had left. And will he needed. There was one place that promised peace and comfort to Ben at this point; it was home.

Home. He set his feet determinedly in motion once again. Home and Sara. The beautiful, soft Sara. He knew his thoughts were fragmented and rambling. His image of Sara as he'd left

65

her this morning—it was this morning, wasn't it?—suddenly gave way to his childhood:

"Benny! Benny!" called his mother from the back porch. He sat high up in the oak tree, secure and safe; but he detected the irritation that crept into her voice. "Benjamin Harrington! You get in here right this minute!"

He flattened himself out on the floor of the tree house lest she come into the yard and glance upward at his hideaway. He pressed closer to the planks as she called out once more. The humiliation, the shame of it. He had been in the bedroom and she had simply opened the door and walked in while he stood in front of the dressing mirror. It wasn't enough that he should be caught admiring his naked body, but that he was handling the pink turgid penis....

"Benjamin!" she'd screamed at him. "Quit that, you nasty boy!"

He'd stared at his mother with fright.

"Don't you know you'll go crazy if you do that?" She'd reached out and slapped him on the cheek.

The sting of her hand had sent him dashing past her and into the bathroom where he hurriedly dressed. The pain wasn't erased by her saying through the door that she was sorry she'd hit him. It wasn't the smack that really hurt; it was having his mother find him naked and playing with himself....the awful shame and guilt stunned him.

Clothed, he'd opened the door and run around her arms and out of the house. Would she ever forgive him? Would he always be a nasty boy to her?

The incident was never mentioned by her again. But she'd changed, he knew that. The old closeness between the woman and her child had gone....

"Yes, Mr. Harrington?" The professor smoothed his goatee as he stood over Ben's desk.

The words didn't come easily. He'd thought he was prepared to do the problem but the formula had escaped him—it was completely out of his memory. Ben gulped. "I can't seem to figure this out."

"Obviously," smirked the professor. "Mr. Harrington, have you considered that calculus may not be your cup of tea?"

Ben was embarrassed. The whole class laughed at him....

Ben's foot connected with a large rock, causing him to stumble, then sprawl in the hot sandy soil. He lay there for what

66

seemed minutes. Everything was swimming before his eyes. At last the blurred vision returned to normal, and he rose to continue the slow trek home.

It was nearing dusk as Ben detoured through an open field that would shorten the route to his house. He could see it now....in the distance, on a street that was strangely empty. The last hundred feet separating him from the sanctuary could have been a mile until he heard her scream.

He knew his wife's voice well, and that was Sara. Sara screaming. Pushing thoughts of his own agony aside, he summoned his last vestige of adrenalin and broke into a stumbling rush toward the house. Reaching it, he burst through the door to the inside.

Sara was fighting madly, twisting her slim pale body away from a man, as she desperately tried to rip away the burlap bag he held in his grasp. With a swift chopping blow, the man's fist smashed into the side of her head, snapping it backward. But still she held onto the bag. He lurched toward the fireplace, the young woman attached to him and screaming uncontrollably with fear. His hand then closed around the handle of one of the fire tools.

Ben saw the metal poker lifted into the air, poised over his wife's head; he saw the cords of muscles standing out in the man's arm, ready to unleash their power into her frail body.

Reaching blindly, Ben felt his fingers on the heavy ceramic vase which adorned the entrance of the house. With a strength that he had never before possessed, he raised the vessel threateningly and squawked in a coarse voice, "Drop it, you bastard!" His voice had an effect.

The man dropped the bag, allowing its contents of silver flatware and rings to spill on the floor as he turned to face his challenger. Standing between him and the doorway was a hideous figure of a man—one arm pulled close to his chest and the other suspending an enormous vase. The lower part of Ben's left ear was connected to his scalp by only a thick slice of tissue, and the skin of his face was a meshwork of wet, bloody cuts. The eyes of the lone survivor of White Water were black balls of hatred set within two dark cavities.

With a darting glance to the woman, the thief raised the tool even higher and began a menacing stalk toward Ben. As he neared the ragged, bruised form, he began to execute a series of half steps, feinting first to the right, then to the left.

Ben stood motionless, moving nothing but the slender threadlike muscles that permitted his eyes to follow the other man.

Guessing as to the weakness of his opponent, the thief pulled the long poker to the apex of the arch, and rushed straight at Ben.

Delaying until the last fraction of the second, Ben thrust his body aside and sent the massive vase crashing into the temple of the man. A dull thud blended with the cracking of pottery, drowning out a subtler splintering that occurred in the plate-like bone that had once covered the man's brain.

Reeling, the thief fell against the wall, then slowly sank to the floor. He was dead before his head touched the carpet.

Across the room, collapsed in a corner, was Sara. Her eyes were wide with fright, with bewilderment, with surprise. Cowering, her dress disheveled from her struggles, she stared at the mangled and bruised man still standing in the doorway. Before making any movement, she asked with uncertainty, "Ben? Ben? Is that you?"

He didn't answer at once, but continued to stand, looking across at her.

Suddenly, Sara realized. "Ben! Ben!" she wailed, as she started in a rush toward him.

Throwing up his hand he shouted at her. "No! No, Sara. Stay away from me!" His outburst halted her flight.

"Oh, Ben. Oh, my God. I thought you were dead. Oh darling, I don't see how...." She reached in anguish for him.

He pulled away from her searching arms. "Sara, don't come any closer! You must not touch me!"

She paused, obviously torn between the desire to touch him and confirm the truth that he still lived, and the urgency in his voice to obey his order. Night was falling, but even in the near darkness she had seen the condition of his ravaged form. "What can I do? Ben, oh Ben, what can I do to help you?"

Ben's last surge of strength to protect his wife had drained the remainder of his energies. A wave of weakness washed over him; yet he knew there was still more to be done. His clothing and skin had received over nine hours of radioactive fallout, and he was an intense threat to Sara. He needed to think, but his mind wasn't working well. He hadn't considered what would happen once he reached home.

"Sara, stay away. It's not safe for you to touch me." He made a hesitant movement, then mumbled, almost to himself, "I guess... the dust...wash as much of the dust off as possible."

Dust particles in the air absorbed radiation and Ben was covered with a visible layer of grayish dust. But washing would only remove the surface matter; nothing could be done to remove the irradiation he'd already received to his tissues. Some of that would be with him longer than he could hope to live. He knew his chances of survival were slim.

Ben walked waveringly through the house and out the rear entrance. Going to the far corner of the lot, he carefully removed his shirt, tearing it away from the shattered arm, and then the remainder of his clothing. After he had dropped the garments, he returned to the house. He could see the stranger still folded on the floor of the foyer as he groggily felt his way into the bathroom.

Sara already had the shower running, and he stepped beneath it. Contact of the warm water on abraded skin caused him to gasp in pain. But it was nothing to compare with the hurt that followed with the thick laying of soap, the soap that was essential for thorough cleanliness. He ground it under his fingernails and into the tiny crevices of his body. Finding himself too weak to stand, Ben dragged a small stool into the shower and sat under the running water, hoping against his better judgment that the water would purify him.

Sara, still hurt and frightened, eased herself down on the tile and leaned against the outside of the shower door. She needed to be near him after this long, horrifying day. Maybe he'd call her for aid—maybe he'd collapse. At any rate, she'd be within arm's reach of him. The warm steam seeped over the door and saturated her clothing with moisture, but she waited patiently for almost an hour.

She hadn't learned to share the Californians' inordinate calmness about earthquakes. Every tremor, no matter how inconsequential, sent a wave of fear through her—as had the one this morning. When Ben was with her it wasn't so bad. He'd laugh and hold her close until the shaking ended. But today she'd been alone, writing a piece for his alumni newsletter, when the earth began shifting. She'd forced herself to remain at her writing table through the ordeal. And it had ceased shortly.

Then, being too unnerved to continue, she had gone onto the patio and gazed out at the Pacific. It was a windless morning; the ocean was glassy calm. In all, the thick haze and stillness seemed to cast an ominous note over the day. The air had grown depressively heavy, she'd observed, and was about to return to the inside when the loud boom rocketed off the canyon walls below the house. At that sound an icy shiver had run the length of her body, raising goose bumps in her skin.

How had she known? Was there some mystical, other sense that flashed the warning to her? She was no believer in mystical powers and yet, as soon as the thundering racket had sounded, she somehow had sensed that this was the culmination of her most dreaded fear, that the sound was somehow connected with White Water. She had immediately run to the telephone and dialed the facility. For the first time, ever, the call did not go through. Then she knew.

It had taken her less than five minutes to confirm the awful truth. A helicopter unit patrolling freeway traffic had witnessed the destruction of the plant—the news was broadcast immediately by emergency frequency. Then units were dispatched to broadcast from loudspeakers before they abandoned the task and the drivers fled the area as best they could. The lack of electricity downed the cell phone towers and internet servers.

Distraught and believing Ben could never have escaped, Sara had thrown herself onto their bed and wept until there were no more tears to come. She had gone through the remainder of the day much like a zombie. With no one to talk to, and the media broadcasting down, she had avoided considering what was to become of her....until the gardener, the thief, had slid surreptitiously into the house.

The shower stall opened and Ben stepped out. His cuts had turned pink and were curled at the edges; his skin was wrinkled and logged with water. With the grime removed, a deep red imprint of his dark necktie was embossed down the length of his chest. The pattern of his belt buckle was burned into his abdomen. Radiation damage was grossly evident.

"Ben?" asked Sara, shaken. "Is it all right for me to touch you now?"

Ben shook his head from side to side. "I don't think so." He dragged himself into the bedroom and gingerly lowered himself onto the bed. "It's best if you don't—for your own sake."

She hastened to him. "Don't you think we ought to try to get you to a hospital?"

He stared at her for a long moment before replying, slowly,

"Morning will be soon enough, Sara. There's no rush now. What's a broken arm in comparison with the other?" He hesitated. "What's it been like since the reactor blew?"

She sat down near him, holding out a glass of juice she had prepared earlier. "Terrible." Then she started telling him the story as she held the glass to his lips.

"None of the stations from Los Angeles are broadcasting?" he asked, refusing more than a sip of juice and weakly stretching out on the coverlet.

"No. But with no electricity we can't even get the distant ones. Everything I've learned has come from a van broadcasting over a loud speaker."

"Are they giving instructions for evacuation?" he asked.

She nodded in assent. "But we can't leave here, Ben. We've got to get you to a hospital."

Ben lay quietly on the bed. "You will have to leave here, Sara... without me."

She reacted instinctively. "No! I'm not going to leave you." She reached out and wiped a wisp of dark hair off his forehead. "I'll never understand how you could have possibly survived the....that force that destroyed the plant."

He was growing weaker as he answered, "Luck.. it was luck. Or no, maybe a miracle....I was blown between two retaining walls. They protected me."

"But you've returned to me and that's all that matters," Sara said, reaching out to him, wanting to touch him.

"Sara, for your own welfare, and the baby's, you'll have to leave here, get out of this. For me, it's....there's not much chance."

"I'm not leaving, Ben. I'm staying with you," she said, almost crying. Should she rely on his judgment as she had in the past? Was tomorrow soon enough to get him to a hospital? His eyes closed, a signal that the talk was ended.

Getting up quietly, Sara left the room and began to search for the first-aid supplies. She was able to collect only a pitifully small stock—several band aids, numerous cotton balls from her cosmetics table, and a nearly empty bottle of alcohol. There wasn't enough even to afford minimal dressing of Ben's wounds, nevertheless she returned to him and gently began bathing the raw cuts with the alcohol. He didn't flinch, even as the astringent met the open flesh—a sure sign that he'd been overcome with utter fatigue, perhaps shock.

71

To Sara, Ben seemed on the brink of death, stretched as he was along the length of the bed, his normally tanned skin angry and red. The terrible fear she'd had of losing him, and the idea that his presence now was only a brief reprieve, weighed like a stone on her. And it was only this very morning that she had complained about getting something meaningful from those meetings with her sorority. How dense of her. The meaning to her life was this man on the bed.

Outside, night had fallen over the land. Inside, the flickering of the one small candle lent an eerie glow to the sickroom. Sara blew out its soft light and sat there in the darkness. Fighting away her tears, she whispered, "God may separate us, Ben, but I shall never."

She could hear the thrashing of his body. His restless, tormented sleep was a reflection of the horror and pain of the previous day. Unable to bear the whimpers that rose from her husband, Sara leaned over and tenderly laid her hand across his brow. It was feverishly hot.

She awakened him as she placed a cool wet towel over his forehead. There was no ice, but the coolness of the moisture caressed him, sapping the heat from his body. Soon he was calmer. The towel quickly dried, and Sara was replenishing the moisture from the basin when she heard his retching begin.

There was nothing in his stomach to mix with the juice he'd swallowed earlier, but the retching continued—long after the last bit of fluid came up. The convulsions racked his body, each spasm taking its toll in energy. He was growing more feeble. Between regurgitations Sara poured more water down his throat. She knew the vomiting had to be controlled. This must be the earliest symptom of the radiation poisoning; he'd need all his energy to combat the later symptoms that would arise. As time dragged slowly on, the vomiting subsided and Ben's fever began to drop.

His condition soon became critical in the other extreme. As the fever disappeared, Ben's normal body temperature also began to drop, until shortly he was radiating more heat than his body could safely lose. He started to shiver. The rigors coursed along his trunk, his limbs; even his head began to quiver. His skin became cold and clammy.

Sara hastily covered him with blankets, yet his shuddering

became even more uncontrolled. She piled on more blankets but the violence of his shaking seemed to increase, again, as the blankets weighed on his lacerated flesh.

Desperate, she whipped the thick layers away from his body and stretched herself alongside him, pressing close to warm him. Then she spread coverlets over the two of them. They stayed, entwined, until the first streaks of dawn crept into the room.

During the long night, Sara had stayed awake, a living barometer recording the changes that were occurring within her husband. As he had grown warmer, she had moved away, allowing the coolness of the air to soothe him. When he'd become too cool, she had snuggled in closer, sharing the heat of her body with him. He had unaccountably lived through the night. Would he make it through another?

At some point during this time Sara's fears and apprehensions had become determination. For once she, Sara Harrington, had full responsibility for another person. She felt that responsibility acutely. Ben's condition would guide her through these next days. His life—or his death—would in all probability depend on her actions.

"Ben," she whispered, "we've got to get you to the car."

He seemed to comprehend for he stirred in a movement of rising. There was no registration of the pain that accosted him—his defense system had blocked the sense receptors of his nerves. He was in shock.

Supporting the greater portion of his weight, Sara moved him off the bed, out of the room, and toward the door. The gardener's corpse, white in death, lay sprawled in the foyer, the side of its temple a mass of dried blood. She led them carefully around it.

Ordinarily the drive to the nearest hospital took at least fifteen minutes. Today it was much less. There were no traffic lights to observe, no traffic, in fact. There were no pedestrians attempting the crosswalks. The thoroughfare was empty of human life. Sara was mystified at the absence of people. Had they all evacuated? Had she been in the proximity of the freeways, she'd have seen the evacuees' vehicles inching forward at a snail's pace, bumper to bumper as the occupants' tempers grew shorter with the snarl of traffic. Everyone with a means of traveling and gasoline had already left.

Sara steered the car into the emergency entrance of the hospital. There were no personnel in sight. No ambulances, no sign of life. The facility looked as dead as the corpse in her foyer.

Quelling the thought that even the medical personnel had evacuated, Sara jumped from her car and ran to the double doors at the emergency entrance. Her shove against them was met with resistance; the doors were locked. Clenching her fists, she pounded on them, calling out in a loud voice. For a moment it seemed there really was no one inside, then abruptly a face appeared through the tiny window to stare at her.

"What do you want?" inquired the mouth.

"Help!" she yelled back. "My husband needs help. Open the door!"

"What's wrong with him?" asked the face.

What difference did it make, Sara was thinking. "He was at White Water yesterday morning during the explosion. He is terribly sick and needs medical attention!"

"I'm sorry, lady, but we're locked up."

She screamed back, "Locked up? Are you insane? A hospital doesn't just shut its door like a shoe store! Open this door!"

"Look, lady, I said we're closed," said the voice coldly.

"You can't be! This is a hospital! You have to accept someone who's injured."

"We can't take your husband," the man stated. "He's contaminated with radioactive materials and we're not admitting any radiation victims."

Sara glared wildly through the tiny window at him. "You're crazy! My husband desperately needs medical aid! He has broken bones and oh, God, just unlock the door, won't you?"

On the other side of the pane the expression softened. "Lady, I'm really sorry, but you see, we don't have a decontamination chamber here. If we admitted your husband he would pollute everyone who went near him, as well as the hospital facility. We just can't allow that to happen. We have patients to care for in here."

"But what about him?" she pleaded. "He needs attention, too."

A visible shrug lifted the shoulders across from her.

"Where can I go? Isn't there some place that has been designated to care for such victims?" begged the distraught woman.

"Not that I know of."

It was unbelievable, this lack of concern, this inability of a medical facility to accept Ben for treatment. "Do you mean that there is no hospital plan to handle this kind of emergency?"

Seemingly disinterested in the discussion, the man answered, "No," and walked off.

The man had left and would not return to her repeated pounding on the door. Angry and disheartened, Sara went back to the car. Ben lay folded uncomfortably on the rear seat, a series of moans issuing from him. His brow was hot to the touch. The fever, a ravage on his body, had returned, resulting in what to her seemed an unconscious delirium. Infuriated with the reception she had received, she started the motor and threw the car in gear.

It was after much searching that Sara finally pulled into the emergency entrance of a second clinic, this one a private institution. Her efforts there produced the same results. The personnel shared an adamant refusal to admit new patients, all of whom would by now have suffered exposure to radiation. The excuse was identical to the earlier one—no decontamination chamber, and risk of contaminating personnel and patients.

It appeared that if the policy of no admittance was uniform, Ben would likely be refused treatment at any medical center. Fraught with anger, her hands shaking almost beyond control, and on legs weak from hunger and fatigue, Sara slowly got back into the driver's seat.

Feeling nearly crushed by her burden, Sara's eyes wandered absently over the dashboard. "Gas!" she exclaimed. "My God, not that too!" The tank was nearly empty of fuel; but where would she find gasoline today? Station after station had been closed as she had driven through the lonely streets. Businesses were obviously tightly shut against the panicky residents. She stared intently at the gauge. No more priceless fuel could be wasted in random driving. She had to find help for Ben soon; or, if she were to continue her frantic search for help—gas.

With stronger determination, Sara started the vehicle forward. In the back of her mind was the location of another hospital, maybe the right one this time. Her thoughts were a flurry of clearly defined ideas, all focusing on plans—plans of how she could force treatment for Ben once she got to this next hospital. She'd lie, she decided. Instead of saying that Ben was hurt in the White Water explosion, she'd tell the attendants that he'd been in an automobile wreck. Then they'd admit him for treatment.

Or would they? The radiation was really the problem, wasn't it? All right, then she'd say that he was the brother of the governor. No hospital administrator would want to turn away a relative of the governor of this state. But, if that didn't work....Well, then, she'd take a rock and smash through the windows.

Lost in her thoughts, as she maneuvered the vehicle along the street, Sara suddenly recalled the name of the hospital— Beckman General. "Yes, that's it, Beckman—it's near the freeway. Please, please let the gasoline hold out."

Activity from far ahead caught her eye. A huge, familiar sign declared the site to be a service station—and one with people, she observed, peering into the distance. It must have had a back up generator to power the pumps. Her heart rate quickened. Was she to be so fortunate, she wondered, as she increased speed. Whipping the car into the filling lane, she braked it to a halt beside a pump. A beefy, hairy man stood at one of the pumps filling a container. In the service bay, nearly hidden from view, were two other men. Suddenly hopeful, she rolled down her window. Then horror overcame her. The service bay was now a violent, bloody example of the inhumanity of man.

A heavy hammer slashed through the air and collided with the side of one man's head, splattering the service bay with blood. Sara, catching only a glimpse of the activity, jerked her eyes away. She felt like retching.

There was not time to be sick, however. The gas thief had his container filled and now focused his attention on Sara. He was near enough that his breath stank and it was his offensive odor that made her first aware of his pudgy hand reaching in to her. Instinctively, she jammed the accelerator to the floorboard. As the car lunged forward, the man's grip on her shoulder was broken and she saw him grasp at the handle where he held onto the door for a second before being torn loose.

In a flash her vision captured the continuing saga in the service bay. One man was on his knees with a fountain of blood squirting from the side of his neck; the other, towering over him, held the hammer. The blood had splattered on the pavement and mingled with the dark spots of grease. Nearby was the final sickness—a hose gushing gasoline from its nozzle. The liquid that was important enough to kill for was pouring into the gutter.

As she sped off into the dismal morning, she was overwhelmed by a feeling of having barely escaped with her life —and Ben's.

Looking back to check on him, then at the gas gauge, she decided to take a chance—they'd have to be able to make it to Beckman Medical Center before the gasoline gave out. She headed in that direction.

Beckman General—Sara's final hope for Ben's aid—was very close to the freeway and not more than ten miles from the power plant. The presence of other patients was evident at once as she drove in at the hospital. Although no one seemed to be entering or leaving the building, there were people outside, and that, to her, meant the facility was accepting patients.

The tires dragged on the asphalt as Sara slammed on the brakes. Ben had not ridden comfortably during their hectic search, but maybe at last he would receive the treatment he deserved.

"Over here!" screamed Sara, her eyes searching for someone in a white coat. "Will you please help me get him inside?" she yelled to those waiting.

No one answered her plea. They sat as if nothing had been heard, as though she didn't exist. She had never before been so completely ignored.

"Oh please! Help us! Please!" she begged.

They seemed not to hear. Could they be deaf? Leaving the car she ran into their midst. "Won't you...?" and then she stopped.

More than a dozen men and women littered the ground. A small form, a child, lay dead not far away. These were the people who had been caught unaware by the nuclear blast. They'd been traveling the freeway at the time, and they were the few who'd escaped immediate death.

Sara recoiled in horror. The direction in which they had been bound was clearly obvious to her. Those traveling south had the right sides of their faces cruelly burned. Those going north had the left sides burned. Whichever side was nearest the plant was the side that had sustained the damage. Flaps of skin had sloughed off and the swollen, reddish tissues were suppurating and smelled badly. Yellowish, pus-like discharges had become encrusted. The odor was nauseating.

They had wandered in from the point of impact. Most must have been waiting since around noon of the day before, Sara reasoned. For relatives or friends concerned enough to attempt locating these people it would have been an impossible chore. Radio broadcasts had warned residents against all freeway travel from the extreme north to the south of the San Mirado area. The verbal cordon effectively prevented persons from going into the area, and it largely prohibited attempting rescue of displaced persons already there.

Local agencies had failed to mobilize units to assist those stranded, and since there were no means for direct communication with homes and families, the whereabouts of these people, and other victims of the disaster, would remain unknown until many days later.

A middle-aged woman apart from the group sat staring vacantly into space. Regaining her composure from the initial shock at the sight of these people, Sara decided that she must speak to this woman. She walked around the others to where the woman sat, and leaning over, she softly asked, "Hasn't anything been done for you?"

The woman laboriously drew her eyes around to look at Sara. "Food and water," she murmured. "They give us food and water."

"Hospital personnel?"

She nodded weakly.

"But there hasn't been a doctor to see you?" asked Sara.

"They told us yesterday that one would be here soon."

Sara winced in imagined pain as she saw the festering burn that had spread like some enormous cold sore across the woman's face and into her mouth. The woman parted her swollen lips as though to speak once more, but Sara laid her hand gently on the woman and shook her head. "No, please. Don't talk anymore....it must be so painful." For the present Sara was inexplicably ashamed... ashamed at being so healthy while these poor souls were in such misery. And she couldn't help them either.

Overhead, the morning sun was just beginning to warm the land. And somewhere lost among those rays of light was the invisible radiation that Sara had begun to absorb into her body. Defeated and exhausted, Sara now realized that her plans to insure Ben's treatment were nothing but wanderings of a fanciful mind.

She returned to her husband.

There was no point in joining this wretched group. They would wait forever, taking their doles of food and water like so many lepers—which they probably were in the eyes of the Beckman staff.

Chapter Seven

Beckman General Hospital, designed to serve not only the adjoining neighboring communities but also the outlying unincorporated area in the vicinity of White Water, was in its third year of operation.

In its brief history it had become known as one of the finer new medical facilities. Aesthetically pleasing to the eye, it was as well planned and richly furnished as any patient could wish. Internally, it was a staffer's delight, its various departments laid out with conspicuous detail for best utilization. Operating rooms were kept at a constant temperature, never varying below 72° nor above 76° F. Treatment and examination rooms received their minimum of four air changes every hour. The most technically modern equipment was available to the highly-skilled personnel.

With respect to the large area it served and the demands of its patients, Beckman General had implemented one of the most efficient, responsive, and systematic emergency health care departments to be found in a local hospital. It maintained continuous, twenty-four hour emergency service; any injured or ill person who presented himself at Beckman would receive a reliable appraisal of the extent of his injury or illness and the proper advice and treatment.

The hospital's administrators, concerned with getting established, had neglected to develop a disaster preparedness plan. They'd been aware of the necessity for such a plan, because it was a requirement for certification of the hospital, but the appropriate time for implementing a disaster program simply had not arisen, although within the previous year Beckman General had dealt with a pile-up of automobiles on the freeway during a heavily fogged morning. At that time, the hospital lobby had served as the triage station—the large space that was immediately set aside for the prompt, brief examinations of the accident victims prior to assignment of emergency attention. The need for a workable disaster plan was recognized then; however, administrative accomplishments evolved slowly.

In these dawn hours, less than a day after the destruction of the White Water Plant, the victims still littered the grounds outside the emergency entrance. Inside, medical personnel heatedly debated the advisability of admitting the radiation victims. The probability of contamination unnerved them.

Dr. Bernard Parsons, a surgeon, was the first to openly criticize the hospital's failure to admit the victims.

The policy made no sense whatsoever to him. They'd gone over this again and again, and still they were unable to reach a decision. Couldn't they see that everything the medical profession stood for was placed on the line this morning?

All staffers had been requested to remain within the building, and most had willingly stayed on, assuming many hours of endless work was before them. It turned out, however, that not only would the staff not be permitted to leave the hospital until acceptable levels of radiation were recorded, but due to radiation hazards no new patients would be accepted. For the whole of the night the staff had been deadlocked on this issue of admitting radiation victims.

The indecisiveness was frustrating almost to the point of causing rage in Parsons. Feeling his neck growing hot under his collar, the surgeon ripped his white jacket off and threw it aside. Unveiling his upper torso revealed an enormously thick chest and broad spanning shoulders. Taller than average, with a shock of brown hair atop a rugged face, Bernard Parsons, stripped to a tight undershirt and white trousers, looked for all the world like a lumberjack. In fact, in the fall of the past year he had taken his vacation in the great woods upstate. To get as far removed from the cares of surgery and medicine as possible, he'd deliberately sought out a small logging town for a rest. It had come as a distinct surprise to the men and women of the village that the barrel chested man with the smooth purposeful stride was not a logger at all, but a surgeon. Someone had humorously nicknamed him Jack—a name Parsons had fondly accepted, even preferring it to Bernard.

Sensing his ire growing, Parsons mentally gave himself a brief reminder that he'd gain nothing with his colleagues, indeed, he'd lose whatever persuasive edge he had, if he gave vent to his anger. He forced himself to assume a tone of reasonableness. "All right, all right! We haven't solved a thing, but we simply cannot ignore those people out there. In my opinion it's a damned sad state of affairs that we've never prepared for this sort of crisis; however, we're still obligated to treat them."

Dr. Cash Archer from obstetrics interjected, "So you want to treat them, Bern? Is that what you're saying?"

"Yes, it is. I'll treat their wounds, Archie, but I need help."

"Where do you propose to keep the patients?" asked the Chief of Staff, Dr. Karl Kranz. He was a great public relations man, but he wasn't convinced the hospital should admit irradiated people, even if someone volunteered to treat them.

"How about the isolation unit?" Parsons suggested.

"Well, I don't know. That's pretty small. There must be twelve or fifteen outside now, and that number will grow," replied Krantz.

"They'd be better inside and cramped than left outside in their condition. Besides, they'll absorb even larger doses the longer we leave them there," reminded Parsons.

Shaking his head worriedly, the Chief of Staff replied, "I'm not sure of this, Bernard. You realize that if we decide to treat those people, part of the hospital will have to be condemned to future use by the rest of the staff and regular patients. And not only will we lose part of our great facility, but you and anyone who chooses to work with you will become contaminated. You will have to be confined to that area we set apart for you. It wouldn't look good."

Jesus, murmured Parsons to himself. This do-nothing kraut should have stayed in medical school. He had no interest in people... .unless they were some group of socialites wanting to be wined and dined out of their contributions. That was Kranz, always the silver tongued administrator....great rapport with the moneyed people. "Dr. Kranz," said Parsons firmly, "as physicians we are compelled to offer treatment to those people!"

Dr. Archer cleared his throat and replied. "Bern, we also have an obligation to the patients already under our care. We can't jeopardize their health simply because there are others needing us."

Parsons leveled a look at Archer. "You're right, Archie... .for once. So I'll tell you what we must do. Some of us will continue with the hospital proper, and some of us will set up an isolation unit for those people outside. That way we can cover all the bases. How about that?"

There were murmurings among the staff, but Parsons knew that none would argue with the logic of his suggestion. He had won his point. The next hurdle would be finding personnel willing to risk treating the patients. "Look," he said, "I have no

81

way—nor desire—to force anybody into risking their personal well-being. But I'm telling you to try to put yourselves in the places of those folks outside. After you've done that, if you feel you still can't help, I promise there'll be no hard feelings. Think about it. What does your conscience tell you?" As he talked, he scrutinized each of the staff seated before him. His gaze fell on Archer who leveled a cool stare back without flinching a muscle. "You have all dedicated your lives to humanitarian labors—well, this is no time to quit," he said, ending his brief speech. The staff sat quietly for a moment, not speaking.

Finally Dr. Kranz spoke. "Bernard, I don't believe any of us can dispute what you say but what you're asking of your colleagues....well, we do need some time to think."

"To think, Doctor?" Or to make excuses, Parsons wondered silently.

"Yes, we need some time to decide. Perhaps if you'd just wait in the lounge for a few minutes...."

Parsons turned and walked out. Time....we need time.....Dammit, there wasn't time! Yet, how often had that frustrating phrase rung through his brain? He remembered the first occasion very distinctly... .it was during his internship at Johns Hopkins. He'd been revved up, bright and eager to start his career, to act. To heal. Then on his third day a good-looking, strapping young man was put on his case load. Tim was a picture of health, the all-American image of youth. His wide smile was infectious; his laugh deep and sincere. "Hi Doc," he'd said. "You're going to fix me up, huh?"

Parsons had liked Tim instantly. He'd sat with the youth and they'd talked about baseball. The Orioles were having a bad season, their worst season in many years, but Tim was sure the team would snap back for the coming year—they had to. He was going off to the Oriole training camp the following summer. The team was going to be his life, his whole purpose.

At that meeting Parsons had listened to Tim and shared in his excitement. And only once did he make any effort to examine the body. For a few seconds he'd palpated the cervical nodes. The one at the angle of the neck was textbook descriptive. It was a firm, rubbery mass, enlarged greatly over neighboring nodes. As soon as Tim left, Parsons had hastened down to the pathologist. It never hurt to check. Maybe the lab report had gotten mixed up, maybe someone else's report had got into Tim's file by mistake. Maybe the node would go down.

"But are you positive, Doctor?" he'd asked the pathologist.

The pathologist had sighed, a flicker of exasperation in the sound. "It's Hodgkins. No doubt about that."

Parsons, perplexed, had had to protest. "He seems so healthy....so vigorous."

"The boy is in remission. In another year he won't be around." His voice grew kinder. "If we'd caught it earlier....if we had more time....we need time to do anything with Hodgkins disease, Doctor."

Parsons had suddenly felt as if he'd had the wind kicked out of him. Later he'd learned that time was crucial—the important factor with most diseases. With most everything, for that matter. Even with Amy. If he'd not been so busy at the hospital he could have spent more time with his wife. And she wouldn't have been so bored. But he hadn't had the time.

He snorted at the idea of comparing his ex-wife with a disease. Well, she had been as devastating to him as a disease. The recollection of unexpectedly coming home that afternoon, and finding Amy and her lover locked in passion, flitted through his memory. The divorce had at least been amicable. No threats, no accusations—just amicable.

Coming back to reality, Parsons pulled out his note pad and dropped to a chair at the table. Time the doctors needed. Well, he'd give them time. He began compiling a list of equipment, drugs, and supplies that would be required in isolation. As the list grew, his attention skipped away only once—once while he wondered how he'd feel if nobody chose to volunteer for the isolation unit. Would he really be able to forgive them for that? He returned to the list. It was growing longer. Would he be able to requisition everything outlined? He had no wish to deprive the patients already within Beckman General, but just how important could a gall bladder removal be in light of the horrendous damage to those people waiting outside?

He'd lost track of the time when a young, feminine arm reached out and removed one of the sheets. "Shall I begin getting this stuff together, Doctor?"

Nurse Sharon Henry was holding the paper. Behind her stood Dr. Max Feldman from Urology, next to him the new intern, Evans, and two aides.

Five. It was a small crew that had come forward—not as many as he had dared to hope for. But five would do. Counting himself, there would be six personnel who would be completely sectioned off from the functioning of the rest of Beckman General. They wouldn't be allowed to enter any other part of the hospital after they'd become contaminated. They'd also be subjecting themselves to hazards that could possibly claim their lives.

Dr. Parsons was at once gratified and saddened by their courage. "Are you positive?" he asked. "Remember, once we step out that door we're committed. There'll be no turning back then."

Their faces were almost stoic. It was too bad Cash Archer couldn't bring himself to join them, Parsons thought. Maybe he should have flung the challenge directly at the obstetrician. But Archie would have let it pass. "Well, what do you say? Any of you can get out now by just walking away." He didn't want any of them to leave, but he needed to know each was certain of his own commitment.

"Shall I get started, Doctor?" Sharon Henry asked as she waved the list at him, answering his question.

He patted her on the shoulder, "By all means, nurse."

"Tell me what I can do, Bern," said the urologist. "It's been a long time since I've treated anything interesting."

The group met together again after the supplies were assembled and deposited in the make-shift isolation unit. Arrangements were made with the regular staff whereby additional materials could be left in a neutral zone to be claimed by members of the isolation staff when necessary. Everything was finally ready.

"Bern, how long will the hospital's auxiliary power system last?" Max Feldman asked. The question made Parsons hesitate. He knew this was a concern of everyone. Utility-supplied electricity had been cut off during the night but the center's stand-by power source had immediately started functioning. He finally answered. "It's hard to say, Max. The generators will only operate as long as we have fuel."

"Assuming the fuel tanks are full, Bern, how long do we have power?"

"I'm not sure. But I vaguely remember hearing something about three days."

"Only seventy-two hours," murmured Max Feldman. "Doesn't give us much leeway. A hospital without power...." He let the subject drop. The seventy-two hours had already begun.

"There's one other thing," remarked Parsons. "The civil defense bulletins warn against water usage. Since the water is contaminated, even in the pipes, diets will obviously be limited to milk and juices for as long as they last—ours as well as the patients. We're fortunate—one of the best-stocked departments in the hospital is the kitchen. However," he added, "we'll begin immediately with a strict rationing schedule for our personnel and patients. Serious patients will be exempt from food rationing for as long as possible." Bern could only speculate what Krantz would do for the rest of the hospital.

He was aware that none of them knew exactly what to expect in their patients. Never having experienced a disaster of this magnitude or scope, and having had no training in treating excessive radiation exposure, it would be anyone's guess as to what would develop with the patients. They all assumed that the number of persons grouped in the parking lot would grow. Little did they realize that before another day elapsed, survivors in the dozens would begin amassing outside the lone, rear entrance.

With Dr. Parsons leading, all six walked out to the ambulance area, to their patients. At a glance it was obvious that three of the injured had died during the night. Others, the most disabled first, were supported or placed on stretchers and carried inside the building for the first attention they'd received since the devastation some twenty-four hours earlier.

Acute, intense doses of radiation produced both immediate and delayed effects. After-effects, and the wide variety of their manifestation, could be a long time in developing; immediate reactions were pronounced and horrible. Of the several who had not been near the reactor and had not received the initial blast of radioactive heat, their symptoms—nausea, vomiting, and diarrhea— were indistinguishable from gastric upsets caused by a large number of rather ordinary illnesses. The knowledge that these symptoms were reactions to radiation poisoning caused Parsons and his staff to approach treatment with new awareness. Medication for treating this aspect of radiation poisoning was the same medication prescribed for upset stomachs and influenza. Vomiting and diarrhea, when uncontrolled, were as debilitating as any disease. When compounded by radiation poisoning, control became all the more urgent.

They were a stinking, malodorous assemblage, these victims of White Water. Liquid antidiarrheals and antinauseants were used freely, but with only limited success. Sharon Henry, a highly skilled, compassionate nurse, had rarely encountered such massive resistance by stomachs to the chalky fluid she poured. Methodically she'd tip the head back and the patient would swallow. Then with equal precision the stomach rejected the fluid, spewing it convulsively out the mouth and nose.

"Dr. Parsons, they just can't seem to hold this down," she shouted.

"Send more in right after they regurgitate," he advised. "They're going to need every ounce of energy they can get, and this constant loss of body fluid is sapping them."

The doctors lent their attention to the most severe cases. Deep lacerations received during the wreckage of automobiles had become swollen with infection. The immediate cleansing of these wounds was attended to. For the victims of radiation burns, there was little that could be done beyond dressing the seared flesh.

Antibiotics were given in any case that remotely suggested need; but the need was great. There seemed no end to open, festering wounds. Shot after shot was injected by the staff until the changing of syringes became automatic. Pain killers and fever reducers were as frequently administered as antibiotics, for without a single exception, every patient had a body temperature that was in or nearing critical range—a boiling fever that resulted from massive infections and inflammation. Superficially, excluding the hideous burns covering only one side of their faces, the victims were much like the typical survivors of a freeway crash—abrasions, bruises, broken bones, and always the vomiting and diarrhea.

A chest wound was open to the critical eye of Dr. Feldman. As a urologist he'd not dealt with this kind of task since his intern days. He was sharpening old skills quickly. "Bern, would you take a look at this?" The huge gaping slit was full of seeping pus.

Dr. Parsons glanced briefly and wrinkled his nose. "That'll take a lot of cleaning, Max. Better start him on a double dose of penicillin."

The small staff worked hurriedly, their actions almost mechanical. They gave minimal thought to anything other than their labors, but they all carried in their minds the fact that the radiation had already begun its devastation on the patients. Some of the victims had greater natural resistance to the damage of the invisible rays and would fare better than others. But in some, the radiation had already attacked the body's cells, tearing apart the cells' structures, and killing the cells outright. Evidence of this fatal destruction lay in three human forms out on the parking lot.

In other patients, passively sitting, taking their medication, the rays had struck their cells, distorting the cell structures, breaking chromosomes and ionizing chemical molecules within the cells. From some of these invasions the cells would recover. From others, cells would begin to divide abnormally, perhaps over years, and the final result would be the long-term after-effect—a malignant tumor.

Eventually Parsons and the staff had all the patients in various stages of treatment. For the first time since the small, select medical group had walked out into the compound to lay claim to the victims there was an opportunity to take stock of the scene.

Bernard Parsons was a man of excellent physical condition. Robust, his strong hands were laced with straps of muscles that allowed him to perform arduous, lengthy operations that often spanned the greater portion of a day. And yet, despite their strength, his hands had begun to shake with fatigue. Catching Max's attention, he motioned and they went into an alcove.

Max slumped wearily against the table in the small, adjoining room. "Damn, Bernie, I didn't work this hard when I was an intern." He attempted a weak smile, without much success.

"We're not going to be any good collapsed. Here, take this," Parsons said as he located them each a can of orange juice.

Max fumbled with the opener on the top. Then lifting the can to his mouth, he drained it in one long drink. The tin can rattled as Max tossed it into a nearby cardboard box. Then he dropped tiredly into a chair.

Parsons stood sipping his juice, reflecting on the day. "You know, it's strange the way attitudes change," he said quietly. "There was a period between the Nineteen Twenties and Forties when heavy doses of radiation were standard treatment for some things."

Max looked up with a flicker of interest.

Parsons continued, "It used to be that young children would be sent in for x-ray therapy....the object being to destroy lymph nodes that were habitually swollen from some inner infection, or in the case of tonsillitis, the tonsillar tissue would be destroyed. Usually two or three large doses of radiation would do the trick, and, of course, the child would have been spared the trauma of surgery."

Max said thoughtfully, "I wasn't aware of that practice, Bernie."

"Oh yes. It was used all right. But it was usually administered to the children of physicians and other upper-crust. Anyway, it much later came to the attention of the profession that there was an abnormally high incidence of cancer of the thyroid among the recipients of such treatment."

"While irradiating the nodes or tonsils, the thyroid also received a dose," suggested Max, caught up in the discussion.

"Right. You know radiation is particularly destructive to that organ. Malignancies developed—slowly, of course—but by now they're being observed frequently in those people who had the treatments as children," said Parsons with a frown.

"I've not read any of this in my journals," replied Max.

"No," said Parsons, shaking his head. "The findings have only recently been circulated." He suddenly grew quiet, lost in thought.

The subject had jarred the urologist out of his fatigue. "I tell you, Bernie, the thought of cancer is really frightening. Too often I've seen its terrible ravages. I used to be on staff with a fellow who'd done extensive radiological studies back in the Fifties. Back then we didn't know much about the hazards of radiation." He paused momentarily.

"Do we know a lot now?" asked Parsons, wearily, as he finally sat beside Max.

"Well, more, at least, But anyhow, this guy was left-handed, you see, and he was always using that hand for positioning the x-rays. So, the hand was frequently exposed in the process. He gave up his studies and went into practice, and it was then that I actually knew him—some fifteen years after he had quit the research.

"Bernie," said Max slowly, "you wouldn't believe that left hand of his. First, he lost a finger from cancer....and then the whole back of his hand became a huge, black malignant growth that spread half way up his arm. God," he shuddered, "if it had been mine, I'd have had the whole limb amputated right to the shoulder."

"Didn't he?" Parsons asked.

"No....he wouldn't. And it probably wouldn't have mattered, I suppose. He didn't live much longer."

The quick-energy sugars from the juice were beginning to renew Max. Now animated and anxious to continue, he asked, "Say, is it true, what I've heard about you?"

Parsons looked up in surprise. He wasn't aware of any rumors going around, and at any rate, he didn't figure the pudgy urologist to be a gossip monger. "I don't know," he answered. "What have you heard?"

Max picked up Bernie's empty juice can and inspected it casually. "Someone told me that you never send a bill to a patient who's terminal. Is that true?"

Parsons ran his fingers through his hair. "Yeah....that's right. Why?"

"Oh nothing. It's just that I've never heard of anyone doing that kind of thing before."

Having no interest in making explanations, Parsons let the comment pass. He was still irked that Cash Archer hadn't come to the isolation unit. Archer was bloated with ego, puffed with self- satisfaction about how great he was. Well, if he was really that good, he should be down here, thought Parsons. After all, Max and the others....

"How is it that you volunteered to work with these patients, Max? You're a family man. Weren't you worried about getting your family out of this?"

The short, stodgy urologist answered rather quickly. "No, Bern. My son's in military school in West Virginia. My daughter is raising hell at U.C. Berkeley, and Louise, my wife, is in a European health spa with one of her friends. I guess you could say that old Dad here was all alone. So I figured....what the hell. Why not do something just for the sake of doing it, for a change?"

Military school, Europe. It must cost Max a hunk of money to keep his family going. "Your wife is in bad health?" asked Parsons.

Max verged on laughter for a second. "Because she's at a health spa? Hell! The name is misleading. It's really a fat farm where overweight gals go to take off the lard." He patted his stomach. "I could do with some of that myself, I guess." His gaze drifted away briefly. "When this is over maybe I'll go with Louise. Yeah, that sounds like a good idea....maybe I'll do just that."

"Dr. Parsons! Dr. Parsons!" Nurse Henry motioned to the physician. "Come quick! You won't believe how many are

89

piling in on the parking lot!"

The respite was over.

Chapter Eight

Their escape from the disaster zone and arrival at the outskirts of Blythe, the small California city bordering Arizona, had not been at all as the Warings had expected. Leaving San Mirado, Frank had imagined that they'd make the trip to the state border by dusk and be across and into Arizona shortly thereafter. But long before the desert community had come into view, the Warings began to realize that some complications lay ahead. To begin with, traffic had been more and more congested as they'd approached the border. Cars lined the shoulders of the main artery, their radiators overheated from steady driving and the hot, late summer sun. The whole area had taken on the aura of some gigantic cattle pen filled with milling people. For as far as could be seen there were hundreds and hundreds of automobile tops shimmering in the heat.

At first, Paula and Frank thought that this spectacle of throbbing human life simply indicated a back-up at the border crossing—too many people trying to cross into Arizona at once. Then, finally reaching a position still on the outskirts of the city, they were forced to draw their vehicle to a halt, the crush of machines and people making further progress impossible.

As night came, the city of Blythe became inundated by strangers. Services were rapidly deteriorating in the business districts. Huge, underground gasoline tanks were emptying. Water hydrants had long lines of people waiting their turns for the precious fluid. Food stores and restaurants were being virtually depleted of edibles. And public restroom facilities had hours ago jammed from over use.

Those on the edge of town just waited to enter. Blocked in on four sides and unable to move, Frank and his family had reluctantly passed the night parked at the side of the road. It had been noisy and unsettling. There was a constant racket of car doors slamming, motors, horns, and talk. Headlights frequently cut through the darkness as the impatient tried leaving. The only comfort was the coolness of the desert air. The nighttime chill had been a blessing, a relief from the daytime heat.

At dawn, unable to sleep and with eyes gritty from fatigue,

91

Frank quietly opened the door, looking out at the littered landscape. Some people had managed to extricate their cars and leave.

Paula had spent the night as restlessly as her husband. Her back ached from the cramped quarters of the car and her mood was petulant. She felt Frank slide off the seat. "Where are you going?"

Shush," replied Frank softly. "You'll wake the kids."

She bolted upright in the seat. They had decided during the night that Frank shouldn't leave them while it was dark, for safety's sake, but with daylight he'd have to get out and scavenge for some food. "Frank!"

"Shush, Paula. I'm going to see if I can't get us something to eat."

"How long are you going to be gone?" she asked sourly.

"Lord, I don't know, as long as it takes. I'll be back when I find some food." With that Frank disappeared.

Paula tried unsuccessfully to settle comfortably into the seat. She glanced back at Kim and Jerry. The two youngsters were soundly asleep. Children....they can sleep through anything. She pulled a tissue from its box and wiped her face. Her skin was oily, badly in need of soap and water. God, what she'd give right now for a tub of hot water filled with bath salts. To luxuriate. This nightmare was a pain.

She stretched her legs, pushing against the floor of the vehicle. There was a soft pop as her right hip slipped firmly into the socket; she winced at the tiny spurt of pain. What a mess this was! Sitting out here in this god-forsaken place, completely surrounded by people she didn't know and would never know, with the smell of human excrement heavy in the morning air— how demoralizing. They'd been fools to rush out like they had. And she'd known it then, yesterday, when Frank was in a frenzy to get out of San Mirado. They hadn't thought to bring one drop of water with them. Yet two large containers of mineral-free water sat at home in the garage. And food? She always kept the cabinets well stocked. She shopped the specials at the supermarket, she clipped coupons—her kitchen was loaded with cans and boxes and jars. She visualized each compartment, each shelf in the cabinets; she knew precisely where every item was located. And they hadn't brought one speck of food with them, not one speck. An old hand carved clock, and a Persian Paw stole, but no food. Paula hated the idea that she'd been so

92

thoughtless as to never consider bringing food or water along. But then, it was Frank's fault, too. He'd started right in rushing them the moment he burst into the house.

"Mom?" The boy's voice was plaintive.

"What is it, Jerry?" Paula asked, turning to look at her son.

"I don't feel so good."

She reached out and touched his forehead. It was hot against her fingers. "Are you sick at your stomach?"

The boy raised himself up, his face suddenly very pale. "I think I'm..." and he lurched toward the window. The retching sounds preceded the vomit by a couple seconds, but in that time the weakened child couldn't get the window down. In the next instant the bile-loaded, foul-smelling regurgitate hit the glass.

"Jerry!" screamed Paula. "For God's sake, get the door open!" Her arm flashed out, and she grasped the handle and pushed. The door swung wide but not before the vomit smacked against her arm. Repulsed, Paula leapt from the car and pulled Jerry out.

He soon stood at the side of the vehicle, retching. When the last heave subsided, Paula used tissues to wipe the boy's face and clothing, then her arm. The youth was trembling and much paler. "Are you going to be sick again?" asked Paula.

Jerry could only nod weakly.

"Then go sit on the ground over there while I try to clean this crap out of the car." It was an impossible task, removing the stench. But at least the solid evidence of Jerry's illness was finally gone. And Kim, snoring softly, had slept through the whole thing.

Paula sat on the ground beside her son for nearly an hour. The earth was cool beneath them, a pleasure after her efforts at calming Jerry and cleaning the interior of the car. Activity around them was picking up. People stepped over Paula's legs as they passed by; they never stopped to talk, which was just as well. She had no interest in anything they might have to say. All she wanted to do was get out of there—through the mob of cars —and over to Arizona, since that was the destination Frank had picked for them. Surely it would be better over there.

"Paula, what are you doing sitting on the ground?"

She looked up into Frank's face. "What do you think I'm doing here?" her voice was waspish.

He seemed perplexed.

Well, God, Frank! Can't you smell the vomit?"

Frank peered in the car and took a whiff. His nose wrinkled. "Jerry?" he asked, nodding toward the boy.

Paula's lips drew tight; she didn't give him an answer.

Stooping down, Frank placed a small sack beside her. "Here. This is all I could get."

"Did you hear anything about what they're going to do to get rid of this jam?" Paula asked, ignoring the bag. "We're never going to get across the border at this rate."

Frank wiped at his. forehead wearily. "It's closed."

"What?" Paula asked loudly.

"I said the border crossing is closed. Arizona has refused to let any evacuees in. They don't want any radiation contamination brought over."

"Well, for God's sake! You mean you brought us all this way to sit outside this stinking town!"

"Paula, how was I to know? I mean, if we'd been a few hours earlier last night we might have made it." He hesitated, dejected. "The best I can tell there's supposed to be some Red Cross relief showing up before long....bringing food and water, I guess."

Paula snorted in exasperation. Seeing the bag she picked it up. She opened it and turned it upside down. A single, flat can fell into her lap. She stared at the can for a second. "Sardines! For crying out loud, Frank! How in the hell do you expect us to eat sardines for breakfast?"

Her outburst caught the interest of several people nearby. They paused to hear what was to follow. Paula glared up at them, quickly getting to her feet.

"Paula," said Frank, "don't yell. I told you this was all I could get."

Paula turned her glare on him. "But sardines...greasy fish!" She looked down into the empty bag then inverted it once more and shook it. Nothing else fell out. Wadding the bag into a ball she threw it away from her. "And there's not even an opener for the can. Just how do you think we're going to get this open? With our teeth?" she taunted, waving the can at Frank.

Frank grabbed the can from her and pitched it into the car. He took her by the arm. "All right, Paula," he said quietly. "There's no need for you to show your butt in front of all these people."

Paula jerked free of his grasp. She was dead tired and hungry. Her temper was on edge and Frank, for his coolness about the whole crazy matter, was not helping one bit. "Just tell me one thing, will you? Why in the world did we have to come this way? Why this...this....whatever this place is."

Lowering his voice as if to set a precedent for his wife, Frank replied, "For heaven's sake, Paula, I've told you a dozen times. I'd hoped that we'd get over to Arizona and stay with Billy Joe until this is over."

"Billy Joe, Billy Joe," snapped Paula. "How's your brother going to help us, Frank? He doesn't have a pot to piss in."

"Paula! Will you please keep your voice down."

"We could be eating breakfast with my parents right now if you'd just listened to me for once. But no," she said viciously, "no, no....not old man Jorgensen. Not a nice comfortable house in Oakland where the air is clean and there's no trouble to worry about. Oh no! You have to do everything the hard way, don't you?"

Frank stared at his wife a long moment. Then he reached down and shook Jerry by the shoulder. "Come on and get in the car, son. You'll feel better inside." Once the boy was in, Frank got in under the steering wheel.

Speaking through the open window, Paula said. 'Okay, Frank. It's obvious that we're not going to get to your brother's house. Now....where are we going? How do we get away from here, anyway?"

Lowering his head on the steering wheel, Frank was near defeat. "I don't know."

A woman's voice carried through the morning air. It was a sound at once familiar to both Paula and Frank. They looked up in surprise as Flo, with Harry behind her, threaded a path to the Warings.

"Paula....Frank," said Flo breathlessly. "I told Harry it was you. I heard you, Paula, from way over there and knew it was you.

The Wintons appeared as tired and disturbed as the Warings felt. "Flo, have you been here all this time?" asked Paula.

Flo nodded. "All night. We got here late yesterday evening." Frowning, she added, "Have you heard? They've closed the border."

"Yes," answered Paula, "we heard." Then recalling that the last time she'd seen Flo and Harry was yesterday after the accident, she asked, "Where's Rickey? You found him, of course?"

Harry stepped forward. "We found him. He was up near the reactor site just where your boy had said he'd be." His face was contorted with worry.

Paula, sensing Harry's concern, asked, "He's all right, isn't he, Harry?"

The big gruff man, normally at ease around people, replied haltingly. "He's...no, he's real sick."

Paula turned to Flo for some explanation. But none was forthcoming. The reactor site—radiation. Paula felt she knew the nature of Rickey's illness. Maybe Frank had been right about the dangers of being near the White Water ruins. "Can you get him to a doctor?"

"That's just it," said Flo, distraught. "It's such a mess here, there's no one to take him to. Can you imagine that?" she said tearfully, turning her head.

"Then what...?" began Frank.

"We're going back," said Harry firmly. "We're going back to San Mirado and wait this thing out."

Frank got out of the car. "Harry, I don't think you ought to do that. You're free of that area now, and sure it's bad here, but there'll be help coming in pretty soon."

Shaking his head stubbornly, Harry stayed firm. "No, we're going back home." He glanced over at Flo. "Everything we own is back in San Mirado, we've got food and water there, and well, it can't be any worse than it is here."

Paula gazed at the people around them, squeezed together like cattle herded in for slaughter. Harry was right about one thing, anyway. Conditions were bad here. And she guessed they were destined to get much worse before this ended. But returning to San Mirado was insane. "You can't go back," she said.

"We have to," answered Harry. "There's no other place for us to go."

"That's nonsense," snapped Paula. "Stay here. Go to another town. Do anything but you're crazy if you return to San Mirado. My God, Harry, there must be people back there who'd give their eyeteeth to be where we are. As bad as it is here...."

"It would be better at home," he said. "Don't you see, we'd be in the house....we'd have beds to sleep on... food. We'd be able to get Rickey to a doctor."

Frank interrupted. "But Harry, there won't be any doctors treating anybody, or if there are, they'll be swamped, too. Damn, man, be sensible! Wait it out here. There'll be food and medical people brought in before much longer. I know there will."

Shaking his head, Harry replied. "I just don't believe the radiation is that bad, Frank."

"Then what's wrong with your son?" demanded Paula.

"Well, he's sick," answered Harry. "But that doesn't mean that the radiation is what's making him sick."

Paula nudged her husband. "Frank, talk some sense into Harry!"

Frank obligingly began when Harry held up his hand. "No, Frank. My mind is made up. If we'd been smart we never would have left there in the first place."

"All right, then," said Paula. "Come with us. We can travel in separate cars or together."

Flo asked. "You aren't staying here?"

"No," replied Paula. She saw Frank cast a glance at her. "We're going to my parents in Oakland."

Frank turned away and got back into the car. His anger at Paula's decision to go to Oakland showed.

"My parents won't mind you're being there one bit," Paula assured her friends. "They'll be glad to help."

But Harry declined. "I'm not going to be a burden on anyone. I've been fending for myself since I was the age of Jerry, there, and I'm not about to become someone's welfare case now."

Helplessly, Paula looked at Flo. Flo shrugged. "Harry makes the decisions in our family, Paula."

Harry grabbed his wife's hand. "Come on, Sugar. We'd best get back to Rickey. He may be needing us."

Paula watched until they became lost in the crowd. That Harry was this dense, this oblivious to the dangers, was inconceivable, but that Flo, a grown woman, would so willingly follow him in such a maniacal adventure was even more incredible, she thought, forgetting her own obstinacy. She'd never let Frank do such a stupid thing, and she certainly wouldn't follow him if he did.

"Well, are you coming?" asked Frank, looking up at her through the window. "Now that you've taken it on yourself to decide our futures, hadn't we better get started?" Frank's sarcasm wasn't lost on her.

The street was empty, totally devoid of life. Not a person was in sight; no child pedaled along on a bicycle; no cars were in motion—it was as though some giant movie set had been placed in suburban San Mirado, but without actors to give the scene life. Harry felt his skin crawl as he looked around in the eerie stillness. Yesterday this row of homes had been bursting with activity. Today there was no one.

Flo moved over until her shoulder touched him. "It's weird, Harry," she said in a near whisper. "I never imagined what a town would be like with all the people gone."

Harry shook a shiver off and glanced skyward. The sun was descending. In another hour everything would be camouflaged by the darkness of night. At another time and in another place this quietude might be welcomed, but not now. They needed people, the security of a familiar face, or any face. Had it been a mistake to bring his family back to this place? Harry rubbed his hands together. The palms were calloused and tough from years of pouring cement, years of making a living for Flo and Rickey. Of course it wasn't wrong to return here. This was their home. This was where they belonged. Yet it was all so strange, this bleakness, this absence of life.

He felt a tingling sensation on his forearm and scratched it. Was this due to radiation? No, it couldn't be. He glanced defiantly at the darkening sky. It's not what everyone said. It couldn't be. They were ninnies to be frightened so easily into running. The radiation, if there really was radiation up there, couldn't be as bad as they said, and certainly not if everyone would simply get inside their homes and stay there. "Get the door open, I'm bringing Rickey in."

As Flo stepped cautiously toward the house, Harry reached into the car for his son. The boy lay inert across the seat. Powerless to move of his own accord, his eyes, dulled by a ravaging fever, watched his father's motions.

"We're home, Rick," said Harry as he scooped the boy into his arms. The lad was too thin for his age. At thirteen he needed more muscle on him. After this, Harry decided, we'll start going to the Y in the evenings to work out. Muscle is all the boy lacked. He's got good bones, and he's strong. A fever won't get him down.

"Harrrry!" Flo's scream slashed through the stillness like a knife.

Unwilling to drop his son, Harry hugged the boy closer and

broke into a lumbering trot to the house. At first he'd thought there was an intruder inside. Instead, only Flo was there, standing in the center of the room.

"Flo! What...?" He stopped. The living room had been stripped bare of furnishings. The tables, sofa, chairs, even the wall-to-wall carpet had been ripped free and removed. "Goddammit!" he muttered.

"The buzzards...the filthy buzzards!" Flo murmured as she walked slowly into the bedroom. She found nothing but four walls and a floor. "Oh Harry, how could they?"

Harry placed his son gently on the floor. Then he carefully removed the one article that had not been taken by the looters. With care and concern for the fabric, he removed the drapery from its hooks and, folding it once, placed it over Rickey.

From the kitchen came the soft cry of Flo. "It's gone....everything...!"

Reaching her side, Harry saw the cabinets standing open. The shelves were bare; every can, box, and article of food had been taken. There would be nothing for them to eat. Flo's sobs tore at the man. He placed his arms around her and pulled her to his chest. "Shhhh... .it'll be okay, Sugar," he crooned. "It'll be okay, you'll see." Gradually her sobs weakened, then disappeared.

"Now what?" she mumbled, her face buried in his shirt. "Oh God, now what?"

He ran his hand soothingly over her back, patting her gently. "We'll be all right, Flo. This won't last long....someone will be coming in to help us."

Flo drew back and snuffled. "Harry, we'll die if we stay here."

"No, no. We won't, Flo. We'll be safe." His mind wandered to the boy in the other room. If the kid hadn't gone toward that reactor; if, for once, he'd done what he was told and come straight home....but no. This was his fault, the father's. He'd given the boy too much freedom, too long a rein. He'd encouraged the son to explore and to question, and yes, even question authority. He felt her head against his chest again.

"Rickey needs a doctor, Harry."

Harry nodded. "Yes. Tomorrow I'll try to find someplace....a hospital where we can get help for him."

"Frank?" Paula's voice broke the quiet.

"Huh?"

"Are you asleep?" Paula asked.

He grunted an unintelligible, "Uh."

Paula lay on her side in a fetal position with her legs drawn up, her back to her husband. It was comforting to be here under the roof of her parents once more. It could be a pleasant, serene existence, being watched over by her father, having the breakfast made, and her mother smilingly calling them to the table—it could be nice. Like the old days. Like the month she and Frank had spent here early in their marriage, before he had dragged her off to the south. If only he'd wanted to stay here, to become a real part of the family. She snuggled down under the warm blanket. No matter how old she got, there'd never be a place as safe and secure as right here at home. She thought of Frank beside her. He hated being here. For a moment she regretted speaking to him. Now she was obliged to talk. "You don't like Dad, do you, Frank?"

"Your folks are nice people, Paula."

"Nice? Is that the best you can do? Say that they're nice people? Christ—the world is full of nice people."

"Let's not quarrel, okay? I said they're nice. What more do you want? Me to lick his feet?" His voice was alert, not drowsy at all.

"Don't get snotty, Frank. It's just that I don't think you show my father the proper respect," she said peevishly.

Frank flopped over on his side, away from his wife. "Oh, shit! At a time like this you're stewing because I don't respect your old man."

"That's because you've pouted around the house all day, acting like he doesn't even exist. You should sit down and talk with him. Ask him about his business or something. Jesus, make some kind of effort," she said. "Do something."

"Why in the hell should I? I didn't ask him to take us in."

"You're here, though." She sat up in bed, prepared to pursue the subject further. "I know what's wrong with you, Frank. You feel like you're a failure when you're around him."

"No, I don't, dammit! What the hell has he done? A piddling company. Bull! That doesn't mean his ass is lined with gold."

"You're jealous," she accused him.

"To hell I am!" he said, suddenly angered.

100

"You're still smarting because of that crack he made about you years ago." Her recollection of the event was vivid. It'd happened at their wedding reception right downstairs. An old friend, too high on liquor, had boomed out at her father, asking him how he liked his new son-in-law. And her father, without any excuse, had retorted loudly enough for everyone within earshot to hear. 'Frank's all right, but he's got no balls.' Not only had she overheard, but Frank had heard as well. His skin had blanched and he'd walked hurriedly away. No, she had never mentioned it to him, nor he to her. But he remembered.

Frank kicked the covers down to his feet. "He never thought that anyone was good enough for his precious child, including me. Jesus, Paula, the only reason we had Jerry in such a hurry was to get the furniture your folks promised us in exchange for a grandchild. I mean, what kind of screwballs were we that we'd have a kid just to please your parents?"

Paula was not a simpering, pouting woman. She said acidly, "Are you sure that's why we had Jerry, and not because you were trying to prove something to yourself?"

"What does that mean?" he asked sourly.

"Nothing. Forget it." Why must they always spoil everything by quarreling. A long silence followed their outburst. It was worrisome, these strange irrelevancies, these dissensions that had begun to creep between them. In this crisis they should at least be able to put a halt to the petty quarrels. At last Paula said, "I read in the Press tonight that the government won't be sending anybody in until the radiation is swept away."

"Good strong winds will have to blow the poison out of the area before anyone will go in—troops, medical teams, or anybody else," Frank replied calmly, welcoming a rest from their quarreling.

Paula shuddered and nudged over against Frank. She touched his leg with the sole of her foot. The bed was warm and comfortable, and for once their argument had ended almost as quickly as it had begun. "I wonder if Flo and Harry really did go back to San Mirado."

Frank lay quietly, unanswering.

Paula was engaged with her own thoughts. "I hate to think of them doing that....going back." A moment passed. "Frank, will we ever return to San Mirado?" She paused. "If we do, I'd like us to get one of those new, Spanish-type houses—out in the de Lorenzo subdivision. A five bedroom, three bath place. You

101

know, with the Spanish brick facade," she added.

Frank heaved a deep sigh. Over the night Jerry's vomiting had become so bad that, with fear and apprehension, he'd taken the boy to the hospital, bypassing the Jorgensens' family physician. He had no sooner stepped inside the house then Paula was before him.

"What did the doctor say?"

Frank removed his jacket. "Jerry hasn't got any radiation sickness," he said, hanging the jacket up.

Paula was obviously worried about something. "Was he sure? Can he be sure?" she asked.

"He's the doctor, Paula. He said there's nothing to worry about...that Jerry just has a gastric upset."

"Then why did he want to keep him in the hospital?"

Frank, annoyance showing, said, "Look, he wants to keep the kid a day or two and build him up. That's all. My God, if you were so concerned why didn't you go with me to take him in?" He started around her toward their bedroom.

"What's Jerry's room number?" she snapped. "I'm going to see him."

"Oh, Paula, for Pete's sake, there's no point in you going over there now. Wait awhile and we'll both go."

Paula held out her hand. "The keys, Frank."

He dropped them in her palm.

She rushed out of the house, slamming the door after her.

Her departure left him with a feeling of emptiness, helplessness. Suddenly it seemed they were growing farther and farther apart. She'd always been high spirited and willful, but now that she had insisted on her parents' home for their refuge she seemed more than ever determined to have her way, to make her own decisions without regard to him or his opinions. Maybe it could be expected. After all, he had married out of his element, as the phrase went. Frank stared at the spot where she'd stood, then shrugged and started to turn away when he noticed the old man watching him.

Mr. Jorgensen peered over the top of his glasses. He was a frail looking old man, reed-thin and pale in his Scandinavian color. But frail looking, only. Frank knew his father-in-law to be as tough as a steel rod, and just as unbending.

"Where's she going?" The question was gritty, almost contemptuous.

"To see Jerry," Frank answered, heading again toward the

bedroom.

"Then why did she call Dr. Hellman?" asked the old man.

Frank paused. "Hellman?"

"Our doctor. She called him before you came in."

Clearly puzzled for a moment, then relieved, Frank replied, "I guess she wants another opinion about Jerry." Sure, Paula was a worrier. Like a dog she'd nag and nag at something until she was satisfied she'd got the truth of the matter. She was worried that the boy had radiation sickness.

Mr. Jorgensen seemed disbelieving. "She made an appointment, Frank...for herself, not Jerry."

Sensing the cold eyes of the old man on him, Frank continued into the bedroom. "Why she's seeing Dr. Hellman is her business, I guess. If she wants you to know she'll tell you." And maybe she'll also tell her husband, Frank added to himself.

He locked himself in the room and lay down on the bed. The woman was exasperating....exactly like her father. And she actually expected him to butter up to the old fool. How could he? How in the hell could he get close to someone when the other drew an invisible barrier between them, then nailed it shut with a bunch of smart-assed cracks about a man not having any balls. Ah, the old bastard. He wasn't worth it. If it weren't for Paula they wouldn't be here....if the old man hadn't been Paula's father Frank would have mashed his face in, wedding reception or not.

Chapter Nine

Cecil Yeager opened his eyes and briefly inspected his surroundings. His presence in the unfamiliar, dingy room momentarily surprised him. Then he remembered. He had crossed the border during the night. No difficulty there. Responding to his immense fatigue, he'd checked into this hotel after stuffing himself on chili and frijoles. That had been a mistake. He had never digested Mexican food well, and the fare served in most Tijuana restaurants was heavily spiced. He hadn't been selective, but had eaten at the first place offering food. This morning he was sorry because the green pepper taste was still welling up from his gut. He'd probably feel better if he could throw it, he thought.

Dressing with haste, he collected his belongings and walked down the rickety stairs to the lobby.

The Mexican behind the desk looked up from his racing form at the American in the crumpled suit. "Como esta, Senor?" he asked.

"Fine," Cecil replied shortly to the clerk. He hoped the man would understand English. "Say, I want to drive down the coast but I need to buy some insurance—you know, for my car. Can you recommend a place?"

His United States automobile insurance policy covered a visitation of no longer than three days, and carried a mileage limit into the interior. Most American policies were written like this, thus the insurance agents made a better than ample living from the foreign turistas who came down to enjoy the climate, the beaches, and the cut-rates on booze.

"Oh sure, Mister. At the border you will find many insurance offices."

Cecil was aware of the disreputable-looking little shanty offices inside the border gates, but he had no wish to return to them. "I was hoping to find an insurance agent here in town," he said.

Shrugging, the clerk replied, "I do not know of such, though maybe you find one. Most Americans stop by the offices at the border, Mister."

Removing his wallet, Cecil paid his bill and thanked the clerk. Perhaps the insurance scheme was an unnecessary risk. It had occurred to him suddenly, and it seemed a good idea at the time. But he was anxious to get deeper into Mexico. Maybe he should scrap the plan and just proceed southward.

In a moment of indecisiveness, he stood on the cracked sidewalk and inhaled the morning air. The light breeze carried an aroma of putrefying garbage from the alley and sent a new wave of nausea racing through his stomach. Unable to decide, by weighing the risk against what he might gain if he succeeded, he finally made up his mind to take the chance, and drove back to the border.

Cecil stopped in front of one of the more respectable buildings on the Mexican side of the gate. It contained not only an insurance office, but a marriage parlor, and next to it, a quick divorce office. The fourth suite was occupied by a bail bondsman.

Stepping nervously into the grubby clapboard building, Cecil was warmly greeted by a suave, meticulously attired salesman. "Yes, sir?" asked the olive-complexioned man as he dragged a chair over for Cecil. "You wish some additional insurance while you visit with us?"

Cecil wavered a moment, then taking a deep breath he rapidly explained his needs.

The agent pulled out a pad of forms and began filling in his signature at the bottom. When he completed his name and the date, he said, "We will require some information from you, please. Your name?"

"Cecil M. Yeager." Cecil spelled it for him.

"And where do you live, Senor?" asked the agent politely.

Cecil hesitated. Should he give his correct address? But then, the agent was sure to ask for his driver's license. "It's, uh, 1214 Adams Street, San Mirado."

The agent paused over the paper. "Senor, the border closed at midnight to all Americans. Until the catastrophe in Los Angeles is over, no one will be allowed to enter Mexico—including our own people who were there yesterday. It is sad, yes, but this is a rule of our Presidente."

Getting the drift of the agent's comments, Cecil immediately objected. "But this doesn't concern me. I have been in Mexico for some time now. I know nothing of what happened there."

Seemingly reluctant to believe him, the agent drummed his

pen against the desk top. "You were not in Los Angeles yesterday?" he asked.

"No, I was here in Tijuana," Cecil answered flatly.

The day was becoming warm. Cecil wiped the perspiration from his forehead and gulped down a ball of saliva. His mouth was cottony inside. "I was right here in town," he repeated to the agent.

Smiling benignly, the man quickly replied, "In that case there is no reason to deny you insurance. Now, we must have the car's make and model, Mister Yeager, and then we will be finished."

Cecil told him the details.

"One other thing, Senor. I am obliged to obtain proof of where you stayed here. It is a small detail that we have been asked to verify since the closing of the border."

Thinking back to the sleepy clerk at the hotel, Cecil decided that a phone call would promptly reveal that he had checked in late in the night and actually spent no more than six hours there. Fumbling with the inner pocket of his jacket, he let his face assume an expression of concern. "You know, I just remembered that I didn't pick up my wallet. I must have left it at the hotel," he said in a worried voice.

"I will be happy to telephone to the hotel for you, Senor," offered the other. "I must call there about you, regardless."

"No, no. I....I will go for it," said Cecil, getting to his feet.

"Let us hope it is there, Mister Yeager. To be in Mexico without identification is not good," said the agent.

Of that fact Cecil was keenly aware. He'd read of many U.S. citizens and their bouts with customs' officials when they couldn't be properly identified. But customs wasn't his problem. He was traveling in the opposite direction. For now, he feared that he had made the insurance salesman suspicious, unless, of course, he was simply being overly sensitive in thinking that the Mexican knew he'd lied. Probably the agent didn't care whether Cecil had come from Los Angeles or not; yet, he had followed instructions in requesting verification of lodging. "I will return once I find my wallet," Cecil said as he walked out the door. He breathed a sigh of relief once he was outside.

As he was pulling the car into the street he glanced into the window of the insurance office. The agent was talking into the telephone, his neck craned to view the license plates on the vehicle.

Cecil sat back and enjoyed the tunes of the mariachi band.

The street musicians were permanently encamped in the patio of the hotel and their renditions of Spanish songs lent a romantic aura to the starlit night. He delicately licked a few crystals of salt from the rim of the glass before taking a drink of the Marguerita. Perhaps he would adjust to the leisurely pace of Mexican living. Ensenada was an interesting city with its warm, sunny days and honey-skinned girls. He had left Tijuana immediately for this town farther south. Here no one seemed to notice just another tourist.

Cecil was particularly proud of himself this evening. His digestive troubles were finally settling down, and he'd brought off a shrewd deal. Being unable to purchase Mexican insurance, he had been forced to discard the plan for driving the auto out into the country and wrecking it, thereby collecting on the newly acquired policy. Instead, he'd passed the word around the hotel that he wished to sell his car. Within an hour a dark, swarthy man had inspected the vehicle and made an offer to purchase.

Unaccustomed to the Latin style of bargaining, Cecil had sold the car on the man's initial bid. For five hundred American dollars, the buyer had a two-year-old sedan. Elated at his good fortune, the man had spread the message of the ignorant tourist, and later Cecil had to become very outspoken in convincing strangers that he had nothing else he wished to sell. The transaction had been altogether exhilarating, for he knew the car to have been radioactive. What could have been simply abandoned in a narrow street had been converted into unexpected cash.

Using a small part of his money, he had invested in a complete new wardrobe—enough apparel to replace those items he'd left behind, and enough to get him started down here. He'd been a conservative dresser all his life, but today, for once, he'd permitted a Mexican clerk to sell him an outfit that he considered slightly garish. He smiled to himself as he remembered the loud shirts and slacks that he had refused before settling on the off-white gaucho shirt of muslin, and the brown pants. He reached up and tugged the open throat of the shirt closer together, aware that it would be some time before he became accustomed to being in public without a tie.

Without knowing the reason, he had taken great pains with his toilet, carefully parting the brown hair in a precise line along the side of his head, and shaving so closely that his skin was as smooth as a baby's. He wore the shirt hanging outside his pants, but it made him uncomfortable. Although it lent a casual air, he was used to the tail being tucked in. Taking one last glance of himself in the mirror before leaving the hotel, Cecil had been delighted to find an image of a man well-preserved for his forty years, with thick bushy eyebrows that hinted at an inner magnetism that he strongly suspected was lacking.

Sitting amidst the evening noise in the open patio, he was strangely nervous—not relaxed as he wanted to be. It was always thus when he was around people. He would tighten up, becoming almost frosty in conversation, and eventually, he would remove himself entirely from the scene. Being a retiring, shy man, making small talk required the greatest effort on his part. He much preferred to avoid such experience. His spirits had been high earlier in the evening, and up in the room he had toyed with an exotic plan or two for spending the next few hours. Thus, he had determinedly brought himself to the patio and taken a seat before the dancing beauty in the red shoes, intent on forcing himself into the swing of things.

He tossed the first Marguerita down and ordered a second. The dark, Latin features of the girl were suggestive of her high spirits. She was a beautiful woman. For a second he was reminded that he'd always been attracted by the exotic beauty of dark women. He had been staring at her as she clicked her heels against the wooden floor and swayed her hips to the rhythm of the music. He was unaware that he had been so obvious until she danced close to him and brushed his arm with her buttock. Then he had jerked away in embarrassment and focused his attention onto the drink as she danced laughingly across the room.

He hurriedly drank and ordered a third. The liquor was something he took for the enjoyment of its effects. The taste was not particularly pleasing to him, but in short time, the tequila was being absorbed, and his taste buds no longer mattered. In college he had referred to himself as the cheapest drunk on campus because it required so little alcohol to make him tipsy. Already it was beginning to hit bottom, sending a lazy, carefree feeling ebbing through his body.

The dancer returned to his table and stamped out a staccato rhythm with her feet as she whipped her torso into a lively series of contortions. Periodically she'd throw her long hair back from her face and snap her head up, revealing the delicate curve of her neck. Cecil watched, entranced. Numbed by the liquor and mass of woman before him, he broke into a broad, devilish grin as she undulated closer and closer to his chair. His palms were growing sweaty and his heart was pounding against the inside of his chest. Her skirt grazed against him during a violent twist of her hips, and he reached out to grab it—a second too late. She laughed as she danced away.

He motioned to the bartender for another drink. The evening was progressing well for him. The waiter obligingly placed the fresh glass on the table and took Cecil's money. The man wore a surly expression as he counted out the change. Cecil noticed this and wondered for a moment if the waiter resented American men with money coming in to flirt with the girls. Not that it should be any concern to the waiter—he was an employee.

Cecil was turning to observe the dancer again when he saw the military uniform of the local policia at the bar. He saw the bartender nod in his direction and point him out to the officer. His back stiffened as he watched the policeman weave a path through the tables and come to test at his side.

"Senor, let me see your identification," said the officer in broken English.

A wave of fear shot through Cecil's body. Why had he been singled out by the officer? "Why do you want to see my identification?" asked Cecil. "Hey, I don't need a passport to be traveling in Mexico, officer."

"Senor." The policeman stared at him, his eyes harsh. "Your driver's permit, please. Now."

Cecil hesitated. To refuse the officer's request would be too dangerous. He reluctantly withdrew his wallet and handed it over saying, "I have been a visitor to your country many times and never has anyone asked me to present proof of my identity."

The officer examined the I.D. carefully. "Are you Mister Cecil Yeager?"

"Yes."

"Come with me."

"Oh no. Now, Officer, I'm only a tourist looking at the sights. I'm sure you've made a mistake."

The man in the brown uniform stared coolly at him. "Come."

"Well, wait. Can't we talk about this?" Cecil pushed his chair away and stood near the uniform so he could speak quietly. "Of course I don't want to cause any trouble, but officer, I think I have a right to know why you're doing this."

He took a step closer and reached out to lay his hand on the policeman's arm. The officer jumped as if he'd received an electric charge, drew his body back and stared with frightened eyes. The reflexive movement of the officer cautioned Cecil. Nothing would be accomplished by offending the man.

"Senor, we will go to the station now," commanded the policeman.

Cecil meekly followed him to the police van. Assuring himself that there was no possibility he could be in real trouble with the Mexican authorities, Cecil felt that outward signs of cooperation would result in getting the confusion speedily resolved. He sat quietly, saying nothing, during the trip to the headquarters.

By night the large adobe structure hardly looked formidable. Soft lights illuminated the entrance as Cecil trailed the officer through the dusty receiving room and into a smaller interrogation cubicle. Several men awaited them.

Appearing to take command, one of them, one with a coarse black mustache and piercing dark eyes, motioned Cecil into a chair. Cigarette smoke fogged the air in the tight compartment.

"Mr. Cecil Yeager," said the commandant, "we regret that this is necessary."

"Well, I think there must be some confusion, officer," replied Cecil. "You undoubtedly have me mixed up with someone else," he said with what he hoped was calmness.

"You sold a car to one of our citizens today, Mister," said the official flatly.

"Sure I did. But that isn't a crime. Why, you people are always buying them right off the lot in Los Angeles."

"Senor Fernando Martinez paid you five hundred dollars for the car," remarked the officer in an accusative tone.

Cecil's calmness swiftly abandoned him. "Yes." At last he knew what this was about. It was the sale of the car.

"Do you have the money on your person, Mister?"

"Yes," Cecil answered quietly.

Extending his hand, the officer ordered, "Give it to me."

"Hey now, wait a minute," protested Cecil, "that was a legitimate sale. Mr. Martinez was happy with the car. He got it for practically nothing."

One skinny forefinger tapped the desk top, a reminder of its owner's position of authority. "Put it here!"

Cecil respectfully laid the folded bills on the desk. "This sort of action must be unusual for even Mexican officials," he retorted.

The officer replied, "We do not rob you, Mister Yeager. You will have your car again. Follow me." With that he led Cecil to the paved compound at the back of the station.

There, two others stood, far removed from the automobile that had been sold to Martinez. Carrying a metal box hooked to a microphone, one of the men strolled over to the car. He flicked a tiny lever and a steady series of clicks issued from the box. Drawing the box away, the clicking grew fainter until at a given distance, it ceased altogether.

Extending the microphone toward Cecil, clicks began to be emitted again, growing stronger as the detecting instrument was brought within closer range.

"As our scientists would say, Mister, you are very hot—very radioactive, like your car."

Everything fell into place. Cecil could see himself in a dingy underground dungeon awaiting a trial that might never occur.

"Nobody sells a beautiful car like that for five hundred dollars —not unless he has a very special reason to get rid of it quickly. And with California tags on it, too. We are not so dumb as you must think, Mister Yeager."

"Look, I didn't know about this. I swear I didn't. I sold it because I needed the money, that's why."

"We do not wish to have you sharing your new..." the officer paused, searching for the right word, "molester with us. We do not wish to have your malady in our country, Mister."

"I meant no harm to anyone, officer. If you think it's best, then I'll just leave." There were other cities beside Ensenada.

"Yes. You will leave. But you will not only leave Ensenada, you will drive your car out of Mexico—back to the States."

Cecil's mind was working rapidly. The car was a hazard to him. "Well, the car is pretty radioactive. I'd just as soon not spend any more time in it, if you don't mind."

The official glared icily at Cecil. "The vehicle is very dangerous, just as you are dangerous, Senor. We wish you out of our country immediately. You will drive your car north to the border crossing, and pass back into the United States!"

Accepting the order as a lesser evil than being thrown into jail, Cecil reached out in an offer to shake hands with the official. The man recoiled at the proffered palm.

"No. No. Do not touch me!" he snapped.

The fright registered on the other's face gave Cecil a

momentary feeling of satisfaction. Perhaps it was because of the tequila, but now that he realized how afraid this man was of the strange radiation, he suddenly wanted to throw his arms around the other, locking them about his body, forcing him to absorb the mysterious rays.

Refusing, wisely, to give in to the foolish impulse, Cecil moved over to the machine and took his place in the driver's seat. It was not until he pulled out from the compound that he understood there'd be a police car escorting him on the long drive to the border.

At the border crossing all eight lanes were closed to traffic. Both in-coming and out-going vehicles were prohibited except for Cecil's, of which, he assumed, they had been forewarned. He chuckled to himself that for once the guards were not in the least interested in checking the car for contraband. He'd seen an automobile of a couple of hippies ripped apart once, on the belief that the trunk, or motor, or something, must be hiding sacks of marijuana. After an hour of searching and nothing was found, the hippies were permitted to enter the U.S. But their car was a shambles.

He had been expected, it seemed. The accompanying patrol car veered to the curb, coming to a stop before the guard station. The barrier had already been removed so that it required nothing more than a single wave from the guard to send Cecil into his homeland.

Driving the freeway between Tijuana and San Diego was a fifteen minute trip—one that he'd made several times in his younger years. He knew San Diego well. He'd been stationed at the naval base as a staff officer for two years. It was a lovely city. He remembered the bright blue skies and cool ocean breezes, the white stucco buildings and the gray ships anchored in the harbor. Climatically, San Diego was a little pleasanter than its big sister to the north, Los Angeles. It didn't have industrial wastes fouling its air, and the serpentine highway systems didn't have to carry thousands of people daily. In comparison, San Diego was still a small city, growing only spasmodically over the past twenty years, and without the constant, sustained enlargement of its sister. But now its beauty was marred by the flood of refugees that had descended upon it.

The masses had become bottled up, the Mexican border preventing them from dispersing any farther southward.

Cecil had often wondered why he hadn't chosen to make his home in San Diego instead of northward. As he drove, darkness obscured the fields to his right and left, but he was aware that stretching along the route were huge plantings of tomatoes and peppers. Later, in the cooler months ahead, the tomato fields would have expansive plastic sheets protecting the tender vegetables from the chill night air.

There was a subtle blending of two cultures within these few miles. The Mexican influence was keenly felt by citizens north of the border and vice versa. Tijuana had blossomed into a sizable town with the advent of military personnel in search of good times and inexpensive items to buy. Toting a pocket full of cash, the marines and sailors found the village an exciting place until military orders finally posted it out-of-bounds.

From such an atmosphere Cecil had just been ousted. What a contrast. Before, the gringoes were beckoned and cajoled into touring their Latin neighbor. Everything was designed to lure the greenbacks out of the wallets and into the chinos. Exiting visitors were pursued right to the gates at the border with promises of "very good watch for little money." Rapidly, it had all ended. For a second Cecil speculated on what the Mexican shops would do until conditions were restored to normal and they once again had customers. Take longer siestas, he thought bitterly before returning to the question of where he could go now—in his search for safety.

The topic in the hotel lounge dwelt ominously on wind patterns—what would happen if the wind turned southward?

"It usually does this time of year. Here, look at the map. See, the wind can sweep down from the Pacific northwest, swoosh across L.A., travel eastward for a short distance, then break southward, coming right down the coast."

"Yeah, but a lot of times it'll blow from the east. If that happens, everything will be dumped out over the Pacific."

"Couldn't it go straight eastward?"

"Only if there's a storm with it. Isn't that right?"

"Lordy, imagine that—fallout being spread across the whole damned nation, from coast to coast."

"Aw, it wouldn't get the northern states."

"Naw, but it'd sure salt down half the country, though."

"What do you think, buddy? You were up there when the

113

plant blew, weren't you?"

Cecil resented the nudge in his ribs. "I don't know what the wind will do—provided it ever blows."

"Oh well, you don't have any sweat. You're home safe. Right?" The big man was becoming obnoxious, as was his custom when around intellectual types, and Cecil certainly wasn't a blue collar. "Right, pal?"

Cecil smarted from the innuendo. "What do you mean by home safe?" he asked.

"Well, you know, you got the hell out of there fast, didn't you?" he asked, a malicious smirk on his face.

"I did what everybody was trying to do," retorted Cecil.

"Looks kind of like running, doesn't it? You get in your own car and drive out—just you. You didn't even latch onto one other person and bring him along, did you?" asked the big man as he stepped in closer to Cecil.

"You'd have done the same thing if you'd been in my shoes." Cecil's reply was firm.

"Nope! That's where you're wrong, pal. I'd have run, sure....but not by myself. I'd have loaded that little old buggy down with my folks and friends before I left."

The room had become very quiet. No one talked, no one moved.

Cecil had a sensation of standing in one of those mirrored cubicles that he'd found at the carnival. Every way he looked he felt eyes staring at him. Every face was turned to him—coldly awaiting his words.

Huge, hairy arms were folded across the man's chest, biceps flexed. "Hell, you didn't have time for anyone else. You hopped in your jalopy and took off, and be damned with everyone."

"It wasn't like that! There wasn't any time to go around gathering up passengers," said Cecil with a hint of nervousness.

"What? You mean there wasn't anybody, not a single soul, who was searching for a ride out? Why, that's hard to believe," the man said sarcastically. "Ain't there lots of old-folks homes up there? I'll bet some of those people would have been happy to keep you company."

Aware that the open antagonism of the other could lead to an angry scene, Cecil replied, "Listen, mister, I don't have any quarrel with you. Now why don't you drop the subject?"

"Naw, I don't think so. There's a squad forming at the armory, getting ready to go to L.A. when it's safe to move.

They're taking volunteers, pal, and I think you ought to offer your services, don't you? Hey, fellows, don't you agree? Shouldn't this yellow-belly come along with us?"

"Yeah, sure, Jake. The dude's going to go right over to the armory," yelled someone from the crowd.

"No you don't, by God. I'm not going to that place again!" said Cecil as he saw the men begin to advance slowly toward him. He felt himself being lifted off the sofa by strong arms. "Wait now! What if the wind shifts down this way? We're all going to be targets," he said, trying to free himself of the arms.

"A bright boy like you figured that out alone, I'll bet," said the man named Jake. "Well, we won't be able to do a damned thing about the wind pulling that radiation over on us, but there's one thing we can do, though, buddy, and that's sign you up for duty!"

Cecil's heart dropped. He had eliminated the idea of staying in San Diego just because of the wind factor—the possibility that the radiation would be carried southward when it was swept away from the disaster zone. Instead of stopping in San Diego he had traveled deep into mountainous country. There wasn't much to the small town, but at the time it had seemed well protected in the hills among acres of avocado groves. And now here he was, trapped once more. They pushed him out the door, prodding when he resisted. The lounge of the dingy hotel rapidly emptied, leaving its clerk wide-eyed and speechless after the confrontation.

The armory was a cavernous building, flooded with lights. Cecil estimated that most of the able-bodied men of the town had signed their names, committing themselves to aid in the rescue effort.

"Bubba," Jake said, nudging Cecil forward, "we got us another volunteer who wants to join us. Sign him up."

"Sure thing, Jake," said the boy with the clipboard. "Howdy, mister. I guess L.A. is going to need everyone it can get once we start rolling, it sure is nice of you to come along, since you're a stranger in these parts. Uh, you don't live around here, do you? Don't remember seeing you before."

"Yeager, here, is from just south of Los Angeles, Bubba. He was there when that reactor exploded," offered the big swaggering man.

"Is that right? Jeezus! Why in the world do you want to go back there? If it was me, I'd have kept right on going—as far as

I could get," said the youth.

"Bubba, you still got that running-off-at-the-mouth disease. You simmer down some and try to get the vitals from Mister Yeager—we want to be sure he's present and accounted for when we get up there. Yes sir, we sure don't want our friend here getting lost in his own home town. Do we boys?" A chorus of assents agreed with him.

Smiling faces acknowledged Jake's play with the boy and Cecil, and the men edged in closer to hear what was being said.

"You got any special kind of work that might be useful in rescue, Mr. Yeager?" asked the youth.

Cecil was cool in his reply. "I'm a chemist, but I doubt you people would have any demands for my skills."

"A chemist?" said Bubba, "Gosh, I don't know much...hey, the high school has a group from their science department that's going in. Wait a second," said the boy, as he dashed off toward a knot of men.

In a couple minutes the youth returned with a member from that group in tow. Assured that Cecil would be confronted by someone else, the others began drifting away, losing interest.

"You say you're a chemist, huh?"

"That's correct," Cecil replied to the newcomer.

The man seemed eager to have Cecil a part of his group. "We could rig the apparatus for water-chemistry tests, if you think you could run them, Mr. Yeager. Clean water has got to be found."

"I could do that, I guess," Cecil answered indifferently.

"Good. I'll get the equipment together for you," said the teacher.

"I said I could," replied Cecil, "but what will you do with the results—once we start recording? We would need to coordinate our findings with other testers. Do you have any plans for doing that?" High school teachers—what do they know, thought Cecil.

The other paused, briefly considering Cecil's remark. "Oh, well, sure. We'd have to be able to feed our findings to someone, I guess."

Cecil envisioned this shoe-string operation rushing headlong into L.A., with no greater scheme in mind than to simply get there. Once inside, they'd be largely ineffective, perhaps even hampering other efforts. "It'd be a good idea," suggested Cecil, "if you contacted the national guard in San Diego. They'd line us up with communication points, I'd expect. Then our test

116

results would be of some use." The teacher was obviously not a thinker.

"That's not a bad idea—as a matter of fact, I'd already considered doing that very thing. Only I was waiting to see if anyone showed up who could do the chemistry part. Of course I'm a teacher myself and could do it, but I'll have my hands full with other jobs," he said with importance.

Cecil replied without a trace of interest. "Then we ought to be able to work together."

"Right. Say, do you know anything about Geiger counters? I think we can take the school's along. We've one that we use in one of the labs, but we've never actually tried it out in the field."

Cecil doubted that the teacher knew anything about the counter. "If it registers radiation in the classroom, it'll do it on the outside, too."

"I'm going to be in charge of this, but I'd appreciate it if you would sort of serve as second in command. Most of the fellows don't know too much about this kind of maneuver, Cecil."

Annoyed by the other's attitude of superiority, Cecil asked, "How is it that you know so much about it—were you in the war?" He vividly recalled his own days of action in the war and the long dark months of therapy for shell-shock that had followed.

"No, I never made it to the military, but I've belonged to the guard for several years, and I'm chairman of my department at school. My principal calls me the best organizer he's had on the staff," said the teacher with pride.

"Well then," answered Cecil testily, "you're certainly equipped to handle this—with all your experience."

The teacher beamed at the double entendre. "Call me Jim. Jim Thompson. There's no need for mister with me, Cecil. I like to keep it on a casual basis, so long as everybody knows who's in control."

Cecil took a long leisurely look at Jim. He impulsively noted that this was one character he'd not easily forget, then he began making mental guesses at the age at which the teacher had surpassed his level of competence. "Your group will be moving in with the rest of these fellows, I suppose."

"Yes, but we're not actually in their unit. We're more specialized," Jim answered. "Sort of elite, I guess you'd say."

"It seems to me that there should be a command headquarters in charge of the entire operation, Jim. Otherwise, how are we going to know which part to enter and what to do?" asked Cecil, showing some interest. "Our rescue squad could easily end up in the same part of the city as another unit, leaving some area unattended."

"That's true," said Jim. "I think I'll get right on the horn and check that out. It sure would be a mess if we moved in and another unit piled right in on top of us."

Cecil was left standing alone as Jim hurried off to his errand. He wiped his brow, thinking of the monumental mess this could be.

"What do you think it'll be like up there?"

"Huh?" asked Cecil as he found a scarecrow of a man at his side. He hadn't noticed the man before. "Where?"

"Up there in the big city," said the other.

"Probably chaos and confusion. It'll be terrible, I'd say."

The beady black eyes stared out from above pock-marked cheeks. "Reckon there's been much looting?" he asked.

"Well, I....sure," said Cecil. "There's always somebody who wants something for nothing."

"Yeah," the man agreed. "Reckon there's been a lot of rape going on, too. What with all those women scared, and not knowing what's happening." His voice carried a wistful sound as he stared into an empty transport truck, not meeting Cecil's gaze. "How do you feel about stuff like that?" asked the scarecrow, giving a leering grin that bared broken, yellowed teeth.

"What?" Cecil asked, not at all sure he hadn't caught the other's drift.

"You know—taking things that other folks have run off and left behind. I mean, they're not going to use it anymore, so there's really nothing wrong with hooking onto it, Right?"

"Personal possessions, things like that?" asked Cecil.

"Yeah, that's it. That kind of junk is bound to be carted off by somebody. The way I figured it, it's there for the taking. Two good men could make a bundle. All they'd need to do is pack it away in a couple choice hiding places. Before long, they'd get hold of a truck," he grinned. "Maybe old uncle Sammy's even, and haul everything out."

Cecil was now fully aware of what was in the other's mind. "What would you do with it?"

"Heck, I wouldn't have any problem. I've got a shed that's four walls and a roof, nothing inside. It'd hold a whole truck load of things—a fortune in goodies," he said, still grinning.

"If you got caught, you'd be arrested," Cecil warned. "You could even be shot for something like that....besides, everything is radioactive."

"Oh, I'd have to have a partner—someone who'd keep a lookout for me just as I'd do for him." The scarecrow looked directly at Cecil.

His intimation was becoming crystal clear. Suspiciously, Cecil said, "You've already got somebody in mind."

"Yeah. From what I've heard, you ain't too popular around here. Me and you, we could work it as a team....and have a little fun on the side, too. Hell, all those chicks ain't going to be dead when we get in there."

Cecil's fist shot through the air, connecting with a soft, thin nose. He felt the gristle crumple under his knuckles as they pushed their way into the flesh. Two small geysers erupted, sending red juices squirting down the scrawny chin of the scarecrow.

Cecil was astonished at his reaction. In his entire life, he had never aggressively attacked anyone. He wasn't a violent man, yet something had just snapped in him, sending him into a low rage.

Backing out of Cecil's reach and using the tail of his shirt, the man started sopping up the blood. "You had no call to do that," he accused. The man's voice became louder and high-pitched as he talked. "A coward....that's what you are. You bastard! You'll be sorry for this!"

Cecil watched as the man staggered farther and farther away from him, still yelling obscenities.

The teacher had returned, catching the last of the action. "What was that about?" he asked.

"Nothing," answered Cecil. "Say, who is that guy?" he asked as he rubbed his bruised knuckles soothingly.

"I don't know him, but I heard someone refer to him as Carter," answered Jim. "He's part of the unit."

"Carter," murmured Cecil. "Is that his first or last name?"

The teacher shrugged. "Who knows. He's just a fellow who is waiting to go along with the rescue squad."

At last the man, holding his shirt at his bloody nose, crept out of Cecil's sight behind a troop truck, leaving the chemist to stare at the olive drab vehicle. That man, Carter, bothered him. Not only was he an unhealthy looking specimen, but there was something furtive, something evil about him. Others might regard Carter as a sniveling sneak of a man, but Cecil viewed him as that and more. He was dangerous. Turned loose in Los Angeles, the man could cause inestimable damage.

"This is it," said Jim, interrupting Cecil's thoughts. "The gear is here and ready to go."

Reluctant to leave his consideration of Carter, Cecil finally turned his interest to another problem that had concerned him. "Jim, has some provision been made for food and water for us?" he asked.

"Gosh!" said Jim, snapping his fingers. "It's a good thing you mentioned that. It slipped my mind."

Cecil wasn't surprised. In fact he had expected this. "Then I think we ought to plan to carry our food and some extra water. Let's try to get some water barrels stored on a couple of those trucks. We'd better be as prepared as we can."

He wasn't exactly sure why, but Cecil felt himself being caught up in the efforts of the rescue movement. His thoughts drifted to the incidents of the past days—of what Calmar Chemical had done to him and how he had tried to even the score with their money, looking out for himself instead of the company for a change. He thought of the Mexican who had been intent on taking all he could get, offering Cecil only $500 for a new car—but Cecil had known the car was radioactive. And Carter, that vulture, perhaps it was the encounter with him that had changed his feelings. Earlier he'd thought of himself as being forced to return to Los Angeles against his wishes. But that was no longer true.. not now. He suddenly wanted to help, to be of assistance.

Chapter Ten

Ben, can you eat something? A tiny bit of food?" Sara pleaded. What else could she do for him beside nourish him? The best she could do for her husband was try to keep him living—at least until she could get medical aid.

He weakly refused the food, just as he had done earlier.

She resignedly left his bedside. She had to get the corpse out of the foyer. Strange..... how methodically her mind was working today. Sara Harrington had been only a typical, passive housewife, content to prepare the meals, do cleaning, and make a good appearance in public. It was important that Ben be proud of her. Decision-making? That was Ben's responsibility. Now suddenly, he could no longer make the decisions. He was totally helpless. If they were not to perish it would have to be through Sara's design.

The body lay stiffly in the entrance. The question was where to grab it. Not the arms. She couldn't bear to touch it. Settling on the shoes, she grasped one in each hand and began to pull.

It was heavy. She'd never known whether Ben had recognized this man or not. Not that it mattered now. The gardener was dead. Would the authorities have construed the gardener's death to have been murder? Or merely self-defense? But then, Sara wasn't really bothered by the legal or moral issues. These were exceptional circumstances.

Dragging the weighty, lifeless form along, she finally had it out of the house and onto the rear lawn. What to do with it? California houses had garages but not basements. Finding the right spot to store a dead person was a problem. Police would undoubtedly want to claim the body—eventually. Meanwhile, though, it had to be put out of sight.

Sara found plastic drop cloths which had been used by the painters and folded them over the form. Then bending down, she began rolling it first one way and then the other, until she had it neatly encased in the sheeting. Satisfied at last, she left the gardener's body securely wrapped and reposing in a far corner of the lawn.

When next she entered Ben's room, she was carrying broth and juice. Against his protests, she gently fed him the nourishment.

Then he dropped into a light sleep.

Sara found the tiny black radio that ran on batteries and carried it into the den before switching it on. She heard the last of the running broadcast on radiation "...can not be seen nor felt. These invisible particles travel at varying rates of speed and that speed determines how far the rays can penetrate into your body. But the dangers are not solely in the rays going through the skin to the organs; eventual damage will show up on the skin itself. These particles will stick to plant life. Do not, repeat, do not eat vegetables that are now growing outside! They are contaminated. Do not, repeat, do not drink fluids that have been exposed to the atmosphere! Above all, people, you risk contamination by your presence in the area. Going outside your house results in irradiation of your body. If you remain in the area, stay as far removed from the outside as possible. If you plan to evacuate, you must do so as quickly as possible. Major routes believed still open to outgoing traffic are...." Sara shut it off.

Her annoyance began to surface as she thought of the broadcast. God, the fools didn't tell you that hiding in the bedroom wasn't going to shield you from the intense rays. Those rays were unavoidable in any chamber short of the old, thick-walled concrete fallout shelters which no longer existed. There was no safe place while the radioactive materials releasing radiation were hanging overhead. They were all exposed by now—some to lesser degrees than others—but every single person within the reach of radioactive dust had begun receiving dosages at 8:46 a.m. on the morning of the accident. It would continue until the poison had blown away or decayed.

She couldn't know how her area was affected. Being seventy miles north, perhaps it would escape the heavy dust. Nevertheless, Sara was incensed that the citizens weren't being told the truth. Maybe that was politics. Or ignorance. Whichever the case, the public never seemed to be given the facts. Had they really known, would the people have accepted theory and gambled on the impossible odds that there'd never be a major accident in a nuclear reactor? Would they have allowed the plant to be constructed regardless? But of course the public's view—informed or not—was rarely heard. Or, if it was, it too often was ignored. Whether from lack of knowledge or overpowered by utility forces, the people had giant nuclear reactors sitting on their doorsteps now. Each one was a potential cataclysm, awaiting a moment of human error or machinery malfunction. Which had White Water been, she wondered.

"Sara?" His call was weak, almost a whisper.

"Yes, Ben," answered Sara, rushing to him. "What is it, darling?"

"I wanted to see you—wanted you here."

His forehead felt abnormally warm to her fingertips again.

"Are you feeling all right?" Ben asked feebly.

"Yes." She placed the wet towel on his brow. "Ben," she asked hesitantly, "what happened at the plant?"

For several minutes he didn't respond. She feared that she had asked the wrong question.

At last he said, "I don't know, Sara." He recalled that Mike had believed he had accidentally caused the controls to be retracted during the shuffle of the earthquake a few minutes before the explosion, but he saw no need to admit this to Sara. It was only a week or so ago that he'd remarked to his wife that possible human errors had been eliminated by recent technological improvements on reactors. Knowing the fears she had for his personal safety around the reactor, he'd continually reassured her, always attempting to allay those fears.

"Ben, you've always insisted that an explosion simply could not occur in a reactor. You've said every authority in the field holds that belief," she reminded him. "You must have some notion about what went wrong."

He lay there in the bed, listening as she probed for an explanation. Weakened by the pain and fever, he could not satisfy her curiosity—for he had no answers. In his exhaustion, he could only close his eyes and reply from his inner darkness, "I just don't know, Sara. It all happened so fast that I hadn't time to think about it."

She bathed the swollen tender skin, the tissues now festering with a seeping yellow fluid as it drained away from his battered ear. "I don't understand it," she persisted. "After the assurances that the plant was perfectly safe, how could this have happened? Was that a ploy to keep opponents of nuclear energy plants silent? After all, nobody in his right mind would want a reactor near him if there was the remotest chance it would someday destroy itself."

"Sara," he answered softly, "I honestly don't think anybody ever expected one to explode—not in a million years."

123

She sighed at the futility, "But wouldn't someone surely have questioned that likelihood? My God, with all the brilliant scientists in this world, you'd think someone would have foreseen this."

The conversation was taking its toll on the man, but her desire to know and to understand was gnawing at her. Ben, even in his infirmity, was asking himself the same questions, searching for answers. He had often wondered what those pilots of the large commercial birds thought when they realized they were going to crash. They had believed in their craft—they continually staked their lives on them. What went through their minds when, in a moment of malfunction, they saw themselves heading toward certain death? Ben thought he knew.

He weakly lifted his hand to Sara. "It's natural to be...confused...we should have been..... prepared, somehow."

She placed her lips against his bony fingers and murmured, "Well, it's unfortunate, but it can't be changed now. We have to live with it, don't we?"

Los Angeles is a mushrooming giant among American cities. It sends its branching hyphae far south into Orange County, eastward toward San Bernadino and north to Santa Barbara. Thus, metropolitan Los Angeles with its eighty-eight satellite cities and several unincorporated areas encompassed a sizeable portion of the almost forty million residents of the state.

By noon of the day following the devastation of White Water Nuclear Power Plant, the news had thoroughly permeated the densely populated region. Unknown by the residents of the area was that the possibility of a major nuclear reactor accident had seemed so remote, so unlikely to ever occur, that there had been no plans formulated to meet such an emergency. By this hour the fact of total unpreparedness was apparent to all—to every woman, child, and man. No single agency—local, state, federal, or otherwise—had been designated to take charge in the event of a catastrophe of this magnitude.

What was the magnitude? The nuclear fuel which fed the reactor had been cleaned over seventeen months ago. In the ensuing period long-lived radioactivity had accumulated inside the reactor, every particle of which was released at the moment of the accident. The exact amount was impossible to measure; however, it was possible that the eight hundred megawatt unit had spewed forth as much radiation as fifty bombs the size of that dropped on Hiroshima. The radioactive dust was now in the atmosphere, waiting to settle out. The environment that received this fallout material would be contaminated with heavy doses of radiation—people, livestock, drinking water, plants, every living and inanimate object.

In addition, a large amount of radioactive materials had melted through the floor of the plant in a liquid form. These would sink hundreds of feet into the earth releasing radioactive gases, much of which would also escape into the atmosphere, adding more lethal potential to the fallout clouds above.

The scattering of scientists combing the area fringes with Geiger counters were recording extremely high readings, much beyond the maximum limits of safety and well into the lethal range. Compounding the problem was the presence of a weather condition which tended to stall the radiation in one place. Without winds, the radiation would not be dispersed.

As a consequence, the southwestern U.S. would receive sufficient radiation to become contaminated. Crops in the fields would be useless as food. People in immediate and nearby regions had reason for rapid evacuation, provided there was someplace for them to go and someone who would be willing to accept the radiation victims. Of the half million who were heavily exposed, over a thousand would die of the direct effect of radiation. Of the remainder, many would develop long-term effects that would gradually be evidenced in increased rates of various cancers and genetic aberrations in generations to come.

Within twenty-seven hours the populace had acclimated its thinking toward one common goal—survival.

Nobody tended shop, made food deliveries, or printed newspapers. Commercial and home utilities were discontinued for lack of supervision. Water still ran through the pipes. However, since the area received its water from open reservoirs it had fast become polluted. Fire stations failed to respond to fires, policemen considered their own personal safety over completion of assigned patrols.

The citizenry was beginning to panic. Fear of insufficient food supplies drove them to plundering the markets. Unable and unwilling to keep their employees on the premises, large supermarkets had their doors barred and managers took refuge with their families.

Food is a major necessity and it was for food and medical supplies that Sara Harrington was torn away from her husband's bedside.

The huge building now had little left of its glass front since frightened mobs of looters had literally kicked their way in. The giant market was still being ransacked as looters propelled themselves forcefully, leaving pain and suffering in their wake. When reduced to basics, individuals become snarling, snappish animals, deadly in their pursuit. Being greedy in their fear, they stripped the products from the shelves, leaving nothing behind.

It took great strength and will to join the melee, but join she did. Sara steered in the direction of the medical supplies and began filling a bag with those objects she wanted. Working quickly, she moved through the aisles, never pausing to select, but reached out and grasped any recognizable foodstuff. Getting jostled and shoved, she lost her footing and ended up piled on the floor. The paper bag split, letting her collection roll out into the aisle. Spectators dived into the assortment and by the time she was back on her feet, the only item she'd salvaged was a box of gauze bandages. Furious, she began pushing her way through the mob once more when a fist closed on her bandages and pulled them from her grip.

The place was being wrecked, and the people took their own share of abuse. An elderly gentleman bent over to retrieve a package and was shoved from behind. His prostrate body was kicked, stamped, then discarded by the mass of pumping legs.

From her position Sara could see the old fellow slide his hand from under his face in an attempt to regain support, and at that instant a thick leather heel came down on his fingers. She heard him moan but saw the futility of trying to fight her way to help him.

A brawl had broken out behind the meat counter. The antagonists each wanted the last hind-quarter of beef as it hung suspended from its rack. Both were husky men, and there was a steady rain of dull thuds as fists met flesh, inflicting raw bruises. The two were evenly matched until one fastened his hand around the handle of a meat cleaver. Sara saw the glint of steel as the ax was hefted high in the air. She shielded her eyes to the downswing. When she again looked, the victor was hoisting the meat to his shoulder. A hind quarter of beef weighs more than the average man can easily handle, but this mighty ant was moving off with his winnings as though it was a cargo of fluffy cotton across his shoulder. He left a trail of bloody footprints behind.

Cartons of food lay about the floor, their sides crushed and contents spilling out. Arms heavily burdened by the weight of booty made last efforts to pile on one additional prize before leaving. What couldn't be carried was often mashed and stamped on the floor. Sara remembered the hose at the gas station, gushing its precious fluid onto the tarmac.

Returning to her task, Sara worked in feverish haste to collect items she needed. Quickly she laid claim to an arm-load of supplies. Cautiously she then wove a path toward the exit. En route she lost several items she'd chosen but finally she made it to the outside and experienced momentary relief to be free of the mob. She glanced at her booty and felt fortunate to have made it out of the building with anything.

Not everyone shared an unreasonable contempt for danger. Some were plainly too panic stricken to force themselves into the wild-eyed mob. Denying their desire to participate in the loot-taking, they stood on the sidewalk watching, then dejectedly walked away.

The building was fast being picked clean. its once full shelves were now the glistening ribs of a fallen animal. Nothing had been spared. Cosmetics, automotive supplies, paper goods— these went as quickly as food.

Sara viewed the sight in amazement. By what manner of reasoning would people select spark plugs and face cream over food? What sort of loss did this represent to the owners? The loss mattered little to her, she decided. Her complete occupation was to see that Ben was cared for as best she knew how. Anything less was beyond her concern.

Noises from somewhere within the house kept urging Ben's brain to awareness. He'd been drifting in and out of consciousness ever since Sara had left his side. He could feel himself slipping into blackness again. Struggle as he might, he couldn't seem to avoid it. It was a frightful thing, this sliding into the depths. It carried him closer to death. He began counting to delay the inevitable sleep. The numbers came out of sequence. He started over with number one, and again the numbers spilled out in disorder.

"Ben?" Sara whispered, caressing his hand.

"Sara?" She had returned. She would help him think clearly.

"Yes, darling, I'm back." She touched his forehead, fearing the heat.

"My arm—Sara, we have to do something."

The limb looked like a log in its grotesqueness. The fractured bones were excruciatingly painful to the flesh....his fingers tumescent sausages protruding from the palm.

"We've got to splint it," he gasped.

Sara blanched. She had expected this but had hoped, even so, that help would come before it was necessary. Steeling herself she left the room to make preparations. When she had collected her materials and convinced herself she was ready, she put the two slender boards and the strips of sheeting on the foot of the bed. She gently took the thick helpless fingers, taut enough to burst, in her own hand. She earnestly forced herself to put away her fear and loathing. She had no choice. He had only her.

He had been watching her closely. "Don't worry about the pain, Hon." His attempt to reassure his wife resulted in a dismal failure as his pale lips began to quiver. The wan, weak smile he intended was aborted.

Strengthening her clutch on his hand she slowly and steadily began to pull the limb straight.

"Oh God, Sara," he panted. "Do it fast! Please!"

Commanding every thread of courage in her body, Sara firmly and quickly lengthened the crooked arm.

"Aeeeiiii!" he screamed as the bones slipped into place.

Whether real or imagined, she heard the jagged ends of the shafts being realigned within the hot flesh. A wave of revulsion shot up her throat.

Ben succumbed to the pain. He lay there without feeling, unconscious and oblivious to the hurt. Huge beads of perspiration rolled steadily off him.

It took a moment for Sara to acquire composure to finish. God how she ached for him! While he was unaware was the best time for completing her task, and with the boards in position she started wrapping the cloth clumsily around the arm.

As a child she'd never played nurse as her little friends had. She'd always had an aversion to medicine, to doctors, to shots. She detested pain and had been a very cranky patient during her one major illness. Now, suddenly, she was faced with the possibility of doing just the wrong things for Ben's comfort—ministrations that would be harmful and damaging to him. How long would it be before the rest of the nation realized the inhumanity of these conditions and sent rescue squads in? For the first time in her life she was solely responsible not only for her own welfare but for that of a mutilated, helpless man—her husband—and the odds were against her succeeding.

128

As Sara kept her vigil the hours passed into late afternoon. She was disturbed that he had not come out of the faint. Was this abnormal? Was he suffering? There had been brief periods when he seemed on the verge of awakening, but then he would relapse into the deep sleep.

A slight flickering of his eyelids brought her attention to him. "Can you hear me, Ben? Ben, are you all right?"

He mumbled something unintelligible.

She bathed his body with wet towels once more. God, how she wanted to cry, to lean forward and bawl her heart out. Instead she kept bathing him. The aspirin she'd fed into him wasn't doing an adequate job of holding his fever down. What had she read about constant high body temperatures and their results? She couldn't recall.

"You did fine, honey," he murmured weakly.

She was startled by the unexpected sound of his voice. "Ben, are you all right? Lord, I thought I'd killed you."

He barely nodded in response.

"Listen, I'm going to fix you something to eat. Food will give you strength. Will you be okay while I'm gone?"

"Sara, we can't use the water," mumbled Ben.

She was certain he wasn't lucid.

"The water is....polluted, now. We can't use it," he repeated.

"Ben, surely the water in those huge underground pipes is safe to drink." It was water exposed to the atmosphere, the newscaster had said—that was the water that couldn't be drunk.

He only shook his head at her comment. "No, it comes from surface reservoirs. It'll be irradiated."

Sara brushed at her forehead in disbelief. "Then for heaven's sake, what are we going to do?? We have to have water," she said in desperation.

"Only well water can be used," he murmured.

"Well water?" Sara began to laugh hysterically. Coughing and spluttering she asked, "Where in the hell does anyone find a water well in southern California? It's too bad we can't drink oil." Her uncontrolled, frenetic giggles ruptured the air.

He gazed helplessly from the bed, trying to reach her.

Shaking convulsively, her hysteria blending with racking sobs, she wailed, "I fought the vultures for a package of gauze this morning. I was pushed, stepped on, and vilified just to steal a handful of groceries. And now I find that we don't even have water to drink. This isn't fair, Ben! God provided us with water

129

to drink, didn't He? Or maybe He didn't. He forgets about us for nine months every year in this stinking desert. What does He think? That we only need water during the winter months and we suck cactus juice the rest of the year? My God, has He forgotten us, too? Oh Ben, why doesn't it rain?" she moaned. "Rain...rain...."

Ben struggled half off the bed and reached out for his wife. He pulled her shivering body, still racked with sobs, close to him. He massaged her back and coarsely crooned to her. "Shush, Sara. We aren't forgotten. Someone will arrive to help us."

"You don't believe that," she said as she shuddered against him.

"We have to believe it; otherwise, we can't go on."

"But the water—oh, if it'd only rain," she cried.

"Rain wouldn't do us any good, Sara. It would be irradiated like everything else," he murmured.

"Oh, God," she moaned. "I'm going crazy—out of my mind! Everything is contaminated! Hasn't anything been spared?"

He shook his head. "But we can't give up, Sara. We can't just roll over and die."

"Oh, why did we, ever come to California, anyway? Why did you ever want to work at White Water, Ben? Good God, what will ever happen to us??"

He slowly sank down on the bed. The worst was yet to come.

A great calm hung in the warm night air, not a peaceful, tranquil stillness, but more a quiet expectancy. In nights past she and Ben had stood together gazing out across the valley—a valley then that was like a nearby galaxy with a million stars. The lights below were gone now. The houses in the valley were empty....and the galaxy gone—nothing more than blackness.

Sara wasn't secure in darkness. She wanted to see the things about her, to know where the next step led. But once the night closed around her, shielding her actions like a loose cloak, she knew she must go through with it.

She stealthily crept over the retaining wall, uncertain as to exactly why she should be so cautious, but cautious, regardless. She was not positive the neighbors had fled their home during the previous day, and she dreaded the thought of being caught in her deed. The narrow rubber hose was soft and flexible. It had given her a brief scare when it lapped up against her calf, causing her to jump, and now she held it away from her body.

Setting the plastic just on the ground so it would be lower

than the gas tank, she squatted alongside her neighbor's abandoned car. She grimaced as the cap of the gas tank squeaked as she tried to remove it. Getting the cap removed was the simple part, the difficulty would be in inducing the gasoline to come up the hose and into the jug. Somewhere in a crevice of her brain was the memory that the fluid would have to be sucked into and along the length of hose. Sara blew into the hose until she heard bubbles popping in the tank. Convinced the hose was immersed in the fuel, she pursed her lips and began sucking. Her eager pull on the interior of the hose brought nothing—but undaunted, she continued. Finally, with a surge, a large amount of the oily, astringent fluid came pouring into her mouth. Gagging and spluttering, she spit it out. It was a loathsome, vile tasting fluid, but discomforts she'd have to bear if she wished to get the gasoline—their passport to help. Tentatively, she resumed the sucking, pulling motion until the fuel was again flowing. This time, she dropped the end of the hose into the jug and had the satisfaction of hearing the liquid splash against the bottom as the container was filled.

Ben's vomiting was unchecked. Lacking proper fluids, Sara had given him the juice from a can of fruit. He'd rapidly expelled that. Of the few remaining tins, the one that sounded the most liquid was a can of green beans. She drained off the fluid and presented it to Ben. The yellowish water went down, but was as quickly regurgitated, and in being expelled, it set off a series of heavings that threatened his very ability to breathe.

She began to panic at her inability to control his violent retching. "Ben, help all you can! We just have to make it to the car!" She would try the hospital again. Maybe, surely, by now, he would be admitted.

Her headlights shed an eerie glow over the hospital grounds. Not unexpectedly there were people still waiting in the outer compound; but oddly enough, they had arranged themselves into a tight knot near the door. On this hot, still night they acted as if their safety lay in huddling together.

A stale stench rose to her nostrils, confirming her fears that these persons also suffered the sickness of radiation. She felt the grasp on her arm, and wrenched away as the voice pleaded for water—for something to drink. From every direction eager hands were stretching to her, imploring her aid. Sobbing moans of agony rose to her ears.

"Miss....water. Help me, please."

She had agitated them by her unblemished, mobile presence. They somehow expected her to assist them, to give them relief. Something she could not do.

Having heard the commotion from the inside, Dr. Parsons flung the door open and peered out. "My God," he said aloud, "where did all these people come from?" His staff had pulled them inside as fast as they could, and yet, two seemed to replace every one that was carried in for treatment. Patients on the inside littered the floor to the door itself. He'd had to step carefully to avoid actually setting his feet on the victims.

Pushing the people aside, Sara ended up directly in front of the doctor.

"Yes?" he asked of the tall, blond woman.

"My husband...Doctor, he must have help," she said beseechingly.

Sara presented an image of a tired, haggard woman. Her eyes were dull and red-rimmed—fatigue evident. It would have shocked Parsons to know that her transition from a beautiful woman to this wearied state occurred exclusively within the past two days.

"Lord, woman, we can't take anyone else in here! We're already spilling into the street."

Parsons, himself, hardly conveyed the typical picture of medical health. He gave an appearance of having stepped out of a slaughterhouse. Bone tired with blood-shot eyes, and a three-day stubble of beard, he was far from being sanitarily dressed in his stained clothing. And he emitted a strong, vile odor that was indistinguishable from that of his patients.

Anger and disappointment were evident in Sara's voice. "You can't take him in? Doctor, do you have even the vaguest idea of what it's like, being thwarted in every solitary thing I try to do for this man? My husband was at White Water Tuesday, and dragged himself home in agony—but he hasn't had a pain killer stronger than aspirin. He's so weak that I can't help him any longer. He's going to die without your help! To die! For God's sake, the very least you can do is give him something for the pain!" Her words rushed out in a torrent, flooding the nighttime air.

Parsons watched her brush searching hands aside, having no time for these other people. He imagined that later she would detest her hostility toward them, but for now her concern was purely for her husband.

"You must help him. Please," she implored him. "Oh, please."

"Where is he?" Parsons asked.

Ben's gaunt, desiccated form was folded in the rear seat.

"There really isn't any space inside, Mrs...."

"Harrington," Sara said absent-mindedly as she looked at Ben.

"Well, Mrs. Harrington," said Dr. Parsons apologetically, "I'm sorry, but I'll do what I can. He'll have to stay in the car, though."

The examination was brief. Dr. Parsons had inspected some indescribable cases during the last day, but this surpassed them all. The sickness was obviously running a steadily intensifying course. Recent emergents were showing evidences of hemorrhaging through the skin. Ben Harrington was in the critical stage now. Having received flash burns to part of his face and hands, the skin was beginning to slough off. Skin grafts would be required, provided he lived, and there seemed small chance of that. Palpating gingerly, Parsons found that three ribs were broken. But there was no blood issuing from his mouth or nose—a good sign that lung damage wasn't extensive. Superficially, the man's tissues had taken the highest exposures of any of the patients Parsons had seen, with the exception of the eight bodies stacked at the edge of the courtyard.

"There's not much I can do, I'm afraid, except administer antibiotics. We're short of medicine...." He gave Ben an injection, then turned to Sara. "He'd be better off at home, Mrs. Harrington. I suggest you take him back. Meanwhile, I'll give you some vitamins for him," said the surgeon, aware that vitamins would at least keep the vital processes up.

"Vitamins? You must be crazy!" snapped Sara. "Vitamins won't keep him alive! I want something for his pain. And more antibiotics—something to kill the infection!"

Dr. Parsons disliked dispensing the precious medicines to such an obviously lost case. Somehow, though, he felt a surge of admiration for the woman. She hadn't quit hoping, hadn't given up. Reluctantly he agreed. "Could you give him the injections if you had the syringe?"

She nodded eagerly. "Of course."

"All right, I'll give you this. Every six hours you fill this syringe up to 30cc and shoot it into his muscle. You won't be able to sterilize the needle other than to soak it in some alcohol between shots. I wish I could give you something for pain, but I

133

just don't have anything, Mrs. Harrington. Here, take this, too. Maybe it'll help stave off the vomiting."

"He's been running a high fever, Doctor. What can I do for that?" she asked in a tone suddenly lighter, less worried.

"What have you been doing?" asked the doctor.

"Giving him aspirin which he usually throws up, and bathing him in cool water."

"Keep giving him the aspirin, but the baths, I don't know. The water is radioactive. You're just exposing him to more radiation." But Parsons would not be able to abate her feeble efforts, or convince her to avoid the cooling towels—they were the only recourse she had to help Ben be comforted even slightly.

"Are you going to check his arm, Doctor? We were sure it was broken so I put a splint on it." She grimaced at the memory.

He carelessly inspected the splints. "You did a pretty decent job, Mrs. Harrington."

"But how about the bones? Can you tell if they're set straight or not?" she asked hopefully.

"Mrs. Harrington, we don't have access to x-ray machines, and quite frankly, the condition of the bones is his least concern, I'd say. There would be absolutely no point in causing him further pain by moving that arm around. Let's leave it as it is, all right?" Dr. Parsons was anxious to be rid of the subject of Ben Harrington. It was a futile case. His attention was demanded with other, less terminal patients awaiting him. The surgeon's nature did not include being niggardly with his skilled services or medications, but the situation was forcing him to make snap decisions on the survivors. Those who appeared at death's door were treated with consideration; but precious drugs were to be used sparingly in their cases. Better to save the medication for others with wider margins between themselves and death.

Sara clutched at his sleeve as he began moving away from Ben. "There's nothing more you can do, Doctor?"

Parsons paused, sensing the desperation in the woman. "No, Mrs. Harrington. I'm sorry."

Sara slowly dropped her head in disappointment.

The doctor collected his instruments. "I'm really sorry. I don't feel any the less helpless than you do—seeing this human suffering and knowing there's so little I can do to relieve it. We're running out of everything and still people are pouring in on us. No water, drug supplies practically exhausted, and personnel who are....well, we're hardly fit to treat anybody now."

Parsons turned and wearily began making his way toward the isolation unit.

"Doctor," Sara yelled after him, "is there any other hospital treating radiation victims?"

He replied through the darkness, "I don't know of one. But then we don't have a communications system anymore."

The doctor gently brushed grasping hands away as they clutched at his jacket, pleading to be allowed inside.

Getting Ben into his own bed sapped the last of Sara's endurance. The fist-sized muscular pump pounded against the inside of her chest. Breathing in short, labored gasps, Sara stumbled through the rooms until she came to the can of food.

Without the liquid, the beans were dried and shriveled from the air. Carefully she bent the lid away and reached in with her fingers. They'd been her breakfast and the remainder were her dinner. She chewed down on the pulpy mass, thoroughly masticating them before plunging them down her esophagus. She was not surprised that with her parched throat, swallowing green beans was similar to peanut butter. The bolus kept attaching to the dry tube, clogging the route to the stomach. Her spine rested against a cabinet door as she sat in the dark, munching, swallowing, then coughing up the bolus, and swallowing again until it finally passed down.

Searching in the darkness, she finally located the bottle of wine. Tilting it, she drank greedily. The wine, why hadn't she thought of it for Ben? She had given him that terrible juice from the beans thinking it would have nourishment in it. As soon as she got her breath back, she would try to get the burgundy down him.

She slid down again to rest on the floor as she consumed the last of the beans. Her thin legs were stretched out straight in front, still trembling from the exertion of moving Ben. Feeling out the one remaining length of vegetable, Sara slipped it into her mouth and mumbled, "God, how I wish the wind would blow."

135

Chapter Eleven

Althea switched the knob, breaking the connection with the radio station. What was the meaning of those numbers? She knew there were different levels of radiation, but what was the real meaning of the numbers? A task force was at last monitoring the fringes of the disaster zone and findings were hourly reported over the radio. But what counted to Althea were the radiation levels here in Los Angeles. What was happening to their bodies—their lives?

The residents didn't need to be told of the stagnant front. They felt the compression, the heaviness in the clouds, the layer of warm air trapped beneath the inversion. How long would the poison hover above them like a toxic blanket? When would it scatter?

Filling the bookshelf were the thick, maroon-colored volumes that her father had bought prior to his retirement. Althea recalled the event clearly. Because Jess Carr had lacked any formal education, he'd planned to spend his evenings making up for lost time. He had extravagantly paid three hundred dollars, faithfully paying them off in installments, for a complete set of encyclopedias—his contention being that once he'd read every book, he'd have better than a college education. He never learned to use a computer. And the encyclopedias were no longer printed. But out of date or not they were a place to start. Internet service providers continued to be on and off in the LA area and her smart phone was directly affected.

She withdrew the correct volume, opened the imitation leather cover, and selected the right page where she began reading. At first she skimmed the printed matter, pausing at times to absorb some important point. The information was largely foreign to her, with her smattering of college science. Beta and gamma rays....alpha particles....penetration depths that sent the invisible dangers through the skin of man into underlying organs....it was almost too much to fathom. Slowly she went back through the pages, digesting what she could and committing other information to memory. In all, there was nothing in the book which eased her apprehension. There were no words as to how one could protect oneself against these hazards. It was useless at this point to read that certain high energy rays could pass through solid concrete blocks five feet thick. It was too late. There was no way that the defenseless population could avoid exposure to the radiation permeating the atmosphere—no way at all.

Finished, Althea allowed the pages to flutter shut beneath her fingers. In reflecting on what she'd read it became evident that this whole incident was a great deal more horrifying than she had originally thought. What degree of safety could possibly be afforded by six inches of stucco wall in a house when radiation could penetrate five feet of concrete? And going out into the open air, needlessly exposing oneself was sheer stupidity. Yet Althea had to take that further risk of exposure. The insulin for her mother had to be found. She'd failed yesterday. Today she'd have to succeed. Althea pressed her head between her palms, as if she could press out her deepening sense of futility. A timid knock sounded on her door.

"Althea? Is it all right if I come in?"

"Yes, Papa." She didn't want to talk to her father right now. The burden of her parents weighed on her like a giant yoke today. She didn't resent her responsibility for them, but what could she do to spare them these dangers? Or find the hormone that her mother must have shortly? Her automobile was gone. Damn Los Angeles, anyway, for being the sprawling city it was. Damn it for making a four-wheeled machine a necessity of life. Damn her own panic and stupidity for leaving the keys in the car.

Her father's expression was one of worry—his face etched in fatigue. The situation was taking its toll on him. Looking closely at her, her father spoke softly, "It's going to be pretty bad, isn't it?" She hadn't fooled him. She never had been able to. "I'm afraid so, Papa."

Minutes passed before he spoke again. "We don't have anything left to drink, darling. I guess we didn't pay much attention to stretching the juices as far as they'd go."

She had prayed for relief before it came to this.

He fidgeted nervously, chewing on some imaginary cud in his cheek. "When do you think they'll send someone in for us?"

She didn't want to say that chances of being rescued before the inversion lifted and the radiation dispersed were remote. Who could be expected to charge into this area and bring food and water to the helpless at this time? "Soon, I hope," she

137

finally replied.

"Althea, your mother didn't sleep last night," he complained. "She walked the floor until daylight....I guess by morning she was so tired she had to get some rest so she finally lay down for awhile."

"I know, Papa. I heard her."

"She's upset, Althea. She's afraid we won't find any insulin for her."

The woeful sound in her father's voice and the abject misery in his face caused a well of depression to build in Althea.

"She'll use the last of the insulin this morning, but after that, what are we going to do?" he asked.

"I'm going to try to get to one of the community hospitals," Althea promised. "I'll leave as quickly as I can." Immediately she began putting on a pair of sturdy walking shoes.

For a moment Jess seemed uncertain. "It may not be safe for you to be out alone....I'm going with you."

"No! No, Papa. You stay with Mama." A seventy-two year old man with a bad heart would never tolerate the exertion. "I'll find someplace that will let me have the medicine."

As Althea completed dressing her father watched her silently. When she had returned from yesterday's trip she had told her parents about arriving at the pharmacy after it had been pillaged and finding Mr. Cole murdered. She had told them the complete story, leaving out none of the details. Until then, the two old people had been inclined to believe that by being seventy miles from the explosion site they were relatively safe from the effects of the disaster. But with the tale told by their daughter they began to realize that there were more dangers than just the radiation. And that was precisely what Althea had hoped to impress on them— that until rescue was accomplished, they must always be on their guard—not only by making themselves as secure as possible from the invisible dangers, but by barring their doors and windows against the pillage which would inevitably begin.

It had been a constant source of concern to her, making her parents understand the full significance of this catastrophe. Convincing their unlearned minds of the powerful destructiveness in radiation, and then convincing them that they must participate in planning their own protection had drained her of patience. But if something were to happen to her, they had to be prepared to care for themselves.

Lou Ella had quietly entered the room. "You're going to try again, Thea?"

Althea crossed to her and hugged the elderly woman tightly for a second. "Yes, Mama. I'm going to Glenview Community."

"Glenview?" rasped Lou Ella. "That's a long way off."

Jess looked up. "Daughter, that's an awful long way from here."

"It's the closest hospital around." Eighteen miles, Althea had determined—eighteen miles of steady walking. If she was lucky she could hope to get back by dark.

Her father grew even more worried. "It ain't safe, Thea....a colored woman walking all alone through that neighborhood."

Althea stepped up to him and hugged him closely. "Don't worry, Papa. White folks are no more frightening than the people right around here. I'll be all right."

Jess Carr had never been an openly demonstrative father but this time he folded his daughter in his arms and squeezed her. "You sure?"

"I'm sure," she answered, turning away. She took money out of her purse and fastened it inside a tiny pocket on her dress. She had no desire to tempt anyone unnecessarily, especially by carrying a purse that might promise some hidden reward. She took one last look around.

"Don't you think you ought to wear something on your head?" asked Lou Ella, her voice showing her torment.

It seemed pointless to Althea; besides, she hated hats. "No, a hat won't stop radiation, Mama. Now I don't want either of you getting upset if by some chance I'm not back by evening. Okay? Promise me that you'll stay in the house and wait?"

Both parents nodded in agreement.

"All right then. Remember, you're to keep inside." She started toward the door, then paused. "And if anybody comes to the house, you're not to let them in. No matter who it is. Even if it's somebody you know, you tell them that you can't let them in the house."

The two old people obviously understood what she said but they were bothered by her instructions, and Althea knew this. They would find it hard to refuse anyone, yet they must, for their own safety.

Walking out of the house, Althea was not at all certain that her parents had a complete understanding of this disaster. Still, the insulin had to be obtained, and she was the only one in the household capable of getting it. They had to be left alone, and she had to make the long trek to Glenview.

The absence of a circulating breeze and the heaviness of the smoggy air was a guarantee that the inversion remained. Her journey toward the hospital had gone smoothly for what she estimated to have been an hour. An hour at her quickened pace, and Althea guessed she had covered four, perhaps five miles. The few people she had seen along the sidewalk had crossed over to avoid her, or had lowered their eyes and rushed on past her, avoiding any possibility for conversation. Althea felt the same way. She had no wish to be detained by anyone—for any reason—and she didn't want to draw near another person. We're all radiation lepers, she thought.

Increasing her pace slightly, she kept her attention focused on her direction. She walked for what must have been another mile, determined only to reach the hospital as soon as possible, when a car pulled up beside her. The stealth with which the vehicle was unexpectedly at her side was startling. She hadn't seen nor expected to see any traffic, when suddenly here it was. She threw one fast, frightened glance at the machine and at the man behind the wheel, and continued her walk.

The car crept along beside her, keeping abreast with her stride. Althea moved away from the street to the far edge of the sidewalk, never slackening her pace.

"Hey! Where are you going?" shouted the man through his window.

Acting as though she hadn't heard, Althea kept her face straight ahead but quickened the pace ever so slightly. She could feel rather than actually see him as he leaned out again.

"I asked you where you're going!" he yelled.

Her heart was racing by now. The man seemed insistent on talking to her, the last thing she wanted from some white man cruising the neighborhood.

The driver reached over and tooted on the horn. Still she kept her face averted. He honked again, twice. "Can't you hear anything?" he shouted at her.

Not knowing exactly what to do but fighting the urge to run, Althea stopped and looked at him. He smiled at her, a not unpleasant smile but one strangely out of keeping with the events and the day. "What do you mean by honking at me?" she asked nervously.

His smile remained but when he opened his mouth to speak

he appeared not to have teeth. "I wondered why you're out walking by yourself."

His comment was valid because she had been wondering herself what was so urgent that the others she'd seen on this journey were outside. Nevertheless, she had no interest in a confrontation with this stranger. She started off, refusing to reply.

The car pulled to her once more and the man again leaned out. "What's the matter with you....you scared or something?"

Scared? Of course she was. Maybe, though, it would be best not to irritate him so that he'd just go on his way. "No, I'm not frightened," Althea answered. "I'm in a hurry."

"Well, where are you going?"

She halted and looked at him again. He sounded normal, perhaps even kind. Was it possible that he had only an interest in helping her? She doubted that. "To Glenview Community Hospital," she replied.

"You sick?"

Shaking her head, she said, "No, not me. My mother."

The man's smile did not lessen as he asked, "What's wrong with her?"

Suddenly this confrontation had become almost ludicrous—she, standing with her heart pounding so loud she could hear it, and that man grinning like a toothless Cheshire cat while he asked his questions. "I don't think you'd be interested in my mother's illness."

"Okay," he answered.

Althea stepped off, eager to be away from him.

"I'll take you there," he called out.

This brought her to a halt. It was going to be dangerous if she didn't get back home before darkness. And to be out in the radiation all day long...."You'd drive me to the hospital?" she asked.

"Sure I will," he answered. "Come on....get in."

She hesitated a long moment. The man sounded sincere.

"Come on," he urged, shoving open the door.

Finally she decided. Perhaps this was one time when she should throw caution to the wind: She wanted to get to Glenview and back home to her parents as quickly as possible. "All right." She slid into the seat with him, but kept her body pressed close to her door.

His smile broadened, but there was no sign of either pink

141

gums or teeth. The man simply had the longest upper lip she had ever observed. "It's good of you to offer to do this," Althea said. "Walking would take hours."

The driver nodded and began to hum a discordant tune under his breath.

She watched as he happily swung the vehicle away from the curb and into the street. His actions were controlled but mechanical. She guessed that he'd only recently mastered the art of driving. She searched for words; perhaps conversation would hide the nervousness she felt. "I really never expected anyone to be interested in helping me."

He nodded in short jerks of the head and continued his disharmonious tune.

His was certainly an unusual reaction to someone attempting conversation. The pounding of her heart was growing louder as Althea remarked, "I suppose none of us would have ever believed this sort of thing could have happened. If we had any inkling...any idea at all....well, without water it can be very bad." Her talking mixed with his low humming. "Had I known the water would be polluted I would have filled my bath tub immediately. At least we'd have had drinking...."

His laughter burst from his chest. She hadn't intended the comment to be humorous, but suddenly this man was laughing as if he'd never stop. Something was amiss obviously with him. Helpless, Althea stared out her window while he laughed. The mirth expanded in him until he was beating his fist on the seat in cadence with his great heaving fits of giggles. At last, after several miles, during which she had neglected to pay attention to direction, his laughter subsided.

"Say, would you like to have dinner with me tonight?" he asked.

Althea swiveled her head around to get a closer look at the driver's face. "What did you say?" she asked, almost afraid that she had heard him correctly.

"Dinner. Din-din. You'll have din with me tonight."

Of course. The man was a nut—a screwball. Had he escaped from some institution, she wondered. "Uh, uh," she gasped in a low stammer, an affliction that haunted her whenever she was overly tense or alarmed, but normally controlled well. "Perhaps you should stop right here. I'll walk the rest of the distance."

Instead of halting, he accelerated. "Oh yes," he said soothingly, "you'll like having dinner with me. First I'll take

142

you to that place—where was that place, again?" he asked, twisting his face in concentration.

Althea suddenly noticed that they weren't headed in the right direction. "To Glenview Community Hospital, but you're going the wrong way. Glenview is north!" she said loudly.

Suddenly he burst out with enthusiasm, "Listen, I've got an idea. There's this really beautiful section of town you should see. It's such a nice day for a drive, wouldn't you like to take a drive?"

Internally Althea was quickly becoming a shaking mass of human tissue. Perhaps she could play it up until she could get him to stop the car. "Oh, I....I....I wish I could but I really don't have the time today," she said, trying to keep her voice calm.

The car raced wildly along the thoroughfare. Tall date palms with their bark hanging in slivers flashed before her eyes, reminding her that they were going away from her destination.

"You know," he remarked, "I always wanted to get on one of these streets and really open her up." He was still accelerating. "Isn't it exciting? No cops to pull me over." He quickly resumed his humming.

Keeping them placating, but adding an edge of sternness to her words, Althea said, "Listen, mister, if you don't slow down you're going to kill both of us. Now, why don't you stop and let me out, then you can drive as fast as you like."

He whipped the steering wheel sharply to the left and the car made a short turn onto a bumpy asphalt stretch of roadway.

"Hey, where are you going?" she asked with added alarm.

His face smiled dreamily as he ignored her.

The road changed to a rut-filled dirt lane that suddenly dropped into an empty river bed. The long, arid summer and fall months had left the bed rock-dry and perfectly passable, but with the exception of bicyclers, nobody ever came here. Arriving in the middle of the river bed, he headed the car directly up its length, intent on a spot that existed only in his mind's eye.

Althea began to formulate a scheme for getting away from this madman. She tightly held onto the door handle, planning to yank it open and tumble out if the fool ever slowed down to a less hazardous speed....or even if he didn't.

"It's lovely, isn't it?" he asked. "Just think, Margaret, we can follow the river forever. Forever...." he said dreamily.

A freeway overpass was above them, casting its shadow on

the crusty floor below as the car raced through it. There was no point in waiting longer. Taking a firmer grip, she pulled the lever and pushed outward. In the next second her body was catapulting over and over the gritty surface of the ground. Contacting the earth momentarily stunned her, but without allowing her body to come to a complete standstill, Althea got her feet under her and began running. She glanced back, expecting to see him behind her. Rather than being pursued, though, she was all alone, racing toward the river bank—a bruised, frightened woman intent on escape from what God and everyone else would judge a lunatic.

The car was nowhere in sight. Having already rounded the bend of the river, it was hurrying away, leaving tiny puffs of dust as evidence of where it had been.

This new area was unfamiliar to her. Pausing at the edge of the bank, she observed a territory so unknown that she may as well have been in the midst of a foreign city. After brushing dirt from her abraded knees and arms, and from her dress, she tidied her fallen hair, then gazed more closely about her. Unaware of how much or how little time she had actually spent within that speeding car, she could only assume from her surroundings that she was now in the Outer fringe of the county—far, far from home. In two directions, as far as she could see, were fields of crops. The last remnants of summer vegetables were still on the ground, awaiting the moment when the human harvesting machines would stalk through the fields, stripping the fruit from the vines. A narrow, dusty road passed between the agricultural blocks, and Althea started off along this road toward the distant houses.

The tomatoes and beans had a peculiar wilt to them today, she noticed—a wilt attributed to both the desiccating heat and to the constant rain of radiation that fell from the sky. Walking over to the margin of the field, Althea stared glumly at the ripe, juicy red globes of food. Continual radio broadcasts had warned against ingestion of irradiated foods, particularly those growing in open spaces. Once they were taken into a body, the radiation would be absorbed by internal organs, eventually accumulating into massive doses that resulted in radiation sickness for the individual. And if sufficiently radioactive, the foods could be as lethal as any poison to a human being.

Yet, hungry stomachs were unreasonable organs, and Althea felt her own empty gut objecting to the absence of food. It had

144

been many hours since her meager breakfast and her throat was parched. The quart-sized organ sent out its volleys of pain and discomfort, disregarding the commands of her brain to be disciplined, to be patient. Without so much as water to stretch its elastic walls, the stomach would continue this until either the desire was satisfied, or the nerve receptors grew too weak to respond.

One large, beautifully shaped succulent tomato hung from the nearest vine. Althea was too smart to succumb to the dictates of her intestines and eat, but she thought of the pleasure it might bring if she could just hold the heavy globe in her hand. Reaching forward, she slid her palm in under the fruit and very gently closed her fingers around it. As she exerted the minutest degree of pressure, the plump tomato ruptured with an ease unnatural to it, and dripped down between her fingers. She stood, holding the soggy mess, and looking at it in surprise. The tomato had been literally cooked in the field, such was the extent of damages done by radiation on the cells of the vegetable.

In disgust, she threw the mess aside and wiped her palm against her dress. It had left a feeling of revulsion in her—the rupture of the tomato. It was to remain long in her memory as the symbol of the devastation that would occur from this disaster.

The road stretched out before her, its dusty path leading back to humanity, she hoped. Each step sent out a little cloud of dust particles as she walked along. The fine granules settled into her shoes, shoes that she had selected for their comfort, but had now rubbed blisters on her heels. Bending down, she removed the brogans and enjoyed the luxurious sensation of the powdery soil against her bruised feet.

A movement up ahead caught her attention. As she drew nearer, she discovered that there were people around, after all. Indeed, a dozen or so men, women, and children had invaded the field of vegetables and were busily intent on filling their buckets and baskets with the soggy food. Lacking the energy to do anything in haste, Althea slowly walked up to them and spoke to the nearest woman. "You're not going to eat that, are you?" she asked.

The woman glanced hesitantly at Althea, then dropped her head. "Yeah," she answered. "What's it to you?"

Althea was not perturbed by the sullenness of the woman.

White migrant workers were usually ill at ease around Negroes, she imagined. "It's dangerous for you to eat this food," she said. "It will make you sick."

"Huh," sneered the woman, "there ain't nothing wrong with this. All's you're worried about is that you won't get your share," and she continued to fill the basket.

Althea protested, "No, it will make you...very, very sick."

"Won't neither," answered the woman. "We've been eating this since the day of the blast—since Tuesday. And ain't nothing happened to any of us yet."

By now several others had come over to hear what was being said Althea closely observed a child peeking from behind the woman's dress. The youngster, like the adults, had an unusually ruddy complexion. The skin of his face and hands was covered with tiny inflamed splotches, lending a sunburned cast to them. From what she had read, Althea knew that this redness was temporary, and because it would go away, the people would wrongly assume there was no connection between the inflammation and the irradiated food. Unfortunately, within a few days, the erythemas, with continual exposure to radiation, would begin to form huge seeping ulcers—ulcers that would be a fertile bed for cancerous growths. "There is no reason for you to believe me," she said quietly, "but that food should not be eaten."

The woman's husband stepped toward Althea threateningly, "You better take your advice somewhere else, sister. Me and my kids are hungry and we're going to eat!"

She realized that trying to convince them was a useless waste of energy, and started turning sadly away. Then she remembered her own objective. "Would you happen to know where Glenview Community Hospital is located?" she asked.

"What's that?" asked the husband.

"Glenview. It's a hospital."

The man obviously viewed Althea with distrust. Her manner was too smooth, her voice was too warm, too soft. "What are you doing out here?" he asked suspiciously. "There ain't no hospitals around this neck of the woods, woman."

"You've never heard of Glenview?"

He shook his head. "Naw. We ain't got no use for sick places."

Althea sighed and resumed her journey toward the distant houses. There was no response to her 911 dialed on her cell phone. The Navigation system pointed her hopefully in the right direction.

"Lou Ella, you can't drink that! You know it'll make you sick." Jess hated to reprimand his weakened wife, but she shouldn't have done it. She'd mixed the sugary, orange-flavored powder with tap water and was sitting at the table drinking it.

"Humph. I don't care anymore; I don't care one tiny bit," the old woman answered.

"Sweetheart, everything will be all right. Wait and see if it's not," said the old man soothingly.

"Where's Althea?" asked his wife. "She's been gone the whole day and half the night. She should have been back by now...unless something's happened to her."

Jess Carr also worried about his daughter's absence. She had been gone much too long.

"How is it that the police can't do their jobs anymore?" asked his wife. "Jess, I think you ought to go down to the police station and report her missing."

In his many years of life Jess had never found policemen particularly helpful. Actually, he and most black people he knew felt they had good reason not to trust cops. "No, Lou Ella. I don't think I should go out. You know what Thea said about us staying inside. Besides, there won't be anyone at the police station."

Lou Ella shut her eyes tightly, a device she'd always used to relay to her husband that she didn't want to hear what he had to say.

"We'll have to sit and wait, sweetheart," replied the old man. "She'll be in, you'll see, and she'll have your medicine."

His reassurances fell on deaf ears. "No, I want you to go report her missing. I can't stand thinking of my little girl out there alone in the night."

"But Lou Ella....it won't do any good. I tell you there's nobody at the police station." His wife was a quiet woman by nature, one who made few demands on her husband. And because she seldom asked anything of him, he was inclined to grant her wishes when she did ask. This, however, was directly against his better judgment and Thea's command.

He peered at her through the dimness. She sat unmoving, her

eyes closed. "Did you hear me, Lou? I said there's nobody at the station."

A tiny droplet squeezed out from under one lid and rolled down her cheek. He saw the shiny tear and was moved. Lou was a strong woman—she never cried, no matter how bad it got.

"Don't worry," he whispered. "I'll go look for her." He felt impelled himself—he couldn't rest, not knowing where Althea was or what had happened. Maybe she was somewhere near and he'd find her. At least he'd be making some effort and that was better than sitting still.

Jess got up and removed his windbreaker from the closet. He slipped it on and zipped the front. To others the night would seem warm but he chilled easily. Going to the door, he cast one look back at his wife. She was motionless, but she'd heard his response, he was sure of that. "Fasten the latch after I'm out," he reminded her, then stepped cautiously into the darkness.

Sometime during the waiting Lou Ella dozed off. When a feeble pounding at the door intruded on her, she was instantly alert. Sliding the latch aside, she cautiously peeked into the darkness. "Jess? Is that you?"

From the opposite side a weight pushed against the door, forcing it open. Althea lurched toward her mother, clutching at her. Her feet were bare, showing huge puffy blisters across her heels and soles. The dress that had been tidy in the early morning was now grubby with filth. A tiny vial of a colorless fluid fell from her fist as she slowly sank to her knees on the floor, completely exhausted.

"My gracious, girl, we were worried sick about you," said her mother. The little woman strained at lifting Althea to her feet. "What in the world happened to you?"

"Mama, your insulin—don't step on it," said the daughter.

The bottle was retrieved, inspected briefly, then dropped into a pocket. "That's not very much they gave you, Thea, not for having gone all that distance to get it."

Althea pushed her mother's hands away, refusing to be helped to her feet. "I'll have to go back when this is gone. They wouldn't give me more at one time."

"Oh, Thea, you look so tired." Lou Ella again tried to lift her daughter.

"No, Mama, let me rest here on the floor."

Lou Ella rushed to the kitchen and filled her glass with the orange powder and water. She stirred it quickly and returned to

Althea. "Here, take a swallow of this....you must be thirsty."

Without realizing, Althea opened her mouth to receive the orange fluid, and felt its deliciousness cascade down her throat.

"There, that's better, isn't it, honey?"

The daughter dumbly nodded, then gasped, "Mama, no! You know it's not safe to drink the water! How could you?"

Tears welled once more in the tired eyes. "I got so thirsty I couldn't stand it anymore," Lou Ella whimpered. "I had to drink it."

"But Mama, you'll have to try! You'll have to steel yourself against temptation!" Arguing with the elderly woman was pointless and only sapped Althea's energy. And now she'd hurt her mother by shouting at her. "I'm sick, Mama....awfully sick. But promise me that you and Dad won't use the water, will you?"

The tears freely flooded Lou Ella's cheeks as she dabbed at the wetness. "Althea, what are we going to do?"

The daughter had been plagued by recurring vomiting since evening. Her body was now weakened by the loss of energy, and a fever was beginning a slow climb, leaving her full of aching misery. "I'll lie here on the floor for awhile, Mama....just leave me here. Maybe I can think of something later."

Sniffling her tears, the old woman mumbled, "Thea, I sent Papa out to report you missing to the police. We didn't know but that something awful had happened to you."

In disbelief, Althea stared at her mother. "Papa is....Mama, there's no police. How could you have let him go?" She felt her body going numb, but she asked, "Why, for Lord's sake?"

"We were worried about you, honey. He should be back by now, though...! guess he just took it slow."

No matter how strongly Althea wished to stay awake, her body refused. She slowly sprawled out on the floor and slid into unconsciousness, murmuring "Papa....Papa...."

As his daughter approached the house from one end of the block, Jess turned the corner at the opposite end. He made his way carefully in the blackness, stepping slowly and feeling the firm concrete before putting his weight down. The short walk had made no unusual demands on him, yet, his body was no longer responding to his will to go on.

The pain slammed into his chest like a sledge hammer then raced up his neck and along his left arm. Beads of perspiration rapidly formed and poured down his face. Clutching his chest,

149

he kneaded his fingers into the bony rib cage, trying to work the pain out. But the ache only intensified. "Lou Ella," he whispered, just before he collapsed on the empty sidewalk.

Light was filtering under the shade. It was the soft, diffuse sunlight of early morning. Althea blinked away the sleep, and listened closely for sounds. The house was still. The air was heavy. There'd been no wind to disturb the quietness outside the frame bungalow just as there were no movements to interrupt the quietude inside.

"Mama?" she called tentatively.

She had laid on the hard floor throughout the night—in the same spot where she had collapsed in an unconscious faint. Her body was sore and stiff, but it was not until she pushed her weight up on swollen, raw feet that she gasped with the pain. It was a metal-hot, searing pain that swept along her body. On trembling, shaking legs, she leaned against the wall and attempted to clear her head. The house was inordinately quiet. "Mama? Mama, where are you?"

She treaded painfully toward her parent's bedroom door and called again. "Mama, are you all right?" Shoving the door ajar, she saw the elderly woman curled on her bed. "Mama, why didn't you answer me?" The old lady's eyes were open. "Didn't you hear me call?" asked Althea anxiously. The grey head made a slight barely perceptible movement on the pillow.

"Where's Papa?" Why hadn't he awakened her, she wondered. At that instant she remembered that he'd been gone when she returned during the night. She moved to her mother's side and took the frail, wrinkled hand in her own. She slid her fingers to the underside of the wrist. Faint pulsations irregularly passed into the delicate receptors of her fingertips.

Hastily, the daughter poured alcohol onto a cloth and bathed her mother's neck and chest. Fumes sent the mother into a small fit of coughing.

"Althea," Lou Ella finally said, "your father is out on the sidewalk....we must go get him." Her voice was tired and weak, almost inaudible, but she attempted to arise from the bed.

"I'll get him, Mama. You stay right here and I'll go call him," said Althea moving toward the door.

"No, you don't understand. Last night when I sent him..." her words trailed off and became momentarily lost. At last they resumed. "When I sent him down to the police station to report on you, he didn't come back." Her voice weakly drifted off again.

"He didn't....what?" Althea grasped her mother's shoulder and gently shook it. "Mama, what are you talking about?"

"I waited all night, maybe I slept some, but by morning I knew something had happened." Large tears again pooled under the swollen lids. "You wouldn't wake up, Althea, so I went out by myself... looking for him." The tiny dams burst and salty drops spilled out.

"You shouldn't have....oh Mama, you...," began the daughter.

"He was dead. There, on the sidewalk—like his heart stopped beating and he just died—not even a block from home. My poor Jess... .Ohhh, my poor Jess."

They cried together, the mother and daughter.

"It was my fault, Althea," she said at last. "I made him go out —he didn't want to."

Through her sobs, the daughter said, "It wasn't your fault, Mama. Papa's heart was bad."

"He tried to tell me that there was no use in...Oh, Thea, why did I do it?"

"Please, Mama. We can't help it now....he's gone."

Realizing that neither really consoled the other, they finally dried away their tears.

"I carried a blanket and put it over him," explained Lou Ella. "I couldn't leave him to lie on the pavement in the hot sun. He suffered so from the heat."

Althea knew what must be done. Walking on aching feet, she managed to get out onto the sidewalk and around the corner to where her father lay. She saw him, exactly as her mother had described him, the yellow wool blanket still covering his body.

The old man weighed only slightly more than his daughter. Yet, positioning him so that she could pull him to the house required most of her meager strength. With the blanket securely wrapped around him and tied at his feet, she worked intermittently, tugging and resting, tugging and resting, until she succeeded in moving him to his own lawn. There, under the shade of the ragged hedge, she left him.

There seemed no end to the pain falling upon her. Now her father's death. How much more could she take? Then she wondered how much more the frail old woman could take. After fifty years of marriage, what happened in the heart of the one who was left? Althea painfully made her way back inside.

"Did you cover him up real well, Althea?" Lou Ella was propped on her pillow, more alert than before.

"Yes, Mama." answered the daughter.

"When will we get help, do you reckon?"

"Soon....very soon."

"The wind isn't blowing, though, is it?"

"No, Mama. Not yet. But it will soon, I know it will."

The daughter leaned close to her mother to dry the perspiration on her face. Then she noticed it—a sweet odor to the older woman's breath. "Mama, you took your insulin yesterday, didn't you?" she asked in sudden fear.

She received a nod in the affirmative.

"Are you sure, because your breath smells sweet." Althea knew the odor indicated improper sugar break-down by the body. For some reason her mother's body chemistry was out of order. But why? "Could you have forgotten to take it?"

"I took it, Thea, only maybe it's not doing much good anymore. The diarrhea is really bad," murmured the woman.

Althea looked straight into the sad pitiful eyes of her mother. "You've been drinking the water, haven't you?"

"I'm so thirsty that I can't help myself, Thea."

Of course. A diabetic's insatiable thirst when the body is not in tune....she'd naturally need fluids. "Oh God, how long will this go on?" moaned Althea. The radiation sickness caused vomiting. "Mama, have you been vomiting?"

Lou Ella slowly shook her head. "Nooo, but I feel so terrible... my poor Jess."

What was wrong with the old woman? Thirst, yes, but why were her body signs so depressed, wondered the daughter. Althea rushed from the room. Stacked in a pile in a bureau drawer were the pamphlets given to her mother by the doctor. She scanned the print, searching for a definition of these symptoms. The black letters jumped at her from the page. Any circumstance which causes a diabetic to rapidly undergo loss of body fluids may quickly bring on coma. Well, now she knew. Mama's body signs were depressed because of the diarrhea—a symptom of the radiation. To forestall a coma, the body's fluids would have to be immediately restored and insulin given. At a hospital the fluids could be intravenously fed directly into the bloodstream, but here, in the house, what could she do? The water. She must get all the water into her mother that she could. This was no time to be concerned with the radiation. And insulin —she had to give her mother more of the precious hormone.

Quickly she went into the kitchen where the instruments were kept. She lifted the syringe and inspected it closely. Deciding on the proper level, she plunged the needle through the rubber cap on the bottle.

By the time she returned to the bedroom, the sweetish odor was detectable from the foot of the bed. The elderly woman breathed heavily, her mouth open as she drew air in between her lips. Althea swiftly injected the insulin. Then, supporting the grey head with her arm, "Here, Mama, try to drink this," and she poured the water through the parched lips. First her father, and now her mother. How long? How long?

The old woman complied hungrily, trying to satiate her gnawing thirst.

"More. Drink a little more for me," said the daughter.

On the third glass, the mother refused. "I can't take anymore, Thea. Wait a minute or two."

"You must, Mama. We have to get as much into you as we can." Obediently Lou Ella took one last swallow.

Slumping back against the headboard, Althea realized how very tired she was. The trip to the hospital, the lunacy of the man in the car, the people in the field—it had left her virtually a lifeless shell. Added to that was the fact that it was over twenty-four hours since she had taken her last morsel of food. Her hands shook with a palsy that she couldn't control. A constant dull ache throbbed in her brain. She glimpsed the bruised, oozing feet and turned her head aside, surprised that she had been able to ignore the pain while caring for her parents.

Her thoughts drifted away in a haze of exhaustion. She recalled her youth, the happy times she'd had—and some of the bad ones. To be a school teacher was her childhood desire, but now she wondered if that had really been what she wanted. The job offered security, and to her parents, it had been prestigious. But it wasn't exciting. There was nothing mentally stimulating about spending five days out of every week with a group of children. Sure, it was gratifying to see them learning, to help mold young minds, but it was mental stagnation for her own active brain.

She'd suspected her discontent for several years, but hadn't faced it, hadn't attempted a new job or given her life a new direction. She'd told herself that at her age it was too late. Well, was thirty-five too late? Now that she was nearing the roller-coaster downhill swing? Or could something be salvaged still? It was a distracting thought—if she made it through this—that she'd give up teaching and do something else she'd wanted to do. It wouldn't take all that much money to open a shop on a small scale, and with any kind of success, it would provide a livelihood for her mother and herself.

A weak, plaintive moan escaped Lou Ella. "Althea?"

The name brought her out of her reverie. "Yes, Mama?"

"I think I can take some more water now."

After drinking greedily, the mother seemed somewhat uplifted in spirit. The abnormal thirst, as in diabetes, was difficult to assuage, especially when a desire for the water was greater than the stomach's capacity to hold it. But it was the shot of insulin that was pulling her slowly back from the brink of coma. The small vial was almost empty of its contents. Althea fervently hoped the remaining hormone would not be required today, for going to the hospital while leaving her mother alone in her present condition was a fearsome choice.

"Thea, do you remember Edward Allsworth?" asked the mother.

"Mama, I don't think you have the energy to talk. Why don't you lie quietly for awhile?"

The bony, wrinkled hand reached over and patted the daughter gently. "There may not be much time for talking left. Besides, you and I, Thea, we never do seem to sit down and really discuss the things that are between a mother and daughter."

"Oh Mama, we've always been talkers—you and I."

"But about the important things," said the mother. "We never discuss the important ones, not like others do."

Her mother was right, they never really talked.

"Edward Allsworth wanted to marry you, Thea."

Edward. Yes, he'd wanted to marry....and it would have been a good marriage, too, despite what people had said. "I thought you and Papa didn't like Edward."

"He was all right," answered Lou Ella softly. "He was....he wasn't a bad sort."

What was it, ten years since Edward? Ten years come November 12. And how many times had he crossed her mind in all those years?

"Thea, did you love him?"

It was a question neither parent had ever asked; nor had anyone else. Did she love him? "Edward was years ago, Mama. I hardly remember him," or the way he always wore his clothes, clothes that fit perfectly and never seemed to wrinkle, or the way he always scooted around her so that he walked nearest the street and she was on the inside.

"But you didn't answer my question," reminded her mother.

Love? He had given her a gold, heart-shaped locket with his picture in it for Valentine's Day. He'd put it around her neck while they stood in the living room that night. The locket was tucked into the little wooden jewelry chest that she kept on her dresser. For some inexplicable reason, Althea felt a tinge of resentment that now, after all this time, someone would bother to wonder if she had loved Edward.

"Does it matter whether I loved him or not?"

For a long while Lou Ella didn't reply. "But he was white, Althea," she said in a tone nearly inaudible.

Yes, and there was no point in rehashing this again—ten years later. Exactly when does a woman become her own person? When does she become strong enough that she's willing to swim against the tide, to disregard well-intentioned advice and make up her own mind? And when it's time to quit being afraid of being a disappointment, to quit living through someone else's eyes. "It may sound strange to you, Mama, but I honestly don't believe skin color makes a difference to people who are in love."

This was wrong, allowing the subject of Edward to be opened. Wishing to stem the tide of old memories, Althea reached for the tumbler. "Here, try some more water. You must be awfully thirsty."

Her mother's thirst was unquenchable as she greedily drank.

"See, you've over-exerted yourself. No more talking for now," admonished the daughter. "You must save your strength."

The aged skin was very dry. Her face felt the warmth of elevated temperature. Gradually, the mother's breathing became deeper, labored. Effects of the insulin were short-lived.

Althea watched over her. Within the following hour, the only noticeable change was in the increased demands for water.

By evening Lou Ella was hungrily sucking air into her mouth. Growing markedly more fatigued, she continued to ask for water, and eagerly drank glass after glass. Without cessation

155

of the diarrhea, the liquid was doing very little toward restoration of the lost body fluids.

Althea resignedly filled the syringe with the last of the insulin. In the beginning she had been afraid that the extra hormone might prove to be too much for her mother; now she was afraid that it wouldn't be enough. As long as the woman was conscious, she could have hope. Generally, unconsciousness could take from hours to days to come, according to the brochure, but once it occurred, then only intravenous fluids and large doses of insulin could save her. Searching until she found the right spot on the leg, Althea shoved the needle through the skin and sat back to wait.

Chapter Twelve

For the residents of Oakland, life went on as usual. The influx of Los Angelenos from three hundred miles south did little to slow the pace of the bay area people. Richmond, Berkeley, Oakland, Hayward, and San Francisco were sufficiently large cities to absorb their share of evacuees without much confusion. It was quite a contrast for Frank Waring, after the Blythe episode. He still was not accustomed to the idea that just a day's drive from his father-in-law's home in Oakland would put him back into one of the most disastrous situations to affect modern mankind.

At the sound of the door closing, he looked up. Except for Kim playing in her room, he had been alone in the house the entire morning with no knowledge of Paula's whereabouts. It was time for somebody to arrive. Unfortunately, it was not his wife who entered, but her parents. Mrs. Jorgensen acknowledged his presence with a glance and swept past him into the kitchen. Her action told him that something was in the air, for she was normally a friendly woman. He turned expectantly toward his father-in-law. "Where's Paula?" he asked.

Mr. Jorgensen walked over to his armchair and took a seat. "It's time you and I had a little talk, Franklin."

Sighing in exasperation, Frank replied, "Mr. Jorgensen I'm still worn out—physically and emotionally. All I want right now is to know where my wife is."

Peering out over his spectacles, Jorgensen answered, "Paula is at Dr. Hellman's."

"Well, all right then," said Frank, starting to rise.

"Sit down, Frank. There's something that needs to be said and I figure this is as good a time as any for saying it."

Here we go, Frank thought. Another round with the old blowhard. But not another scene of no-balls, m'boy, that's for sure. "Okay," he said, dropping back down, "shoot." Best to get it over with, finished.

"Paula has been telling me what it's like in San Mirado, Franklin. Now understand me, I'm not criticizing you. But

157

Paula's used to having nice things. She always had everything she wanted when she was living here. She even had her own car when she was too young to legally drive it. Now I know you do the best you can for your family, but I happen to believe they deserve a little more than you have given them."

Frank hadn't moved so much as the tiny muscles that cause his eye-lids to blink.

His father-in-law continued. "You say you're an accountant, but what you're doing is fairly ordinary bookkeeping work, and your salary shows it."

"Paula told you how much I made," said Frank flatly.

"Of course she did. She's interested in getting ahead, my boy. But what bothers me is that you're planning to move them to Arizona so you can bide your time with your brother. He's never made it, if what Paula says is true, and I can't see how you hope to do any better."

"Billy Joe gets along."

"That's not good enough, Frank. A man has responsibilities to himself and his family. Why, you'll be forty years old before long, and you still don't have anything. Not even a job, now, though that's a blessing in disguise, in my opinion."

"Paula and I were doing okay. Maybe I didn't make a fortune at Calmar, but I never had to ask anyone for help."

"But you weren't getting anywhere. If you'd taken my advice when you two first married, you could have worked your way up in the company. To an executive position by now, Frank. But no, you had to do it your own way and look what you've achieved. Nothing."

"What else did Paula tell you, Mr. Jorgensen? She's apparently felt free to discuss things with you that she won't with me," he said with bitterness.

"Well, that's natural, Franklin. She was always a daddy's girl. You know, she's in a position to inherit quite a large sum of money should anything happen to me. I want to make certain that. she handles it wisely, that's all."

"And you believe she could do that, if I worked for the family company," said Frank.

"Let me put it this way. Paula and I have talked it over. She knows my feelings on the subject and she's inclined to agree with me, to the point where she has already said that she's not going with you to your brother's."

The old man's statement caught Frank by surprise. "When

did she say that?" he quickly asked.

"Just this morning, while we were downtown."

So that's why they had all left together—Paula and her parents—they couldn't talk with him in the house. "Well, she's going whether she wants to or not."

"Now, Franklin, be sensible about it. This is her home. She's happy here, and she doesn't want to leave it. She never did, not even after her marriage when you dragged her off to a one-bedroom apartment in that dumpy housing development full of destitute Mexicans. Given her choice, she's going to stay this time. And she'll want you to stay with her."

How could he argue with her father until he was sure of Paula's feelings? "Maybe we'll be going back to San Mirado," Frank answered lamely. "She mentioned wanting a new house there."

"When will that be? You don't know when the danger will pass, much less whether you'll have a job or not. No, it's time you decided to play it smart. For once, do it my way, Frank."

Frank felt his temper rise. "Why should I do it your way? Paula knew I would be an accountant when she married me, and she also knew that I didn't want to become another cog in the family wheel. I just don't happen to see licking your boots as leaving me much self-respect, Mr. Jorgensen. Furthermore...."

"Hell fire," snapped the older man. "When are you going to get some sense in that head of yours? Here I am trying to set you up in business—a break you're not going to get anywhere else— and all I get in return is a slap in the face. Christ alive, I told Paula years ago that you'd never amount to anything!"

His hands knotted into balls as Frank worked his anger down. Of all the things Paula's father could say, the offer of a job was the least expected. It was too bad that the old man couldn't have made it without any strings attached, and without the derision he seemed to feel he had to cast on his son-in-law. "Not amount to anything, Mr. Jorgensen? Well, maybe not, by your standards. But I've always been my own man, by God!"

"And it pleases you to say that—when you don't even have the money to pay your son's hospital bills?"

"Who said I don't have the money?" Frank snarled.

"You did....when you checked the boy in you told admittance that you didn't have the money...that you'd get it together somehow."

"My God," he said, "the people at the hospital know what's

happened to us. They know I have insurance and I'll pay the rest when I can get the money out of my bank. I don't know why it won't work with an ATM but it doesn't. I guess because no one is at the place and there's no electricity there. And my credit card won't work either."

Jorgensen smiled benignly behind his glasses. "Well, my grandson's bill is taken care of....you don't have to be bothered by that."

Frank jumped from his chair and began pacing the floor. "You went over there to that hospital and stuck your nose into my business....what a presumptuous old ass you are!"

"Now you listen to me, Frank Waring! You can't talk to me like that in my own house. No sir! I took you and your family in because you had no place to go."

"Bull! You took us in because you've never been able to let go of Paula. You never did want her to leave this house, did you?"

"I want my daughter to have a good life....and it may interest you to know that I had hoped that I would find a son in the man she married."

"A son?" asked Frank, incredulously.

"Yes, a son."

Frank laughed. "Shit. Lucky the son who gets manipulated by you."

Jorgensen lowered his voice. "I can see now that it's impossible. You'd never fit into my company, Frank. Never. We need bright, ambitious men and you simply don't fill the bill."

Frank felt a hot flush rush to his skin. He ached to hit out at the smugness on the other's face. "We're leaving here as soon as I can get Jerry out of the hospital."

"Paula and the children are not going with you."

"No? Well, we'll see."

"They're not leaving with you, Frank," said the father-in-law. "I'll place money on that."

He sounded so positive that Frank was momentarily uncertain. Had the old man failed to tell him something? "My wife and my kids go with me."

"Nope," answered Jorgensen. "Not this time. Not with the baby."

That single word caught Frank off guard. "What?"

"The baby. Didn't you know Paula is expecting? She got the doctor's confirmation on it before you left San Mirado."

160

Frank mumbled, "She didn't mention it to me."

"You're not very informed, my boy. But then you never were."

Frank was paying the taxi driver when he saw her descending the steps. She had that determined march-time walk that clued him in to her mood. The thick glass door of the hospital cast her reflection after her, outlining the purposeful swing of her body.

"Paula! Wait!" he shouted, running after her.

She paused only long enough to allow him to fall into step with her. "We've got to have this out, Paula. Your old man has been hammering at me ever since you left the house."

"I'm in a hurry, Frank. Jerry needs some pajamas and other stuff." She started off across the street.

He grabbed her by the arm, spinning her around to face him. "Jerry can wait until we finish this," he said angrily.

She shook him loose. "Not here in the parking lot, for God's sake. I don't want everybody staring at us."

Together they walked on toward the car and slid into the seat from opposite sides; he, brimming with anger, she, collected.

"I want you to explain to me why you've done this... ." Frank began, "pouring our private affairs out to your father. It's getting where everything he says ends up humiliating me, Paula. Jesus, don't you think it's time you acted like an adult and quit crying on his shoulder?"

Paula drew back and glared at him as she spoke. "You're a fantastic snot, Frank, did you know that? I've spent the best part of my life watching you crawl around in a rut, and I'm fed up to my chin with it."

"All right. All right! But tell me, not that old bastard. Damn, I can't believe you even told him how much money I was making."

Paula shrugged. "Why should that concern you, anyway? He'd help us if you weren't such a prick. He'd set you up in the business and we could begin living like we should."

"I thought we'd hashed this out long ago, Paula. How is it that we're fighting over your folks again?"

"I don't know, Frank. It's just that sometimes you trigger the worst in me." And she returned the favor, always.

"We were doing fine when we were so far away from your

parents that we never saw them. Now, all of a sudden, we're taking their hand-outs and I'm feeling like pure hell. Damn, Paula, people back in Los Angeles are dying from some foul crap in the air, and here we are bitching at each other. My God, we ought to feel lucky just to have gotten out of that mess. What's wrong with us, anyway?"

She gazed out the window for a long moment, then answered, "I tried with you, Frank. I agreed to let you have your own way, while I sat in that stinking subdivision swapping lurid tales with Flo. Well, that's behind us now. This explosion at White Water has forced me to face the facts."

"You can't blame the radiation crisis for forcing us into this, Paula. You're well aware that you never had reconciled yourself to San Mirado—or me either, I guess. You were always searching for something better," he said testily.

"Yeah? What kind of searching did I do, Frank?" she asked as she faced him.

"Flo's husband probably knows more about that than I do." His answer was sullen.

She'd have slapped him, but sitting under the steering wheel made the movement impossible. Lowering her voice in a sinister warning, she replied, "That's a filthy accusation that could only have been made by a son-of-a-bitch, Frank Waring."

"Do you deny it?"

"Certainly I do," she snapped. "Although I can't see why I should bother."

"Why didn't you tell me about the baby, Paula? I have a right to know since I'm the father," said Frank. "I am the father, aren't I?"

"I could kill you for that," she said venomously.

He disregarded her threat and asked, "Why did you confide in your father but not me? My God, I'm your husband."

A tired, bored sigh escaped her lips. "Because I wasn't ready to tell you. And that's just as well, I guess," she answered. "I went in to check with an obstetrician this morning. He thinks the pregnancy should be aborted."

"Aborted?" Frank asked in stunned disbelief. "That's murder! No, there'll be no abortion on a child of mine!"

"It's not even a child, yet, Frank. It's a tiny glob of cells about the size of my thumbnail," she said quietly.

"Glob, hell! It's human life! What does that butcher give as his reason for ordering an abortion?"

"Dr. Hellman says there's a good chance that the baby, even if I carried it to full term, could be horribly deformed because of my exposure to the radiation."

"Well, I won't stand for it. It's a sin and a criminal offense. No," he shook his head emphatically, "I won't stand for it!"

"It's neither a sin nor a crime to terminate a pregnancy on an embryo that might never live."

"You can't be sure that it'll be deformed. It could be a perfectly healthy baby."

"Dr. Hellman will know. He expects hideous abnormalities in children of mothers who were exposed in the first three months of pregnancy," she said. "He thinks the risk is too great for the child."

Slowly the realization began to sink in. "How far along are you?" he asked.

"Over two," she replied.

He obstinately shook his head. "No, Paula. I'll never agree to it. Not ever, not on a child of mine."

Paula answered flatly. "I'm not sure you'll have any choice in the matter." The days of his importance were rapidly passing.

"Oh yes I will. A wife can't even be touched by a surgeon without her husband's approval."

"And you'd withhold it, I suppose, and bring a helpless, marked child into this world?"

"Yes, I would," he stated. "I sure as hell would."

"Huh, that's precisely what I told Dad you'd say. Maybe he was right about you all these years, Frank, and I was the one who was wrong."

"Answer me one other question, Paula. The other night when we talked about returning to San Mirado after this was over, you said you wanted a new house—one of the de Lorenzo places. Why did you change your mind so quickly, to not even considering going back?"

She pondered his question. "It's difficult to explain. In a way, I believe it's what you feel when you refuse to work with Daddy, Frank. You realize how much I want you to join the business, but it's more important that you live your life your own way, without being under the dictates of my father."

"Well, I'm surprised that you understand," he said.

"For me, the situation is similar. It's not that I don't love you, for I do... .but I want something more, something gratifying to me, personally."

"And you think you've been walking in my shadow, is that it? You need to be more than just a housewife?"

"Oh, I like being a wife, but can't I also be other things? Someday Daddy's estate will be ours... .if you want a part of it. Then, I'd like to be able to have an active role in the business, make some decisions. Use my brain. Is that such a crime?" she asked.

"But look where we are, Paula! You want this and I want something a hundred and eighty degrees opposite it. Obviously we can't both be satisfied," he argued, "when we're so far apart. So one of us has to give in."

"Compromise, Frank, not give in," she said.

"No! Either you or I will have to forfeit, Paula."

"That's a strange word—forfeit. It means one of us has to be penalized. Is that it, Frank? Will one of us have to be penalized in order that our relationship can survive?"

Dejectedly, he asked, "Put like that it doesn't sound very pleasant, does it?"

She sadly shook the hair from her face. "No....it doesn't."

Chapter Thirteen

There are certain background noises that are taken for granted; the whir of tires against warm concrete, the low buzz of human activities intermingling with bits of conversation, a door softly clicking shut. At Beckman General Hospital, staff and patients alike were cognizant of the abrupt cessation of the motors and the purring of ventilation systems. Death of the electric buttons connecting the nurse's stations with various departments and rooms was observed with the sudden loss of all the hospital's lights. For minutes, talk stopped as each person evaluated the unusual quiet.

It hadn't been unexpected. The hospital's stand-by power system could continue only so long as the fuel held out. The staff knew they worked on borrowed time. Once the auxiliary system was switched on, the personnel had been diligent in cutting power usage as low as possible, and they had fervently hoped that public power would be reinstated before the emergency system used all its fuel. Now there was simply no more oil to burn. Time had run out.

In the isolation unit, Dr. Parsons was suturing a twelve-inch gash extending from the upper chest to the right ear of his patient. The cut had been clean, having occurred as the boy, a radiation victim, fell through a window in the rear of a neighboring house. The type of accident seen in the past couple days had distinctly differed from those normally admitted. No longer were people driving their cars into each other; they were spending more time breaking and entering.

"What the hell!" Parsons yelled as the lights went out.

"That's it! The generators are dead!" said Max through the darkness.

"Goddamit, I can't see a damned thing! Somebody get me some light!" Parsons felt the last four inches of gaping wound under his fingers. "Some light, damn it! Sharon, isn't there something around? A flashlight?" he bellowed.

"We didn't get flashlights in our inventory, Doctor," answered the nurse as she fumbled toward him in the darkness.

"Oh hell, who'd have thought of flashlights in a hospital? Well, I've got to close this boy, and I sure as the devil can't do it in the dark."

"Here, Doctor." Sharon Henry snapped on the butane lighter that she carried in her pocket.

Parsons peered through the weak beam at her. "You're a smoker, huh?"

"I was when I had time," answered Sharon.

"Humph....cigarettes are bad for you, girl, but I'm damned happy to see that little torch of yours right now." He bent in closer to his work. The faint illumination was sufficient to allow him to complete a slightly crooked row of stitches in the skin. After he dressed the wound, he turned to the nurse and gave her an appreciative smile. "My kid sister could have done a prettier job of stitching than that," he said.

"In the dark, Doctor?"

He released a long tired breath. "I wish I had a sense of humor right now—then I'd tell you what I excel at in the darkness, nurse."

Sharon showed the same bone-weary exhaustion that she had heard in his voice. During the last seventy-two hours, days had merged into nights with hardly an awareness of the change. Sleep and rest were luxuries snatched in small amounts by the personnel within the isolation unit. Arrival of daylight was always announced by increasing numbers of patients waiting on the outside.

Those admitted never really recuperated before their release from the special ward, but massive overflowing of the facility compelled the staff to administer treatment and send them away. All but the most extreme cases were handled in this manner. Admitted, examined, treated, and sent away. Unfortunately, the vast majority suffered from forms of radiation sickness, conditions for which the medical staff had no cure. The grotesque pile of loosely-wrapped bodies was growing larger by the day, as those whose lives had terminated were placed beyond the outer walls of the hospital, and closely draped with canvas.

Parsons moved over and pushed the door to the outside open, admitting weak moonlight to the interior. The aged, the infirm, the very young—every conceivable cross section of people— were grouped at the outer door. "Good grief," said the surgeon as he peered through the night at the masses on the parking lot, "why don't they just stay in their homes. They'd be much better off in their houses than straggling through the streets, trying to find a hospital."

"They're scared and they're sick. It's natural that they'd want help," said Dr. Feldman, groping his way forward.

"Yeah, but if they only knew how little we can do for them, then they would lock themselves in and concentrate on trying to stay alive until this is over."

"When will that be, Bernie?" asked Max.

Dr. Parsons' broad shoulders seemed to have narrowed over the past couple days, pulled together as they had been by his ever-busy hands. Lack of proper food and rest, coupled with a steady, grinding pace that never let up, were leaving their mark on him, despite his natural physical stamina. But he never slacked his pace willingly, always driving himself to see the next patient, to ease as much suffering as he could. "Lord, how I wish I knew, Max. When I have time to think of it, I tell myself that we have to get relief soon, that the radiation can't hang there over us forever. But I don't know. With the loss of electricity we've really had it." Feeling his way back to the examining table, his mind raced with ideas of how to put together sufficient lighting to continue through the night. Lighting, the one thing they must have. "Well, we can't do anything in the dark... and there's no use in bringing in another patient until we can get some light to work by."

"How about alcohol, Bernie? We can throw together some makeshift alcohol lamps," suggested Max.

"With what? Jars?" asked Parsons, interested at once.

"Sure, why not? Punch a hole in the lid and feed some sheeting strips down into the alcohol. It'll burn."

"Yeah....that's not a bad idea....but we'll have a holocaust if that fire gets away from the wick and into the liquid," he said, as he began to search for the vessels.

"We'll make the wicks a tight fit," said Max as he joined him. "They'll sure be better than no light at all."

The two physicians quickly began the chore, collecting jars and sheeting. Max gouged the holes in the lids and twisted the cloth into wicks; Bernie stuffed the thick cords through the lids. Sharon poured the alcohol. They worked as a well-organized team.

"Dr. Parsons, you're awfully nervous," said the nurse. "Are you all right?"

He paused, annoyed that the stubborn cord wouldn't enter the perforation. "I'm running a touch of fever, but nothing more

167

serious."

"It's the radiation, isn't it?" asked the nurse.

"Well, we couldn't hope to avoid it, Sharon. I'd be surprised if others of us don't have some symptoms. You, maybe?" asked Parsons, intent on threading the wick.

"Headaches and nausea, Doctor."

Max asked quietly, "I wonder how long we can go on at this rate?"

No one bothered to answer him as they set the cigarette lighter to the first lamp and a weak flame flared up. "All right," said Parsons, "let's bring in the next patients."

A big man stepped forward, working his way through the gloom to the table. A woman walked frantically to keep pace with him, trying to hold on to the boy he carried in his arms. Parsons took one look at the lad, checked the angle of his jaw for a pulse, and said to the man. "I'm sorry....your son is dead."

Harry stood immobile, transfixed to the spot. Suddenly his lips began to quiver. Moving up from behind, Max took the boy from Harry and started toward the outside with the body.

"Harry. Harry," said Flo, "come on. There's nothing we can do for Rickey now."

Parsons understood their helplessness. Every death was now becoming a personal loss to him. But children....they were the hardest to give up. "Wait," he said. "Since you're here I ought to check you."

Flo had Harry by the arm, steering him in the direction of the exterior. "It doesn't matter, Doctor...not now."

"Yes, but..." the couple had walked out into the darkness.

For a long, solitary moment the surgeon could only stare after the departing couple. Their pain reached out to him. If they'd brought the boy here sooner; if he'd had more time with the youngster....Parsons shook himself. There were too many, too many. Fifty physicians were needed here....a truckload of supplies. Death came so easily....he turned to the next patient just as a commotion caught his attention.

A thin, disheveled woman pushed past the intern and staggered into the room. She searched the near darkness wildly, then stumbled to him. Her face was instantly recognizable to Dr. Parsons, only it seemed to have aged since he had observed it earlier. Now she was a woman weary, ill, and on the verge of madness—if the strange glint in her eyes meant anything.

She clasped him by the front of his dirty jacket, yanking him into her body. "You've got to help me, Doctor! Please, you have to do something." Her arms jerked spasmodically as she held onto him.

He gently attempted to break her grasp. "Now, now, try to be calm, Mrs. Harrington. Try to stay calm."

She had no more tears to shed, but dry sobs still racked her as she poured out her plea. "The medicine is gone, Doctor, and he's in such pain. Can't you give me something for his pain?"

"Mrs. Harrington, we don't have anything. We haven't had for a long while," Parsons said.

She sank down on her knees and fastened her arms around his legs. "There is no one, if you refuse to help me. I beg of you, have mercy on my poor Ben!" she cried.

The others turned their backs to the rending scene. The woman's humility, her self-abasement was a private experience to be shared by her and the man of whom she pleaded.

Parsons gently but firmly lifted her to her feet. Tenderly he brushed the matted hair from her tear-stained face. "All right, Mrs. Harrington," he said softly. "I do have some morphine." He backed away and unlocked a white metal cabinet. In his hand was a small squat bottle. His reserve—for the ultimate emergency—the last of the precious drug. He placed it on the table.

"I can't give you all of this but wait a second and I'll draw out enough for one injection." The woman was both pathetic and admirable in her insistence to save her husband. Such a wife every man should have, thought Parsons.

Bending toward the sink he selected an instrument with which to withdraw the fluid. "I'm sorry that this is the best I can do," he said with genuine regret. Needle poised, he turned to the table to find that she was gone....and the bottle of morphine had disappeared.

Sara raced through the darkness of the house, bumping against the wall as she hastened to him. "Ben, darling! Ben. It's me. I'm back." Swiftly she pushed through to his bedside. By the flickering of a candle, Sara loaded the tube with the narcotic and plunged the needle into his arm.

He received the needle without a hint of awareness. Its fine sharp point split the microscopic nerve filaments, causing short waves of pain that were completely lost in his greater anguish. Physiologically, his systems, his vital organs, were deteriorating. Breathing sluggishly, he moved very little now, but lay still, almost comatose. Unable to take nourishment for the past twenty-four hours, his condition had steadily worsened.

"Ben, can you hear me, darling?" asked Sara as she tenderly ran the wet towel over his neck.

He hadn't spoken in the last day, but soft distressing moans had issued from him, an indication to Sara that the breach between life and death was narrowing.

"The medicine will help, Ben. You won't hurt now."

Sara traced the outline of his brow, pausing to gently caress the tight skin. Parched, cracked lips and the stubble of beard reminded her of his long hours of agony. She murmured soothingly of their lives together, how they had met as young adults, of her happiness with him. Her voice grew sweeter as she recounted glistening moments of pristine bliss that she had shared with him— of the times of exquisite tenderness between woman and man. Whispering softly, she crooned, "Please hear me, Ben. Please know that my life had no meaning until you, dear." Finally she sobbed quietly in the dimness of the lone flickering candle, breaking the string of endearments.

A series of harsh, gurgling wails escaped his throat, sending Sara into terrified alarm. Reacting violently, she clutched at him. "Oh mercy, Ben! Hold on, darling! I'll give you another shot." Another? She couldn't remember when she had given the last one. Was it too soon for another? Time had no measurement over the past few days, and there was no way of knowing how much time had elapsed since the first morphine was given. If she gave him too much narcotic....but he was in tremendous agony. She must give him relief—it was all she had to give him now.

She quickly, methodically, loaded the instrument a second time. After the briefest hesitation, she shoved it into him. It was done.

Shortly he grew quiet, but his pulse beat in spasmodic jerks that seemed to grow stronger, as though the heart were labored.

It was a Friday night; a night that might ordinarily have found the Harringtons entertaining at a small dinner party or at the theater. Recalling the past, Sara slumped back in the chair and used a towel to wipe the mixture of sebum and grime from her face. She heard him breathing, more calmly now, and continued listening as long as she could.

Discontented with her toiletries, but too weary to do more, she laid her head on the padded arm of the chair and dropped into a light, restless sleep. How long she'd slept she didn't know, but the strange unearthly call snapped her to consciousness.

"Sarrrraaaaa."

Instantly awake, her eyes wide with fright, "Yes? Ben?"

There was no answer.

Hadn't he called her name? Maybe she had dreamed it, but she didn't remember a dream. The night was deathly quiet, an uneasy, unnatural stillness. God, if only the wind would blow.

Suddenly, the stillness pressed upon her. Sara lurched toward the bed, to Ben. He made no movement. But he was cooler. Ah good, the fever was going. He would feel better now. Without the fever....the fever? She flattened her palm over his brow, then his chest. She laid her cheek against him. Icy sensations coursed through her. He had no body heat. None. He was dead. She lifted her head and sat back. Ben was dead.

A crashing, shattering noise—like an aluminum sheet slapping against a wood frame—jarred her to her senses.

She looked wildly around, expecting unmentionable horrors to descend on her, to steal her life from her.

The clamor repeated itself. Then she knew. The ventilation ducts in the ceiling were being buffeted—buffeted by wind. The wind was blowing. At last.

Chapter Fourteen

News that the thermal inversion lifted spread like wildfire through the populace on Saturday. Late night radio and television stations across the nation had broken into their regular programs to make the announcement. The message was flashed to the command posts where rescue squads awaited.

Within the disaster area, change in the climatic condition was signaled by strong northerly winds that swooped cool air into the metropolis where they nudged under the heavy, stale blanket, and carried the pollutant southward. Prevailing air currents rolled high along the Pacific coast before veering oceanward in the vicinity of Baja.

Wind currents are predictable, but temperamental, forces in southern California. Usually cool moist air descends from frontal systems originating over the northwest Pacific. However, opposing flows occasionally develop from warmer latitudes and sneak in from the southern Pacific region. And often periodic drafts blow in from the northeast Nevada area. Rarely, a current dashes straight across the lower half of the state from the ocean and makes a bee-line for the east until it hits first higher elevations, then drops to lower altitudes. The latter course would have meant devastation to one of the two richest agricultural valleys in the state, and the fallout would have settled over a moderately densely populated area.

As it happened, however, the direction the wind ultimately carried the radiation was coastally, allowing minimal amounts of the fallout to deposit along the route to San Clemente, Oceanside, San Diego, and into northwestern Mexico before steering oceanward. Fallout would be dropped into the waters of the blue Pacific, where it would eventually become a factor in the food chain of the marine organisms. That the radiation in all probability would end up in the albacore, bonito, and other tuna —a major source of canned fish—and eventually in the gastrointestinal tract of man was a certainty, but it was the least of the present worries. That it was being brushed onto the ocean and not deeper into the nation was sufficient cause for restrained elation among the people.

Anticipation of the lifting of the thermal inversion had

resulted in a massive mobilization of special rescue forces under federal jurisdiction. In collaboration with these forces were smaller units organized at local levels around the perimeter of the disaster zone. The coordination of the forces had begun on Thursday. Ground crews had begun a movement to the outer fringes of the radiation field, and once arrived, they threw out their tents and set up bivouac, awaiting further advancement until a wind shift came to disperse the bulk of the radiation.

On a given signal, air units would be quickly dispatched from far-off bases. As a reconnaissance squadron, the planes had been equipped with special recording instruments with which rapid calculations on the radiation levels could be made. Instructions to the pilots of the crafts had been to fly within recording range, and carry out a series of readings. Under no conditions were the fliers to take their craft into pockets of densely radioactive fields, phenomena that were generally expected by scientists because of the natural, basin-like geography of the area.

Once the advance squad gave the go-ahead, ground forces would begin their entry into the zone. Municipal water tank trucks from surrounding cities had been loaded with their life-saving fluids and pulled into position. Medic squads from across the nation, with vast supplies of medicines and drugs, formed a waiting vanguard. Batteries of scientists—chemists, physicists, biophysicists, biologists, and environmentalists—mingled at the forefront. Troopers, whose single command was to restore order, stood ready in their khaki uniforms with their oiled and shiny rifles nearby. In all, it was a formidable force that stood patiently waiting the singular order—the order to move.

To the southeast, in the tiny hamlet nestled at the foot of the low mountain range, the helicopter set down. The craft had been dispatched from San Diego with material for the group organized at the armory. The last of the packages was being lifted from the craft when the crackling of the radiophone drew the pilot's immediate attention. "The word has come!" he shouted excitedly to the men standing beside the plane. "The wind is up! It's time to go in!"

In fact, instructions had been specific to the young pilot—he was to proceed directly to the disaster zone and begin his report on the radiation levels. Unfortunately, the remainder of his crew was back in San Diego. Anxious to be one of the first in, he determined to take off northward as soon as he could get someone aboard to do the readings. Leaning out of the plane, he

173

shouted to the men below, "Hey, I've got orders to move, but my crew is at the base. Is there anyone here who can read this Geiger counter and wants to go in with me?"

The prospect of arriving at the scene before the radiation was widely dispersed appealed to no one. Quickly the knot of men began to break up, with each one moving out of earshot of the pilot.

"Listen," he shouted at them, "I don't know anything about this box and it won't do a bit of good for me to go into L.A. without getting the readings. Come on! Don't any of you know anything about a counter?"

Cecil had already been assigned to go in on a troop truck— the destination for encampment had already been designated— and he was interested in keeping tabs on the skulking form of Carter. Yet, from deep inside came the urge to stay apart from the departing backs of the same men he had encountered in the lobby—the ones who were now hastily withdrawing to the security of the olive-green trucks. It was time to forget his childish fear of planes. Stepping forward, he hoisted himself into the craft and said, "I'm Cecil Yeager."

The young pilot smiled and shook hands. Without hesitation, he pulled out the outline of the route he had been scheduled to take over the big city. "I guess we're ready to go then, Cecil. By the way, I'm Arnie."

It was with calm deliberation that Cecil had hauled himself aboard the plane to return to the very area that he had so futilely tried to avoid. He was composed as Arnie deftly maneuvered the copter into the zone. Even with the best estimates from men who should know, still nobody knew exactly what to expect. As one of the first aerial units into the area, Cecil imagined that he felt much less trepidation than others to come. After all, he had lived with the fear of radiation since Tuesday morning, and by now, he'd been numbed into acceptance. The others were just beginning to worry.

Suddenly ground features began to take on a familiar cast as Arnie angled the chopper to do an aerial scan of upper Orange County before continuing on to Los Angeles International Airport where the first radiation reading would be taken. They were flying low, and from their elevation could clearly see there was no normal movement of people or traffic below.

Cecil viewed the desolate interlocking freeway system. Ordinarily, morning and evening rush hour traffic would be hooked bumper to bumper as the vehicles crept along to off-ramps, or, getting a free stretch, darted ahead to make up for lost time. Often when an automobile was pulled out on the shoulder, it was an occurrence that for some unexplained reason, intrigued passing motorists. Invariably, the passers-by would reduce their speed, backing up traffic while they craned their necks until their curiosity was satisfied. Today, nothing moved on the giant highway system.

Arnie nodded at the scene below, "What do you think of it, Cecil? Do you reckon everybody is too sick to get out? Or do you suppose they are all..." and he left the word unsaid. A young man in his prime didn't like to consider death.

Cecil stared down at the scene, "They're probably sick, all right. And too scared to care about trying to leave now."

The helicopter circled once over the Angels Stadium then crossed the multi-laned Santa Ana Freeway. Arnie dipped the craft toward the rising peak of the Matterhorn. He glanced below. "Look, Cecil," he said, pointing at the towering make-believe summit, "the last time I was in Disneyland, it was so crowded there must have been twenty thousand people there. I took the kids on the monorail and we toured the whole thing. It was a madhouse that day," he said sadly. "Man, it's sure dead now."

Not one sign of life existed in the huge amusement park. The place that was famous world-wide for its attractions and its rides, in four days had become a graveyard.

Arnie shook his head as they hovered over the park. "I can't believe it. I never thought anything could shut off life like that explosion has done, Cecil. You just never expect a thing like that to happen, I guess."

Softly, his voice inaudible among the roar of the rotors, Cecil answered, "Yes, no one ever thought this would happen."

"What?" yelled Arnie, aware that Cecil had spoken.

"I said....nothing, Arnie. Forget it."

L. A. International Airport lay to the northwest and Arnie guided the plane in that direction. The major airport serving metropolitan Los Angeles was bounded on the east, north, and south by tracts of housing. Residents had long complained of the noise of the big jets as they took off and landed, polluting the air with the howl of their engines and leaving their trails of noxious fumes as they raced across the sky. To the west of the airport, though, was clear, blue Pacific water. Cecil saw the glimmer of

175

the waves long before the chopper approached the landing strips.

The airport was laid out in the shape of a horseshoe with the open portion of the shoe lying eastward. It was into this region that they flew, directly in toward the tower and between the runways flanking the north and south sides. In the center were the terminals, and to the inside, a street through which traffic normally coursed. Parking lots filled the extra space in the middle of the horseshoe, and it was onto one of these that Arnie intended to lower the plane. Vehicles still dotted the lots, evidence that owners had failed to return to them.

The chopper made one slow loop around the terminals and returned to a bare space that Arnie had selected for setting it down. With a whir of blades, the craft was lowered to the ground. Suddenly, seemingly out of nowhere, there was a man frantically waving his arms at them.

Carefully, they settled into the lot nearest the man. As soon as the whirl of the propellers ceased, the man ran up to the side of the craft. Arnie piled out of the cab, and Cecil, with a firm grasp on the Geiger counter, followed.

The man had reached Arnie first, and was enthusiastically pumping the pilot's hand in welcome. Cecil placed the counter on the pavement and was preparing to make a reading when he sensed a mass of humanity moving toward them. In a fraction of time they had come pouring out of the terminal and were streaming across the lot. At that moment Cecil thought they were to be deluged by the rush of bodies, but it quickly became apparent that the crowding, pushing mob was bent on reaching the helicopter, and Cecil and the counter were simply small obstacles standing in their paths. Finding himself rudely shoved aside, he reached out blindly and latched onto the handle of the counter. With it in tow, he pushed his way through the pack until he was beside a very startled Arnie, and several yards from the plane. The man who had greeted them began frantically yelling at the top of his lungs, asking the mob of people to calm down, to control themselves.

His request for reason went unnoticed by the mob as more and more jammed themselves against the chopper, shoving to get inside it.

When Arnie saw the tiny cab packed with some eight or nine flailing bodies—a space that normally held three—he rushed forward, joining in the melee. The lower half of the last person

176

to try to get aboard was protruding from the door, and this, Arnie grabbed. Tugging mightily, he managed to yank the man free. Immediately he fastened onto another and began pulling at him. In the meantime the lone man of the welcoming committee continued to yell, finally raising his voice above the din.

Eventually the realization that the helicopter wasn't going to transport any of them out of the area without a pilot, and the continuing plea to come to their senses, caused the rioters to gradually wind themselves down. Then, with abashed and slightly embarrassed looks on their faces, they began to depart the packed craft, and regroup nearby.

At last the chopper was empty. A hush fell over the tamed mob. The portly fellow who had waved at them before they landed, stepped out away from them. By his demeanor, and his self- assurance, this dominating man became a spokesman for the assemblage. "We got carried away for awhile there," he said in half-apology. "But you can see how anxious we've been. You see, we had about decided that there wasn't going to be any rescue."

Cecil was impressed by the man's composure. "How many of you are there?" he asked.

Turning toward Cecil, the other replied, "Last Tuesday when the flights were canceled, we were over eighteen hundred in this terminal—by my estimation. The majority beat it out of here on foot and whatever, so that by now there are around six hundred left. Most of them are inside there," he said, pointing.

"And you all gathered here in this terminal?" Arnie asked.

"Of course. There was no other place to go. We were in transit to various places—I was on my way to Tokyo when this happened—so we were stranded."

Trying to be encouraging, Arnie said, "You will all be picked up, but we were just sent here to take some measurements on the radiation levels. We have no way of getting you out in that craft. It's too small."

"Yes. We understand that," answered the man. "Can you tell us how extensive this is—how bad?"

"We're not sure, yet," answered Arnie. "I guess we won't know until the advance squads get in here and establish some order to things."

"Are many people....dead?" inquired a woman from the group.

"We have no way of determining that at this time," he

answered. "It'll very likely take weeks before we can say. But once the radiation level is sufficiently low, rescue squads will be pouring in for you."

It was then that Cecil noticed the physical appearances of the victims. Rigors of their ordeal plainly showed on their countenances. Physiological deterioration was prominent in a few, but most visibly suffered from lack of food, water, and rest. Beyond that, they showed fewer of the signs of radiation sickness than he had expected to see. But then, these people were probably the healthiest of the survivors.

"Some of our people are suffering awfully," said the spokesman. "Why don't you come over to the terminal and see for yourselves?" he asked, motioning them toward the building.

Carrying the counter, Cecil fell into step with Arnie and the speaker. They crossed to the terminal entrance, quickly forming a file. Automatic doors no longer swung open from the pressure of a foot on the rubber mat. Instead, the group trailed through a huge hole in the glass and quietly walked a long hall to a concourse at the base of the escalators. There, lying about on red plastic seats from the waiting lounges, were the remainder of the travelers. An awful stench pervaded the stale air. Huge blister-like lesions were common on many, but the odor didn't seem to originate with the festering skin disorders, or intestinal upsets that many had suffered.

Arnie seemed to think the stench excessively strong as a weak but audible gag escaped his mouth. Quickly he threw his hand up as though to stifle another such reflex, and turned his head away.

Motioning them to follow, the spokesman led Archie and Cecil to a narrow room at the side of the concourse. Privy to the means for opening the door, he unlocked it, but held on to the knob. "We didn't know what else to do with them," he said, "so we decided to just store them for awhile." With that he pushed the door wide and the most malodorous air wafted out to them.

Flicking on a flashlight, he cast a beam across the interior of the chamber. Lying in rows, were the bodies of those who had succumbed over the past four days.

"That's really something, isn't it? Look at them. Most of them appear perfectly fit," the group leader observed.

They did form an eerie collection there on the cold floor. Superficially, they seemed like absolutely healthy people who had, with alarming suddenness, died. No bandages and no

178

broken, misshapen limbs were present. There were no open wounds, no purplish bruises. Except for the pallor of death, and fixed expressions of pain on their faces, they appeared to be asleep.

The ghastly waxen bodies and sickeningly sweet odor of decaying flesh was enough to send Arnie stumbling back out the door to the concourse.

In Cecil's mind was the incongruity of the generally more able persons he had seen upon arrival and these dead testaments to the ravages of radiation. "How strange," he said, as he observed them.

The spokesman agreed. "It was really hard to believe. They'd begin to feel sick—by Tuesday night and Wednesday was when we first started noticing them—and then they'd get very weak. Within a day they'd become so helpless that they couldn't move. They'd complain of pain. Then, without any other warning, they'd die. Just die." said the man as he played the light on them.

"By Wednesday, you say?" asked Cecil. "In such a short time?" He was thinking that the radiation would have been exceedingly high to cause such early deaths.

The other nodded. "I was lucky, I guess. I knew a little about radiation. I was a lance corporal in World War II and my company ended up in Japan right after we dropped those two A-bombs. I'll never forget the sight of some of those poor devils—it's haunted me for all these years."

Cecil understood. "The devastation must have impressed you."

"You're not kidding," said the spokesman as he steered Cecil out of the small room and into the concourse. "I was a tinhorn medic at the time and we got some of the Jap casualties to treat. You know, ever since then I've read nearly everything I could lay my hands on about radiation."

"Are you a doctor?" asked Cecil.

"No. I run an import business, in Dallas. That's why I was on my way to Tokyo. You may have heard of me if you've been in Texas. My name is George Fenimoore Kingsley of Kingsley Enterprises."

"Glad to make your acquaintance, Mr. Kingsley. I'm Cecil Yeager. The pilot of the chopper is Arnie."

Arnie was finding the odor repulsive to his sensitive stomach. His brain held an image of the rows of bodies and the

179

recollection caused goose bumps to race down his arms. By all calculations there must have been at least three dozen forms incarcerated in the darkened chamber. He had sought an area of fresh air since leaving the gruesome chamber, but had yet to find it. "I'd like to do a check on the upper level," he announced as he started up the frozen escalator. The others fell in behind him.

"You know, last Tuesday was a fair day for traveling," said George. "By nine o'clock in the morning, the terminals had very few passengers in comparison to what they'd have been like on a Saturday—or Friday afternoon. I had an hour lay-over and was in the waiting lounge reading when the public address system brought the bad news."

"That must have been a hell of a shock to you," suggested Arnie, taking the steps two at a time.

George appraised the younger man from under his hooded lids before he replied. "Shock? Hell, it scared the daylights out of me. But you know, most of these jokers acted as if nothing had happened—that is, for awhile. When all incoming and outgoing flights were canceled, they began to get the message."

"How did they act?" asked Cecil with interest.

"Why, just like a bunch of rats leaving a sinking ship," he said. "First, there was a lot of talk and yelling, then someone broke out running. The next thing I knew everybody was running and screaming. They trampled anybody who got knocked down....just stomped one old lady to death."

Cecil asked, "What were you doing, George, with no place to go?"

"Well, I was like some others. Caught here, out of pocket, we didn't have any choice but to stay put. There wouldn't have been any point in checking into a hotel, anyway," he said.

"Actually, that concourse is probably one of the safest areas people could have been to avoid a lot of the radiation," commented Cecil. "Down there in the center of this huge building you'd be shielded by several rather thick walls and floors. Presumably, many did stay down in the center of the terminal. Otherwise, there'd have been more casualties than there are."

They had reached the upper level by now, a level almost completely walled in by thick, tinted-glass plates.

"Yeah, I knew that," George replied. "But for the life of me I couldn't convince some of those folks to go down to the concourse. They'd sit in here, gazing out through those tinted glass windows, talking nonsense—like any minute they expected a big jet to pull up and take them aboard."

The men were standing a floor above the concourse and were staring out across acres of pavement. To some, a favorite pastime at any airport was watching the jets being steered along the white lines until they were even with the passenger ramp— or listening to the huge engines being revved, in preparation for flight. For them, the excitement would be hard to recapture after today.

George remarked, "Frankly, I'd bet that nearly every one of those people in that little room below had spent most of his time right here by these windows."

"It's difficult to persuade some people that something—like radiation—that they can't see and can't feel, is harmful to them," murmured Cecil, gazing out over the field below.

"Don't I know that!" George replied.

They moved back down to the concourse, and threaded their way out toward the terminal entrance, anxious to get back outside.

Streams of morning sunlight were scattering over the airport, highlighting the broad Century Boulevard, and lending an air of normality to the entire complex of pavements and buildings. Climatically, it was going to be a pretty day.

George stepped in closer to Cecil, and leaned toward the box-like instrument Cecil carried. He put his hand out, touching it. "What does your counter say?" he asked.

Cecil flicked on a tiny switch and checked the numerals on the dial. "Here, on the Street, around one hundred rads."

"A hundred. I, uh, never did get the hang of that word rad," George said. "What does it mean in relation to hazard potential?"

Cecil had acquired a healthy respect for the Texan. In all probability, the man had been responsible for saving many of the hundreds of lives now awaiting relief in that building. "Rad is the term used to describe a given amount of absorbed radiation." Cecil's cheek twitched after he completed the statement—it always twitched when he had given an explanation of something that had no relevancy, no coherency to the listener. "Rad is often used interchangeably with roentgen. Whereas rad refers to absorption in soft tissue, roentgen refers to a measure of radiation exposure in air," he explained. "This machine is old. Now they use a newer term called millisieverts.

They all are just a measure of what radiation is out there."

George was still looking at the speaker, waiting for the moment when something would be said that he understood. When he realized that Cecil had finished, and that no other elaboration was intended, he shrugged his shoulders, a weak smile on his lips. "Well, I guess I'm too dense for your kind of talk, Cecil. I was just wondering about how dangerous it is out here right now."

"Maybe an example would shed light on the subject," Cecil hastened to add. "For instance, it is believed that a dose of radiation in the range of four hundred fifty rads would result in death for the majority of people. Above that, very, very few, if any, would survive doses as high as one thousand rads."

The statistics were sinking in, as George listened with his head slightly bowed.

"However," continued the scientist, "very few, if any, would die following exposures up to two hundred fifty rads."

"How high do you suppose it got during the thermal inversion?" asked the Texan.

"I wouldn't even want to guess, George. Eventually, the radiation extreme will be calculated, but I don't think we'd have any means of knowing precisely—it'll just be an educated guess."

"That people have died from the radiation is fairly conclusive proof that it got high, though. Up to four hundred fifty or above?" asked George.

Cecil didn't wish to demoralize the man, but still he wouldn't lie to him, either. He'd give his own estimate. "Yes, I'd say it got well above four hundred fifty. But I wouldn't want to speculate on the upper level." Noticing the other's concern, he said, "You're in good shape, George. Very good shape. I wouldn't think you should worry. Down in the concourse you were reasonably well protected from the radiation, and generally speaking, the smaller the dose, the better it can be tolerated."

The older man lifted his gaze to Cecil. "I understand that there's a ten-to-twenty year latency period for the development of cancerous tumors—from radiation exposures. That's what we, who survive this, have to look forward to. Some future, huh?" he said bitterly.

Cecil couldn't deny the truth of those remarks. He couldn't find anything appropriate to say. The silence was embarrassing.

"When will the rescue team arrive for us? George finally

asked.

Glancing at his watch, Cecil replied, "It's after eight o'clock. They were instructed to start rolling at the same time we got our orders to move. Of course, they're traveling via the highways, and not too fast. But I figure they should reach the city in a couple hours, at the latest."

George nodded.

"Arnie will call in for a medical detail to be flown to you folks, though," promised Cecil. "As soon as he phones, a squad should be in the air within a few minutes. So it shouldn't be too much longer, George."

He and Arnie returned to their helicopter, gave a short salute to the lone man on the sidewalk, and flew off in the direction of their second destination.

Once clear of the airport, Arnie put in the call to his command center. He rapidly relayed the news of the conditions they had found at the site. Although Cecil could not hear the conversation at the other end, he knew by the pilot's comments that instructions for proceeding directly to the second reading site had been somewhat altered. When the call was terminated, he asked, "What's changed, Arnie?"

The pilot answered, "Seems someone is worried about the condition of the County Art Museum. We are to go straight there and report on what we find." His tone indicated bewilderment.

Cecil didn't question him further, but sat back in the bucket seat and routed their journey on Arnie's map of the city. He hastily pinpointed the area, then checked the scene below.

"Isn't it on Wilshire, Cecil?" asked the pilot as he searched for familiar structures.

"Right," said Cecil. "I think we're over the boulevard now. Veer eastward and we should spot it pretty easily. It's by Hancock Park."

Wilshire Boulevard cut its swath through the business district of gleaming modern buildings, its peculiar absence of people and traffic marking this as an unusual day. They followed the street for no more than a couple minutes when Cecil spotted the park below. "That's it, Arnie," he said, pointing. "That's Hancock Park, and the La Brea Tar Pits next to the museum."

The park was its lovely serene self of natural foliage and lush beds of flowers bordering the expanse of brilliant green, if somewhat overgrown, lawn.

Arnie seemed impressed, not by the beauty of the park so

183

much as the huge pits of black bubbling tar. "We sure don't want to set this bird in the middle of one of those pits, Cecil," he said as they slowly circled the area. "Which one is the museum?" he asked.

"The white building there," Cecil replied.

Without hesitation, Arnie lowered the craft into the center of Wilshire Boulevard and cut the rotors. Before moving from his seat, he looked toward the many steps leading up to the front of the museum.

Cecil detected the hesitation, almost a reluctance, in the pilot to go inside, but he didn't say anything.

Finally, Arnie heaved a sigh and unbuckled his seat belt. "Well, I guess I'd better go on in," he said.

"Do you want me to go in with you?" asked Cecil.

Arnie seemed relieved. "Yeah. I wish you would. I....the commander said that there might be some kind of trouble in there, Cecil."

Cecil watched Arnie checking around the cab of the chopper — the sort of thing that might be done if he were searching for a weapon. Indeed, Arnie's fist closed around the handle of a wrench, and then he started exiting the plane.

Unwilling to ask his motive for the wrench, Cecil got out and walked side by side with Arnie up the flights of stairs. They paused at the entrance to the museum. Its glass doors had been smashed to slivers. Cecil looked expectantly at Arnie. The young man had paled, and his fist clenched the wrench until his knuckles were white under the skin. Together, they walked on through the foyer, their feet making crunching noises as they carefully eased over the shards of glass.

They hesitated at the inner door, and listened. There were no sounds from within. Using the head of the wrench, Arnie pushed the door in, and they stepped cautiously inside. The main chamber was an ordinary, empty viewing room. Its gray walls, the repositories of masterpieces of paintings, had been gutted.

Cecil moved over to the nearest framework of a painting. It was a large square case that had been built nearly flush with the wall. Covering it had been a three quarter inch thick plate of plexiglass, a special precaution taken to prohibit defacing of the work. The painting was now gone—as were all the others that had been on display. He didn't need to ask Arnie the significance of this bit of thievery. He knew.

Arnie mumbled under his breath, "Every God-damned one is

gone." When at last he turned to Cecil, he said, "This is really going to raise a stink. Jesus, is it ever! Cecil, this was a Russian exhibition, and now every one of their damned paintings has been stolen!"

"Yes, I know," answered Cecil. "I was in here looking at these two weeks ago. The exhibit was a collection of impressionistic art—Picasso, Gauguin, Van Gogh—they're priceless pieces."

"And they're gone," Arnie reiterated. "I got to call in about this, Cecil," and he hurried out the door.

Cecil took one fast reading, duly recorded the radiation level, and trailed Arnie back to the chopper.

When his report to the command center was completed, Arnie asked, "What do you make of those paintings being gone, Cecil?"

It was a nebulous question from the youthful pilot. In his precise manner, Cecil formed an answer. "If you're thinking about the diplomatic angle, I'd say the Russians are going to be very upset by this. They haven't been all that eager to make cultural exchanges with the United States, anyway. And now, with such a valuable collection gone....well, I'd imagine they'll come out with some nasty accusations about how those paintings disappeared."

"You're thinking this will add some heat to the cold war?" suggested Arnie.

"Undoubtedly," Cecil replied. "There have been masterpieces on loan to the museum before, but these were the first ones that had to hang behind those extra thick plates of glass. The Russians made a big to-do about special packing for shipment and special protection while the paintings were on display. It almost seemed that they expected the art-work to be sabotaged somewhere along the way."

Arnie said, "But there must have been guards stationed with the exhibit, then. Someone beside the regular museum staff."

"No, I don't believe there were. At least, not when I was in here to see them," answered Cecil. "Not that it really matters whether guards had been here or not. Once White Water went, everybody would have been expected to make himself his primary concern."

"Well, it looks like somebody was enterprising enough to get in there and take every blasted painting. Man, he must have been crazy to come into the radiation for them."

Cecil fastened his seat belt before replying. "I don't see it as

185

having been such a gamble, Arnie. Not when you weigh the hazards against the value of the paintings. Not for someone who had a plan to remove them quickly, then get away."

Arnie looked at his partner quizzically. His face showed respect for the shrewd brain of the chemist. "You sound like you could have done it yourself, Cecil," he said lightly.

Cecil checked the belt and settled back in the seat. "No, not me, Arnie," he answered. "But I do have an idea about the system. I've always thought that if you understood the system, you could beat it." His gaze returned to the front of the museum, and came to rest on the scum covered reflecting pool. "That's what it really takes to stay ahead," he added.

For Arnie, the subject was getting a little deep. "We've got three more reading sites to cover, Cecil. I guess we'd better get on with it," he said, not completely understanding Cecil.

"Arnie, when we're finished, I'd like to be dropped off at the spot where my friends are to be." Cecil used the term 'friends' loosely. What he had in mind was re-joining the volunteer crew from the little mountain town.

"Sure," Arnie replied. "No problem. Our work will be over after the third stop."

In the recesses of every mind there lurks an indomitable fear of the unknown. It may lie dormant in courageous souls, only to rear its ugly head over the foot of the death bed. In others, it surfaces unexpectedly on a darkened street in the late of night, and in some, in the middle of a sunny morning. To those men traversing the roadways on a clear, warm California day, fear had been well hidden, placed far and deep in the crevices of gray matter. As in others before them, they had no knowledge of the sort of things to expect within the irradiated area. But as the trucks and jeeps hauled them nearer, more than a few hearts began to entertain doubts and fears.

As a militia, the members had been taught to think in terms of wartime experiences. But for many, this was their first real military effort. Consequently, as instructions were relayed and segments of the troop procession would peel away from the security of the long procession, lonely anxieties invaded the troopers. This wasn't an action of war. There were no alien men bombarding them with missiles from behind thick embankments. Each man carried a weapon and his job had been clearly spelled out. Working in a buddy system of twos, they were to locate and report on persons within each area via their

186

about more seedy sections of the city was nowhere to be seen.

Far ahead, in the glare of the pre-noon sun, a lanky figure darted across the pavement and toward one of the residences. Carter? And if so, which house was he headed for? Cecil quickened his pace and closed the distance between where he had stood and where he thought the man to have been.

If Carter's objective wasn't any particular house, the long, covered form lying near the hedge of this little bungalow would certainly have attracted his attention. Cecil, short on breath from the exertion of running, walked over to the bundle. From its length and thickness, he did not have to peek inside to know what it contained. This was the vicinity where he thought he had seen Carter. Yet, nothing moved. There was no sign of him now. Cecil considered what the scarecrow had told him. In light of that, vacant houses would offer the greatest prospects for looting. But Cecil doubted that Carter genuinely wished to find all the houses vacant.

Any effort on her part would be fruitless now, thought Althea. She had maintained a close vigil over her mother during the endless night. Once the elderly woman drifted into unconsciousness, forcing liquid down her throat had become an impossibility. Near dawn, her vital signs had further weakened, leaving the daughter no choice but to stay helplessly by as her mother gradually entered a comatose state. With no means for administering intravenous fluids, and no insulin, death was inevitable.

Her breathing, the greedy gasping of air, was less labored, less pronounced, as the pulse rate grew increasingly weaker. To an uncritical observer, the symptoms might have appeared as a remission, but Althea recognized the changes as a sign that her mother was slipping into a slow, if painless, death. It was now painless, because the body is uniquely endowed with the ability to enter into a state of profound insensibility when confronted with extreme and extensive suffering.

The sound of the kitchen door being softly shut did not go unnoticed by Althea. She had been unaware of the stationing of a rescue unit, as near as three-and-a-half blocks from her home over an hour ago. Therefore, any intruder entering uninvited surely would have sinister motives.

She felt shivers of fright course through her body at the unexpected sound. Speedily, she crossed the floor, reached the door of the bedroom and was shoving it closed when an

189

explosive force smashed into the door, shoving her back against the wall.

Stepping into the room was a misshapen, disfigured gargoyle of a man. Greasy black hair fell into his face, partially hiding the gash of a mouth and its jagged, yellow teeth. His torso was little more than a skeleton covered with grayish white skin, and submerged beneath loose fitting, dirty clothes. "Ah ha, what have we here?" he cackled. "A poor lady in distress."

He moved closer to Althea, beckoning to her with long dirty fingers.

She stepped backward, her hand wildly searching for an object, something to hold. "Stay away from me!" she threatened.

He advanced toward her, his face split by a leering grin. "Now missy, don't you go getting upset. Carter doesn't like his women to get loud." His grotesque smiled broadened.

"Stay where you are!" she shouted as she moved away from him. "You stay away from me!" She saw him as he lowered himself into a partial crouch. There was nothing to use as a weapon, yet she knew that he would hurtle himself toward her, and she prepared herself for it.

As she had anticipated, his skinny body shot out at her. But as he lunged, she hastily stepped aside, and eluded him. "Get out of here! You have no business in my house!" she yelled.

He straightened himself. "Heh, heh, heh. You don't really want me to leave, missy. Oh no, you'll like me."

She managed to get the boudoir chair between them, but this put her with her back to the corner, completely at his mercy.

Grinning fiendishly, he grabbed the chair and sent it into her, pinning her in place. "Aha! Now I've got you!"

Trapped in the corner, her mother on the bed a few feet away, Althea watched his drooling mouth as he leaned toward her. His tiny eyes were bright with a feverish excitement as he jettisoned long bony hands forward, and knotted his fingers in her clothing. Then he kicked the chair aside, and pulled her to him, hideously laughing all the while.

She lashed at him with all her strength, leaving four trails of raw flesh imprinted on his face.

His laughter continued as his fist bit into her cheek, spinning her head sideways.

Five days of grief, pain, and a lack of nourishment had left her physically debilitated, but it hadn't damaged her determination. She twisted free and launched her razor sharp fingernails straight at the orbit of his eye. A warm clear fluid flooded over her fingertips, and his laughter changed to screams of pain.

The darkness that fell over the collapsed eyeball added intense anger to his pain. Lashing out as the humor flooded down his cheek, his blow caught her again on the side of the head, and this one staggered her, leaving her brain a maze of flashing lights. Her legs buckled. Her body crumpled, and she felt the floor under her and above, the squirming bony creature shoving her farther down. Unable to escape, she felt the blows raining on her body, pummeling it into submission. Her strength to resist left her as the blows repeatedly slammed into her head and chest. She felt consciousness begin to slip away.

Then his weight was abruptly gone. Standing over the intruder was a stocky, squarely built man whose foot was directly between the other's shoulder blades, and his hands in the black oily hair. Pressing the foot in, he simultaneously yanked the head back. A dull, but distinct, snap was heard emanating from the vertebrae of the intruder's neck.

It was quiet in the bedroom. The assault, the din, had ended.

Althea's attacker was on his side, completely motionless, but mumbling incoherencies. His salivating lips were all that moved.

Cecil stared at his handiwork, then at Althea's—at the eyeball. The woman, still slightly stunned, began getting upright. He reached for her and gently helped her into a sitting position. "Are you all right?" inquired Cecil.

"Yes. I...I, guess," she answered uncertainly.

She avoided looking at the vacant, deflated eyeball in the body, but gaped at the strange position of her attacker's head. "He...His head is strange."

Cecil stared down at Carter. "Yes."

She looked up at the man who had rescued her. "Is his neck broken?"

"Uh huh. I believe so," he replied without interest.

She scrutinized the big man. "Are....are you with a rescue unit?" she asked, hoping desperately he was.

"Yes," he answered quietly. "Troops are coming in all over the city." Cecil's palms were sticky with grease from Carter's hair, a repulsive feeling that he eliminated by wiping against his trousers. "I'll get this guy out of here for you."

"It wouldn't be wise to move him, if his neck is broken, would it?" said Althea, trying to be lucid.

"No, ma'am. It wouldn't," he answered, still looking at Carter. Althea winced as she pulled her feet under her. Cecil helped, but it was an effort for her to get up. Her left foot looked particularly repugnant. In the scuffle the outer side had ruptured from the small toe back to the heel and was now a yawning wound that released a mixture of yellow and red fluids on the carpet. The foot was worsening, but for the moment, there was a more important matter. Hobbling, she went over to her mother's bed and felt the limp wrist. "My mother is dead," she finally said. "She has been in a coma and she died while...." Her voice gave way to soft sobbing.

Cecil looked at the gray hair and the worn wrinkled features of the elderly woman. "She's at peace," he said softly. Aware of the sobs, he dragged the chair over and waited until the daughter collapsed into it.

Unintelligible mutterings still came from the man on the floor. Returning to Carter, Cecil took an ankle in each hand and began pulling toward the open door. His tug at the ankles pulled the body straight, and a short gasp left the man—the very last sound that Carter made.

Althea had covered her mother with the sheet and was waiting when the chemist returned. Her tears had not quite dried, but her composure was regained. "Is he dead?" she asked.

"Yes," he answered. "I removed him to the yard." Suddenly he seemed uncomfortable in the small bedroom. "Are you ready to leave?" he asked, avoiding her eyes.

She hesitated. "I don't want to leave my parents here. My father is dead, too; he's in the garden. What can I do for them?" asked the woman with concern.

"You're our first consideration," said Cecil. "The government has established recuperation spas throughout the state. Everyone who is willing, will be sent to one. But before that, you ought to be examined by a doctor."

She was now a haggard, trembling, emaciated woman whose fine, dark features were accentuated by her gauntness. But despite her thinness and the pain, and fear that even yet showed in her eyes, the beauty of the woman was readily noticeable to Cecil.

"No, I can't abandon my mother and father. I couldn't rest at all, not knowing what was being done for them," she said.

"Don't worry. I'll take care of them for you," he promised. "I'll make certain that they're decently buried and the sites marked. When you return, if you decide to, you'll know exactly where to find them."

Althea searched his face. Then hesitantly she took a step. Moving on the spongy pustules encrusting her feet caused both limbs to become aching, throbbing clubs. She reached out to Cecil. He slid his arm around her waist, and suspended hers over his shoulder. In this manner, Althea was gently led to the encampment of the medical unit.

Nearly sixty miles south of Log Angeles, in an unincorporated area, the Harrington home sat on a large plot of land, commanding a sweeping view of the ocean. It was a setting from which Ben and Sara had often drawn peace together.

Sara admitted the men into the living room with just a hint of formality, stopping short of inviting them to be seated. Their rapid arrival had been unforeseen, and Sara was slightly discomfited by her unkempt appearance before them. Educated in Europe, and prepped for a life as a gracious lady, she had deeply rooted ideas as to how one coped with problems; appearances were important. A well bred, cultured person always presented a stiff upper lip in the face of adversity. And here, she had been momentarily caught off guard.

One of the men, sensing her discomfiture, got right to the point. "Mrs. Harrington, since your husband was at the reactor when the accident occurred, I believe his, uh, his body would be of special interest. I hope you don't mind, but I've requested that the chief pathologist be here for Mr. Harrington's removal."

Sara, though wondering about the significance of what he'd said, raised no objection. She sat down with the two men, sensing some semblance of order returning to her life; the nightmare was now drawing to a close. They talked, politely avoiding further mention of Ben's body, as they awaited the arrival of the medical examiner.

Admiration was plainly obvious in the men as they observed Sara's controlled efforts after the long, arduous ordeal. She was dead tired, hungry, and thirsty. Small aches dully throbbed in her body. She was disheveled and grimy after the past four days. Her husband was dead in a room down the hall. Nevertheless, she calmly and with preciseness for detail, recounted the events of the accident, as described by Ben, and the horrors that

193

followed. She talked without interruption for almost an hour.

A whirring of blades informed them of the medical examiner's arrival. Shortly, the chief pathologist stepped into the room, his hand extended. "Mrs. Harrington, I'm Dr. Elrod Seevers from the Surgeon General's staff. I'm sorry we had to meet under these circumstances." He was a balding, short man, wearing black horn rimmed glasses. "Your husband was a supervisor at White Water, I've been told," he said in his rapid-fire speech.

Sara nodded in assent, wondering what action he planned.

The pathologist aggressively pushed ahead with his idea. "While you may consider this an indelicate suggestion, it is my opinion that your husband's remains would be invaluable to medical research, Mrs. Harrington."

She stared at him, as one might who viewed a poisonous snake from the other side of a glass partition. She hadn't realized that such a request would be made of her. With a quick flash of anger, she said, "Dr. Seevers, your proposal is contemptible—an insult to Benjamin Harrington's memory. The man gave his life for his work. It's too much to expect that his body would be a contribution to science in addition."

Her unruffled composure belied her simmering interior and caught the pathologist unaware. He had anticipated her immediate compliance. "I apologize to you," he said quickly. "However, there is great likelihood that the course of this nation's future and its reliance on nuclear energy for peacetime uses may be decided from this recent catastrophe. Any information gleaned from this terrible tragedy must be weighed with regard to the best interests of the American people." He spoke in haste, as though there were much to be done, and this was only one of many tasks facing him, that Ben's was only one of many bodies to claim.

He paused to allow his statements time to be mentally digested before continuing. "Naturally, no one desires to pressure you into granting us the medical use of his body against your wishes. The decision is entirely yours to make," he stated.

A silence followed as Sara considered his arguments.

Two aides entered the room, carrying a stretcher on which rested a long, empty canvas bag. They hesitated, uncertain, then moved out into the hall until their superior was ready to issue instructions, to tell them to take the body or leave it.

"Where would he be taken—out of state, I presume?" asked

Sara at last.

"Oh yes, to Washington, D.C." He hastened to explain, "The condition of his tissues after all his exposure to the radiation could tell us much about the sort of damage done, and thereby, perhaps, lead us to devise medications and treatments to allay such effects," he remarked as he glanced at the watch on his wrist. "Thus far, we have nothing to combat radiation sickness."

Sara wasn't to be rushed into making a hasty decision, however. "Wouldn't you think that a more acceptable method than dealing with the effects of radiation would be to simply prevent those facilities from producing radiation—from being developed—in the first place, Doctor?" she asked in a biting voice.

"Yes. Yes," he agreed readily. "But I am only a man of medicine, Mrs. Harrington. I'm not politically motivated. Such things as safeguards for nuclear reactors is not my concern." He hesitated, seemingly reluctant to spend more valuable time in discussion with the woman. He glanced at the aides waiting in the hall, then back to Sara. "My concern is with locating the proper subjects to provide a basis for research."

It was a cold, hard statement that he'd made, speaking of the victims of White Water as though they were so many research animals. To be studied, autopsied, and converted into statistics. With revulsion Sara thought of Ben's final importance divulged in the tale told by his poor, mangled tissues. A wave of nausea spread through her, and was rapidly fought down. "Isn't it interesting, Doctor," she asked, "that until Tuesday, this sort of accident had been declared an impossibility?"

Peering through his thick lenses, he observed the woman sitting across from him. He considered the question momentarily, then finally remarked, "Shall we say that what was formerly impossible, has happened? And now the question in most minds is exactly what kinds of damages have been done."

Sara thoughtfully tugged at a rent in her dress. "You seem to be a very busy man, Dr. Seevers."

He removed his glasses and dried the perspiration on the frame. "Yes, there is much to be done," he replied as he replaced the spectacles.

"Then I will not take more of your time, Doctor. You may take Ben's body with you."

Seevers showed no surprise at her decision. Wiping his brow with a handkerchief, he said, "Thank you, Mrs. Harrington.

195

Yours is a compassionate and noble gesture, one of which I'm sure your husband would approve." After a slight hesitation, he added, "There is no reason why you could not have services for Mr. Harrington before assigning him to us."

"Yes, I'd like that," said Sara. "We are from the east coast originally and we have relatives there. Yes, we'll have a private service for Ben back in Connecticut," she said at last.

"In that case I will arrange transportation for both you and your husband," said the pathologist.

His habit of referring to Ben as though he still lived was annoying to her, but she was reconciled to placing both of them in the doctor's seemingly capable hands for the present. "Are there papers that I must sign declaring my permission has been granted," she asked.

Dr. Seevers nodded, "Yes, but they need not be dealt with today. There is time enough for that, Mrs. Harrington."

He flicked his hand to the aides; they, in turn, moved quietly into the bedroom to begin their grisly chore.

Ben's death was forever in her thoughts, but now there were other considerations. "Dr. Seevers, what sort of protection has been established for our homes and belongings that we are leaving behind?" Not that she had any intention of staying, but she hated to think that the beautiful house with its collection from six years of marriage would be looted and stripped.

With calming reassurances, he replied, "Sentries will be posted throughout the whole sector, I'm told. Military personnel will be designated to guard against the unlawful taking and destruction of property. Mrs. Harrington, you needn't worry."

A far away look passed quickly over her face, then she said, "it's impossible to imagine this vast area being abandoned. Why, millions of dollars in possessions will be left behind as people flee their homes."

"I'm certain many, many residents will not leave," said the pathologist. "There is no place for them to go, and for a variety of reasons they'll choose to stay, I think."

"But how?" she asked in disbelief. "What will they do for water, for instance?"

The little physician repeated what he had been told. "According to the latest decision made, emergency supplies of water and food will be trucked in. Sources of community water that were contained in reservoirs will have to be expelled through the sewers into the ocean. It's not usable as it is.

Refilling the reservoirs will take quite awhile. And until unpolluted, clean water is made available, the citizens who stay must make do with having it hauled in to them."

The impact of lack of water was to be keenly felt for the next several months, not just to the populace who would be forced into a strict, skimpy allotment for the barest of emergency uses, but for commercial and industrial purposes, there would be no clean water available.

"Eventually electricity will be restored, I suppose?" asked Sara, recalling the feeble flames of alcohol lamps at Beckman Hospital.

"Engineers and crews are being brought in to put the oil-burning plants back into operation," he replied, "but for a very minimal output. For Los Angeles and these smaller cities to get their feet back on the ground, it is going to take longer than we thought, I'm afraid." Seevers glanced at his watch a second time.

Sara had grown tired of the conversation. The physician was anxious to be about his gruesome business and she was eager to have an end to the movements and the muffled conversation in Ben's bedroom.

Hearing the aides finishing their chore, Dr. Seevers took Sara away from her chair and turned her aside so that she would not see the aides as they came by.

The canvas bag, taut from its contents, was borne slowly through the hall, through the front entrance, and into the helicopter.

To him, the chore was completed. "Mrs. Harrington, when you are ready we can depart."

"If there is time, I'd like to gather a few items to take along," said Sara.

"Of course," he replied. "We'll wait."

Sara started out of the room, then paused and said to him, "By the way, Doctor, there is a man, a body on the rear lawn. He was our gardener. I couldn't very well leave him here in the house, since he died Tuesday," she said with detachment. "Perhaps you will want to look at him."

The pathologist accepted her statement without any show of concern. "He has been outside since Tuesday, you say?"

"Yes. For four days," she said as she walked out of the room. Summoning his aides, he ordered them to prepare the remaining corpse for removal. "And rush it up," he added.

197

As assistants to the pathologist, the two men had often performed unpleasant tasks. But the prospects of bagging a body that had lain in the hot sun for several days promised to be their most repulsive encounter.

"Shit," mumbled the younger member as he strolled across the flagstone patio, "why doesn't he do it himself if he wants to drag every rotten carcass back with us."

His companion poked him in the ribs, "Hush! You want him to hear you?" he asked, glancing back toward the physician.

"I don't give a damn. When I took this job I didn't know everything that went with it, so I don't figure they're paying me enough for this kind of work," answered his friend petulantly.

"Aw, quit your bitching. Nobody is making you hang onto the job," replied his companion as they stepped into the yard.

"Jeez, lookee there! Somebody rolled the dude up like a mummy!" said the younger man. "Bet he stinks when we get him out of that plastic." He stared through the wrapping at the corpse.

They cautiously began the process of unwinding the translucent covering, anticipating the moment when a foul odor would escape from the package and soil the air they breathed.

"This dude is going to be a mess to get in the bag," remarked the complainer, cutting the plastic away in layers.

Finally the body was free, its wrappings to the side.

"Man, look at that!" exclaimed the youth. "I can't believe it!"

"Hey, I'd better call Doc Seevers. He'll want to see this one before it goes in the sack," said his companion, rushing off.

Returning with his superior in tow, the two walked directly to the corpse. The doctor dropped to his knees beside the body and began a visual examination of the face, hands, and hair. "This is hard to believe. According to Mrs. Harrington, this man has been out here since Tuesday, but he surely doesn't seem in any state of decomposition—not at all what you'd expect."

"That's weird, really weird, Doc. He's in perfect shape, like he could have just died."

The physician, still stooping, gazed thoughtfully at the excellently preserved form. "She said she'd rolled him up in a plastic sheet. Was it tight, boys? Did the sheet fit him snugly?"

"Like a glove. She really did a job on him. But why didn't he... decay?" asked the younger man. "I'd have figured him for rotten."

"Yeah, I can't figure that either," commented the other aide.

"I once helped load a guy that had been drowned, and had washed onto a bank. He'd been there about a week when we got the word to pick him up. Wow, I'd never smelled anything like it." He shuddered at the memory. "He was falling apart when we got to him."

Dr. Seevers stroked his chin as he continued to stare at the corpse. "You know, boys, this is very interesting. Yes indeed. Mrs. Harrington covered him tightly preventing air from freely circulating around the body. That would reduce the rate of growth of decay bacteria. Then, radiation was constantly pouring down into the man, irradiating and killing any decay organisms that ordinarily would have resulted in deterioration of tissues. In essence, the body was preserved by irradiation."

"You make it sound like a new method for preserving food," remarked the young aide.

"No, not new. Irradiation of food was used as a means of conserving texture and taste a decade ago. It prevented spoilage successfully, but never did quite catch on as a preservative. I recall seeing pork chops that had been kept unrefrigerated, in paper for several months. They were still fresh enough, yet no one volunteered to cook and eat them."

"They wouldn't have been harmful, would they?" asked the aide.

"No, of course not, It's just that no one in our group wanted to try them out," he answered shortly.

"Well, that guy's head is not in very good shape. That's a hell of a bruise over his temple," noted the other aide.

Drawing closer to the inert form, the physician carefully scrutinized the wound. At last he stepped away and said, "Bag him." As he turned back toward the house, he called out, "Mrs. Harrington! I'd like to talk to you."

Sara filled a large purse with personal items but paused in her packing when she heard his call from the patio. "Yes, Dr. Seevers?" Her tone verged on haughtiness.

"This man, your gardener—his, uh, remains are in superb condition, Mrs. Harrington. Much, much better than we had expected."

Since the woman offered no comment, the doctor elaborated further. "You did a splendid job in covering him, a splendid job," he said, watching her carefully.

"Should I say that I am pleased, Doctor?"

Her flippancy had surprised the doctor somewhat, causing

uncertainty as to how the issue should be discussed. After all, the woman had undergone great mental stress, and yet had managed to show real composure in arriving at the decision to donate her husband's body for medical exploration. Insistence on her clarification of the method of the gardener's death could prove to be inhumanly cruel in light of her earlier traumas.

"I hardly know where to begin," he stammered. "I...."

"You are concerned over how the man died, is that correct?"

"Yes. That bruise on the side of his head, it seems...."

Again she interrupted him. "Perhaps I'd better explain, Dr. Seevers. You see, last Tuesday, things became hectic for those of us living close to White Water. By evening, the word had thoroughly circulated about the dangers. Presumably, those who had decided to stay on rather than run, were fairly panic-struck. Looting and stealing had already begun and I....well, I naturally thought Ben was dead," she said softly. "It was nearly dusk when the gardener burst into the house and began throwing my silver and jewels into a bag—a total shock to me."

"He had worked for you some time, Mrs. Harrington?" asked the pathologist.

"Yes. Several years." She paused in her narration to reconstruct the actual events, then continued, "Anyway, when I discovered the thief, I tried to stop him. He became abusive, then threatened my life. He was reaching for a tool from the fireplace at the exact moment that poor Ben miraculously staggered into the house." Once more she paused. "You can imagine my surprise to see my husband, Doctor. He was in dreadful shape, but alive. Seeing the gardener threatening me with the tool infuriated him and he..." she hesitated, "well, he..."

"He killed the gardener, Mrs. Harrington?"

Sara answered softly, "Yes. As unbelievable as it sounds, he smashed the man's head with a huge vase."

Silence followed the end of Sara's narration. An explanation had been given, and satisfactorily, to her mind. She was aware that there would be suspicion attached to the man's death, so she had told the story quickly, and to the point.

To Dr. Seevers, the tale had sounded logical and conclusive. His purpose was not to enforce the law, nor did he seem inclined to report this infraction of the law. Nothing could be accomplished by compelling this woman to repeat her tale before authorities.

"Has he a family in the area?" the doctor asked.

"I really couldn't say. We never talked about anything other than the yards," Sara answered.

He hesitated for a moment. Then finally, he said, "We will take him to Washington with us. I'll fill out the proper notice of death and present it to local authorities once they're operative again. Eventually his family will be notified," he said.

"Thank you, Doctor. Now, give me another minute and I'll be ready." Turning, she walked rapidly back into her bedroom.

Sara was anxious to be gone. The past few days had nearly destroyed her memories of the lovely home overlooking the blue Pacific. Without Ben, the home no longer existed—it served no purpose. With her packing completed, she hesitated before the mirror. God, what a wretch, she thought. A white bone comb lay on the dresser. She snatched it in her hand and sank the teeth into the matted knots of blond hair. A shampoo. If only she could wash it. The teeth had snagged. With growing impatience, Sara yanked at the tangles, and a whole hank of hair fell out of her scalp. It hadn't hurt. Actually she didn't remember tugging particularly hard, but there it was—a long blond skein hanging from her comb. She stared in disbelief. Then, deliberately, she sectioned out several smaller strands, and gently pulled at them. They, too, ripped free of the scalp. With dismay, she realized that she was losing her hair. Something was causing the roots to die and the strands to drop off her head. Very, very carefully she selected one last strand, a strand from near the back of her head. Exerting only the most minimal of effort, she gave a light tug. Again the hair pulled loose from the scalp. Throwing down the comb, she clutched the heavy purse in her arms, and taking a final look around the room where Ben had died, she walked out.

Dr. Seevers was waiting as she stepped into the hail and said, "I'm ready to go, Doctor."

Chapter Fifteen

Two Months Later

'Washington, D.C., in December can be a bleak, dreary city. Frigid air hung over it on this chilly morning leaving a powdery coat of crystalline frost on the ground. By ten o'clock puny rays of sunlight had dissolved the frozen moisture on all but the shady sides of buildings, but the chill remained.

Cecil rested in a slightly hunched position on the rear seat of the taxi. As a Californian, he had maintained a wardrobe of light weight suits and summer clothes. Now, the outfit he wore was unsuitable for warding off the cold, and adding the lining to his raincoat had not increased his protection sufficiently. He turned the poplin collar up around his neck.

Washington had changed over the past twenty years. Not the city itself, though it had enormous new buildings, but the towns surrounding it had changed. During his military years, he had served a brief appointment within the huge, brown complex that was the Bureau of Personnel. Directly across Columbia Pike from the Bureau stood the gray compound of Arlington Barracks, one of the several naval outposts within the Washington area, and behind it, Shirley Highway stretched into Virginia. Commercial buildings had sprung up from what used to be broad, well-manicured expanses of lawns and foliage.

He instructed the driver to go slowly around the clover-leaf at the Pentagon so that he could get a better view of the structure that housed the military empire of the country.

Arlington Cemetery was the same impressive, sobering sight as always, with its row upon row of small white markers, geometrically spaced and labeling each plot as the final resting spot of an American soldier. John F. Kennedy was there. Before leaving, he'd visit the monument of the assassinated president, and go to the Tomb of the Unknown Soldier to witness, once again, the changing of the guard. Was the guard still changed, he wondered, or had that been eliminated? Listening to that lone bugle, hearing the smart slap of rifles in salute, it made him proud to be a citizen of this country.

The taxi crossed Arlington Memorial Bridge, moved slowly around Lincoln Memorial, and continued east on Constitution Avenue. The driver was sensitive to the shivering, pale man who had hailed him from the hotel. From his mirror, he had watched Cecil. "You've been here before, buddy?" His passenger was lost in thought and reflection at the scenes. Clearing his throat, the driver tried again. "You act like you're seeing D.C. for the second time."

"Huh? Oh, yes. I lived here for a short while—years ago. It has really changed."

"Yeah, I'll bet. Some things stay the same though. You ought to see the cherry blossoms in the spring."

"I hear they're some sight to behold," Cecil remarked. "It was summer when I was here before. I used to go to band concerts that were held on a barge sitting on the Potomac, right beside Arlington Memorial Bridge. They were something, too." How vividly he recalled the sway of the barge and the music.

The taxi pulled to a stop before the building and the driver said, "Here's your address. Luck to you, mister, and enjoy your reunion."

Cecil tipped the driver and hesitated before ascending the steps. The government office building was not one of the new ones. Its age was established by the ancient weathering of the stone, and the strange V's that substituted in the place of U's on the overhead lettering. It was a typical structure in the capitol. Checking the buttons on his coat, he started up the stairs. Through the doors and down a hall on his left, referring to the letter once more to make certain he had the right suite, he entered the offices.

The receptionist was courteous as she greeted him. "Oh yes, Mr. Yeager. We hope you had a pleasant trip."

"I did, thank you. However, I hoped to do a little sightseeing while here, so I declined your accommodations and selected a hotel in Arlington," he said with politeness.

Her bright cheery smile flashed back at him. "Oh, that's perfectly all right. The Senator only wanted to insure that you wouldn't be inconvenienced, that's why he thought all of you people would appreciate having arrangements made for you. When the meetings are finished, I will provide you with a chit to fill out, Mr. Yeager. You can be reimbursed for your food and lodging at that time."

"There are others here, also?" he asked.

203

"Yes indeed. Although it is early yet, one lady arrived a half hour ago." She nodded toward a mahogany door. "Perhaps you'd like to meet her," she replied as she pushed back her chair.

"Don't get up." He smiled. "I'll find my way."

The large rectangular chamber was designed for informal conferences. One end was filled with plush easy chairs and couches. Toward the opposite end extended a heavy wooden table, its sides flanked by chairs. The motif was harmoniously thought out, with just the proper degree of comfort, but not too much. Semi-transparent drapes admitted only a vestige of exterior light; lamps dimly illuminated the peach colored walls. It was a comfortable room, Cecil thought as he noticed the woman at the far end.

Her lonely figure sat, sunk deep into the cushions. The lamp nearest her had been turned off. On the floor by her side were a pair of crutches.

Cecil peered toward the woman, aware that something about her was vaguely familiar. He moved closer to her "Althea?" he asked tentatively. "Is that you?"

She raised her head at his voice. "Yes. Who...?"

"It's me. Cecil. Cecil Yeager."

"Cecil! For heaven's sake. I can't believe it's really you. What a surprise!" she said with genuine warmth.

He walked to her and dropped down by her chair. "Althea, I had no idea you'd be here."

She touched him on the shoulder. "My, you're looking fit these days, though paler than I remember you."

"It's this cold weather," he answered. "I can't take it. My bones rebel when the temperature slips to freezing."

She fingered the fabric of his coat. "Well, you need heavier clothes. This raincoat won't do at all for this climate, Cecil."

He grinned sheepishly, pleased that her concern had shown through. "What would you think if I told you that I hated to spend the money on an overcoat that I'd wear for less than a week?"

"I'd think you were a very thrifty, but somewhat cold, man," she answered lightly.

He laid his hand over hers. "Althea, why didn't you reply to my email or texts?" he asked with sudden seriousness.

She didn't respond to his question.

"An envelope with a check to cover your parents' expenses,

and a thank you—well, I'd hoped for more than that. Some news about your welfare, your plans, you could have sent me something."

"I, I....I didn't think you'd care, Cecil. You did an awful lot for me, and I didn't want to become burdensome to you," she said, dropping her eyes.

He appraised her neatly coiffed hair, and the thin sensitive face. "Of course I cared. I had already decided that once these meetings ended, I'd go to visit you. Luckily, I don't have to wait that long," he said, giving her hand a squeeze.

"You've been very nice...but..."

Impulsively he continued, "Listen, now that you're here, we can make this a pleasure trip. I lived here for a few months once, and I've always wanted to return. Althea, this is an exciting city! There are such interesting sights—and we'll see them all!"

She picked the crutches off the floor. "I'm afraid I won't be able to tour Washington with you, Cecil," she said softly. "These are very cumbersome things."

He glanced first at the wooden staves, then down at her bandaged feet.

"They haven't healed, you see. Doctors keep saying that anytime now they'll be back in fine shape. And for awhile, the sores do start to heal. But soon, they split open and become raw wounds," she explained. "These crutches are to keep me off my feet as much as possible."

"Well, you shouldn't have been asked to testify," he said gruffly. "You're obviously in no condition to be moving around a strange city by yourself."

She laughed quietly. "Oh, you're too concerned," she said with fondness. "We grown girls often travel in foreign cities. But the sticks and the feet are a handicap, I'll admit to that."

"At least I get to see you again." His face brightened.

She let her hand drop. "Yes. This trip was probably just the medicine I needed, Cecil. I had been so despondent, so distressed, that I didn't want to leave the sanctity of the hospital. Then, resting at the spa was such an easy escape, that I didn't want to leave it either. This request to appear before the investigating committee sort of coaxed me out of my lethargy."

Cecil dragged a nearby chair over and sat in it, close to her. "How do you feel generally, Althea?"

"Tired. Tired all the time. But I have an excellent appetite lately, so I should put on a few pounds and begin to feel better."

His thick bushy eyebrows suddenly lifted at a thought that entered his mind. "All right now, I've got it all worked out, down to the last detail. Here's what we'll do. I'll rent us a car. When we're finished here each day, we'll take off on a driving tour of D.C. It's not a bad way to see the city, in fact, it's a lot easier than walking, I promise you."

"Cecil, you are silly. Me, a virtual invalid..."

"We'll see Alexandria, Althea. It's a beautiful old colonial town, and Mt. Vernon, where Washington stayed. Hey!" He snapped his fingers. "I'll rent a wheelchair. Then every place that we want to inspect more closely, I'll just zip out the magic wheels and away we'll go," he said with a boyish enthusiasm.

"Are you listening to me, Cecil?" she asked.

"And the Smithsonian. You haven't seen anything until you've seen the Spirit of St. Louis and those dinosaur bones, and the gem collections. It's a wonderful city, Althea."

"Cecil, stop it!" she commanded in a soft, but firm voice. "You haven't heard a word I've tried to say, have you?"

"No, I haven't Althea. And furthermore, I'm not going to hear any excuses from you about why you can't do this or do that. After White Water you're entitled to a vacation, lady, and this is as good a place for it as any. Not warm like home, maybe, but otherwise, it's loaded!"

A pleasant, perplexed smile illuminated her face as she listened to him. "What about the expense, then? I didn't bring much money with me," she protested. "My share of the...."

He held up his hand, as though forbidding her to think in this vein. "Let's say this is on Calmar Chemical Company."

"Oh, are you going back to them?"

"Well, actually, they are opening a new site in San Diego, and they've offered me a slightly better job." His mind flashed to the day when he had relieved them of the money in the safe. Evidently, the company had chalked that loss up to one of the numerous hazards of the day.

"Will you move there, Cecil?" she asked.

"I'm living there now, Althea. You know, you'd like it in San Diego, too. It has a nicer climate than Los Angeles."

For a brief moment she was remorseful. "I'll never again live in Los Angeles, I know that as a certainty," she said.

The receptionist interrupted to usher a lady with several pieces of hand luggage into the room. Cecil and Althea paused to observe the stranger, then quietly resumed their discussion in lower tones.

Depositing the cases near the doorway, Paula Waring walked over and peeked through the drapes at the grounds outside. There was nothing of interest there, but the action gave her something to do until she could shed the discomfort of being in the presence of people she didn't know, and who obviously were not anxious to introduce themselves.

She was tired and irritable from loss of sleep. She had not intended to take a late-night flight, but the bridge was jammed, and getting over San Francisco Bay had been inordinately time consuming. Consequently, she'd missed her scheduled flight and had to be re-scheduled on the only available space in the early hours of the morning. With luck, today's meeting would be brief and she could hurry on to the hotel.

A recent edition of a popular ladies' magazine was on the table, thoughtfully placed there on an impulse, in this very masculine, business-like room. She carried it to a chair, and began flipping its pages. The entrance of a fourth person caught her attention and she looked up.

"Hello, Paula. I was wondering whether or not you'd decide to attend."

He was standing just inside the door, with both hands sunk deep into the pockets of his overcoat.

"Frank," she said tersely, "hello."

He walked slowly forward, moving a chair near to her, where he took a seat. "You're not very glad to see me, I can tell by your expression."

She lifted one arched eyebrow and waited until he had settled down in the cushions. "I expected you."

"How are the kids?"

"The children are fine."

"Are they in school? Do they like it?"

"Yes and yes. Frank, I...."

"I hope to visit them before long, Paula, if that's satisfactory to you," he said.

"Of course it is. Visiting them is your prerogative as their father. Besides, they ask about you."

Twenty-eight hundred miles away from the scene and they were still antagonists, subtly throwing verbal blocks at each other.

Frank casually glanced at her midsection. "You've gotten rid of it—the baby?"

207

She ignored his question and stared coolly back at him.

"Well, have you or not?" He raised his voice, causing the low murmurs at the far end of the room to suddenly cease.

"Hell yes, of course I have," she hissed. "You surely don't think I would fail to go through with it because of your objections. Ha! You over-estimate your influence, Frank."

Visibly sagging, he laced trembling fingers and leaned closer. "Can't we at least be friends? After all we meant to each other, can't we remain on friendly terms and quit this snipping at each other, Paula?"

She hesitated before answering and then said, "Sure, why not? I don't have any bitterness toward you."

"I've missed you," he said. "We were together for so long that, well, I guess you became a habit to me."

She sadly shook her head from side to side. "A habit. What do you know about that. You have an absolute knack for saying the wrong things, Frank."

"Now what the hell have I said to set you off?" he asked.

"A habit," she repeated. "But naturally. That's the same as being taken for granted."

Searching for safer territory he finally inquired about her parents.

"They're doing fine. And how's Billy Joe and Connie?"

"Great. Just great. Paula, I've got a realtor working on selling the house. He thinks he has a customer about ready to sign."

"That's good," she answered with interest. "Is he willing to pay our price?"

"There's a problem with that. See, we didn't have much equity in the house, and well, property values in San Mirado have really taken a dive."

"Because of the White Water mess?" asked Paula.

"Sure. What else? Anyway, the buyer is offering eight thousand under our asking price," he said with a grimace.

"Eight thousand! Good Lord, we can't take that! After paying the realtor's fees we wouldn't come out of it with a penny. Not only that, we'd actually owe some!"

"I'm afraid we won't have much choice," answered Frank. "Suddenly nobody wants to live around there, Paula. This buyer is a speculator, according to the realtor."

"Frank, surely someone would be willing to assume our loan. Why, to take over our mortgage and move into a nice place without any outlay of cash—that would be a tremendous bargain."

"Yeah? Well, it wouldn't unless we found somebody who wanted to live in that area pretty badly. So far, that region is far from being a mecca to weary house hunters."

"We won't sell for his price, I'll tell you that right now." Her words had poured out flat and hard.

"Then I assure you that I'm not about to keep making payments on that house, Paula. Frankly, I don't give a damn if the bank repossesses it or not." His voice was quiet as he spoke.

She became subdued when she realized he really just didn't care about the house. "I don't want to let it go for nothing. We did put a lot of improvements into it, and we ought to try to get something out of it, Frank."

"Look, Paula," he said with decisiveness, "I've done everything possible. The trouble is that nobody wants to live there. Hell, we're not by ourselves, you know. Nearly everybody has their place up for sale, but there simply are not interested buyers. And it's much worse in L.A."

"The furniture—what did you do with it?" she asked.

Frank removed his all-weather coat, and loosened his tie. "I hauled what was left to Billy Joe's. Before I got back to San Mirado, someone had broken into the house and thoroughly ransacked it. They stole practically everything that was worth stealing."

"Oh Frank. No! What kind of bastards would do that, anyway?"

"Greedy ones, Paula. Practically every house that had been abandoned by the owners was gutted. I ran into Cooter Avondale, from down the block, remember? He said that thieves had taken every stick of his furniture, right down to and including the carpet. Can you beat that?" he said, shaking his head.

"Did you hear anything about Flo while you were there?"

"Uh uh. But then I wasn't there to pay calls on the neighbors."

"I often wondered what they did. Flo and I were having coffee that morning when it happened," she said wistfully. "She was a nice gal. I tried getting in touch with her but she hasn't responded to my texts or emails."

Peering around the door, the receptionist smiled pleasantly to the four and remarked, "I'm terribly sorry that the Senator has been detained. However, he sent a message saying that he'd be here within the next few minutes. I'll be at my desk if there's anything I can do for you." Another show of pearl-white teeth, and she disappeared.

"Frank, when will it be normal, do you suppose?"

"What? San Mirado?"

"The whole region—San Mirado, the coast, everything."

"I don't have any idea, Paula. There used to be some large dairies in the county, but those animals have all died or been put to death. Their milk was contaminated, anyway. But, it was a strange scary feeling that I got from just traveling through there the other day. Everything was so different. It was almost spooky."

A tall, stunning woman walked silently across the padded floor and took a seat in the one remaining spot. She sat equidistant from the others and the center of the room.

The buzz of voices halted momentarily, then resumed as the talkers ignored the newcomer.

Sara didn't object to being excluded from conversation. There were monumental decisions that had been made in the darkness of the night, and once made, she could now relax to some degree and await the outcome. She recalled the discussion with her physician.

Harry had been the family physician for years. He had cared for her sister's children, watching over them from fetuses into the rowdy youngsters they were today. He had treated every illness of their family that was within his realm of practice. And when the time came, he personally chose the specialists that were to be called in. Thus, she had the greatest confidence in his ability, and had willingly consulted him immediately after the service for Ben.

Because of her confidence and her faith in him, he had been surprised and slightly annoyed when she had adamantly refused the fetal x-rays or a sonogram. "Sara....dear," he had said, "you are only borrowing trouble. I have already given you my assurances that it is highly unlikely any malformations will develop after the third month of pregnancy."

But she had sat on the edge of the examining table, tucked the loose-fitting white gown tightly around her, and shook her head, "I don't care, Harry. I simply don't want any more disturbance of the baby-not from anything."

He had persisted, "Sara, a sonogram is not radiation - it is sound waves that form an image. And an x-ray delivers only a minute amount of radiation. It cannot possibly harm you."

She had been obstinate. "No."

Being close to the family allowed him the privilege of saying what he thought. His features softened, and he asked with kindness, "Is it a fear for what the film might reveal, Sara? Is that it?"

She didn't respond to his questions, but stared forlornly at the floor.

"Sara, with your past history of being unable to carry a child to full term, we must pay close attention or you may end up losing this one. Now, I know you want this baby, and I want to help you. But dear, we must know where we stand. I can understand your fears. However, I think we can be optimistic in believing that your exposure has not harmed the developing child."

She had faced him as he leaned against the cabinet, his arms folded. "Then if you are so certain the baby is normal, why insist on the sonogram or x-raying it?"

"It's standard procedure," he answered. "It's just part of keeping tabs on both the mother and child during the pregnancy."

"No, Harry. I won't have it," she said with finality. She suspected the physician was entertaining some doubts about the wisdom of her having this child. But when she tried to trap him into admitting to it, he steadfastly denied any doubts and encouraged her to continue carrying the child. Regardless of her personal fears, she did want Ben's baby, but she would not permit exposure to more radiation or other medical procedures.

Harry had shrugged, "Well, the pelvic measurements still must be done. I think while we are preparing for those, we should also withdraw a sample of amniotic fluid."

She looked up at his mention of the amniotic sample. "What does that mean?" she asked.

"I'll insert a needle into the amnion, the sac containing the baby, and remove some of the fluids. It's a simple technique, Sara. Absolutely painless."

"And what will it prove, Harry?"

"Oh, a variety of things. Not the least of which is the general health of the fetus." He expected her to agree readily.

"No," she said. "I don't want that, either."

For the second time that morning the physician had been surprised by her lack of cooperation. "You are using that same

211

bull-headed determination to thwart my skills that other pregnant women use. Because you are with a child, this makes you a special person, my dear, and as such, you now know more than the physician," he said tartly.

His accusation was neither harsh nor cruel, but she knew he was tremendously irritated. Sara sighed, then answered, "I'm sorry, but, well....I desperately want this child, Harry, and I don't want to take unnecessary chances with it. No needle, no x-ray, no sound waves." She gave him a weak smile, begging for understanding.

He had finally agreed to do it her way.

Returning from her reverie, Sara glanced to either side and noticed that no one was paying the slightest attention to her. Deftly she removed the gold compact from her purse and flicked it open. She studied the lines that seemed to have become permanently etched in her face. It was a more mature reflection that she saw now. A little wiser beyond her years. But the cheek bones had remained good. It was a nice thin face that would soon become fat if she stuck with that diet the doctor had given her. She touched the puff to the tip of her nose and over her chin. The chin was pointed. Or was it? A vision of the old hag she had seen in a movie flashed through her mind. Once more she glanced at the others, and discovering that she was not being observed, she quickly patted the blond wig before straightening it a fraction of an inch.

"Good morning, ladies and gentlemen, I'm Senator McCauley. My sincere apologies for being tardy." Senator Orin McCauley had bounded into the room and come to rest in their midst before they had time to know he was there.

As the Senator graciously introduced each person, Frank Waring looked around the room, seeing Cecil Yeager for the first time. Cecil avoided Frank's look of recognition. Funny, thought Frank, you'd think he'd want to be friendly. Still, maybe he didn't want to be reminded either.

Althea just barely nodded to Paula Waring. Maybe later she would ask Mrs. Waring about Kimberly she thought... now the Senator had everyone's attention.

The Senator was unusually short in stature, no more than five and a half feet tall. In a generation of teenage amazons, his own sons were well over six feet in height, tributes to nutritious food, exercise, vitamins, and their long-limbed mother. Being dwarfed by most of the people he encountered only reinforced the little

212

man's aggressiveness, however. Tenacity, a nimble athletic body, and a sharp, probing mind had gained him a reputation as a fighter on the hand-ball court and a wily opponent in the halls of justice. A successful career in corporate law had provided the impetus for an equally remarkable career in politics. Now functioning as a United States Senator, he had been assigned the mission of spearheading the investigative search into the causes and consequences of the destruction of White Water Nuclear Power Plant.

"I want to thank you for agreeing to come here," the senator said. "You are not the only group to meet with us, there are others; but, you have been requested for very specific reasons. Mrs. Harrington, quite obviously, is here because Mr. Harrington was a supervisor working at White Water at the moment of the explosion. We would hope that through her association, she will be able to add pertinent information about the nuclear facility. Others of you will no doubt shed light and share your insights on other aspects of the accident."

He looked deeply into each face, anxious to put them at ease and acclimate them to the next few days, to what they should expect. Continuing, "This series of meetings with you will be informal. Your depositions, your statements, will become a part of a formal hearing that will follow later. You may be interested in knowing that the press is barred from these meetings, but your testimonies may be issued upon completion of our discussions. Do any of you have any questions?"

"Senator McCauley," asked Cecil, "exactly what is to be the scope of your investigation, or do I have the right to inquire?"

"You surely do, Mr. Yeager," answered the Senator. "Our intention is to do a complete and thorough study of the destructive force of the White Water facility and what caused the plant's disintegration, if possible. We're also delving into that plant and its parent company, West State Utility, and into the handling of radioactive fuels, their wastes, whether safeguards are sufficient or not, and the relationships to other plants already in existence. Ultimately, our findings will pave the way for formal hearings on the advisability of nuclear installations as sources of power for civilian use."

"That's an impressive undertaking, Senator," Cecil remarked.

"Yes. And one that I'm sure you will agree is absolutely necessary, that should have been done, in part, years ago. Now, if there are no further questions, perhaps Miss Haydn could arrange an appointment for us to meet again, this time on an individual basis."

Sara found the little statesman strikingly individual in his attack on the problem of White Water. She remembered that Ben had met the Senator the very day before the explosion and had thought him bothersome, a bit too inquisitive for his, Ben's, taste. How odd that Ben had felt that about the man. She found his businesslike manner inspiring, and his approach to people, perhaps short on patience, but refreshing, nevertheless.

"Will we be required to be here long, Senator, more than several days?" asked Althea in her well-modulated voice.

"Oh, I wouldn't think so, Miss Carr. Generally, you'll respond to our questions and add anything you wish, and that's it. Finished," he answered. "Thank you very much, all of you. Uh, Mrs. Harrington, I'd appreciate your remaining with me for a few minutes, if it's convenient. I'm most eager to hear your comments."

Relieved that the Senator had wanted nothing more than to meet them and establish appointments for personal conferences, the others quickly prepared to leave.

Anxious to assist, Cecil slipped the coat around Althea's shoulders, then solicitously held the pair of crutches while she carefully got to her feet and fitted her arms over them. Once all was in order, the two slowly made their way out of the chamber.

The Senator and Sara had watched quietly at the ministrations to Althea. When at last the couple had left, following the Warings, McCauley swiveled his chair around to Sara. "Mrs. Harrington, you won't object to having our conversation recorded, will you?"

Sara replied gracefully, "Not in the least, Senator."

"Good," he answered, as he pushed a button under the edge of the table. An electronic apparatus containing a small recorder was ejected from underneath. "Re-playing occasionally reveals certain things that even the best secretary misses. Are you comfortable?" he asked.

"Yes. Quite."

"More coffee?"

Sara nodded to him. "Yes, thank you. Black."

With the cups filled, the Senator punched a tiny lever on the machine and the reel began turning. He was commiserative when he spoke. "Your experience was traumatic, it would have had to be, Mrs. Harrington. Do you have plans for returning to the west coast, to your home?"

"No. There would be no point, not now," answered Sara. "Although I may be compelled to make one trip concerning the disposition of my house."

"Yes. I've heard that there are enormous losses in personal and real property sustained by residents of the area."

Sara inclined her head in agreement with him. "There's no demand for homes around there. People are scared of the area now. They don't want to be associated with it."

"Well, long-term radiation is a powerful factor—it'll destroy the tourist industry in the area for years. But worse than that is the fate of that whole section of the state."

He abruptly changed the subject. "Mrs. Harrington, did your husband ever indicate, by any means, that safety controls at White Water were inadequate?" He looked straight at her as he spoke.

She had been expecting this, for what else could the Senator want from her? "Ben was a believer, Senator McCauley. By that I mean that he had confidence in nuclear reactors. He believed that they were the answer to the energy problem for all industrialized nations."

"Did he never have doubts, though, about the total safety of such a potentially dangerous device?" he asked, still watching her.

She traced the outline of the base of the cup as she considered the question. "May I offer an opinion?" she finally asked.

The Senator replied, "Of course," and leaned back in his chair.

"My husband was highly skilled at his work. He was a brilliant man, Senator. Yet, because of his dedication, his devotion, to the prospects of nuclear power, he was confined to a relatively narrow channel in his thinking. It is my belief that he never allowed himself to consider alternatives that arose whenever scientists discussed the pros and cons of nuclear power facilities. I also doubt that he ever lent any degree of credence to the theorized dangers and hazards of a severe nuclear leak, he was so convinced science had perfected the process." She directed her eyes at him, unwavering.

"Those hazards are no longer in theory, Mrs. Harrington."

"No, of course they are very real. But there had been leaks of radiation from nuclear installations before White Water, only not on this scale, of course," she added.

215

The Senator had listened intently as she talked. "Yes, unfortunately we can't seem to profit from small accidents—the lessons are only learned after we've been hurt. And yet, Mr. Harrington must have appreciated the dangers of radiation—with his formal training, he'd have to have been aware of the deadliness of such a thing when uncontrolled. Don't you agree, Mrs. Harrington?"

Sara replied, "Oh, I'm positive he understood that, but he had such blind confidence in technology that he thought it had attained a level of supreme excellence, that it had truly eliminated all possibilities of mechanical and human error."

"Humph. Sounds as though Mr. Harrington figured there was very little else to be learned, that the summit had been reached."

"Or perhaps he had simply committed himself to one way of thinking and stayed loyal to that cause," she said in defense of her husband. She thought the Senator very brusque in his questioning.

"That's very risky when a man is focused in one direction to the extent of blocking out all other views, Mrs. Harrington. Particularly in scientists," stated McCauley flatly, almost mocking.

Sara tugged at her coat, fastening it closer to her body. It was an act that was performed without conscious thought, when one feels himself threatened, or inspected too carefully.

"Your husband survived three days after the blast. He managed to return to his home without any assistance, any aid. He was an extraordinary man, an extremely intelligent man. He must have had some inkling as to the cause of the disaster."

"As I said, my husband never expected that sort of thing to happen, Senator. You must remember that Ben was desperately ill by the time he reached home. We spoke of the accident only once, and for much of the remainder of his days he was incoherent and in agony," answered Sara, recalling Ben's terrible moans and the broken limb.

"Yes. Well, it is regrettable that any evidence of the cause of the disaster was totally destroyed with the explosion. Our men in the field have found precious little to help answer our questions," remarked the Senator.

Aware that her responses, while perhaps not very helpful, had been given readily, Sara felt inclined to ask a question of her own. Senator McCauley and Senator Jackson had caused some degree of concern to Ben. She recalled the visit by the

216

politicians only the day before the destruction of White Water. She interjected, "Ben mentioned having met you at White Water, Senator McCauley. Just prior to the accident. At the time he believed that your purpose in being there was at the request of an environmental group. Was he correct?" She knew she may have breached political ethics and was guilty of being an inquisitive woman, but the presence of the politician had caused her husband some concern.

The Senator checked the burnished sheen on his well manicured nails. It was not his practice to confide in people, to inform them of his reasons for actions he had taken. Yet, this was a gracious woman who sat across from him. She could easily have declined his request to come to Washington and tell her story. She deserved the truth. "Mrs. Harrington, despite what your husband may have thought, Senator Jackson and I were at White Water at the invitation of the president of West State Utility Company. I believe that it was the president's intention to publicize our tour of the facility—after it was made, of course. We went to White Water out of curiosity, and nothing more."

"I see," said Sara with unexplained relief.

Senator McCauley glanced at his watch, then shut off the recorder. Since the investigation had begun he had been a busy man. "Mrs. Harrington, I appreciate your cooperation and your patience. We will discuss this again, but not today. I have an important meeting with the president of West State Utility Company and I'm most anxious to hear some responses from that gentleman." Indeed, his eagerness to talk with Sara had delayed him.

Sara retrieved her purse from the floor. "I'm afraid I haven't been very informative, Senator. Believe me, I'd like nothing better than being able to relate the causes for White Water."

A flicker of a smile passed over his face as he shook her hand. "You have been helpful, Mrs. Harrington. Now, Miss Haydn will phone a cab for you."

217

Senator McCauley's chauffeur steered the limousine into the circular driveway where he brought it to a smooth halt before the brownstone house. Inside, Sara fastened the warm fur coat at the throat, and stepped out. This was what she had dreaded, this being dragged out into society before she was ready, before she was prepared to re-enter the life of a single woman.

She had done battle with her conscience over whether or not she would attend this dinner given by the Senator. And it was not until her first night in Washington that she decided to accept the invitation. The affair was given in honor of those persons testifying from the Los Angeles area, but it would have been easy to refuse. After all, she was in mourning. Instead, she had gone to an exclusive shop in the city and bought a dress.

Once she was in the foyer, a maid took the mink from her shoulders. She was met by her hostess and led into the drawing room. She was the last guest to arrive for the gathering of some twenty politicians, their wives, and her new acquaintances from the west coast.

The two women paused, and in that moment Sara was aware that she was being scrutinized by every person present. For one frightful second she was convinced that it was a ghoulish interest maintained by the others that caused them to stare at the wife of the dead Ben Harrington. Then she looked closer at their faces and realized that she had been wrong. The men plainly appreciated her beauty, and the women, well, at least they were aware of her.

Her black chiffon dress was floor length with full sleeves that tightly gripped her thin wrists. It fit loosely about the body, successfully hiding the small bulge that was forming in her abdomen. Devoid of jewelry, the dress was a striking contrast against the pale skin and the platinum blond hair. Huge, oval brown eyes, shadowed by many sleepless hours over the long nights, lent an ethereal loveliness to the woman.

The Senator's wife accompanied Sara as she introduced her to the guests. Congeniality was the theme of the evening as each person made a special effort to meet the heroic survivors of the infamous White Water catastrophe.

Cecil had arrived with Althea. In the three days that they had been in the nation's capitol, the chemist and school teacher had become steady companions. While Althea spent the morning with Senator McCauley, Cecil sat waiting patiently in the rental car for her return. They saw the sights together, and dined

218

quietly in out- of-the-way restaurants. He had become adept at whipping out the wheel chair and helping her slide into it for strolls through historic sites. Inexplicably, he had become very attentive, very protective of her welfare. She, in turn, willingly allowed him to care for her so that their relationship was becoming a symbiotic one for their mutual benefit. His gain was in having, for the first time ever, the knowledge that a woman not only needed him, but relied on him. Hers was in being cared for.

They had been deftly separated by a matron of good intentions. While Althea was being regaled with mundane conversation about the 'better universities,' Cecil stood with a martini in his hand, talking with Senator Tanaka, but keeping Althea in constant view.

The junior senator from California remarked, "As a chemist, Mr. Yeager, you must have some concrete opinions as to how this business of nuclear energy can be resolved."

Cecil watched Althea take a proffered drink before replying to the others' comment. "Not really, Senator. Right now my chief concern is getting my life back together again."

"Sure. I understand that. Very well, in fact. You see, although I'm an American-born Japanese, relatives on my father's side were in Nagasaki in 1945. After the big bomb ended the war, Father began trying to get them into this country. For years his hands were tied, but finally he did manage to bring his brother over. My grandparents were killed during the A-bomb blast on Nagasaki, Mr. Yeager."

Cecil was only partially listening, he realized. Finally he turned his attention fully to the speaker. "What were you saying, Senator?" he asked. "Something about Nagasaki?"

"That life goes on," answered Tanaka thinly. "That was all." Looking at the yellow skin, the oriental expression, Cecil was annoyed at himself for having wanted to elude the conversation. Besides, when would he ever meet so many influential men again, all in one room? Taking a sip of the drink, he said, "There was a time, just a couple years ago, Mr. Tanaka, when it was blasphemous to even question the civil use of nuclear power. The proof of that is in the billions of dollars poured into nuclear research while solar, geothermal and other power sources are given sums that are embarrassingly small in comparison."

"Ah ha, you do have ideas," said the Senator. "I couldn't imagine that anyone could go through what you people did without coming out with strong opinions on nuclear energy."

"Oh yes," said Cecil. "I have ideas, hundreds of them." He paused thoughtfully. "But does it really do any good, Senator; does it really forward any cause by my standing here telling you what I think about nuclear power?"

Tanaka seemed perplexed. "I beg your pardon....I don't seem to follow you, Mr. Yeager."

For a split second Cecil sensed that he was bordering on hostility toward the politician. Why Tanaka, a man he'd never met before and would doubtlessly not see again? "Wouldn't you agree, Senator, that we had been amply warned about nuclear energy, that as a nation—public and politicians alike—we should have expected that somewhere, nuclear power would turn against us?"

The Senator replied slowly, nodding. "Yes....I see."

At that moment announcement was made that dinner was to be served. Cecil suspected Tanaka was eager to end their exchange. The man quickly excused himself to join his wife in the dining room.

Cecil was disappointed to discover that his seat was not next to Althea's. He glanced down the table at her, and smiled reassuringly as a gentleman slipped the chair in under her.

"How do you do, Mr. Waring," said a high, nervously feminine voice. "We didn't meet earlier. I'm Mrs. Algernon Jackson, Senator Jackson's wife."

He accepted her introduction with a trace of amusement. "How do you do. I'm not Mr. Waring, Mrs. Jackson. I'm Cecil Yeager," he said to the slight, fragile-appearing woman.

"Huh? My goodness, I could have sworn you were pointed out to me as Mr. Waring." As though to reassure herself that he told the truth, she leaned over to see his place card. "Well, my goodness. How could I have made a mistake like that?"

He smiled at her half-heartedly as he held her chair. "People are always getting me mixed up with someone else." That was the truth. He had always been a shy, nondescript person who was never remembered by name, but other than being a giddy young wife, there didn't seem to be much about Mrs. Jackson that would be memorable, either.

"You must tell me all about your experience, Mr. Yeager. It must have been terribly interesting," she said absently.

"I....we..., there isn't much...."

She leaned beyond him and talked with animation to the lady

220

on his left, her fluttering hands accenting her remarks.

Near the head of the long table sat Sara Harrington next to Senator Tanaka. Anne McCauley had evidently given some thought to the placement of her guests. In Cecil's case the order was less to his liking than he had wished.

"Now what were you saying Mr., uh... .Yeager?" asked Mrs. Jackson. "My husband made me promise not to monopolize the conversation, but gracious, every time I meet new people I just can't hush until I find out everything about them. We have only been here over a year, you know. Before that, Mr. Jackson was very big in our home state, and we were always, always having to entertain. Why, you were one of the men who discovered that the entire Russian exhibition of paintings was stolen. How exciting that must have been for you, Mr. Yeager."

He wondered how he could respond to a comment like that. "Exciting, Mrs. Jackson? Actually, I considered the discovery to have been rather sobering. After all...."

"Oh yes, yes. My husband says the Russians are in a positive dither about it. They seem to think we staged the whole thing just to steal their valuable works of art—which is sooo silly. As I told Algernon, if we Americans had wanted any paintings, we could have bought our own. We have far more money than the Russians, anyway."

To Cecil's immense relief, the soup was served. His appetite was suddenly ravenous as he bent forward, enjoying the broth.

Mrs. Jackson dipped her spoon in and out of the bowl, swishing the greenish liquid around, but never pausing in her monologue. "You just won't believe the problems of living in Washington."

Cecil now understood why she was such a frail, delicate-looking woman. She never ate.

"We have had the most difficulty in finding a good school," she continued. "Private, of course. We wouldn't consider sending our children to public school. I always attended a private school, as did my husband, Senator Jackson. Algernon told me that if we couldn't find an acceptable institution, we'd just have to send the children to English boarding schools. They're very posh, you know, very posh."

The soup dishes were removed and huge platters of baked salmon were brought in.

"As I was saying," continued Mrs. Jackson, "there is nothing...."

Cecil shut her out.

Paula Waring was far removed from Frank, to his irritation. They had arrived at the dinner together, having spent very little time with each other over the past three days, and now, this evening, she seemed to be avoiding him completely. He grew sullen as he watched her with the other guests. She was excited by the affair, and at times almost flirtatious—to his great annoyance. How could she do this, when there was so much left unsaid between them?

Across from Frank, near the host, sat the regal Sara Harrington.

"Is it true, Mrs. Harrington," asked the member of the House of Representatives who sat on Sara's left, "what they say about convertibles?"

"I beg your pardon?" she replied, "I'm afraid I didn't catch your question." She wondered briefly if she'd lost the art of chitchat.

"That the natives don't drive convertibles in southern California," said the man bending nearer to her.

She smiled pleasantly at him. His comment was a mark of the guests' attitudes toward her—stick to inane comments, don't refer to unpleasantness. "As a matter of fact," she answered, "my husband and I moved there with the idea of taking long drives in the evening with the top of our convertible down. When we arrived, we quickly learned that virtually no one drives such cars."

"Why is that?" he asked with seriousness. "The terrible smog?"

"Oh, our smog is really not as bad as New York City's," said Sara. Then she continued disinterestedly, "Southern California was originally desert and it gets very cool in the evenings. Other than that I don't suppose I've ever given any thought as to why convertibles aren't popular cars in California." She smiled again at him. "But they aren't."

The food was excellent and the dinner was progressing nicely. Sara was surprised that she could be briefly lured away from morbid thoughts and caught up in some rather satisfying exchanges with a few of the guests.

She had turned slightly toward the gentleman seated next to her and was listening with interest, when the waiter presented the platter to the diner on her right. She heard the clatter of the serving spoon as it rebounded from the table, and was aware that the waiter was frantically scrambling to keep the platter from dropping. What occurred in the next instant was a total shock, however. The waiter, in his haste to hold the dish upright, had pulled his arm into her, into her hair. She felt the tug, and quickly reached up to prevent further damage, when the cold draft swept across her scalp.

Her wig was off her head, and hooked onto a button on the waiter's sleeve, dangling like a platinum animal in a trap.

"Ahhhh!" Murmurs arose from the throats of the diners.

"Oh my!"

"The poor dear."

Suddenly the room was as quiet as a tomb. The exclamations quickly died as the guests sat there, stunned, by the bald, slightly shiny pate of the beautiful Sara Harrington. There was nothing so incongruous as this lovely woman suddenly without a single hair on her head.

The waiter made strangulated sounds as he futilely blended profuse apologies with clumsy efforts to remove the platinum hair piece from his cuff.

Mouths were agape at her dilemma, shocked by the unveiling.

Sara reached out and took the waiter by the arm. She expertly untangled the silver strands from the button until she had it completely free of the cuff. Holding the hairpiece in her hand, she said, "You will excuse me, please." And with that, without great hurry, she walked from the room, the wig resting on her palm.

Blinded by beginning tears, she broke into a run once she reached the hall. Without direction, she rushed unseeing along the corridor.

"Miss... Miss. In here," called a quick thinking maid.

She heard the invitation and saw the maid motioning to her. Following the beckoning arm, at last she was secure within the flocked walls of a tiny dressing lounge. Thankfully, she collapsed.

She was alone as tears of humiliation poured down her cheeks. How could she ever face those people again? How could they ever forget the glossy bare scalp that she saw reflecting back to her each day? Doctors had assured her that losing the hair was often a consequence of exposure to radiation, that it often happened to persons undergoing medical radiation therapy, and that it would grow in, eventually. As a blond, they said, she was more susceptible to hair loss after exposure to radiation than someone with darker hair color would be. Sara had carefully observed Althea's hair. She hadn't lost hers, it seemed. At long last Sara moved to the vanity. Sitting before the mirror, she saw the tear streaked make-up, the filmy black dress that she had thought was perfect for the occasion. What must they be thinking of her, she wondered.

Minutes passed before the diners retrieved their forks and began slowly, dispiritedly picking at their food. Any real or superficial cheerfulness was gone from the affair. For many, the sight of Sara's hairless scalp was the closest inkling they had of the horrendous episode in the woman's life. No woman, barely thirty years old, is bald-headed without a very traumatic reason. It was one thing to be told that her husband had died, and she had survived one of the world's most critical accidents, but it was quite another matter for them to see, with shocking clarity, a result of that accident.

There was hardly a sound heard in the dining room. The waiter, aghast at his awkwardness, asked to be relieved. Anne McCauley decided to go to her guest, but only after giving the poor woman a chance to recover. She expected Sara to want to leave immediately, and she could not blame her.

Every woman momentarily thanked the Supreme Being that what she had just witnessed had not happened to her. Every man felt a fleeting desire to place a protective arm around the chiffon shoulder and make a pledge to the lady that all was well. The spirit of the affair was dead—indubitably dead.

Eventually, near the end of the now interminable meal, a soft rustle from the doorway caught their attention. There stood Sara, every bit as striking in her platinum hair and black dress as the moment she had first entered the house.

There was a scraping of chair legs against the floor as the men, all of the men, got to their feet in obeisance as she returned to the table and hesitated beside her seat.

Sara inclined her head in a short, courteous nod to them.

She hadn't chosen to leave, thought Anne McCauley. What guts! She shoved her own chair back, and in one swift motion, the men and the women were all standing, waiting, until Sara reclaimed her seat.

"Ladies and gentlemen," announced McCauley, "I propose a toast—a toast to the most beautiful, gracious lady of the evening —to Mrs. Sara Harrington." He lifted his glass to her.

In unison, wine glasses were hefted above in a tribute to Ben

Harrington's courageous wife.

The remainder of the dinner went smoothly.

Upon its completion, the women met in small groups to praise the act, one that they were sure they could not have performed. More than a few suppressed a desire to plainly ask Sara how she had done it, had returned to the dinner.

Off in the corner, being introspective, Orin McCauley wondered at the deeds that impressed man. Had these people heard Sara's own account of the events following White Water, or Althea's, would they have been more impressed than they had been by the sight of Sara's bare head? It was impossible to explain, but this was a society that measured a woman's value by her degree of beauty, and by little else. In this case, each woman present had inadvertently put herself in Sara's place, and was shamed by being uncovered. But the men? Maybe it was their male egos that reminded them that there was a defenseless woman, one that they had somehow failed.

As the evening was drawing to a close, cars were summoned, and farewells given. Despite attempts at gaiety it ended on a somber note.

Since they occupied rooms at the same hotel, Paula and Frank had ridden in the same car. The chauffeur held the door as they slid onto the seat.

"Paula," said Frank, "I'd like to talk to you. There are not many days left here, but I think that if we try, maybe we can work something out before we leave Washington."

"Frank, listen to me," answered his wife.

He peered at her through the darkness of the night.

"There is nothing to be worked out between us. It's over. Finished. Done."

"That's not so, Paula. Because you want something that you didn't find in our marriage doesn't mean the marriage was a failure," he said, still straining to see her.

"No. But if I didn't find it satisfying then, there is no reason to believe that it will be now. Nothing has changed, Frank, except that we were forced out of our rut," she replied.

"For the sake of the kids, I want to give it another chance. They deserve that much, don't you think?"

"The children don't have anything to say about it. They know. They've already been told that we'll be applying for a dissolution of our marriage. They're not the first kids a divorce has happened to." She looked out the window at the night.

"But it's unnecessary, Paula. We can't throw away fifteen years of our lives," he pleaded. "That would be foolish."

"That's not the point. We're not throwing away anything. We're just putting a stop to a relationship that has gone cold and indifferent."

"I don't feel that way about you," said Frank.

The car stopped in front of the hotel and discharged them. They walked silently up to their floor.

"Did you hear what I said?" he asked. "I said I don't feel cold and indifferent toward you."

She unlocked her door, refusing to look at him.

"Paula, please. Can't we try?" His voice was soft, pleading.

She was inside and was starting to close the door when he put his hand against it, holding it back. "Wait, Paula. Let me come in for awhile and talk. Just for awhile."

"Frank, I..... If you come in you'll want to stay the night," she said.

"Yes," he answered. "Yes, I will."

His hang-dog expression was hard to resist. Paula stepped aside and allowed the door to be opened.

The meetings with Senator McCauley had gone much more smoothly than had been expected. He had been courteous and sympathetic, keeping them before his recorder no longer than absolutely necessary. His staff had met their obligations to the Californians with consideration and helpfulness. But for all that, they were anxious to be leaving Washington. Sara had immediately embarked on her return trip to her family's home in Connecticut. Paula and Frank had caught separate flights shortly after their last conference with the Senator. And now, the last of the group struggled into the air terminal with an assortment of packages and hand luggage.

For Cecil and Althea, the trip had been a combination of business and pleasure, the latter having become more acute because of their time together. Having fulfilled his plan for seeing the historic capitol once more, Cecil was perfectly willing to get back to the warm, winter days of southern California. Standing before her, his collar up against the chilly breeze that swept in each time the big doors opened, Cecil shivered slightly.

Althea noticed his shuddering, put the crutches firmly against the floor, and stood up. No matter that they had only a moment ago selected this spot to await their flight. "We must find a warmer place to sit," she said. "Neither of us needs to end up with a cold, do we?"

He grabbed the bags and moved off behind her, several chairs away. "All right, now?" he asked.

Althea smiled. The chill had been invigorating to her, but he was shivering. "Sometimes I think I'm hardier than you, Cecil. To me, the nippy air is refreshing. But of course, you're still wearing a summer raincoat."

"I know. I know," he replied. "I need someone to help me decide what to wear. I need a woman's touch, I guess."

"How is your headache?" she asked. "Did you take something for it?"

Over the past few days their relationship had taken on tones of something more than mutual interest in each other. Just as he had developed a deep concern for her, she, in turn, had quickly adapted to his sensitivities. He smiled, remembering, that for a continuing cough in his chest she had treated him with a special concoction designed to end the hacking.

"Here," she said, removing two aspirin. "I want you to take these."

He dutifully gulped them down.

The holiday season was just getting into full swing, travelers passed back and forth, their arms loaded, as they searched for their departure gates, or met incoming planes. Cecil had watched them as they carelessly stepped near Althea's bandaged feet. He had seen the awful wounds, and was concerned that someone would unwittingly mash into them, causing her pain. He leaned forward and extended the nub of the crutches slightly, a caution to strollers. "You know," he said, "I've given some thought to your insurance problems, Thea. Before we land, I'm going to tell you what to do once the insurance agent arrives."

"All right, Cecil," replied the woman.

"And if he gives you any static, you call me."

"Yes," she answered. Then after a moment she continued, "It's very kind of you to help me. I honestly don't know what I'd have done without you. From the day you came into that house....when that man...." her voice drifted off.

Cecil had been watching her, but at the mention of Carter, he turned away and pretended to observe the people in the terminal.

227

Finally she spoke in a soft voice. "It's odd, don't you think, that we have never discussed him?"

Although he knew perfectly well to whom she referred, he asked, "Who? Carter? The man I found attacking you?"

"Yes," she answered.

Aware that she observed him, Cecil continued to look about at the people. Why was he unwilling to discuss Carter? It was not as if he had forgotten the man. Or his foot between Carter's shoulders, or the snap of the man's neck. He had certainly felt no exhilaration in what he had done to the scarecrow, but he'd had no regrets, either. Carter's death was simply a consequence of his action—and of the times. "What's to be said, Althea?"

She worried with the handle of her purse for a moment, collecting her thoughts. Then in a nervous tone she said, "I've wondered if you were ever questioned about his manner of death, Cecil."

At last he turned to her and looked deep into her eyes. "My report explained how he died, Althea, in rescuing you. Did you expect more to be made of the incident?"

"I hoped not," she replied, meeting his gaze directly. "I really hoped not."

As he returned his attention to the passers-by, he heard her gently sigh. There would be no further mention of the wicked, drooling man who had beaten her practically senseless, then had attempted her final humiliation. He took a long draught of air and said, "You know, Thea, the best part of these past two months has been in finding that once again I have control over my life. Do you know what I mean?"

She laid her hand on his arm, "Yes, I know. During that week of White Water none of us could do anything but be swept along in its wake." She paused, "Yes, it is nice to think that we are again our own masters."

They sat silently for several minutes, watching the crowd.

"I wish you'd come to San Diego, Thea. It's such a beautiful city."

"No," she answered. "I make changes very slowly, Cecil. I'll stay on in San Mirado."

"You'd like it there in San Diego," he said. "I'd find you a little place next to my apartment. We'd be together a lot."

She slowly shook her head, making no reply.

After awhile, he asked, "We get along all right, don't we, Thea?"

She smiled. "Yes. We get along fine, Cecil. But I won't make myself a burden on you. I won't allow you to be my guardian any longer."

The loud speaker announced their flight, putting an end to the conversation. Cecil paused momentarily, as though wanting to say more, then reluctantly got to his feet. "That's us."

Chapter Sixteen

Six Months After White Water

It was over. Finished. Everybody had gone except for the two of them. Theirs had been the last case on the docket, but instead of rushing out as had the others before them, they had heard the pronouncement, and remained in their chairs until the chamber emptied. After fifteen years, they had developed mutual habits, similar methods in reacting to situations, which even now, still bonded them together. A single declaration by a man in a black robe couldn't undo the routine which had become second nature over the years.

He walked over and sat down beside her.

"Well, that's it, Paula. Are you happy now?"

"It had to be done, Frank. You know that."

"Yeah, I guess, since you had obviously already decided on it." He was bitter, and it showed in his speech.

"Did you hear what the judge said?" asked Paula. "He said ours was the most amicable interlocutory he'd ever granted. The next time we're here, it'll be for the final divorce decree."

"I thought it was called a dissolution," Frank said.

"Dissolution. Divorce. They amount to the same thing."

"I'm glad you waited," he said. "At first I thought you wouldn't."

"You wanted to talk, didn't you?"

A custodian stuck his head inside, saw the man and woman in conversation, and backed out.

"You know something, Paula? I really believed in us, in our marriage. I never figured it would end this way."

"Yours is a blind faith, Frank, the kind that belongs in religion, not in a marriage."

"It carried us through fifteen years," he reminded her.

"People have to be realistic about marriage, though. There's so much sharing to be done, that has to be done, that the more realistic two people are, the better their chances are for success." She spoke firmly.

"I'm not so sure I believe that. To face reality is one thing, but if you dig too deep, you may find some things in the other person that you just can't live with. That's what happened to us. Until then, until that mess at White Water, we were doing fine," Frank replied.

"White Water really brought it out in the open, didn't it?"

Frank laced his fingers together, the digits becoming antagonists, pulling against each other, as he worked out his inner tension. "Psychiatrists say that certain things become traumatic for people, reducing their capacity to cope. A marriage breaking up, loss of a job, having to relocate—these are very stressful occurrences to most people," he said. "I guess we are no different."

"You're right, I guess. In one single day we were hit with two of those, Frank. Your job, having to suddenly move. No wonder our nerves were rattled."

"And now the end of our marriage. I think the only thing worse that could have happened would have been death," he said thoughtfully. "We're lucky there."

"Yes, we are," she agreed.

"Say, on the way here, I passed by San Mirado area. The freeway exit is still blocked off - can't get into there. They say it is still too radioactive to occupy. Ran into Cooter last week. They are still in California, living further down south. Can you imagine that?"

"Did they ever get any of their belongings back?" she asked.

"Naw. Had to buy everything new. Nothing was salvageable. Boy, was he sore! Said he should have barricaded his family inside the place and stuck it out instead of running."

"Didn't he know how many died from the radiation?"

"Oh yeah, but the government keeps promising they'll clean everything up."

"Cooter is stupid," she said matter of factly.

""I heard that Flo and her husband moved to Texas. Did you know that's where they came from originally?"

"No. But I really liked Flo. God, she could tell the funniest stories I ever heard," answered Paula with a hint of sadness.

"I wish now that I hadn't let the house go back to the mortgage company. If I'd kept up with the payments I could have probably moved back to San Mirado when all the cleanup is done," Frank announced. "It was a nice place."

Paula looked at him, shaking her head. "You don't get it, Frank. It's NEVER going to get cleaned up, no matter what the government says."

He threw her a disgusted look. "It's great for you to run around dishing out advice. How do you know everything? I don't have the money to buy another house. In case you have forgotten, Paula, the money tree went out with Santa Claus."

"Crap, no wonder the judge thought ours was a peaceful divorce, there wasn't anything to fight over," she snapped at him.

"Except the kids."

"Oh well, why squabble over them? Children are always better off with their mother, there's no question about what's best for them. Besides, a father rarely wants the responsibility of the kids, anyway," she said. "At least none that I've heard about."

"That's not true. I told you that I'd take them. That I wanted them. But no, nothing doing."

"You know that they belong with me, Frank. With your appreciation for the female form, you'll very likely be married within a year." Her face broke into a tight smile at the barb.

"For God's sake, where did you get a hair-brained idea like that? I've never chased the skirts in my whole damned life," he retorted. "Jesus! What a thing to say."

"Come on now. Are you telling me that you haven't had any dates in the last four months—not even one?"

"No, I haven't. Not a date. I got together once or twice with this gal who works in Billy Joe's office, but that was all."

"Huh. That's pretty hard for me to believe."

"What about you? Have you been virtuous ever since that night in Washington?" he asked, forcing her to remember that last time.

"What are you getting at, Frank?" she asked suspiciously.

"Your innocence, Paula, your innocence. You didn't exactly try to protect your honor when I spent the night with you."

She gave an exasperated snort. "How childish! We were still married and you did beg me to let you in."

"Yeah, and I've often asked myself why you did that. For me it was simple. I hoped we could patch up our differences. Yet— within two months—you filed for divorce. Why did you sleep with me, anyway?" he asked as he stared at her.

"Curiosity, maybe. Or one last stab at making it work."

"Bull, you can be more honest than that."

"All right then. Maybe I was just in the mood, Frank, and

232

you were convenient!"

Her reply smarted. He gulped back the knot of anger rising in his throat, and fought to control his temper. This last conversation wasn't going in the direction he had wanted. It wasn't easy, sitting here in this big empty chamber, trying to reestablish some rapport with this woman he loved.

"Here we go again," he murmured under his breath.

"What?"

"Nothing. Nothing."

"Frank, look, there's no point in us badgering each other any more. It's ended. From now on we are nothing more than two people who happen to be the parents of the same kids. Let's leave it at that."

"Is that really the way you want it—nothing more than that?" Was it really this easy for her, he wondered.

"Of course. Why else would we have divorced?"

"I can't believe, Paula, that after all those years, two children, and all, we mean absolutely nothing to each other now. That's incomprehensible, completely incomprehensible to me."

"To you, but not to me, Frank." In a moment of weakness, she reached out and touched his arm. "I'm sorry, really sorry. I hope you'll believe that. If the marriage, if our goals, or whatever, had just been big enough to include my own dreams, then maybe it would have lasted. As it is, it's finished for us. Whether you'll accept this or not, I am very sorry that it has ended this way." She spoke with a rare, genuine warmth.

Frank carefully examined the fair Scandinavian features, the blond hair, hazel eyes. "You know something, you even look like your father, Paula," he finally said.

"Is this another snotty crack you're making?"

"No, it isn't. It's a fact, and it kind of surprised me that I hadn't noticed the resemblance before."

"In that case, thank you," she answered shortly.

"You and your old man ought to get along fine. You're sure alike in more ways than appearance, too."

"Suppose we let this subject drop. I'm not interested in having a quarrel with you, Frank."

He straightened his tie and stood up. "Yeah. You're right. We may as well call a truce, huh?"

"Let's do. Frank, Jerry said that you had asked him to spend the summer with you. I don't feel good about that."

"Why? What's wrong with a teenager spending the whole

233

summer with his father?" he asked with annoyance.

"He's not a teenager, yet."

"He's thirteen."

"Well, I don't want him running wild while you're working during the day. That's the way a kid picks up bad habits."

"Hell fire, Paula. You can't keep him tied to your apron strings always!"

"And I won't let you make a hoodlum of him!"

The sound of the custodian brought a halt to their heated words. They waited expectantly for him to leave, but he did not. "I'm late, folks. If you don't mind, I'd like to get my cleaning done in here," said the old janitor.

"Oh, we're sorry we detained you," replied Paula, showing her compassion for the tired old man and his weak watery eyes. "Come on, Frank. Let's go so he can do his work."

Frank shoved the little gate aside, letting Paula precede him along the aisle. Once out on the street, they paused.

"Where's your car?" he asked, looking up and down the street.

"In the lot. Where's yours?"

"By the curb."

They glanced toward their vehicles. It would have been too much of a concession for either to go to the other's car to finish the discussion.

"Getting back to Jerry," said Paula. "Why do you want him with you when you don't even have a home, Frank?"

"Connie and Billy Joe would like to have him visit. They have already said that. Besides, as soon as I get on my feet I'll be moving into my own place—probably before summer."

Paula scanned his face, "You haven't mentioned Kim. How do you think she will feel when her brother goes to you and she hasn't been invited? She's going to be hurt, Frank."

He looked at her in mock surprise. "That's the very thing I told you, Paula. I said this would hurt the kids, that they'd be the ones who'd suffer. And you reminded me that they expected divorce— that it didn't matter."

"Well, I don't like the idea of you taking Jerry and not his sister. That's not fair to her."

It was a problem that defied solution, this matter of the children. "I guess it isn't fair, but I can't have them both at the same time. I'll just plan on taking Kim after Jerry returns here. Is that okay? Or have you decided to let him come to me at all?"

Frank could tell by her expression that she had made up her mind. She always told everything through her face. "How about it?" he asked.

Paula glanced toward her car, aware that it was late and she ought to be going. "Frank, you can have Jerry for the summer."

"Are you sure it's all right?" he asked.

"Certainly. You're a fine father." She patted him lightly on the cheek and hurried off to her automobile.

He throttled an impulse to call after her. But instead, he watched her until she rounded the corner and was lost to sight. Sighing, he unlocked his car and slid into the seat. Summer. He'd see her in the summer.

Cecil walked along the white sandy beach, keeping above the water line. It was a gloomy overcast day with a chill wind blowing in off the Pacific, a day that would attract no one, not even kids in shiny black wet suits, to the area. Normally, April would have brought out the teenagers and beach bums in droves, but not this year. The long stretch of sand was empty.

He ducked under the frayed twine of a volleyball net, and continued toward the rocks. He hadn't frequented the beach often, having always felt conspicuously out of place among the semi-nude, tanned healthy bodies that frolicked or lounged in the sand. His only other trip here had been made on the spur of the moment, and had left him regretting it. Not that he had any reason to regret it, but the shock of seeing the honey brown body with its two firm mounds of breasts bared had stunned him for a moment, and he had unwittingly been caught staring. The girl's smart suggestion had sent him rushing off the beach.

There were no signs of old campfires, no colored towels littering the view today. Sadly, the entire beach was a wasteland in need of warm bodies, surf boards, and life. Not too different from the rest of the countryside, Cecil reasoned. Huge fields, once lush with vegetables, were now pastures of wild grass, proliferating for the lack of tilling. But what was the use in tilling a field that couldn't grow edible foods?

A cluster of fucus lay in the sand. The tough, leathery ribbon-like thallus of seaweed was tangled and knotted from its beating by the surf. Walnut-sized air bladders were present among the sticky thongs. Cecil dropped his foot on one of the bulbs and pressed down until he heard the popping sound under his shoe. Tiny gnats swarmed around the mess, forming a dark screen as he pushed the pile aside. As an afterthought, he stooped down and separated the thick filaments, searching for fragile brittle stars cloistered within. The delicate pink and orange marine animals were nowhere to be seen. Sadly, he walked on.

Ahead of him were large dark boulders, normally submerged by the tide and invariably coated with dense layers of barnacles. Today they stood dry for the tide was low, one of the lowest of the year. Jumping from stone to stone, he edged out to the most distant rock and climbed atop it. From there he felt above the ills of his world. Damp air soaked through his blue windbreaker, causing him to shiver. Rather than seeking shelter from the dampness, Cecil sat down on the big rock.

A few gulls floated in the gray sky. There was little food to be scavenged from the shoreline—evidence of the destructiveness of the radiation on marine life. Colorful, flower-like anemones and starfish, common tideline inhabitants, were absent, leaving tiny crabs alone and isolated. Cecil watched the fiddler crabs scurrying about in empty snail shells, oblivious to the big man towering above them.

He sat there in solitude for over an hour. At last, he realized that evening was drawing near, and since he didn't wish to be late for visiting hours, he hunched deeper into the jacket, and trekked the lonely trip back along the beach, then to his car.

It was a distressing concern that had gradually encroached on his peaceful existence. Thoughts of Althea kept taunting him, distracting him. He missed the proper exit from the freeway, as the nagging, persistent thoughts continually interfered with his concentration, reminding him of his vulnerability. Again he exited onto the wrong street.

Out of patience, he swung the car into a sharp U-turn in the middle of the block, and headed toward a flat, sprawling complex of medical buildings. A white, square sign identified the facility by its new name, Beckman Radiation Treatment Center.

Her room was in the south wing overlooking a field of parched yellow grass. She had been awaiting him throughout the day even though he wouldn't arrive until visiting hours. He was that kind of man—prompt, precise.

Two empty paper cups rested on the aluminum bed tray, an indication that medication had been given.

236

"Hello, Althea." He glanced at her fine features, crowned by thick dark hair. This was the first time he had seen her tresses loose, and not done up in the chignon. A gray streak had appeared among the darker strands.

"Cecil. I'm glad you're here. It has been so long."

He seated himself across the room. "Not since we met in Washington," he said. "Exactly four months ago." He shifted about uneasily. Was it going to be hard to find things to say now? In Washington, and until he had left the plane, they'd had a steady running conversation.

"You're thinner. You've lost some weight," she remarked.

"Yes," he replied. "I have."

"Come closer and let me get a good look at you."

Obediently he walked over to the bed.

"I like you in those clothes. They're very casual. Do you know I always picture you in a suit and tie?"

He colored slightly. "I decided it was time I started enjoying life a little more, Thea. So I began a new image, I guess you'd say." She seemed tired and weary to him, although he could not have expected anything else. "Your eyes look tired. You're not sleeping well, are you?" he asked.

She presented a flicker of a smile. "Not very. But you—I want to hear about you. What business do you have in Los Angeles?"

"Oh, it's nothing. At least it's nothing important. It can wait until you tell me why you were transferred to Beckman."

Her large black eyes dropped to the sheet, avoiding his stare.

"Althea, what's wrong?" he asked.

She tore a tissue from its box and it was then that he saw the tiny pools of tears that had collected in the corners of her eyes. Her tears moved him, he wanted to touch her, but he refrained. "Tell me. Maybe I can help, Thea. I did once before, remember?"

"No, no. It's not that. I'm not expecting you to help. There is nothing you can do," she answered despondently.

"But you emailed me. You said that you did want to see me again," he began. "You said...."

"Maybe I was wrong. I probably shouldn't have contacted you— not after all this time."

"Nonsense. It was you who had said that we shouldn't see each other, not me," said Cecil.

"You were too serious, Cecil. You wanted—well, you want

237

something that I'm not sure I can give," she said, blotting at the tears.

"What? Friendship, companionship? Look, we're not senile. There's plenty of time for us to enjoy living." His words had come out harshly, something he hadn't meant. He wanted to be tender and gentle, but wasn't sure how.

The tears had dried. She was composed as she searched his face for some hidden meaning. "I have missed our conversations—our long talks, Cecil. What do you do with your free hours now?" she asked innocuously.

"Read. Sleep. Putter in my garage. Play on the computer. Search out new places to take interesting photos." At the mention of the photography his face brightened. "I work with digital material. I have some fabulous photoshop programs. They do everything. Some of my photos have been published in magazines, Thea."

"Haven't you made new friends—friends at Calmar? Around your apartment?" she asked.

He idly toyed with a snap on his jacket. "People don't interest me all that much. You know that."

"They should, though. You are such a strong man. Kind. Considerate. You have so much to offer to friends."

He looked past her, out at the darkening night. "I've never had close friends—not before you. When I'm with them I don't know what to say. I can't make small talk like other people do."

"We talked," she said. "For nearly five solid days you and I talked about everything under the sun. Didn't we?"

He nodded. "And that's just it. You're the only person I've ever known that I could really communicate with."

"But that doesn't mean there aren't others around with whom you can share your interests."

Shrugging, he said, "I haven't looked for them, though, and actually, I don't really need anyone." It was a cold, hard assertion, put in such a way that no further discussion was invited. Suddenly the room was too small, choking him. "Why did you contact me, Althea? Why? Or are you sorry that you did?"

"When I wrote the email I wanted to see you, Cecil. I know now that it was unfair of me—selfish of me—but I was so far down, so depressed. I felt that if I could just talk with someone for a few minutes, someone who really understood my aloneness, that I'd be heartened, and could face the days before me."

He laid his hand across hers. "You've been through a lot, Thea. Much too much. What is it, Thea? Tell me."

"Dr. Parsons, my surgeon, is going to amputate my left foot, Cecil. He said that there was no other alternative. Not after six months."

Instinctively he drew his hand back. "Amputate? Your foot? But why?"

"The blisters—the radiation. It won't heal. There is nothing else to do but remove it," she choked. "I... it's....oh, it's horrible!" she cried out.

"Well, but my God, Althea, an amputation, it's bad, of course, but...." He hesitated, reluctant to say anything that could be misconstrued, misinterpreted. "It could be...." and he stopped short of saying the word worse. "Could it be the surgeon made a mistake? Maybe you should consult someone else—get another opinion."

She was suddenly strangely quiet; there were no outbursts after that one admission to being frightened.

"Doctors have made errors before, Althea. Perhaps another method of treatment by someone new...another doctor...."

"Dr. Parsons only confirmed the opinion of the physicians who have treated me over the past six months, Cecil. It's very definite to these men that allowing the condition to remain would be further damaging to my body."

"The other foot—what about it? Isn't it healing?" he asked.

"Yes. Slowly. They think."

"Then, I can't believe they won't give this more time."

"No. The decision has been made," she said with finality.

He walked around to the window and stood, staring out into the darkness. He was shaken by the news. Althea was almost reconciled to the amputation, but to Cecil, the prospect had jolted his system. He wanted to weep for her, but how could he do that if she wasn't crying for herself? Little did he know that her sobbing had lasted half the day that the decision to amputate was made. By now her tears were gone and left in their place were visions of her future without the aid of one limb—a bleak empty future, it must have seemed to her. Still turned toward the night he asked, "How can you accept this with such calmness?"

"I've known for several days. I've had some time to make mental adjustments. In a way, I suppose I'm lucky. While thousands have died, I survived to lose a foot."

"It could be worse," he said quietly.

"Once I didn't think so. Once I thought I'd rather die than be left a permanent cripple. But the desire to live can't be shoved aside that easily."

The man was silent, his back to her.

Noises from the hall seeped through the closed door.

"When is it to be done?" he asked.

"Tomorrow. In the morning."

A metal cart was being pushed by the room, causing a rattle of wheels against tile flooring.

"What time?" asked Cecil.

"Ten o'clock."

A voice, muffled by the walls, its words indistinctive, permeated the room from the hallway.

"I... Will any of your family....Will your Aunt Bertha be here?" It seemed important that someone be waiting for her. There must be someone who would welcome her out of the anesthesia, welcome her return to the world.

"I haven't bothered telling my aunt and uncle. There is nothing they could do. Not now." She recalled the last time she had spoken with her aunt, that day, in her parents' living room, while her mother and father listened.

Finally he turned to face her. "I'll be here. I'll be right here in this room after the surgery." Reassuringly he stepped over to the bedside, and touched her gently on the shoulder.

She grabbed his hand and pressed it to the side of her face, grateful for his concern.

"Later we can discuss what must be done after you leave here." He pulled the chair up and sat down. A single light shone from the head board, casting a dim circle on the floor. He stretched his legs out until they were illuminated, leaving the rest of his torso in semi-darkness.

"There was one chore that I'd hoped to complete before—before this," she said. "My parents' house. I asked to be driven by there on the way to Beckman—it's in such disrepair."

"You surely don't intend to go there, Althea."

"No. But it needs to be boarded against intruders. The old neighborhood was in shambles, and it's just a matter of time until everything inside the house is stolen."

Cecil hadn't the courage to tell her that looting happened long ago, and there was probably nothing left in the old place. "Someday property in that area will be worth something again.

240

If you can hang onto it, you might eventually sell it for what it's worth," he said.

"Oh, I'm not even worried about whether or not to sell it. But I shudder to think that my parents' personal things will all be gone before I can get to them. Cecil, have many of the people stayed? What's it like in the city now?"

"Many stayed, mainly because they'd lose everything—efforts of a lifetime—if they left."

For awhile, her financial position had been overwhelmingly depressive. "The government's insurance doesn't pay for the losses, not a fraction of the losses. I used to worry myself sick about it, until I decided that if the insurance doesn't cover it, it just doesn't," she replied sadly.

"No. It couldn't possibly. Lots of folks just dropped everything and left, though, just cut themselves loose from houses, possessions, like they didn't care. I couldn't believe it, driving in this morning. Acres and acres of farm land, all full of weeds, shells of commercial and industrial buildings where thriving businesses once operated. It's ghostly, Althea. Yes, like an immature ghost town of the west."

"It'll snap back, won't it, Cecil? Los Angeles can't die. It has to revive!"

"Oh yeah, I suppose. But it'll take a while."

"Senator McCauley has announced that the formal investigation will begin next week," she said.

"Really? When did you hear that?" he asked.

"On the radio, this morning. I liked him, didn't you, Cecil? Didn't you think he was sincere at getting to the bottom of this?"

"He's sincere, all right. And smart. I hope we see some drastic changes resulting from that little man's efforts."

The door opened a crack and a nurse peered in. "Althea, can I get you something?" Noticing Cecil, she continued, "Ah well, I see you have company. How nice."

"Thank you, no. Everything is....fine," answered the patient.

"Are those pills taking effect, yet?"

"Some. I'm beginning to get drowsy."

"Remember to buzz me if you have any trouble falling asleep. We want you rested, you know."

After the nurse had gone, Cecil began digging for his car keys. "I guess I'd better not keep you awake, then," he said and rose.

"You didn't tell me why you're in Los Angeles—what brought you here," Althea said. "Some sort of business?"

"It was nothing," he answered.

"But you emailed me that you had important business here."

"Well, it wasn't very important, after all."

"Oh, I see. Cecil, will you really be here tomorrow?" she asked.

"Of course I will. Right here in this spot." He tugged the blanket up under her chin. "I'll be waiting right here."

"Then I'll see you tomorrow?"

"Yes. You will. And by the way, I'll go to the house and have someone nail boards over the doors and windows for you."

"I....I... How often have I thanked you for something you've done for me?"

"Don't worry, Althea. Everything will be all right. You'll see."

The night had been endless for Cecil. He had tossed around, failing to find sleep, until he'd finally given up, and dressed for the coming day. In street clothes, he sat in a chair, holding a book in his hand, but not reading. He wished he were at his apartment. This strangeness of a motel room—well, he had trouble sleeping in any bed not his own, and he just wished he were back in San Diego. The sooner, the better.

But of course that wouldn't really resolve his problems, to ignore them. He had come here planning to ask Althea Carr to marry him, and now he was acutely aware that the situation had changed. Not his fondness for the woman—that was still there. Fondness, though, was hardly a proper reason for marriage. There was supposed to be love, that intangible state of emotion that Cecil was not sure he had ever experienced. He felt elated and proud when he had fulfilled her need, but, that wasn't love. Encountering a burst of gratitude from her after he had performed some menial, masculine function always inflated his self-importance and left him more determined than ever to have the pleasurable experience repeated. Perhaps the feeling was akin to those same desires he had sought to satisfy from his parents when he was a small boy. When the rewards had been gratifying, he had continued his infantile stunts until admonished by his parents to quit fooling around and go out to play. Their admonishments had crushed him, but he'd never failed to do their bidding. And here, years later, when the memories of his parents were faint, he was still seeking approval.

He slammed the book shut in disgust. Self-examination wasn't a practice that he particularly enjoyed. But marriage? He needed that....he needed her. That she was black meant nothing, for after all they had been through, such a minor factor as skin color was easily transcended.

The night air was cold and wet. Some thinkers sit quietly to meditate, but he walked. He walked down the block, past the coffee shop, and on toward the single neon sign that emitted an eerie glow in the fog. A year ago he'd have hesitated before taking a midnight stroll anywhere in Los Angeles; in fact, he probably wouldn't have done it at all. Now, after White Water, he no longer feared the darkness of a big city. Tonight, and for many to come, these empty streets would be safe for a lone pedestrian. He grimaced at the thought of how base some men could become, sinking to unparalleled depths to forward their own gains under the cover of darkness.

Shrubs had become overgrown forests around the tired-looking shop fronts. Cecil felt irritated that the tenants who had moved back in to resume business didn't take greater pains to get their places tidy and trim. They seemed not to care about external appearances anymore—a completely opposite attitude from that before the incident at White Water. Los Angeles and its daughter cities had become outcasts, anathemas, to visitors and tourists, and as such, had lost their spirit, their verve, almost their desire to recover. Lacking physically demolished structures to satisfy the curiosity of the morbid, the towns had nothing to charm the people in from far away. Furthermore, a constant fear of radiation hung over the area even yet.

He was anxious to be gone from here. It was foolish for him to have come. Primping like a high school boy, he'd rushed up to Los Angeles, intending to declare his devotion to the woman and make her his own. Silly fool! A near helpless woman who'd have to be carefully treated for months, who'd be nothing but a burden until she'd mastered the art of handling a synthetic limb —he didn't need a woman like that. On the other hand, she made him feel like a giant. She listened to him. She shared his ideas. She knew what was happening in the world.

It was no good. It wouldn't have worked. He strolled

aimlessly in the night, wishing for the sunrise.

They wouldn't let him wait in the room. Instead, he sat in the lounge, making inquiries every ten minutes about when he could see her. Being barred from her room was distressing, since he'd promised her that's where he'd be when she was returned from surgery. What would she think when she didn't find him there?

It was late in the afternoon. Had something gone wrong? Was she all right?

"Mr. Yeager, you can go in now," said the nurse. "She'll be very drowsy for the rest of the day so don't be surprised if she drops right off to sleep. We would prefer that you remain only for a few minutes."

He tiptoed in. She was covered by a thick white blanket, her left foot conspicuously missing. The room was a gray shadowy cubicle, looking more tomb-like than like a repository for the living. He had forgotten the flowers. He'd have to get some for her.

"Althea," he whispered softly. "It's me. Cecil."

She uttered the least audible of sounds. "Yes. I know."

"Are you...are you okay?"

"Ummmm." Other than the slight motion of her lips, she lay still as a stone.

He stood over the bed, watching her. Deciding that she was asleep, he crept to a chair and gently lowered his body into it. He'd wait.

Minutes dragged into an hour. A nurse came in and checked on her patient, noticing the man sitting motionless by the door. Her duty completed, she quietly left.

He nodded. Loss of sleep from the previous night overtook him, and he dropped off into a light slumber.

Someone else entered the room to glance at Althea, but he ignored the nurse. Quickly he dozed back off. In what seemed like seconds, a light was turned on, and both a physician and a nurse were standing by her bed. The nurse was inserting a thermometer into Althea's ear, designed to get the temperature in a fraction of a minute.

"She looks alert. Right, Althea? You can hear what I'm saying, can't you?" asked the physician.

Her eyelids flickered in acknowledgment of his question.

"Good girl," he said as he extended the disc of the stethoscope to her chest. He moved the disc once before he found the right spot. He listened closely to her heart, then smiled down at his patient. Removing the stethoscope, he draped it around his neck. "You're doing just fine, my dear. Just fine." He scratched a note on her chart.

"Uh, Doctor?" said Cecil as he ventured toward the bed. At his question the physician turned in surprise. "Oh? Ah, yes, I'd forgotten you were there."

"I'm a friend of Miss Carr's, and I wondered if, uh, how long she'll be in here," Cecil said.

"That's hard to say. Depending on how well the tissue heals, it could be two weeks to a month," answered the physician.

"I see," Cecil murmured softly.

"And of course on how strong her will is to get out of the hospital and up and around," the doctor added.

The nurse commented on the evenness of the patient's temperature, and busily began tightening the coverlet across Althea's chest.

An aide stuck her head in and spoke briefly, "Dr. Parsons, Dr. Archer would like to see you in OB when you've finished your rounds."

"In obstetrics?" asked the physician. "Are you sure you've got the right guy, miss? I'm an old sawbones who never gets a call to OB.

"Yes sir. You, Doctor."

He patted his patient's arm, "I'll be in to see you early in the morning, but I don't believe you'll be having any problems developing, Althea. Now it's a matter of time for healing. Time, my dear." To the nurse, he said softly, "Watch her closely."

Shortly the physician and the nurse were gone, leaving Cecil and Althea alone.

He walked over to stand by her.

"You waited," she said.

"Yes," he replied. "I said I would be here."

"I was afraid that you wouldn't—that you'd leave before I got fully awake."

"I wanted to talk to you."

"You're sweet to have stayed."

"Thea? Are you....can you understand me plainly? Can you hear me?"

"Yessss. I'm awake, Cecil." Her reply was faint, almost

245

whispered.

"I have something very urgent that I must say to you," he said. "I know this may seem like the wrong place, and the wrong time, but I can't stay here for long because I have to get back to my job. And I wanted to tell you before I left."

"Tell me what?" she whispered.

"What the business was that I had in L.A." His voice faltered as he searched for the correct words.

"Yes?"

"Thea, I want you to marry me—or us to be married, I guess that sounds better. Just as soon as it can be arranged," he blurted out.

She didn't respond directly, but lay there quietly, looking at the big man whose hands were shaking.

At last she answered, "No, Cecil. You're a generous person, but I don't want your pity, and I won't burden you with my infirmities."

"Nevertheless, I'm cleaning up my place for you. When I return here, we'll discuss the arrangements," he stated firmly.

"I'm not sure this is the thing to do, Cecil. I...."

He placed a finger across her lips, stilling her protests. "Oh yes, you'll see." He bent down and kissed her cheek. "I must go now. But I'll be back...dear."

In making the transition from a facility geared toward serving a community's needs to a radiation treatment center specializing in radiation cases, Beckman had temporarily lost many of its original functions. Patients with ordinary ailments were presently sent to other hospitals, allowing the staff at Beckman to concentrate on those admissions which had become abundant over the past six months—radiation victims.

Bernard Parsons was now the Chief of Staff, a result of his pioneering with radiation medicine, and it was with some degree of wonderment that he arrived in the office of Dr. Archer immediately upon completing his rounds. "Hi, Archie. I thought obstetrics had been turned over to the midwives and you were looking for a job," he joked.

The obstetrician beckoned his colleague inside. "I was beginning to doubt that we'd ever get any more fat ladies around here until today. But I've got something I'd like to get your opinion on. A new arrival—early this afternoon."

Dr. Archer was a tall, handsome man in his early forties. With thick blond hair and an easy smile, he became the source of many fantasies for his patients.

"Yeah? A pregnancy?" said Parsons. "Well, that's way out of my field."

"I don't think so, Bern. You've treated the symptoms of radiation sickness... .this ought to be right up your alley. At least you can tell me what some of this means," he snapped his finger on the stiff folder on his desk.

Dr. Parsons sat down, suddenly interested. "What do you have, Archie?"

"Not a hell of a lot, unfortunately. She was admitted because of early labor pains, but she has been under the care of a physician from out of state. I called him to get some history on her after she told me she'd been in this area during White Water." Indicating the folder, he said, "This was all I could get by phone."

He handed the papers to Dr. Parsons who began skimming the data.

"She's a primipara?" asked Parsons without taking his eyes off the printed matter.

"Uh huh. And since this is her first one, it could be a long while before she delivers."

After looking through the medical history, Dr. Parsons said, "I can't believe she's trying to have this child."

"I know. She's asking for trouble," agreed Archer. "Bernie, what's the deal on those wild fluctuations in her white blood cell count?"

Holding the folder nearer the lamp, the physician saw a record of treatment following White Water. For the first two months white cell numbers vacillated to extremes, several thousand below to several thousand above the normal count. Three transfusions had been administered during the low reading periods. Eventually the WBC had stabilized. Parsons replied, "We found the same thing happening in our patients, Archie. No doubt radiation had mysteriously affected the bone marrow and lymph glands where the cells are made. But how, I don't know."

"Look at the hemoglobin stat," said Archer. "When I first saw that I didn't give it a second thought because nearly all pregnant women develop some degree of iron-deficiency anemia. The fetus frequently demands more iron than the woman can provide," said Archer. "Later, I got to thinking something wasn't right."

"What are you concluding? That this case is in some way special?" asked Parsons.

Dr. Archer answered, "Lack of iron is evidenced in pale hemoglobin, but it is a certainty that where the blood is too iron poor, the oxygen supply to the fetus is reduced. As you know, it's the iron that carried the oxygen in compound through the bloodstream." He paused for a moment. "Yes, Bernie... . she's a special case all right."

"According to her physician, she had oral doses of medicinal iron, Archie. That should have corrected the anemia promptly."

"But it didn't. She was nauseated by it and had gastric cramps so she was switched to intravenous iron."

"And?" asked Parsons, anxious to get to what his colleague saw as the crux of the patient's problem.

"Apparently that did the trick, but only over several months. Several months, Bernie! That's a helluva wait for severe anemia to be corrected, especially for a pregnant woman."

"Our radiation patients who had been heavily exposed invariably became anemic. I suspect that since radiation had interfered with the developmental rate of white cells, causing those wide fluctuations that we saw so often, then it could have in some way affected the red blood cells. They're produced in marrow of the bone, too," Parsons said.

"The question is, was her anemia a consequence of pregnancy or a result of the radiation?" asked Archer.

Dr. Parsons was thoughtful for a long moment. "Who knows? But it means that the fetus has been improperly supplied with oxygen for what—nearly two-thirds of its life?"

"Yes. That's it. So, you know what lack of oxygen to a brain does. It's probably the number one cause of mental retardation," said Archer. "That baby could be in bad shape."

"Have you looked at the fetus?" Parsons asked.

"No," replied Archer. "She won't allow any sonograms or x-rays. She's adamant about that."

Dr. Parsons glanced back at the folder. "She ran a constant fever during the rise and fall of the WBC, which later dropped to low grade intermittent. She must have felt like pure hell during that time. Several of us down in isolation were going through the same thing, and we were miserable." Hesitating,

248

Parsons asked, "What is her general status now?"

"She says she has never gotten her stamina back. Always tired. But of course that goes right along with the condition of pregnancy, especially when coupled with anemia."

"Hmm. Tiredness, malaise—classic symptoms of radiation sickness. Within two weeks after the release of the radiation we began getting hundreds of cases of that very thing."

The obstetrician wrinkled his brow in concentration. "That shouldn't have been too hard to control, Bern. Did everybody suffer it?"

"Most did," Parsons answered. "Very few missed the tiredness altogether, though, and depending on the degree of exposure, those symptoms gave way to new and different ones within weeks. The route taken by the sickness became almost standard, beginning with the primary stages of nausea, diarrhea, vomiting, tiredness. Most of the casualties died during the first few days after the fallout—before they ever got to fever and blood disorders."

"Actually then, this woman had all the symptoms of radiation sickness, and she had them throughout a vital part of her pregnancy," said Archer. "If she'd only let me take some tests..."

As Archer rambled on about the woman's refusal, Parsons recalled an infant he had seen in his early career, a child suffering from a condition supposedly induced by radiation. The vision that he hadn't been able to erase from his memory was the tiny, tiny head—no larger than a woman's fist—sitting atop the infant's shoulders. "Archie, have you ever seen a microcephalic idiot?" he asked, for that's what the baby had been.

Archer halted in his monologue: "A microcephalic idiot? A pin head?" he asked.

"Yes. The bottom rung of the ladder of intelligence, one of the most severe of the mentally deficient," Parsons answered.

"Well, no. I haven't" he admitted. "Say, what does that have to do with this?"

Parsons hesitated while he rubbed the grit from his eyes, then he said, "Under normal conditions, the chances are less than one in twenty five thousand that a woman would have such a child."

"So?" urged the obstetrician.

"So a study was done on the offspring of Japanese women who were in mid-pregnancy and within a mile of the atomic blast that devastated Nagasaki, Archie. Of the two hundred five babies born to those women, seven were microcephalic idiots. Seven, Archie. A far cry from what might occur normally."

"Boy, you're not painting a very bright picture, Bernie."

"You mean that I'm pessimistic?" asked Parsons as he handed the folder back. "Yeah, I am. One of these days you'll begin pulling out babies that you'll think have been marked by the devil. That's when we'll start seeing what awesome damages can result from exposure to radiation. Frankly, I don't think what we'll find will be pleasant."

"The rate of abnormalities will increase, you're saying."

"Greatly! No doubt about that."

"All right, Bernie, but about my patient. What do you think?"

"That you and your patient had both better cross your fingers, knock on wood, and pray like hell." he said solemnly.

"Aw, come on Parsons. Level with me."

Parsons grinned sourly at Archie. "I wish to God I could be optimistic about her. But....say, will you do something for me?"

"Sure. Name it," answered the obstetrician.

"I'd like to assist when she delivers. Okay?"

"No problem. I'll have you paged."

"Thanks. What's her room number?"

"Eleven—it's on the delivery floor."

"Right." The surgeon began pulling himself out of the chair.

"Hey, hold on a second. You aren't leaving, are you? You haven't told me anything yet," Archie complained.

"What's to tell? I don't have any experience with radiation-affected pregnancies. But, I have a hunch we'll be getting them."

Archer walked around to stand before Parsons. He was expressively sober. "You can be a sad-faced buzzard sometimes, Parsons. If everybody listened to you we'd be saying our rosary every day instead of once a year."

Parsons was upright, face to face with Archer. "That bothers you?"

"You know what I mean. It just can't be all that bad. God, man, you sound like we're going to be paying for this forever."

"We will, for several generations. But frankly, I'm surprised to find a non-believer right here in the midst of this mess. You've got a short memory, Dr. Archer."

"Let's say I prefer to look on the brighter side—and there must be one," replied the obstetrician.

"Well, look all you like, but don't ignore the facts. They're

250

brutal, you know. Or at least you would if you'd been in that isolation unit with us for five straight weeks."

"There's no need to get sore at me, Parsons. Some of us had other obligations to meet. We couldn't lock ourselves in isolation with you and forget the practices we'd built up."

"You're right," Parsons answered shortly. "What was that? Eleven?"

"Yeah, eleven."

The door of room eleven was ajar so he walked quietly in.

Her features confirmed the medical record that he'd just read. Soft brown eyes, alert to the movements around her, watched as he drew near.

"You don't remember me, do you?" he asked as he reached her bed.

Rich full lips parted slightly, revealing a hint of a weary smile. "Of course I remember you, Dr. Parsons."

"Bernard. Call me Bernard. How are you feeling, Sara?" She glanced at the mountain of flesh protruding from her abdomen. "Tired. I wish it were over."

"It won't be much longer now. But I must say that for a lady beginning labor, you look in good shape. Different from how I remembered you, though."

She made a motion toward her hair, then let her hand return to rest by her side. "I lost my hair. It dropped out."

"Yes, a lot of mine did, too, but yours is coming back in much faster than mine." He smiled at her as he inspected the blond strands, hardly more than two inches long, which carpeted her scalp. "It's thick, with beautiful healthy color. I'm jealous."

She looked at him quizzically, as though trying to remember more detail. "That's odd. I don't recall your hair at all."

"Well," he said, pretending huffiness, "I certainly had a lot more than this. A lot more. It used to just drive the nurses crazy, seeing all my coarse distinguished locks that required constant female attention." He smiled mischievously.

She caught the gist of his game and her countenance broke into an amused grin.

"However," he added, "you never stuck around long enough to have a close look at me."

Her smile faded. "Were you mad at me for taking all the morphine and running?"

"Of course not. Those were difficult days—for you more so than most of us. I've wondered about you several times, you

251

know. I read that you'd been in Washington talking to Senator McCauley."

"Did you know the formal inquiry begins next week?" she asked.

"I heard that. But I'm surprised that you returned here, especially right now. I'd have thought you would have stayed on the east coast where you'd be free from all these reminders of the past."

"My being here does seem inopportune, doesn't it? Here, at Beckman, which I hardly knew existed until a few months ago?"

Leaning on the foot of her bed, he asked, "Would I be nosey if I asked why, Sara?"

"Oh," she said after a moment, "there are several reasons. Ben had some papers in a safety deposit box. I thought I should have them with me."

"Surely they could have waited until after the baby was born and you felt well again," he commented.

"No. I wanted them now, in case something happened."

"Something happened? Hmm, what could go wrong with you? Why would you be worried about your pregnancy? Or, isn't that what bothers you?" he asked.

"Not really," she replied slowly. Then, "Well, maybe. You see, I have a terrible feeling about it, as if something is not quite right."

"You shouldn't worry. Obstetrics is a very modern, up-to-date science. Even the most difficult pregnancies are handled routinely."

"The feeling, though, I can't get away from it, Dr. Parsons."

"Ah. Then it wasn't the desire for your husband's papers but something else that caused you to return."

"I suppose so. Subconsciously, I must have wanted to be here when the baby is delivered. That doesn't make much sense, does it?"

"I've heard of stranger things in pregnant women," he answered without any sign of the humor that would ordinarily have accompanied such a statement.

"Beckman is the place for radiation victims, though."

"True, but...."

"And you're in charge," said Sara.

He searched her face for the underlying meaning to this conversation. Her pink-hued lips were replete with invitation, but that was unknown to the woman, who felt in her face

252

nothing more than a warm flush as occasional contractions occurred. Her slender fingers lay across the white sheet, their nails burnished with a lacquer of identical color to the natural tone of her lips.

In seriousness he asked, "What bothers you about this pregnancy?"

She searched for the explanation and then admitted, "It's hard to say. When I told my physician, he wanted to take several scans and tests. And, it's ridiculous, but I just can't allow any more radiation to enter my body. Nor do I want the other tests. Stupid, isn't it?"

"Refusing the x-rays? Not really. No, I don't blame you, but that's not the only way to see what the fetus is like. This feeling you have...?"

"The kicking, for instance. I had always been told that the baby will do a lot of moving about—kicking motions—felt by the mother. I haven't noticed anything like that. In all these months, I haven't felt a thing that was like that."

"Did you tell Dr. Archer?"

"Well, I haven't talked with him all that much," she answered. "Sara, would you mind if I listened to the heartbeat?" he asked.

He was a surgeon with a better than average record at problem-solving. Still, what could he hope to learn by hearing a fetal heartbeat when in a few hours he'd see the baby?

Receiving her permission, he applied the stethoscope and listened intently for a couple minutes. Finally he stepped back from the mound of flesh and smiled reassuringly. "It sounds fine to me, Sara. There's nothing at all unusual about the fetal heartbeat."

"Then why don't I get the same kind of jolts I've heard other women describe in their pregnancies?" she asked with concern.

"You have felt some motion, haven't you?"

"Yes, but very slight—nothing like I expected," she said.

"Well, Sara, I don't know. But I'm sure everything will be all right. And it won't be too much longer until you'll be a mother with a trimmer figure than you have now," he said with a lightness that he did not feel.

She seemed unconvinced that there was no cause for concern. "I wish I could be sure."

"You're borrowing trouble when there's no need to. Let's just wait and see what happens, okay?"

"There's not much choice for me, is there, Dr. Parsons?"

"Oh, I remember you as a fighter. I say you struggling against insurmountable odds, while lesser people gave up. This thing won't get you—not you."

"Dr. Parsons..." Sara began.

"Bernard."

"Bernard, what thoughts did you have after I stole that whole bottle of morphine from you?"

"Hmm, as I recollect, I was past the point of having thoughts. I was a robot, going about my tasks as mechanically as though I was remotely controlled by some unknown being."

"By taking the entire bottle, did I leave you....did I cause anyone to suffer?"

"Everybody was suffering, Sara. One unit of morphine wouldn't have made much difference."

"It helped Ben. It made him unaware of the pain so that he... he..." she faltered, unable to continue.

"I'm sure it did," he hastened to complete her thought. "You know, I've read your recent medical history. It must have taken tremendous will power for you to attend those investigations. You probably should have been getting complete bed rest instead."

"Fatigue was my biggest enemy during those first months; and it still is. But I had this compulsion, I guess you'd call it, to do my share, to add whatever I could about the conditions here. I often wonder why I was compelled to be there, to talk with the Senator, and the only suitable explanation is that because I have lost so much, I'm desperately anxious that the incident at White Water not be repeated."

"Was it worth it, Sara—giving your account to Senator McCauley? Will it cause any changes do you think?"

"Until the formal inquiry is over, we won't know what to expect. But one experience like I've had is enough for a lifetime," she asserted. "More than enough, actually."

"Not that anybody ever noticed, but most of the physicians in this region signed a petition protesting the operation of White Water until safety factors could be positively guaranteed. Of course, nobody paid any attention to us," he said sadly. "That's always the story—nobody pays attention."

"Bernard, what will happen to Los Angeles?" asked Sara.

"Time is the answer. In time, it'll slowly revert to a normal city—the same gigantic sprawling city of six months ago," he

254

answered. "Its scars will disappear. Eventually."

"Do you really believe that?" she asked.

"That it'll regenerate its lost parts? Sure, in that respect a city is more durable than the men who made it. After all, it's not the only city to have been destroyed—it's just unique in the method of its destruction."

"You have great faith," she said matter-of-factly.

"In mankind. Yes, I do. When people collectively put their brains together, there's no limit to their accomplishments."

She looked at him thoughtfully. "There's not much recorded history of people collectively putting their brains together, though."

"That's perfectly true, Sara. However, we've been rudely thrust into an age where the failure to exercise our brainpower could result in our annihilation. We have a choice. Now we simply use our right to make it."

They both realized that the subject of exercising rights had been open long before the destruction of White Water.

A visible twinge of discomfort passed through her body. "Umm. They're coming more often—the pains."

"Dr. Archer doesn't expect labor to progress this quickly," said Bernie with sudden concern. "I'm going to give him a buzz."

"Wait!" Sara asked as the last of the pain left her. "Wait, Bernard."

"Yes?" he asked.

She smiled weakly at him. "I know this doesn't make much sense, but will you stay with me in the delivery room? It's unusual, but I'd like it if you were there."

He laid his hand reassuringly on her thin shoulder. "I had planned to assist Archer. I've already seen to it, Sara. I'll be in the delivery room with you."

Fitting the cap down over his head, Dr. Parsons watched his colleague from the corner of his eye. "Why didn't you slow the labor, Archie? For her first, didn't you think it was progressing too rapidly?"

The obstetrician was tying his gown. "Six hours is pretty quick for a first, but the fetal head was showing through the entrance of the vagina—quarter-size—so I figured what-the-hell, we'd go on with it."

There was nothing for the surgeon to say. This was out of his domain.

They moved into the delivery room which was being readied for the patient.

"Isn't she here, yet?" Archer asked a nurse.

"They're bringing her over. It'll be a minute."

Anesthesia machines with their tanks of gas were pulled over to the delivery table. The overhead surgical light would not be turned on until the woman's shaved pelvis was scrubbed with antiseptic and covered with a sheet.

Dr. Parsons inspected the large mirror by which the patient could view the proceedings. Its presence, its function, made him uneasy. "What kind of anesthesia are you giving her," he asked Dr. Archer as he turned away from the reflector.

"Meperidine was given up in the room."

"No. I mean during the delivery. Did she have any preference?"

"She didn't mention having a particular choice. A saddle block will do."

"She should have scopolamine," said Parsons.

"What? I don't see any necessity for completely blocking out her memory of the birth. A lot of women want to see what's happening, and want to feel it—at least they want to feel some of it."

"Nevertheless," said Parsons, "I believe it would be wiser if she slept through the whole thing."

"Aw, come on, Bernard. That's ridiculous. Besides, it's not advisable to give sedation at this stage. We need her awake enough to do some pushing."

The doctor was insistent. "Look, Archie, I'm not trying to tell you how to do your job...."

"Don't then," snapped the physician.

"But I think it would be smarter to slow the delivery a bit, than have this woman mentally charting everything that's happening in here."

"Parsons, if I'd known you were going to be a pain in the ass I wouldn't have let you in here!" Archer began checking the instrument tray, ignoring the surgeon.

Parsons reached and nudged the tray aside. "Will you put her out or won't you?"

Wheeling around, his eyes smoldering with annoyance, Archer said, "Man, I can't figure you! Why is this so important that you're standing here arguing with me?"

"For the life of me, I don't know," answered the surgeon.

256

"But I wish you'd just do it my way, and put her out."

"Many women want to see their babies immediately, as soon as they're born," Archer protested.

"And some women have unpleasant memories from their pregnancies," said Parsons in a voice suddenly grown cold.

The double doors were shoved open as Sara was wheeled in. She was draped for the occasion and fully awake.

Arrival of the patient should have ended their discussion, but for Bernard it was not ended—not until he had his way on the anesthesia. "Well, Archer?" he asked.

Archer's eyes glared over the top of his mask. "Parsons, you don't know a damned thing about this. Now either shut up or get out!"

"Then you won't knock her out?" asked Parsons in a low voice.

"No!"

The surgeon was not defeated yet. He stalked over to the mirror and bent it out of line with the delivery table.

Dr. Archer observed the action, but allowed the mirror to remain in an angle.

Sara was assisted onto the table. Both feet were placed in the stirrups as she lay down on her back. Metal handbars were raised along each side for her to later grasp and push against during the heavy contractions. With final adjustment to the stirrups, the lower part of the table was slid in under her pelvis. A nurse stepped forward and swabbed the lower abdomen and inner thighs with antiseptic. The entire area was then blanketed by a sheet containing a window for the vaginal opening.

At the last minute Dr. Archer had decided against the saddle block and opted for a local anesthetic. The anesthetist moved into position and administered the agent to the area around the vagina. This would effectively block the pain receptors and would leave Sara capable of the pushing movements necessary to help extrude the baby.

Since her entrance into the delivery room, the tension between the two physicians had lessened. Parsons had been satisfied in insuring that Sara wouldn't see the actual birth, and he stepped aside to give the obstetrician plenty of room to work.

Allowing the anesthesia to take effect required a few minutes and the surgeon walked over to stand by Sara, momentarily sharing in the short wave of fear that flitted across her face.

She watched his eyes as they darted back and forth over the

top of his own sterile mask, and saw one lid drop into a long wink at her. That she had asked him to assist was proof that he inspired confidence in her, that his being here was consoling.

The vaginal opening was becoming distended from the baby's head. "We're ready to begin," announced Dr. Archer. Reaching for the tray, the obstetrician chose a scalpel and with a flick produced an incision which enlarged the opening further. With the episiotomy completed, there would be no danger of random tearing of the mother's tissues as the baby began its exit. "All right, Sara, let's bear down now," said Archer.

Sara clenched her hands even tighter around the bars and inwardly pushed. The inner tension was clearly evidenced in her face.

Bernard had moved to stand behind Archie, content to be out of the way and a spectator.

The top of the child's head appeared slowly, moving outward by a fraction with each contraction.

"Bear down, Sara! Come on. Push."

Sara's grunt was audible as she followed Archie's instructions.

"Harder, Sara! Harder, now!"

More of the same gutteral sounds issued from her.

Slowly, slowly, the tiny head, wet and smooth from fluids, inched into the world.

"That's a good girl," Archie said encouragingly, "a good girl."

The small face was turned towards the floor, in his hand.

"Come on, Sara. Once again," he said. "Once more, now."

The head was free, and Archie carefully rotated it to the left, turning the body ever so cautiously until the shoulders were correctly positioned. Fluids dripped between his gloved fingers as he gingerly maneuvered the tiny body through the last of the birth canal.

"Again, Sara. Just as little more," he said. "Come on now, Sara. Just a little longer." His voice was soft, almost a croon to the expectant mother. "Here we come," he said.

The shoulders were shoving through, widening the vaginal gap even more. "Ahhh, here we come."

Abruptly the shoulders popped through with unusual ease. Dr. Archer stared down at the infantile form supported by his hand. In disbelief, he glanced up at Dr. Parsons, who by now was making sure the mirror had not become re-aligned to Sara's view.

A faint gasp was heard from one of the nurses who was assisting Archer.

For what must have seemed like minutes, the animation of the medical persons was suspended.

Sounds indicated Sara was still laboring at expelling the infant, and it was these noises that finally reminded Archer of his task.

The abdomen with its thick slimy umbilical cord was just coming into sight when the doctor regained his speech. "A little more, Sara." He choked over the words, then cleared his throat. "Push, Sara!" he said.

And it was free.

All eyes turned to look at the child. Parsons, Archer, the two nurses—only the anesthetist stood by Sara.

Across the gloved hands of the obstetrician lay a miniscule human being. From each tiny shoulder extended a knobby bud, less than an inch long, with several stubby projections. Opposite miniature male genitals were two other buds, again no longer than an inch. In all, it looked like a diminutive doll, without arms or legs, but with a distinctly-formed head atop the red-stained torso.

The room was quiet, empty of adult expression as they stood in somber disbelief.

Parsons saw the shock registered in the obstetrician, who was transfixed as he held his charge. "Slap him!" he urged. "Now, Archer!"

His command jarred Archer into frenzied action. Failing to find lower limbs by which the infant could be suspended, he shuffled the baby from one hand to the other.

"Slap him, dammit!" repeated Parsons.

"I... .I can't. There's no way...!"

"Turn him on his belly and slap!" Parsons yelled.

Archer stood helplessly shifting the child for a more secure grasp when the nurse reached out for the tiny bundle.

"It's no use, Dr. Archer. He's dead," she whispered.

She took the baby from him and held it.

Archer snatched up a gleaming sterile instrument and clipped the umbilical cord.

Dr. Parsons heard the faint, plaintive call of his name.

"What is it? What's happening?" Sara asked.

The nurse moved away from the center of activity. "Bernard, where's my baby? I want to see it," demanded Sara. He quietly closed his fist over her warm sweaty knuckles. "Sara, the baby is... the baby is dead."

"Dead? Oh, noooo," she wailed as she threw her arm across her eyes, trying to stop the rush of tears.

"It was....there was nothing to be done for the little thing," said Parsons. "There was nothing to be done."

"My God how I wanted that baby. Ben...oh, Lord, it was all I had of Ben....all that was left," she cried.

Archer quickly ordered a syringe, and injected a fast-acting sedative into her arm.

She was rapidly becoming delirious. "Where is my baby? I want to see it!" she screamed.

"Sara. Sara! Don't! You had a little boy. But please, Sara, it won't help for you to see him," said Parsons.

She shook his hand off her shoulder and started pulling her body upright on the delivery table.

"Keep her still!" ordered Dr. Archer. "I'm not finished down here!"

"My baby. I must see him! Where is my baby?" Bernard held her against her struggles. "All right, Sara. Relax and I'll bring the baby to you."

"No! I'll find him myself," she panted.

The surgeon shoved against her, pinning her to the table. "You wait now, Sara. Stay right here. Don't move, and I'll bring your baby to you."

A nurse stepped in and replaced him. She talked soothingly to the prostrate woman, calming her until the sedative took action.

The obstetrician had removed the afterbirth. The pancake shaped, spongy placenta and the vestiges of membranes were dropped into a pan.

Bernard lifted the infant. Using a surgical towel, he wrapped the cloth tightly around the body, concealing all but the head. Cradling it on his arm, he eased back to Sara's side.

She was calmer now.

"Sara," he said, glad that the sedative was working, "Sara, here is your baby."

She looked at Parsons, then down at the child. She made no effort to take her baby from Bernard but, after a long moment, turned her face away and broke into a gentle sob.

Dr. Archer sutured the incision closed, making neat, precise stitches; taking infinite care to reduce the episiotomy to a thin, clean scar—almost as if removing any visible sign of the birth would also obliterate the memory of it.

The child was taken out. Shortly afterward, Sara was wheeled into a recovery room.

It was a later hour that found the two physicians sitting at a desk with cups of steaming coffee.

"Parsons, that was the only time in my career when I absolutely couldn't do a thing but stand there," said the obstetrician.

"With the baby?" asked Parsons knowingly.

"Yeah. I couldn't do anything but stare at that poor, deformed child. I....I've never delivered anything like it before."

Dr. Parsons absentmindedly dropped in another cube of sugar. For the moment his thoughts were elsewhere, with Sara Harrington.

"You anticipated some problems with the delivery, didn't you?" asked Archer. "I did. From the patient's past history, I figured there'd be at least transfusions needed for the baby, but....Parsons, are you listening to me?"

"Huh? Yeah. I heard you, Archie."

"What did you think we'd find?" he asked.

"I didn't have any ideas, really. I suppose Sara was the one who was most convinced that something was wrong." He now knew why she hadn't felt the normal kicks and jerks characteristic of limb movements.

"I'd sure like to have an autopsy of that child, though," said Archer. "Without it, we'll never know if they were radiation induced deformities or not."

Parsons replied absently, "She won't permit an autopsy."

"How do you know?" asked Archer. "Have you mentioned it to her?"

"No, of course not," said Parsons. "But I'm sure she won't go along with it. She asked me to arrange for the child's cremation."

"Well, there won't be any cremation yet. Not until I've asked her about an autopsy," stated the obstetrician.

Looking up from his coffee, Parsons said, "I don't want her harassed about this, Archer. You go on and ask, but if she says no, then that's where it stands. No pushing, understand?" His words carried threateningly across the table.

"Without the examination we'll never know whether the deformities resulted from radiation or what," Archer replied testily. "Absence of arms and legs doesn't necessarily result

261

from radiation. Thalidomide produced the same anomalies."

Dr. Parsons was finding the obstetrician increasingly irritating. "Sara Harrington certainly never took thalidomide, and whether the radiation caused the malformations is beside the point, Archer. What I'm saying is that she shouldn't have any more agony now—certainly not a further reminder of that baby. You should just forget the autopsy."

Dr. Archer disagreed. "Nope. I'm going to ask for one. She has nothing to lose by permitting it."

Sighing, the surgeon pushed the coffee mug aside and propped his arms on the table. "You know, she's not aware that the child was deformed. When you go in to talk with her about the autopsy, she's going to wonder why—and she'll ask. What are you going to say, then, Archie? That the child had no limbs?"

Shrugging, the obstetrician replied, "Why not? She's got a right to know."

"Right! For God's sake, man, hasn't it occurred to you that for her it may be best if she didn't know?" Bernard felt his voice rising to a crescendo, but made no effort to temper it. "The woman stayed with a dying husband, exposing herself to radiation. She came to this very hospital twice for treatment of him and each time was turned away. She watched him as he slowly and agonizingly died, and there was nothing she could do to prevent it! Archer, I'm telling you to leave her alone! Don't even mention an autopsy to that woman! Do you hear me?" He felt his hands quivering with anger as he finished the outburst.

It was evident by Dr. Archer's expression that he had not reckoned on such a heated argument from his colleague. Pulling himself to his full height, he snapped back, "What in the hell gives you the right to tell me what to do, Parsons? Just because you're the chief of this staff doesn't mean you can start pushing me around. I was in this hospital long before you ever got here and I'm not about to be treated like some young intern, by God."

Parsons retorted, more heatedly now, "I have the right, and in this case I'm telling you to lay off." Suddenly, his tone softened, "Lay off, Archer, or I'll have your job—I swear to God."

A deep flush of blood suffused Archer's neck and continued on up to his cheeks. "Oh, so that's it! You're still holding it against me because I didn't volunteer to serve in the isolation unit—to play martyr with you! I knew that somehow you'd try

262

to get even with me, Parsons, but I never figured you to have to sink this low to do it!"

Had the accusation been on target? Bernard wondered. Was Archer right or was the man suffering a guilt complex from his own decision not to work with the radiation patients? Sure, he recalled that he had harbored some nasty thoughts about the staff members who had turned their backs on him and his small crew. But it wasn't a long-festering resentment, dormant over the past few months, that had finally surfaced. No, it was something stronger than resentment, something he felt about himself. He hadn't been bothered at the time—at the moment he had decided Ben Harrington couldn't be saved—by his decision to withhold the antibiotics for patients with a greater chance of recovery. His assessment of the man's recovery potential had been made professionally, and there was no need to regret his choice. Yet, he did. He often wondered—since Harrington had miraculously escaped death once—if he might not have avoided it again with the precious antibiotics. No matter how he tried to shake the feeling off, he always returned to the unwelcome thought that he had played God and determined, almost guaranteed, Ben Harrington's death. It was an unpleasant vision, the picture of himself arranging the life and death of people. "You're wrong, Archer. Despite what you may think, you're wrong!"

"Bull! shouted Archie. "You're just worried that you can't handle the job of Chief of Staff, and you're going to try to cover your inadequacies by picking on me—me and the others. There'll be others, won't there, Parsons?"

Now, in the heat of anger, Bernard began to see that he had been right about Archer. The man did suffer guilt pangs about his role, and coupled with that was his growing resentment that Parsons had gained the appointment of chief administrator. Recognizing the truth in both himself and his associate, he wearily replied, "I'm not out to have your job, Archer. Frankly, I don't give a damn whether you're on this staff or not, but I'm not interested in taking your job from you. All I want is to make certain that Sara Harrington is allowed to recuperate in as much peace and quiet as this facility can provide." He looked up at Archer, still poised before him. "And that's exactly the way it's going to be. Understand?"

A long, suspenseful moment passed as the two men stared at each other. Finally Archer exhaled a slow breath and answered,

"Yeah, I got your message." With that, he walked out of the room.

Bernard heard the door close after Archer. It had been an unusual day, the sort of day that occasionally happened to medical people, the kind that they always wanted to forget—the constant dealing with the illnesses that plague man, the never-ending contest with death—and the toll was great on the surgeon. It was not during the aftermath of the White Water incident, but later, that he'd had momentary impulses to take off his white jacket and walk out of the hospital forever, never to look back, and never to return to the vocation that had gradually become more demoralizing that satisfying to him. It was no longer enough to just get through each day. There had to be more than that. What had happened to the old ideals, the old enthusiasm? When had it begun slipping away? And why was it so hard to re-capture? His body ached from fatigue. He was totally exhausted.

The traveling suit felt strange after the months of baggy, loose fitting maternity clothes. But it was a comfortable, good sensation that Sara had, knowing that she still filled it out in the right places.

Sara adjusted the chaise and gently unfolded her body along its length. Her dress was entirely incongruous with the patio and the lazy, warm sunlight that filtered through the morning haze. It was a serene, gentle time of day and it had brought her out to enjoy her last few hours of California, relaxed and alone in the secluded area behind one wing of the hospital.

Her thoughts skipped ahead to the near future. She wondered when Senator McCauley would contact her. On their last meeting he had said that once the formal investigation was underway, then he'd get in touch with her. Well, he was in his chamber today, beginning anew with his attempt to weed out the causes and evaluate the effects of the disaster. She must be there when his call came. More so than ever before, it was imperative that she take her place before those committees and agencies that the Senator deemed importantly open and receptive to the facts of White Water. White Water... .it had provided impetus to an anti-nuclear movement, but maintaining the momentum would rest with the people, the ones who were concerned. To sway, and keep permanently fixed, the federal government, the Atomic Energy Commission, and private industry, would become an all-consuming task—one in which she was eager to be a part.

"Hello there," he said. "How did you manage to get out here? This place hasn't been used in months."

"Good morning, Bernard." Sara smiled warmly at the tall, thin physician. "I spotted this little nook on one of my frequent rounds through the corridors. It's delightful."

"But seedy," he said, glancing around.

"After that gloomy room, this is a regular heaven. Besides, I simply could not stay inside any longer."

He pulled out another chaise and took a seat. "Only five days, Sara. Are you positive that you aren't pushing this a bit—this desire to leave us?"

Her soft laugh flowed through the morning air with a touch of feigned gaiety. It was an unconvincing display of humor. "You may think this is the greatest spot on the west coast, Doctor, but I assure you that it is not. Oh, don't misinterpret that, Bernie— I'm eternally grateful for all you've done for me. Believe me."

"But five days... .I question if you should be this active and should undertake such a lengthy trip so soon after the birth," he said with a hint of worry.

"Dr. Archer believes that it's perfectly all right. He says the quicker a woman gets out of the child bed, the faster she recuperates."

"Archie is a horse's patoot."

"Oh Bernie, you couldn't be that unchivalrous. Dr. Archer is a fine man."

"Uh huh. But he's still the south end of a north bound donkey." This time she genuinely laughed. "Are you absolutely certain that you're not too busy to drive me to the airport?"

"Not a chance, not a chance. I haven't been out with a beautiful woman—in let's see—about eighty years."

She looked at the fibers of silver hair growing in among the darker ones. With his small trim mustache, Bernard Parsons was a very distinguished-looking man. "How old are you, anyway?" she asked.

"Ah now, have I ever asked you anything that personal, Sara? Or would you have answered me if I had?"

"Well," she replied in mock annoyance, "it would be impolite to ask a lady her age. Besides, she'd lie to you."

265

Bernard chuckled. "I'm forty-one."

His age surprised her. "My goodness, you look...."

"Yeah. Older."

She had been thinking of ten years older.

His attention was caught by a wheelchair being pushed down the hall. "Hey! Hey, you two. Come out here for awhile and enjoy the sunshine."

He jumped up and shoved his chair aside so that Cecil could roll Althea into the sunlight.

"We can only stay a second," announced Cecil. "We have some important plans to make."

"Haven't I heard via the grapevine that you two are getting married?" asked Sara.

"Yes, we are," Althea replied.

"Yes, we are," echoed Cecil.

"Congratulations to both of you. I hope you'll be very happy," Sara said. "Will you be leaving soon, Althea?"

"In another week. Another seven days. It's awfully exciting, you know. Cecil has been working on the apartment. We'll live in San Diego." The words came rushing out of her mouth.

"Uh, listen, I hate to cut this short, but we must get with it, Althea," said Cecil fondly.

They bid Sara goodbye and left.

Sara sighed, and glanced at her watch. "It's about time we were leaving, Bernard."

"Hmm. Your folks will pick you up at Kennedy Airport?"

"My sister will. Dad hasn't been well lately and he and Mom hate to travel into New York."

"I was in Connecticut once. Overnight. I stayed at a friend's house in Bridgeport."

"Did you?" she asked with interest.

"We had a clambake on the beach that night."

"It's beautiful state, Connecticut," answered Sara.

"Oh yeah. I'd like to see it again, sometime."

"Well, if you do make it back East, you must be sure to visit with me, Bernie."

"Do you mean that?" he asked.

"Of course. You've been such a tremendous help to me, the very least I could do is offer to show you around my old home town."

"You know," he said thoughtfully, "I'm taking a month's vacation in August. Maybe I'll really drop in on you."

266

"Good. I'd enjoy visiting with you."

"Guess I'd better get your bag to the car, then."

"Bernie?" She'd said his name quickly.

"Yes?"

"I wanted to ask you about....the..." She hesitated. Should she ask? Did she really want to know? Would it better not to know? Sara looked at Bernard intently.

"About what, Sara?"

She fumbled with the gold wedding band on her finger, turning it slowly around and around. There was little new that could be said about her baby, she decided. Had there been more, this tender, gentle man would have told her. She reached out and placed her hand on his arm. "Will you come to see me?"

Parsons smiled. "Plan on it."

A SHORT HISTORY OF THE DEVELOPMENT OF THE NUCLEAR POWER PLANTS

On December 20, 1951, at the Experimental Breeder Reactor EBR-I in Arco, Idaho, USA, for the first time electricity - illuminating four light bulbs - was produced by nuclear energy. EBR-I was not designed to produce electricity but to validate the breeder reactor concept.

On June 26, 1954, at Obninsk, Russia, the nuclear power plant APS-1 with a net electrical output of 5 MW was connected to the power grid, the world's first nuclear power plant that generated electricity for commercial use. On August 27, 1956, the first commercial nuclear power plant, Calder Hall 1, England, with a net electrical output of 50 MW was connected to the national grid.

As of January, 2015, there are 439 nuclear power plants that are operational in the world with another 69 under construction. The United States has 104 of these plants, France has 59, and Japan has 50. (2)

U.N. Secretary General Ban Ki-moon warned that the world must prepare for more nuclear accidents on the scale of Chernobyl and Japan's Fukushima plant. He said the grim reality demands sharp improvements in International cooperation (3)

(2) European Nuclear Society web site home page. **www.euronuclear.org** , April 21, 2011
(3). Los Angeles Times. April 21, 2011. UKRAINE - U.N.'s Ban gives nuclear warning

The following is an excerpt from the sequel
to "The Nuclear Catastrophe", which
begins several years following the accident
at San Mirado. A nuclear accident in
Fukushima, Japan, has occurred.

#Betrayal
A nuclear fiction novel of survival

by

Barbara C. Griffin Billig

Dedicated to:

All my supportive social media friends on twitter, facebook, google, pinterest and more, and to the inspiring preppers and survivors, and those writers who are trying to alert us to the dangers in the world.

Special thanks to my good friends Nancy Van Volkinburg, Beryl Elman, Larane Nesbitt, and Anne Bierly who were interested enough in my writing project to read the first draft of #Betrayal. Michelle McKeeth helped so much with the editing. Their notes and observations are incorporated into the final manuscript.

Also thanks to my twitter pals, '@FactsCount', '@1CaptD', '@ThatArcher' and '@KevinMeyerson' (who lives in Japan). We have exchanged a lot of tweets. And thanks to all the rest of you I have gotten to know and exchanged interesting and useful information.

And finally, a thanks to my husband, Edward Billig, an outstanding electrical contractor who can build anything...and provides me with the time and support to pursue writing.

This novel is a sequel to:
"The Nuclear Catastrophe"
A fiction novel of survival

PROLOGUE

The white walls and the white linens surrounded her. The bareness of the room was overwhelming, not cozy and comforting. For the moment she was alone. Sara watched the clock click away and wondered if these were the last moments of her life. She wanted some more morphine but was afraid if she increased the dosage she wouldn't wake up again. She fingered the pump. The pain hit her with an intense wave.

As the relaxing drug flooded her body she floated away. Help, she was too young for this! And she thought back...Sara thought back to her first baby who had been born after the devastating San Mirado nuclear catastrophe. When her child was delivered they had wrapped it in a towel and given it to her to hold. They thought she didn't notice. But she did – she could feel it was too small and too thin. Ben's baby – their son. Delivered in the presence of Dr. Bernard Parsons.

It had been the nuclear catastrophe that could never happen. Her then husband, Ben, had been the supervisor of the local nuclear power plant. He never failed to assure her how safe the nuclear plants were, they had thought of everything in the planning. They were fail safe. They had thought of everything except the earthquake that had frozen the control rods. The control rods that couldn't be lowered into the core of the nuclear reactor to slow down the speed of the atoms splitting. The control rods which were necessary to keep the reactor from overheating. The reaction kept increasing in speed, releasing more and more heat as more and more atoms split, until a terrible explosion of pent up energy and overheated gases blew the place apart, causing a meltdown and a tremendous release of radiation.

People panicked and drove in the wrong directions, clogging the streets, trying to flee. They couldn't believe their precious phones no longer worked, or the bank automated teller wouldn't give them any money. The things they took for granted disappeared in an instant and they were not prepared.

And now years had passed. She was married to Dr. Bernard Parsons. And now they had Fukushima. The Fukushima nuclear catastrophe that everyone said could never happen. Just as it had been said the nuclear catastrophe could never happen in San Mirado. Would they never learn?

CHAPTER ONE

Dr. Bernard Parsons sat at his desk in his suite of medical offices adjacent to the hospital. His white lab jacket hung open over his open collared dress shirt and neatly pressed pants. He was a handsome man, but the past years involving the San Mirado nuclear disaster had aged him somewhat. He had already done his morning rounds for his patients. He had visited with Sara, his wife, in her private hospital suite, and made sure she was as comfortable as possible. Once again he had been reassuring to her. He was hoping for a miracle. The phone rang several times before Bernard could reach it. It was his direct line which bypassed his secretary and receptionist. "Hello, Bernard Parsons here," he spoke into the telephone.

"Bernard, how are you? Just calling to see what's happening?" Sam Baxter said. Sam, of Baxter Investments, was a successful businessman in the real estate and investments market. He was the 'go to' person for getting ahead with your money. He had five sons from his first wife, who were in business with him. His second wife, Elise, had no children. But it was because he was insistent about her not having a child. And secretly, just to make sure he had his way, he had, as insurance, had a vasectomy. That served two functions. One, he could cheat without the fear of getting stuck with one more kid, blackmail, and/or a divorce. And two, Elise – who was incapable of taking care of anything – was prevented from having the child she constantly talked about wanting. She worried obsessively about who was going to take care of her when she was older.

"You have over $50,000 cash in your investment account," Sam said. "One of your bonds was called at par and you haven't been spending as much lately, so you should put this to work. We have a good bond, in-house from a trust. The kids who are now in control want to cash everything out now since the father has died. They will sell it below market. The smell of money is driving them to get this done quickly. You can buy it for eighty cents on the dollar – 50,000 in the block."

"So who's behind the bond? What's it rated" asked Bernard.

"Oh, you know I'm going to go through all the particulars with you. Just wanted to let you stop me dead in the water if you had other plans for the cash," Sam responded. "It's a bond for the Moorpark, Ca. school system, rated AA, and insured by Ambac. Moorpark's a very upscale city, very healthy financially. Yield is 5% tax free."

"As long as it's not Sacramento," Bernard said. "Go ahead." Then he paused slightly, not knowing whether he wanted to broach the subject or not. "How are the kids?"

With a sigh, Sam answered, "Doing well. I have to monitor their transactions and since there are five of them it takes a lot of my time. They've brought in a lot of business, got to give them that. But they just don't believe that things can go wrong. And they resent my looking over their shoulder."

"We will have to have dinner one of these evenings when things settle down at my house," Bernard said.

"How is Sara doing?" Sam asked.

"Realistically, not so well. But I'm always hopeful for a remission or a miracle. Listen, gotta run, my nurse has buzzed me several times...patients are waiting. Thanks for calling, Sam." Bernard hung up the phone and pressed his nurse's intercom button.

Fuji woke up hungry. The drab concrete block walls around him had no decoration and stared back at him silently. He blinked to clear out the sleep from his eyes. Other people were starting to move around, up from their cots. Soon the noise level would move to such high decibels people would gladly go outside to get away from it. But it was cold outside and almost as cold inside.

The government had been giving them rations since they had

been evacuated from Fukushima, but they were hardly edible. First the authorities had said it was no problem for them to stay in the area. Then after two weeks they were told the area was very radioactive and there were mandatory orders to evacuate. He wondered how much radiation they had been exposed to.

Fuji thought about what he would do today. They needed a place to live. They had a home near Fukushima, Japan, but now they were no longer allowed to go there. They also needed clothes. Now he had no job. His wife and two children were alternately scared, hungry, bored, angry, and confused. They were sleeping on cots with hundreds of other families in a big warehouse. There were two bathrooms inside, outside were portable toilets, and one makeshift outside shower with only cold water.

"Fuji...," his wife said, "are you awake? I'm going to get the children up and go stand in the food line."

"Okay. I'm going to see if it is possible to shower."

"Have you heard anything? About what's happening?" Shisa asked.

"I'll try and find out," he replied. Slowly rising, he got off his cot in his rumpled, soiled clothes and began making his way to a door leading to the outside. A government agent would be there later he had heard. Possibly they would have some clothing to give out. It meant standing in line again for hours to take your turn. Some people had money or had relatives they could stay with. Fuji and his family were poor. They had no nearby relatives. They had no money. And now they had no possessions.

He stopped to piss on the way by closely hugging the wall and hoping no one would notice. At the shower there were only a few men as most people were in the food line. He took his place in line, hoping they wouldn't run out of soap in the dispenser, or the paper towels, before his turn came. He hoped the sun would warm the cold air. Maybe he could get an extra shirt since there were no coats.

"Did you hear anything?" he asked the man in front of him.

"No one seems to know anything except we can't go back now. The earthquake and tidal wave wiped out most of the area, the radiation from nuclear plants contaminated the rest."

"But we can go back?" Fuji said hopefully.

"Who knows? There's not a lot left there. Where did you work?"

"I worked at the power plant", Fuji said.

"The nuclear plant? The one that blew up?"

"Yes, the Fukushima nuclear plant."

The other man shook his head and left Fuji standing there as he walked quickly away.

Bernard was sitting in his offices after the last patient had left and the employees had gone. There was not much of a push to get home since Sara was in the hospital located beside his medical offices. He would get dinner from the hospital cafeteria and take it up to eat with her. It couldn't be any worse than what she was being served. Hospitals were famous for their bad food.

Bernard sat and looked over the latest offering from Sam's company. His kids were pushing second loans on houses secured by real estate. Supposedly it could never go wrong with real estate constantly pushing upward in price. He thought back to the last catastrophe, when the nuclear plant in San Mirado, California, had blown up. Real estate values went to nothing in the area after all the radiation contamination. Didn't make any difference whether you held the first loan or the second – you were out of luck. The lenders lost their money, the homeowners lost their houses. Insurance didn't cover radiation disasters.

But, as the kids pointed out, these weren't in Southern California, but in the suburbs outside San Francisco. He and Sara had moved there after getting married to start a new life together. And the government obviously believed nuclear was clean, safe energy or they would have closed the plants down. Just because there had been an accident in Fukushima didn't affect the values here.

Bernard pondered whether he believed all this. He and Sara had been in the middle of the last disaster.

Bernard thought about the fact the United States was recognized as a world leader, a world power, perhaps the strongest of all the nations with the most modern technologies. Yet, as a doctor he contemplated why the United States didn't lead the world in having the lowest mortality rate among infants. And it wasn't even a close race. With approximately 188 countries reporting, the US was only number 34. And a lot of the countries ahead of the US had no nuclear power.

In fact it had been theorized that the health of the United States population had been compromised by all the above ground nuclear testing starting in the 1940's, then the underground tests which followed, and the massive leaks of radioactive material. Australia, with no nuclear industry, was ranked 18 in the report.

Interestingly, the Japanese, who had been subjected to two massive nuclear bombs and had 55 operating nuclear plants in a small country, was number 3 in lowest mortality rating. It would be revealing to see what happened to their rating over the next ten to twenty years after their massive Fukushima nuclear accident. But the documentation showed the United States, in those years of testing nuclear bombs in the atmosphere and oceans, had detonated over one hundred million times the bombs which had been dropped on Japan. The US was first in the production of radioactive pollution.

Bernard opened the hospital room door softly, to see if Sara was awake. He hoped she was, but if she were sleeping he would return later. Her eyes were closed. Even with no makeup she was still beautiful, her features perfect. She had naturally blond hair and big dark eyes. The lashes were heavily fringed and surrounded those eyes, giving her a dramatic look. Slowly they opened and a smile came to her face. She lifted her arms to him, to touch him. He bent over and kissed her cheek.

"I have good news, Sara," he said quietly.

"And what is that?" she asked still smiling.

"Well, you have improved in how you are feeling, so we must assume the chemo and radiation have done some good. The tumor hasn't grown. You could very well be in remission at the moment. But the tumor is inoperable and is still there in your brain. There is a new experimental procedure available. A doctor with your same tumor tried it. He figured it was his only chance to survive. His tumor began to shrink. Duke University has begun a larger study with good results for these glioblastomas.

"Is it painful?" she asked.

"No, not really. It requires an injection into the tumor, but it's done with anesthesia. You would have some soreness in the scalp area after, but that's about it."

"What is being injected?"

"Polio virus. They have shown in mice the injection of the live virus into tumors shrinks them. First we would get your polio vaccination updated so you didn't get polio. Then we would do an injection of the live virus into the tumor in your brain. Hopefully it will work for you as well as it has for this doctor."

"What kind of doctor is he?"

"Interestingly enough he is a cardiac surgeon. When he got this brain tumor and was diagnosed with only six months to live he started doing research. This guy wasn't a smoker; he only drank minimally and kept his health an important part of his life. So why did he get this tumor? He found a medical paper published wherein twenty-two doctors had all gotten this same type tumor in the same side of the head and the same placement. They were all doctors who had radiological studies going on while they were doing surgery."

279

"That's rather scary, Bernard, you being a surgeon."

"Does make you think. But anyway, he then found the study with the polio virus injection and decided to make a try. For him, it seems to be working."

"Well, can I have a little break from the hospital before we try something else?"

"Why not. I'll ask your doctor to make a final determination and sign you out. I will discuss this with him and perhaps you can even leave today."

Sara's eyes lit up and then tears formed in them. She squeezed Bernard's hand tightly. "I can't wait to get out of here."

Sara stared out at the view from the back deck of their home. They lived high in the hills north of San Francisco. She had missed looking out at the bay, the boats coming and going, the sunrises and sunsets. Bernard was close enough to his hospital so commuting wasn't a problem. And there was no nuclear plant close to them. That had been a factor in their choice of where to live.

She also missed the activities she had shared with her friends. When she became ill, first with the headaches, then nausea, finally vomiting, Bernard had insisted she have a MRI. It had shown the tumor, an aggressive malignant type, located in her brain in an inoperable location. It was hard to talk with her friends about this.

They had called and she had simply chosen not to discuss it. "Let's not dwell on this," she said. If Bernard wanted to tell them he could. But their questions were depressing, and certainly she had no answer to the one which was repeated over and over – what are you going to do? Even though the doctors said radiation and chemotherapy had little effect on these tumors she and Bernard decided they would start with that route. Since his offices were at the hospital, it was easier to check in for a stay there while she received treatment. They had no children and had decided they didn't want to take a chance on bringing a damaged child into the world after their radiation exposure from the San Mirado nuclear catastrophe which had occurred while they were living in Southern California. She thought about all those young Japanese women now heavily exposed to the radiation released when the Fukushima nuclear reactors melted down in 2011...and sighed heavily, thinking back on her own experiences.

But if she were going to continue her life, she had to rise above these thoughts and move on to what she enjoyed. She picked up her tablet and began to type an email to her friends. "I'm out of jail! I'm coming down to visit next week. Call me if you can go out to play. Sara"

CHAPTER TWO

The restaurant was large with open glass windows and shiny mirrored tables. Light and reflections bounced off the hard surfaces. Elise Baxter looked around from her tiny table where she sat by herself. Things were whirling in her head. She knew those people were looking at her. Was one of them Saundra? Saundra hated her. What she needed was a dog. But 'he' wouldn't let her have one.

She gathered up her jacket and threw money on the table. She couldn't stand them watching her anymore. She finished her glass of wine in one gulp and strode toward the door. She was tall and darkly beautiful, with features perfectly placed, her clothing expensive and stylish. She would go home to plan her next   move.

"Goodbye, Mrs. Baxter. Hope you enjoyed your lunch!" said the hostess as Elise left. Elise did not acknowledge her, but kept moving without making eye contact.

After Elise had exited through the door, the hostess heard someone calling to her. She turned and greeted one of her favorite customers. "Hi, Saundra", she said as she went over to a table of six women. "And, Sara!" she said excitedly. "You're back!"

Sara smiled. "Yes, for the moment. Glad to be here. We just take one day at a time."

"Was that Elise Baxter who just left?" Saundra asked. "I haven't seen her in months," she casually remarked to the other women at the table.

"Yes, she came in by herself," the hostess replied.

"I don't know what is up with her. She used to do a lot of things with us. Now, nothing," Saundra commented.

"Well, have you spoken with her?" asked one of the women at the table, Julie, a tall blonde wearing an elegant hat and expensive jewelry.

"I called and her husband Sam answered and said she wasn't available. I haven't heard from her since." Saundra shrugged with a lack of understanding. There actually had been more to the event but she didn't wish to share it publicly.

"Well, that's strange, but I always liked her. Do you think we did something to offend her?" Julie asked.

Another one at the table spoke up. Lila, originally from Vietnam, was married to a wealthy real estate mogul. This had gotten her citizenship. He was 20 years older but the marriage had lasted. She spoke in a heavily accented voice, "We went on all those outings together- Santa Barbara, Beverly Hills, Malibu....she never said anything, she seemed as if she had a good time."

"Do you think we should call her?" Julie asked sympathetically.

"Do whatever you feel comfortable with." Saundra Sommers stared thoughtfully. Seeing Elise brought back all the memories of what had transpired between them. She wasn't surprised Elise had not spoken to her. Elise couldn't reach out. She basically sought attention by trying to get you to come to her. She had joined their ladies charity group and would disappear, then complain no one had called her. When months had passed she would rejoin, hoping someone would welcome her back.

"I will call her," said Lila. "We are getting together for your birthday luncheon. She will come."

"We have to go," said Julie. "We have the Childen's Charity Board Meeting. The money from our fundraiser is going to the Fukushima child refugees this year. You know we will catch hell if we are late." She paused, then said, "Sara, are you good to get back to your hotel?"

"Yes," she replied. "The hotel car is picking me up. It should be outside about now."

The women stood and left as a group, gathering coats and purses, chatting and hugging as they pushed out the hotel door into the mild California winter weather.

The Japanese Minister of Public Affairs, Tan Tanaka, was sitting behind his desk staring out at the view over Tokyo. It was panoramic. His offices on the twenty-fifth floor were so high in the building the people below on the streets resembled tiny, tiny dolls. It helped when he didn't have to distinguish between those doing well and those impoverished below. He liked being far away from the people. It kept his decisions on a more intellectual level rather than an emotional one.

His phone buzzed and as he picked it up a familiar face burst through his office door. He heard his secretary say, "Mr. Kurosawa is coming in regardless of my request he be announced."

"So, I see," he replied. "Thank you. I will take care of Mr. Kurosawa." He set the phone down as Kurosawa and another Japanese man strode over and stood in front of his desk.

"What the FRICK is going on here?" the head of CEPCO, the Japanese Citizens Electric Power Company yelled loudly. "Thousands of people are out in the streets demonstrating against nuclear power, volunteers are out everywhere measuring radiation levels and posting them on the internet - even in the West Coast of the United States. Unmanned drones are flying over the Fukushima-Daiichi site taking pictures which are being published across the world. Can't we shoot these down or something? They are in our air space! Can't the demonstrators be controlled?"

"Please to sit, Mr. Kurosawa. And I would be pleased if you took a seat, also, Mr. Yamado. Could I provide you with tea or Saki?" he asked.

"No, let's just get on with it," he said shortly. "What are you

284

doing about all this?"

Tanaka sighed, but felt he might as well tell them the news. "The UN has hired an electrical consultant from the United States to take an independent look at what has happened at the power plant." The Japanese Minister Tanaka looked disgusted as he made the announcement.

"How independent? We don't want to get away from the story that the tsunami caused this. Tsunamis are rare – happen infrequently. We will just get better back-up generators for next time so we won't have the problem of the control rods not being able to be lowered. Our story is the back-up generators failed." Kurosawa's face was red and his fists were clenched.

"Oh, no one is going to find out it was the earthquake that caused the control rods to jam. How are they going to find out if we don't tell? This independent expert is going to get paid a lot of money to just rubber stamp our findings. We have to do it this way. If this disaster is linked to an earthquake we could be out of business. All our reactors are sitting on earthquake faults." Tanaka smiled reassuringly.

"I don't even want to hear *anything* akin to that" said Mr. Yamado, who was representing the Japanese Yakuza, the country's mafia type organization. His 1950's rat pack style of dressing looked comically retro. He was wearing a shiny tight-fitting suit with pointy-toed shoes and sported longish pomaded hair. "We have billions invested in those plants. Who is going to give us our money back? The government made us a guarantee when we paid the money. I'm sure you value your health and the health of your families," he stated. The man glared menacingly.

"Well, stay away from the radioactive zones then if you want to talk about health," Tanaka testily responded. "And speaking of zones, what are the plans to make reparation to the people we have had to evacuate out of the Fukushima area? There are at least 150,000 displaced people, maybe more."

"None that I know of," the Japanese Mafioso responded. "We have enough expenses to take care of with these plants fully melted down. What's going on with the insurance claim? How much are we going to get?"

CHAPTER THREE

Bryce sped down the road at high speed, looking for a radar unit or a marked car. The bike slowed as he approached the turnoff to his offices. Deftly hitting the remote clicker that opened the gate as he downshifted, he managed to time it so he didn't have to stop and put his feet on the ground. The Harley Wide Glide was comfortable and easy to maneuver. And since the sissy seat had been taken off the back of the bike he didn't have to throw his leg into the air as a ballet dancer would to get over the high backrest when dismounting the bike. Much safer, he thought, though it meant no riders on the back. And the girls were always eager for a ride.

He strode toward the entrance to the offices, taking his gloves and helmet off as he went. The gate was closed now and the parking lot supposedly secure but he didn't believe in leaving things to chance, so he was taking his riding accessories inside with him, rather than hanging the helmet on the handlebars with the gloves inside. His helmet cost almost one thousand dollars. He refused to buy a cheap helmet when you only had one head. It was full face and was made by the same designer who made the helmets for the race car drivers. They said you could drop eggs in the helmets from a two story building and the eggs wouldn't break. He had seen guys who rode with half helmets or beanie helmets who ended up with broken teeth from flying rocks and jagged scars on their faces from road debris. Just because you ride doesn't mean you have to do it stupidly.

Inside, his offices were on the top floor of a three story 50,000 square foot glass office/warehouse building. They were beautifully furnished, but in a very masculine manner. He strode over to the closet and hung his leather jacket up and put the helmet and gloves on the upper shelf. It was Saturday and he didn't see much activity on his way through the building. If he had to come in to work at least he could do it on his motorcycle, to put some excitement into the day.

He booted up his computer and brought up the contract for bid which had come in Friday. The United Nations was insisting independent consultants be brought in to evaluate the Fukushima nuclear disaster. The nuclear power plant company, CEPCO, was being held responsible for the disaster at their plant in Japan. CEPCO had been forced to agree to the hiring of a company, a team to act independently. Hundreds of thousands of people had been displaced from their homes; the soil and structures were still contaminated with radioactive materials; cleanup, such as it was, had been ineffective and improperly done. Over two years had passed and there had been little if any remuneration given to those without homes and jobs.

The bid for the contract called for Bryce and his team to write a complete report on what had been accomplished so far and what remained to be done, outlining the procedures to which his field of expertise pertained. He couldn't believe CEPCO had sent in crews to wash down buildings which were contaminated with radioactive dust from the fallout after the nuclear meltdown and explosion. They had then let all the water contaminated from the improper washing run into the sewers and out to the ocean. No wonder the fish over there were too hot to eat. He idly wondered how many were swimming across the ocean to be caught someplace else...someplace deemed safe, perhaps all of the West Coast of North America.

Scanning through the pages he highlighted areas he thought were not clear and then forwarded it to the company attorneys to peruse. Bryce Anderson was 40 years old, an electrical engineer and electrical contractor. Their company did design and wiring on large commercial structures such as hospitals, hotels, high rises, and nuclear plants. Much had been made of the fact the back-up generators, designed to pump cooling water to the nuclear fuel which was fissioning, had failed during the earthquake and ensuing tsunami. But the earthquake had frozen the control rods in place, so the nuclear reaction could not be slowed down. The lack of electrical power to pump the cooling water then became the final step in the disaster.

Bryce thought about who he would take with him on his team. There was a lot of resentment over the fact he was a partner in the company at his age, one of the largest privately held electrical firms in the United States. But he was smart and a diligent worker. He also stated what he was going to do and kept his word about his commitments. Maybe his marriage hadn't worked out as well as his job. But succeeding in business took a lot of effort and time and his wife hadn't believed she was getting enough attention. He hoped the younger guy she was living with now was making her happy, in his former house, and with his former money.

This book may be purchased at :

http://www.amazon.com/dp/B00IX1L94Y

ABOUT THE AUTHOR:

Barbara Griffin Billig graduated from Washington University in St. Louis at age nineteen with a degree in biology and a minor in chemistry. She taught for several years in St. Louis before moving to Southern California. There she owned a variety of businesses including pet shops, restaurants, and a real estate brokerage firm. Deciding to take a sabbatical from the business world for several years she wrote, in conjunction with another teacher, Bett Pohnka (1935-1991) "The Nuclear Catastrophe" to heighten awareness of the potential problems associated with nuclear power plants. This fiction novel, originally written in 1977, eerily portrays what ultimately came to pass with 3 Mile Island, Chernobyl, and the Japan Fukushima nuclear reactors meltdown. The original hardcover first edition is still in libraries throughout the United States. This 4th edition was written post Fukushima.

After several years of research following the Fukushima nuclear disaster the author felt compelled to write a sequel, which resulted in "#Betrayal". Lies, greed, murder, and power struggles all intertwine as the aftermath of the disaster unfolds. In fact, the aftermath is almost worse than the original disaster. The question becomes: "Whom should you trust?" Understanding the events of yesterday is preparation for the future.

"Nuclear Road Trip-Onward to Destruction" was written with Michelle McKeeth and released in December 2014 as a fiction novel. The dangers of the nuclear waste storage pools have been largely ignored. Mother nature, incompetence, or terrorism could bring about a large enough disaster to have to evacuate eight million people in the Chicago area. ISIS has plans to make it happen.

Please feel free to visit Barbara Billig at any of the following web sites:

Web page: http://www.barbarabillig.com

Follow on Twitter:
http://twitter.com/barbarabillig

Blog:
http://www.thenuclearcatastrophe.blogspot.com

Facebook:
http://www.facebook.com/BarbaraBilligTheNuclearCatastrophe

Pinterest:
http://pinterest.com/barbarabillig/nuclear-catastrophes/

Google + : Barbara Billig Nuclear Fiction Novels of Survival

Email: barbarabillig1@gmail.com

Books by Barbara Billig

The Nuclear Catastrophe (a Fiction Novel of
Survival) is also published as:
THE DISQUIET SURVIVORS of The
Nuclear Catastrophe in paperback

#Betrayal, a Nuclear Fiction Novel of Survival

Nuclear Road Trip-Onward to Destruction
(with Michelle McKeeth)

These novels may be found on Amazon.com
as e-Books or in Paperback

Thanks for Reading!